PRAISE FOR
MALICE DOMESTIC 1

"Elizabeth Peters has coaxed from a baker's dozen of interesting authors the 'traditional' short stories written exclusively for this softcover collection. You'll especially like Sharyn McCrumb's lampoon of the literary community in 'Happiness Is a Dead Poet' . . . Witty, cheeky, sardonic, deliciously sarcastic."

—*Buffalo News*

"An outstanding collection of original tales . . . Brevity is no detriment to characterization here. . . . The contributors avoid cliché while remaining true to the genre . . . celebrating the traditional mystery."

—*Publishers Weekly*

"Pull up your coziest armchair, brew yourself a pot of Earl Grey, and settle in to enjoy as these sleuths, both amateur and professional, solve crimes of murder and mayhem."

—*Prime Suspects*

"You will relish all these stories like tasty morsels."
—*Chicago Sun-Times*

Elizabeth Peters Presents MALICE DOMESTIC 1
Mary Higgins Clark Presents MALICE DOMESTIC 2
Nancy Pickard Presents MALICE DOMESTIC 3

Available from POCKET BOOKS

NANCY PICKARD

presents

MALICE DOMESTIC

3

An Anthology of
Original Traditional
Mystery Stories

POCKET BOOKS

New York   London   Toronto   Sydney   Tokyo   Singapore

An *Original* Publication of POCKET BOOKS

POCKET BOOKS, a division of Simon & Schuster Inc.
1230 Avenue of the Americas, New York, NY 10020

ISBN: 1-4165-0708-6

This Pocket Books paperback printing September 2004

10 9 8 7 6 5 4 3 2 1

POCKET and colophon are registered trademarks of Simon & Schuster Inc.

Cover art by John Zielinski

Printed in the U.S.A.

Copyright Notices

Contents

Contents

Malicious Domesticus

Nancy Pickard

If you'll think back to your childhood, you'll probably remember your first lesson in "malice domestic. . . ."

When I was five, I loved visiting my friend in her big, white, rambling home with the adorable playhouse out back. But I was terrified of her huge father, who roared at her mother (who only spoke of him by his last name), while we cowered in their sunny, cozy breakfast nook, drinking milk and eating cookies.

Malice domestic!

I once had another friend, Amy, who had, it must be admitted, a nasty jealous streak. One day I wanted to introduce her to another pal of mine, Susie, a pretty little girl whose face had not yet grown big enough for her two front teeth. Not to put too fine a point on it, Susie had buck teeth. Knowing my friend Amy all too well, I begged her beforehand not to mention Susie's teeth when I introduced them: she *promised* me that she wouldn't make fun.

"Amy," I said to her, "this is Susie."

Pretty, trusting Susie smiled.

Treacherous Amy stuck out her own top teeth over her bottom lip, like Bugs Bunny.

Oh, God! *Malicious domesticus!*

There were no ax murders in my childhood—and I hope not in yours. No serial killers. No international spies. No private eyes or undercover cops, unless you count the one who dressed up as a clown to visit schools to talk about traffic safety. There was goodness aplenty, but there was malice, too . . .

"Little girl?" called the man from inside the shady entry-way to the church that I was passing as I walked home. He was standing on a stepladder, staring at eight-year-old me. "Little girl, would you come in here and help me change this light bulb, little girl?"

"N-no," I stammered.

I don't remember what he called out to me next, because I was running, running away. . . .

Malice domestic.

I know of a minister who ran off with a parishioner's wife. Don't you? Doesn't everyone? I remember the boy who hung himself when we were all in high school. Don't you? Doesn't everybody? Now, years later, I know what was *really* going on behind closed doors at the apple-pie home where the popular girl lived. Don't you? Now we know why she tried so hard to please all the time. Now we understand, with sympathy, what lay behind that perpetually brilliant smile of hers. Now we know why she got pregnant and married and left school before she graduated.

She was escaping Malice Domestic.

And probably running right into the arms of more of it.

It's frightening precisely because it's so close to home. It's important because, to quote an ancient Chinese source of wisdom, "The family is a direct reflection of society, being its smallest unit." Malice domestic is threatening because it's so ordinary that it's often invisible, like a bogeyman in the closet in the dark of our childhood rooms. Is it really there? Did we imagine it? People wouldn't really do anything like that on *purpose*. . . . Would they?

Oh, yes, they would . . . and in these pages they will.

This anthology is the third in a series that was originally inspired by the Malice Domestic conventions that are held annually for fans and authors of mystery and suspense fiction. At the conventions, the Agatha Awards are presented to the writers who are deemed to have cooked up the Best Novel, Best First Novel, and Best Short Story in the "traditional" mystery genre for that year. (Last year's Short Story winners were Charlotte and Aaron Elkins, whose story, "Nice Gorilla," appears in the second volume of this collection.) What's a "traditional" mystery? In short, it's one that traces its lineage through writers like Elizabeth Peters and Agatha Christie more than it does through private eye writers like Raymond Chandler.

It was, in fact, Chandler who wrote that "Down these mean streets a man must go." But we fans of the so-called traditional mystery novel know that all it really takes is one mean person on a perfectly nice street. And it doesn't have to be a man who walks down that street, it could be a woman or a child or even an animal, and any of them could be victim or villain.

That's malice of the domestic persuasion.

As you'll soon see, there is deliciously, wickedly, fascinatingly, horrifyingly, even humorously, infinite variety to the species *malicious domesticus.* So pull up an easy chair . . . in your perfectly safe home . . . and turn off all the lights but your reading lamp . . . and curl your feet up under you and enjoy these stories of mystery and humor and suspense, telling yourself all the while, knowing from experience going all the way back into your childhood, that it could never happen to you or to anybody you know. . . .

And if you believe that, I have a bridge I'd like to sell you.

Nancy Pickard

MALICE DOMESTIC
3

The Dying Light

Taylor McCafferty

I died a year ago today.

I reckon there aren't a lot of people here in the tiny town of Pigeon Fork, Kentucky, who've died and lived to tell about it. Of course, that's why back when it happened, I didn't tell a lot of people about my dying. Nobody would've believed me. And if they didn't believe me about the dying part, they sure wouldn't have believed me about the rest of it.

When I first woke up from dying, I was still so drowsy from the anaesthetic that I started to tell my husband all about it. Right away, though, Carl began to look at me funny. Real worried-like. So, even in my doped-up state, I knew to shut up.

I turned over and turned my face to the wall, but Carl didn't leave like I hoped he would. He just kept sitting there by my hospital bed, patting my arm. "I'm sure sorry, Elna," Carl said.

Carl must've come straight over from the hardware store because he was still wearing the white dress shirt, the navy blue slacks, and the name badge over his left shirt pocket that his dad always made him wear to work. Carl Laswell, the badge read, Vice President. Carl was running his hand through his short-cropped, sandy hair. "I mean it, Elna," he added. "I'm sure sorry about the baby."

When Carl said that, I shut my eyes. Tight. I didn't open them again neither.

I must've dozed off after a while because when I opened my eyes next, Carl was gone. I'd moved around in my sleep some, and I was now lying with my face toward the window. I could see it was getting dark outside.

I was thinking clearer by then, and I knew, of course, that I didn't want to talk to Carl about my dying. I sure wanted to tell somebody, though. It wasn't like you died every day.

So when Aunt Rae walked in right after visiting hours started up, I decided I'd tell her. I took one look at her thin face stamped with its usual no-nonsense frown, and I knew Aunt Rae was the perfect one to tell what had happened. She'd let me know in a hurry if I was talking sense or not.

Aunt Rae always has been a real sensible kind of person. She and Uncle Merle brought me up after my mama and daddy were killed in a car accident the year I turned seven. I would've liked to have been able to say that ever since the day my parents were killed, Aunt Rae has been like a second mama to me. That isn't exactly the truth, though. That's not to say, mind you, that Aunt Rae didn't do the very best she could, because I know she did. It was just that Aunt Rae was a good ten years older than my mama. Where my mama had been little and cute and full of laughter, Aunt Rae was tall and thin and, as best as I could tell, had to work hard to crack a smile.

It's difficult to believe Aunt Rae and my mama were even relatives, let alone sisters. From what I remembered of Mama, she'd always been quick to give you a hug, and she'd always smelled of *Evening in Paris* toilet water. Aunt Rae always stiffened up every time you hugged her, and she always smelled of mothballs. I hate to say it, but hugging bony Aunt Rae was a lot like trying to cuddle up to a coat hanger.

Aunt Rae never did have kids of her own, either, so that

probably explains a lot. I figure Aunt Rae must've been genuinely bewildered as to how to go about taking care of a little seven-year-old girl who cried all the time for her mama.

Fact is, I might've thought less of Aunt Rae for being the way she was, if it weren't for one thing: Aunt Rae didn't have to take me in. She could've let them put me in a foster home or an orphanage, or she could've pawned me off on some distant cousin or other. Aunt Rae and Uncle Merle didn't hesitate a minute, though. They took me right in, and all the time I was living in their house, I never heard one word of complaint about it.

That's why I truly believe that Aunt Rae did the best she knew how. And, if she was never real loving with me, well, it just wasn't in her nature to be a warm and fuzzy type person.

Uncle Merle, on the other hand, was a different story. A big, jowly guy with a round, red face and a huge beer belly, Uncle Merle might've made up for some of the affection I was so sorely missing. In fact, I can remember when I first came to live with him and Aunt Rae, every once in a while Uncle Merle would toss me up in the air and catch me in those great, big, muscled arms of his. Laughing, of course, all the time he was catching me.

Oh, yes, Uncle Merle was definitely the warm and fuzzy type, all right. Only trouble was, with all the drinking he kept doing over the years, Uncle Merle started pretty much overdoing the fuzzy part. In fact, what I mostly remember these days when I think of Uncle Merle was him sitting out on the side porch, creaking back and forth in the rickety old swing, and drinking himself into a stupor.

While Aunt Rae, of course, stared at him through the screen door, her thin mouth pinched into an even thinner line than usual.

When Aunt Rae came to visit me in the hospital that day, Carl must've already told her about the baby. She was looking real uncomfortable even before she got to my bedside.

In fact, she stood there in the doorway to my hospital room for a minute or so, fussing with the lace at her collar.

Aunt Rae was wearing what she always seemed to wear—a long-sleeved, calico print dress with a skirt that reached all the way down to her ankles and a neckline that started right under her chin. A no-nonsense dress, if I ever saw one.

Aunt Rae was carrying a big bouquet of zinnias in practically every shade of the rainbow. I had no doubt those zinnias had come from the flower bed outside her kitchen window.

I don't think Aunt Rae realized I'd already seen her, because as she stood there in the doorway, she drew a heavy sigh and clucked her tongue a couple times. Then, squaring her thin shoulders, like maybe she was steeling herself for something pretty awful, she bustled on in.

The first thing Aunt Rae said was, "Oh, you poor thing." She kissed the air right next to my face and clucked her tongue some more. "Here," she said, "I brung you some flowers." She held out the zinnias for me to see. "To cheer you up," she added.

I tried to smile. "That was right nice of you, Aunt Rae. They're real pretty," I said.

Aunt Rae gave a quick nod of her head, as if to say, *Of course, they are,* and then she said something that I knew very well that she meant to sound comforting. "Don't worry, sweetie," she said, patting at the sheet next to my arm. "You and Carl will have other children. You will."

I just looked at her. Aunt Rae was actually acting as if the baby had been mine and Carl's all along. As if Jimmy hadn't been the father.

Of course, that was like Aunt Rae. She'd always been good at sweeping dirt under the rug and forgetting about it. She'd actually told me more than once that Uncle Merle drank for medicinal purposes only. As if maybe Aunt Rae actually believed that Uncle Merle's doctor was named Jack Daniels.

"You and Carl will have a lot more children," Aunt Rae went on, punctuating her words with an emphatic shake of her pepper-gray head.

I didn't say anything. I wanted to, but I knew not to. There was no use in getting Aunt Rae upset all over again. Lord knows, she'd been upset enough.

Besides, I sure didn't want to talk about Carl and me. I took a deep breath and started in. "This morning the baby wasn't the only one who died, Aunt Rae," I said.

Aunt Rae had started bustling around the room, the way she does, looking for a water glass to put the zinnias in. My words, though, stopped her right in her tracks. "Why, Elna," she said, turning to face me, "whatever do you mean?"

"*I* died, too," I said, and then I started in, telling her as much as I dared. By the time I'd finished, those zinnias in Aunt Rae's hand were looking a little limp.

I told her how during surgery, all of a sudden, I'd woke up. How all at once I wasn't unconscious anymore. I could see everything that was going on, and I could hear everything. Just as if I wasn't under an anaesthetic at all. Aunt Rae really looked alarmed at that, but I held up my hand, as if waving her concerns away. "Oh, I didn't feel any pain, Aunt Rae, or anything like that. It was like I wasn't in my body anymore."

In fact, I'd awakened staring into a heating duct in a corner of the ceiling of the operating room. I didn't tell Aunt Rae that part, though. She was looking as if she was hearing a whole lot she couldn't believe as it was.

That day in the operating room it had taken me a moment to realize where I was, but then I sort of rolled over to look at myself, way down there on the operating table with all the doctors and nurses bending over me. And I heard them say it.

"She's gone."

"We've lost her! There's no pulse, no blood pressure!"

I watched them running around down there, all excited, and I knew instantly what had happened. I'd died. If I hadn't already had a pretty good idea what had just occurred, I think I would've guessed it when one of the doctors started hitting me on the chest, screaming at me. "Come on, damn it, come on!"

I watched that doctor actually hitting my chest with his fist, but I didn't feel a thing. Not pain, not fear, not anything. Oh, maybe I did feel a little curious—and yes, a tiny bit anxious. For one thing, I was wondering where do I go from here? If I'm not in my body anymore, do I spend the rest of my *whatever* staring into a heating duct?

It wasn't exactly the way I pictured spending eternity.

As soon as that thought crossed my mind, though, it began. The scooting—or, at least, that's what it felt like. "I was sort of scooting through this long tunnel toward this real bright light," I told Aunt Rae.

By then Aunt Rae's mouth was actually hanging open. "Bright light?" she repeated.

"It was like this light was God," I said.

Aunt Rae looked downright relieved to hear this part. At last, she was hearing something she could relate to.

Ever since Uncle Merle had passed away two years before, Aunt Rae had gotten real religious. Can you believe, she went to prayer meeting on Wednesday night, choir practice on Thursday night, Sunday School and regular service on Sunday morning, and still another church service on Sunday night? And she was always after me to go with her. All this because Uncle Merle up and had himself a fatal heart attack—a man who hadn't stepped into a church a day in his life.

"God, you say? You saw the Lord?" Aunt Rae said. Her watery blue eyes were now glued to my face.

"I guess you could say that," I told her. "I saw this light, and I knew it was God. And then I got to the end of this here tunnel thing, and I heard the words, 'Not yet,' so I went back." I looked away so Aunt Rae couldn't see my face. "Then I woke up in the recovery room."

After all that, Aunt Rae actually had the nerve to look disappointed. I think maybe she'd been hoping that what I had to say was going to be something that could be written up in the *National Enquirer.* So I hurried to tell her the rest.

"And, Aunt Rae, I felt the baby go by me. I felt his little soul slip past mine at the end of that tunnel. That's how I knew the baby had—had gone. And that it had been a little boy."

I swallowed the lump in my throat, determined not to start crying again. I'd been crying already when the doctor in the recovery room had walked in to tell me the sad news.

That doctor had actually turned pale, because before he'd even had a chance to open his mouth, I'd told *him.* "I know," I'd said. "I already know. My little son is dead." Mine and Jimmy's son, I'd thought, wiping away tears.

After what I'd just told her, Aunt Rae was looking every bit as pale as that doctor. "Well, good heavens," she said. For Aunt Rae, this was as close to a curse as she would ever get. But she still had that look on her face. That look you give somebody that you think might be telling you a pack of lies, but you don't want to upset them. In case the reason they're telling you all these lies is that they're sick.

Real sick in the head.

So I started telling Aunt Rae the thing I knew she'd want most to hear. "And, Aunt Rae, I saw Uncle Merle."

Just as soon as the words were out of my mouth, I wondered if I should've told her after all. Aunt Rae actually caught her breath, and her eyes started showing the whites all around. "Your Uncle Merle—?" Her voice was a whisper.

"He looked real good, Aunt Rae. He looked happy."

"And he was in heaven—?" I almost laughed at the surprise in Aunt Rae's voice.

I didn't have the heart to tell Aunt Rae that I wasn't real sure exactly where I'd been. So I just said, "Uncle Merle was there, with the light." I smiled, remembering. "And it was so beautiful, Aunt Rae. It was the most beautiful place I'd ever been. There were all these gorgeous colors, and everything there seemed to be making this wonderful music."

Aunt Rae looked as if she might cry from sheer relief. "Oh, thank the Lord," she said, clasping her bony hands together. "Thank the dear, dear Lord."

"I saw Mama, too. And Daddy." My parents had been dead for almost twelve years, but they'd both looked just as I remembered them. "They were all waiting for me, Aunt Rae. Waiting and smiling."

Aunt Rae smiled then, too. My mouth had gotten real dry all of a sudden, so I reached over to the nightstand for a glass of water. But Aunt Rae didn't even notice how bad my hands were shaking, she was that excited about what I'd just

7

told her. Until visiting hours were over, she kept pumping me for more details. Particularly about Uncle Merle. "Elna, you've made me feel so much better about your uncle," Aunt Rae told me right before she left. "You have no idea how glad you've made me."

The next week I was real glad, too, that I'd decided to tell Aunt Rae, because she started bringing me all these books she'd checked out of the Pigeon Fork Library. I knew, of course, what she was really doing. She was trying to take my mind off losing the baby.

That was okay with me, though, because those books told me everything I needed to know. Page after page described the exact same thing I'd gone through. The moving through the tunnel, the light, the meeting up with folks who'd passed on.

An NDE—that's what those books called it. A Near Death Experience. The NDEs in those books even described the things I hadn't told Aunt Rae about. Like the slide projector I'd seen. Of course, it hadn't been a real slide projector, but that's as close as I can come to describing whatever it was.

It was as if slides of your life—scenes just as you'd seen them when you were alive—all flashed right before your eyes. That slide projector had started up just as soon as I got to the end of the tunnel. While the projector ran, the light stood next to me and said, "See? *See?*"

And I saw all right. I saw Uncle Merle riding me around on his shoulders when I was eight. I saw Aunt Rae fixing my hair in long, blond braids the Easter I was twelve. And I saw me and Carl starting to go steady.

That had been the year I turned sixteen. Carl and I had been dating almost a month by that time, and I'd been convinced he was all I could ever want. At six foot two, Carl was good looking, smart, and had just been elected president of the Pigeon Fork High senior class. When he asked me to go steady, I didn't hesitate a second. In fact, in those slides of my life flipping past, I saw me looking practically ecstatic as Carl slipped his senior ring on my finger.

And then, a few slides later, I saw me meeting Jimmy.

It had happened during my senior year in high school. Carl had graduated the year before and was working at his dad's hardware store in town.

It was, in fact, at Laswell's Hardware Store that I first laid eyes on Jimmy.

Of course, I couldn't tell Aunt Rae about this part. Because Aunt Rae wouldn't listen to anything about Jimmy. If you even mentioned his name in her house, Aunt Rae's mouth would get all pinched up, and she would stomp right out of the room.

I knew without even thinking about it that Aunt Rae wouldn't want to hear how many of my slides had Jimmy in them.

It's funny but when slides of your life flip past you like that, you can see real clear how things were. You can especially see how things happened the way they did. I watched all those slides, and I thought, *Oh, Jimmy, if I'd known then how everything was going to turn out, I'd have run in the opposite direction.*

Oddly enough, it had been Carl who introduced us. Carl, my husband-to-be. And Jimmy's half brother.

Jimmy's mama and Carl's dad had been divorced when Jimmy was just a baby. Right after the divorce his mama had taken the baby and gone off to California somewhere. After she left, Carl's dad must've had his new wife, Darlene, all picked out, because Carl was born less than a year later.

That made Jimmy only a year and a half older than Carl, but the way Carl talked about him, I'd always pictured Jimmy as much, much older. And much, much wilder.

All the time we were going steady, Carl was always telling me tales about how his half brother Jimmy who lived out in California had gotten himself arrested for stealing a car. Or how his half brother Jimmy who lived out in California had hopped a freight train going east because he'd taken it into his head one day to see the Grand Canyon. That time nobody had even known where Jimmy was for months. "That Jimmy is crazy, that's all," Carl told me. "Crazy as a loon."

Even Darlene, Carl's mother and Jimmy's stepmom, said

the same thing. Darlene Laswell had been only sixteen years old when Carl was born, and sometimes it seemed when I was talking to her that Darlene and I were practically the same age.

For one thing, Darlene sure didn't look as if she were much older than me. She had a thick mane of chestnut hair tumbling past her shoulders, an hourglass figure, and brown eyes fringed in lashes so thick she never had to wear mascara. And she always insisted that I call her Darlene, not Mrs. Laswell. "I never met Carl's half brother," Darlene told me, "but I heard me some tales about him. That boy's crazier than a June bug."

To somebody like me, who'd spent all her life in a town of only fifteen hundred people, Jimmy had sounded crazy, all right. And more than a little scary. When Carl told me that Jimmy's mama had died, and that Jimmy was coming to live with him and Darlene and his dad, I'd actually dreaded meeting him.

The night I met Jimmy, Carl and I were on our way to the movies. We'd stopped by Laswell's Hardware Store because Carl was supposed to pick up the receipts and take them over to the bank that evening. That was how reliable Carl was. He was not yet twenty, and yet his daddy trusted him with a money bag containing thousands.

Mr. Laswell had just given Carl the receipts, and all three of us were still standing out in front of the store, just shooting the breeze, when the best-looking guy I'd ever seen came walking out of the store.

Jimmy had on real tight faded jeans and scuffed-up cowboy boots, and he looked as if he hadn't combed his black hair all day. For a second he just stopped and stared at me. And, even though I was holding Carl's hand, I couldn't seem to pull my eyes away from Jimmy's dark green ones.

"Well, well, well," Jimmy said. "Who do we have here?"

Carl said real quick, "This is *my* girlfriend, Jimmy. *My* girlfriend, Elna." Carl emphasized the word *my* both times.

Jimmy said real soft, "Lucky guy." That's all he said, but Carl's head kind of jerked toward him.

Darlene was, at that moment, just coming out of the store

in back of Jimmy, and she must've heard what Jimmy said. She kind of sauntered up to him and gave him a long, sideways glance through those thick lashes of hers. "Oh?" Darlene said. "And do you think your daddy's a lucky guy, too?"

I couldn't help but notice that Darlene's little question caused Mr. Laswell's head to kind of jerk toward Jimmy, much like Carl's had just done.

Jimmy never did answer Darlene. He just smiled some more, his eyes still resting on mine, and pretty soon Darlene gave out with this funny little laugh. Like maybe she'd just been kidding and she didn't really want an answer anyway.

Mr. Laswell, however, didn't seem to find any humor at all in the way Darlene was still looking at Jimmy. Jimmy's eyes, on the other hand, were still on mine when he turned and headed back into the store.

Once Jimmy was gone, the rest of us kept on standing out there, acting like everything was just the same as it had been.

Only, of course, it wasn't.

For one thing, all the time I was still standing out there in front of the hardware store, I could hardly concentrate on whatever it was that Mr. Laswell and Darlene and Carl were now talking about. And I was having an awful time trying to ignore how fast my heart was pounding.

Not to mention, there now seemed to be a real strained tone to the conversation going on around me.

Oh yes, the day I died and I watched all those slides of my life flip past, it was so easy to see how inevitable everything was. It was obvious, really, watching all of us, what was going to happen.

Shortly after Jimmy moved in with the Laswells, Carl up and bought a house of his own. Carl started pressuring me to marry him right away, too, but I kept on telling him that I wanted to finish high school first. Now I realize that, even at the very beginning, Carl must've sensed what was going to happen between Jimmy and me, and Carl had been trying his best to head it off.

But there wasn't anything Carl could do. Some things are just meant to be. One Wednesday evening, not too long after

Jimmy's and my first meeting, I was standing outside the Pigeon Fork First Baptist Church waiting for Aunt Rae, as usual. Everybody else had pretty much gone, but Aunt Rae was still inside, talking to the reverend. After every church service, Aunt Rae always took her time saying good-bye. It was as if Aunt Rae could never quite get her fill of holy words, and she always needed just a few more to take with her.

While Aunt Rae was getting her final dose, I was just standing there, waiting, when—of all people—Jimmy Laswell came sauntering down the church steps. I hadn't even known he'd been at the service.

For a second Jimmy just stood there. Then he took a deep breath and reached for my hand. "You sure are beautiful," he said.

I must've turned bright red. I pulled my hand away and said, trying to sound real casual, "I didn't know you went to church."

Jimmy just smiled. "There's a lot of things you don't know about me. Why don't you go out with me and find some of them out?"

I just looked at him, my heart starting to pound just like it had done in front of the hardware store. It seemed as if it took me forever to be able to speak, but I finally managed to say, "I couldn't. I'm going steady with Carl." I tried to sound kind of offended that Jimmy had even asked, but to tell you the truth, all I sounded was excited.

Jimmy gave me a look that seemed to see right into my soul. "You feel the same way I do, don't you?" Jimmy said, reaching for my hand again. "You know we're supposed to be together."

I didn't have to answer. He could feel my hand trembling in his. "Come on then," Jimmy said. And, almost as if I were in a trance, I went with him.

After that day, I guess I must've been in a permanent trance. I was so much in love I couldn't think of anything else. I tried to feel guilty, or mean, or something, when I told Carl the next day that I couldn't go steady with him anymore. But the truth was, all I felt was happiness. I felt like I might explode with how happy I was that Jimmy wanted *me*.

"You're going to be sorry. He'll break your heart, Elna," Carl told me, his eyes glittering with unshed tears. "Mark my words. He doesn't care two cents about you. I'm the only one who really loves you."

I barely heard Carl. All I knew was that *Jimmy* loved me. After what seemed like a lifetime of feeling lonely, I'd finally found someone to love who loved me back. I'd never felt this way with Carl. So what if Jimmy was a little wild? That only made it that much more exciting to be with him.

"Jimmy's just playing with you," Carl told me a couple weeks later. Carl had actually shown up at the high school, and had waited for me after my last class just to tell me this. "Getting women to fall for him is just a game with Jimmy. Why, you ought to see the way he carries on with his own stepmother!"

I'd just stared at Carl. He wasn't telling me anything new. I'd already heard the talk, of course. In a town the size of Pigeon Fork, there was no way you weren't going to hear the talk about Jimmy and Darlene. The way I'd heard it, though, it had sounded as if the carrying-on was more on Darlene's part than Jimmy's. People were saying Darlene was practically throwing herself at him. In public, mind you. Jimmy had been hired on as a stock boy at his dad's hardware store—where, of course, Darlene worked in the office—and, according to all the gossips in town, Darlene flirted with Jimmy right in front of customers and all. "Carl," I said, lifting my chin, "the way I heard it, your mama ought to be ashamed of herself!"

Carl had looked at me as if I were talking nonsense. "You just won't see, will you?" he said.

But I did see the day I died. Seeing those slides go by, seeing me and Jimmy laughing together, seeing us spending every spare minute with each other, it seemed as inevitable as everything else that I would end up expecting Jimmy's baby. Before, with Carl, I'd always found it easy to be sensible. Carl and I had agreed that we were going to wait until we were married, and we'd waited.

With Jimmy, we never even talked about marriage, but it was as if I couldn't get close enough to him. We hadn't been dating six months when one night I ended up at Crayton County Hospital, doubled up in pain. The doctors there were real nonchalant about it. They told me not a thing was wrong. I was just pregnant, that's all. They gave me some pills to take, and they sent me home.

I guess I dreaded telling Jimmy worse than doing anything in my whole life.

Jimmy and I were sitting out on Aunt Rae's side porch, in Uncle Merle's old swing, when I broke the news. Jimmy did a quick intake of breath, swallowed once, and then he said, "It's okay, Elna. It is. We'll just get us married right away, that's all."

I thought I would shout with joy. "Jimmy, do you—do you mean it?"

Jimmy looked at me, surprised. "I love you, Elna. Of course I mean it." He ran his hand through his dark hair. "I don't make much at the hardware store, but we'll do all right, you and I. We will."

That Friday night was the happiest night of my life, sitting out there in that rickety old swing with Jimmy's arm around me, planning our life together.

The next day Jimmy was gone.

When I hadn't heard from him all day, I called up his dad's house. "Jimmy isn't here," Mr. Laswell told me, his voice hard and angry. "He up and left town this morning."

"Wha-a-at?" That was all I could get out.

"There's money missing from the cash register, too," Mr. Laswell went on. "Evidently, Jimmy just helped himself and then took off."

My heart started doing a dull thud. "I—I don't understand. He—"

Mr. Laswell went on as if I hadn't even spoken. "Jimmy's no son of mine. No sir. No son of mine would do what he did."

"But, Mr. Laswell, Jimmy wouldn't—"

Mr. Laswell interrupted me. "Oh yes he would. You don't know that boy like I do. He's stolen before—and, believe

14

you me, he'll take what's yours if you don't watch him." Mr. Laswell's tone was bitter. "Look, Elna, I'm his own father, but I'm telling you the truth. Jimmy's no damn good. Never has been. You're better off without him." He drew a ragged breath. "Hell," Mr. Laswell muttered, "we're *all* better off without him."

I could barely speak. "But, Mr. Laswell—"

Mr. Laswell interrupted me again. "I tried to talk him out of going. I didn't know about the money yet, of course. But you know what? Jimmy just laughed at me. He said he had a hankering to see Owensboro."

Owensboro was over two hundred miles away. I actually felt for a moment that I was going to faint.

I hung up that phone, feeling as if my whole world had just ended.

Right after that, Carl phoned. "Elna, my dad just called me. He said you were real upset. I—I wanted you to know that—well, that I'm awful sorry." You could tell Carl also wanted to say I told you so real bad, but he didn't. Instead, he said, "I can't hardly believe it. I talked to Jimmy last night, evidently right before he took off, and I didn't have any idea what he was planning on doing."

Carl's voice seemed to be coming from a very long distance away. "And, uh, Elna," Carl went on, "uh, last night Jimmy told me something else." There was a long silence on the phone. Finally Carl said, "He told me about the, uh, the baby and all." Carl's voice was now every bit as ragged as his father's had been. "I don't know, Elna. I reckon Jimmy just wasn't ready to be tied down by a family."

Carl went on saying some other things, but to this day I don't have the slightest idea what they were. I don't even remember hanging up the phone. All I remember is thinking that I might actually die from the pain.

Aunt Rae was walking past just as I hung up, and of course, it only took one look at my face for her to know immediately that something was terribly wrong. She kept at me and at me until I finally told her. When I did, she exploded. "I knew that Jimmy Laswell was a no-account. I knew it from the first!" She started in on me right then, trying to talk me into giving up the baby for adoption. "I will not have that no-account's kid in my house. I will not have it!"

Aunt Rae made it all too plain that if I decided to keep Jimmy's baby, I was on my own. And yet, somehow, I couldn't agree to give the baby up. I kept thinking, this baby's all I've got left of Jimmy, and I'm going to keep it. Besides, one day he might be back. I told myself that over and over.

Even when a small voice inside me whispered it wasn't true.

Five nights later, the doorbell rang, and I ran to answer it. It wasn't Jimmy standing there, though. It was Carl.

Carl must've noticed how my face fell, because he set his jaw before he said, "Come on, Elna, there's something I want to show you." We drove to his house, and Carl took my arm as he led me inside. There, just inside his front door, Carl stopped and then just stood there, waiting for my reaction.

I didn't know what to say. Carl had redone the entire inside of his house. He'd put up real pretty floral wallpaper and laid carpeting that looked like wall-to-wall green velvet. He'd gotten himself some new furniture, too. On the new oak coffee table in front of his new couch, there was a huge vase filled with daisies and pink sweetheart roses.

"I wanted to make this the kind of home a woman could love," Carl said. "Marry me, Elna. I still love you. And I'll treat this baby just like it was mine. I promise you I will."

Carl took hold my hand then, but I couldn't help it, I pulled away. "Carl, you're a sweet man, but I—I can't. I don't love you the way a wife should."

"You'll learn to love me," Carl said, almost pleading, but I shook my head.

I expected Carl to give up after a while, but he didn't. Every single day after that, Carl kept asking me to marry him. Over and over again. Finally, one rainy night after I was starting to show, Carl told me, sounding casual, "I heard from Jimmy today."

My heart nearly leaped out of my chest. I guess I couldn't keep the hope out of my eyes, because Carl looked as if I'd slapped him. His face was grim as he took something out of his pocket. "Jimmy's got himself a new girlfriend, Elna. He sent me her picture." Carl's eyes were riveted to my face as he handed the snapshot to me. It showed Jimmy, his hair a little longer than I remembered, and some long-legged blonde. Both of them were standing by a motorcycle.

"Jimmy couldn't even take the time to write me a letter. Just that note on the back," Carl said.

I turned the picture over and saw, scrawled carelessly across the back, the words, "Hi, you all! Doing fine!— Jimmy"

I stared at those words, and I actually felt dizzy. I wasn't a handwriting expert, of course, but it sure looked like Jimmy's writing to me.

I guess right that minute I started hating Jimmy every bit as much as I'd loved him. He was a no-account just like everybody said, and he'd used me. All the time we'd spent together had been a cruel lie. When I handed that picture back to Carl, I'd made up my mind. "If you still want me, Carl," I said, "I'd be proud to marry you."

Carl and I were married two days after I graduated from high school. I thought that we'd put all this awfulness behind us—that Carl and I and the baby would become a real family. I didn't once let myself even think about Jimmy. Carl never mentioned him anymore, and I sure never asked about him.

As far as I was concerned, Jimmy had become nothing more than a painful memory. I even tried to think of the baby that I was carrying as just mine and Carl's, the way it should've been right from the start.

And I tried to tell myself that everything was going to be all right.

That slide projector I watched the day I died, though, showed me how it really had been—my body growing more and more swollen as my pregnancy dragged on, long and painful. Slide after slide showed me lying in bed, trying not to cry.

Eventually, I decided that all the pain I was in was my punishment for ever getting involved with Jimmy in the first place. In my seventh month I reckon I got punished a little more. They rushed me into the emergency room, bleeding real bad.

It was in the hospital that morning that the baby and I died. I guess maybe something had been wrong from the start. Surely, you're not supposed to have that much pain.

They say in those library books that Aunt Rae brought me that a Near Death Experience like mine changes a person— that it makes you see things different from the way you did before. I know that's true.

When I finally came home from the hospital, it seemed as if even Carl's and my house looked different. I walked into the living room, sank down on the sofa, and just looked around me. At the wallpaper. At the carpeting. At the fresh flowers on the coffee table. Once again, there were daisies and sweetheart roses all done up real pretty in a huge vase. Carl must've ordered them from the florist special.

Carl was running around, getting me pillows and putting my things away. It made me want to scream, watching him run around like that. Finally, when Carl came back into the living room, I said, "By the way, Carl, have you heard from Jimmy lately?"

Something seemed to flicker in Carl's eyes, but he answered me right away. "Why, uh, no, Elna, I haven't heard from him. Dad has, though."

I blinked. "Your dad?"

Carl was nodding. "Dad said Jimmy phoned him a couple days ago and told him that he was thinking of going south. To Nashville, maybe."

I just stared at Carl for a long moment. "You didn't talk to Jimmy yourself?"

Carl didn't even blink. "Nope," he said. "Nope, I didn't."

I kept right on looking straight at him. "Well, I did," I said quietly. "I heard from Jimmy when I was in the hospital."

Carl's eyes got real wide when I said that. "What?" Carl's voice suddenly sounded like he had sand in his mouth.

I nodded, my eyes still on his. "Jimmy had apparently

found out what had happened and all, and I reckon he wanted to make sure I was okay."

I was still staring straight at Carl the whole time I was saying this.

Carl, of course, was now looking at me a lot like Aunt Rae had when I'd first told her about my dying. Like maybe he was hearing things he couldn't quite believe.

And yet, just like with Aunt Rae, I was telling the truth.

Carl moved to sit next to me on the couch. "You talked to Jimmy in the hospital, and you didn't even mention it until now?"

I glanced over at the flowers on the coffee table. As a matter of fact, I'd talked to several folks in the hospital that I hadn't mentioned to Carl. "I thought it might upset you," I told Carl, "if you knew I'd heard from Jimmy."

Apparently, I'd been right about that. Carl looked downright upset, all right.

It was later, when I was pretending to nap on the couch, that I heard Carl out in the kitchen, talking real low on the telephone. I kept right on pretending to be asleep when Carl hurried out the front door.

And then, of course, there wasn't anything left to do except wait.

Until the sheriff phoned.

The sheriff told me it all happened just the way I'd told him it would. On the way out of town, Carl stopped by the hardware store and picked up his dad.

Then Carl and Mr. Laswell drove quite a few miles outside of Pigeon Fork down a winding country lane that dead-ended in heavy woods. The two of them appeared to have been arguing some on the way, so the sheriff was pretty sure that neither one of them even had the slightest notion they were being followed.

At the dead end Carl and Mr. Laswell had gotten out of their car, walked into the woods, and led the police directly to Jimmy.

Carl and Mr. Laswell hadn't even bothered to bury Jimmy. They'd just rolled him into a ditch and covered him up with leaves.

At the trial, the coroner testified that Jimmy had died of multiple blows to the back of the head.

I went to see Carl just once, when he was still locked up in the county jail here.

"Carl," I said. "I want you to know, it was me who told. I called up the sheriff when I was still in the hospital, and I told."

Carl's face sort of crumpled, and then he managed to say, "But how? How did you know?"

I had my answer all ready even before he asked. "Jimmy told me," I said.

Carl had looked at me then as if I were crazy, but once again, I was telling him the truth. The day I died, it wasn't just Uncle Merle and Mama and Daddy that I'd seen, standing there in the light.

I'd also seen Jimmy.

He'd been standing there next to the others, looking at me with love in his eyes. As soon as I saw him, I knew. I knew that the snapshot Carl had shown me months before had been taken before Jimmy had even met me. And I knew right then that Mr. Laswell had lied to me the day Jimmy disappeared.

I'd looked at Jimmy, standing there with the others, and I'd actually reached out for him, even as I'd felt myself being pulled back. Back to life without him. "Not yet, sweetheart," Jimmy had said. "Not yet."

When I'd opened my eyes in the recovery room, of course, I'd started putting it all together. That's why I phoned the sheriff while I was still in the hospital. I didn't tell him about seeing Jimmy and the light, of course. I knew the sheriff would probably never believe any of that stuff. Nope, what I told the sheriff was just my suspicions. I also told him it would be a real good idea to put Carl under some kind of surveillance the day I came home from the hospital.

At that time, of course, I hadn't been totally sure that Carl was guilty, but I'd sure known for certain that his dad was. Mr. Laswell had decided something had to be done to make sure he didn't lose Darlene, and he sure enough had done it.

It had been Carl himself who'd made up my mind about

his part in all this. Carl had made up my mind when he'd phoned his dad the second he thought I was asleep.

In the last twelve months, I've been real busy, what with the trial and all. It helps, I think, to keep busy. I've particularly had a lot to do since Mr. Laswell and Carl were convicted of capital murder, and both of them sentenced to death row.

Mr. Laswell and Carl are supposed to get the electric chair, but I've been fighting real hard to keep that from happening. I've been getting petitions signed, and talking with what seems like hundreds of lawyers. I've even been giving speeches all over Kentucky. I've been doing everything in my power to get their sentences commuted to life imprisonment.

Everybody keeps telling me what a wonderful woman I am. They even wrote me up in the paper as an example of how forgiving a person can be. Aunt Rae told me that she thinks it's on account of my Near Death Experience that I am the way I am these days. It seems she checked out those same library books that she brought me in the hospital, and she's read in quite a few of them that having a Near Death Experience like mine often makes a person more kindly and loving toward their fellow man. Aunt Rae tells me that she believes my dying has made me into some kind of super person, able to look past all this "earthly strife" and to see things on a "higher plane."

Aunt Rae is partially right. It definitely is because of my Near Death Experience that I'm working so hard to save Carl and Mr. Laswell's lives.

I've been dead myself, you see, and I know how it is.

Dying's too good for them.

Cast Your Fate
to the Wind

Deborah Adams

My later encounters with unnatural death weren't pleasant, but certainly that first—when I was quite young and still willing to believe in fairy tales—was the most difficult.

I had just whiled away two years at Tragg-Davis College to be near my fiancé while he completed his degree. My home economics courses were instructive, if dull, and my room-mate, Keebe, was shocking but enlightening. She insisted that she was there to earn a degree, and that marriage had no place in her future. She supported causes that I'd never even heard of, and she believed that President Kennedy was the savior of our country. By late summer I was forced to acknowledge that some of her unorthodox views had rubbed off on me.

In early September my parents invited Tommy's family for an informal dinner in celebration of our engagement. They'd chatted and smiled and planned for hours, with a sort of surprised delight that suggested they'd only just learned of our impending marriage. In fact, Tommy and I had started going steady in high school and had been making plans for over two years while we waited for him to graduate from Tragg-Davis.

I remember spinning wildly around the house that night, babbling on and on about china patterns and the merits of bridesmaids' dresses designed so that they could be worn again and again. By the time we girls retired to the kitchen to clean up and wait for the men to bring the party to an end, I had a nudging headache and I was just trying to keep that smile on my face without bursting into tears. Pre-wedding jitters, I supposed.

The men were in the living room, discussing Tommy's hunting trip for the fiftieth time at least. It wasn't as if they hadn't heard the stories already. The trip had been a graduation gift to Tommy from his father, and had taken place at the same time Valentina Tereshkova was orbiting the planet. (I'd listened to my parents discussing the story one muggy morning. My father said it just went to show that the threat of communism had not passed, because they'd gotten into space before us and what sort of people were they anyway, to subject a lady to the unknown dangers of space? My mother said Valentina was no lady.)

It was also the same time I'd planned to be married, having dreamed all my life of a June wedding. But Tommy had earned his vacation and his father had made all the arrangements without consulting my fantasy life, so I'd rescheduled the wedding for November, the Friday before Thanksgiving. It wasn't a big deal, and Tommy, of course, didn't care when we got married. All the same, I couldn't quite get over the feeling that my wishes had been tossed aside without a thought. I tried explaining it to my mother, thinking surely that she would see my side of it, but she pointed out that men need their time alone and that I was being selfish to carry on about it so much.

The evening would have been easier and more fun for me if my brother, Davey, had been there, but he was working an extra shift that night and couldn't possibly get away. Davey had been on the police force for over three years and loved his job. More than that, he was doing well at it. I couldn't understand why, with a good job and a decent salary, Davey hadn't married yet. He'd have made some lucky girl a wonderful husband.

And Susan's husband, Jamie, the successful young lawyer, was tied up at his office. That left only Tommy, his dad, and mine, to hold down that discussion of hunting and guns they'd carried on all through dinner, which Jamie would have loved because he owned an expensive gun collection and loved showing off his knowledge of the subject. Susan, without her husband, was trying as hard as I to salvage some enjoyment from the evening, but her restlessness gave her away.

"Lily, as soon as you get back from your honeymoon," Susan said as we put away the last clean plate, "we'll go shopping for furniture. Now don't let anyone talk you into taking their crummy old castoffs. It's better to have an empty house than to fill it with a bunch of secondhand junk nobody wanted in the first place."

Susan could think of such things. I never understood how Tommy's sister could be so different from him, always spending money even before she married a lawyer. For starters, she'd insisted on having a car for her high-school graduation. Then she'd gone off to an expensive private college, which was just silly because there were easier, cheaper ways of catching a husband. And she'd wound up marrying Jamie, who'd lived just down the street from her all their lives.

But she was no snob, and I liked her for that. Susan was pretty and fun and born with a knack for fitting into any crowd. She was a perfect wife, a perfect mother, a perfect woman. More than anything, I wanted to be like her. And there she sat in a pale pink sheath, her golden hair poufed, with a perfectly matched pink bow above her bangs. When I'd complimented the outfit earlier, Susan had waved her hand as if it didn't matter and said, "Oh, I got this at Spengler's this afternoon. They're having a sale. You should run by and pick up a few pieces for your trousseau."

What Susan didn't understand was that I couldn't afford

Spengler's prices, sale or no. Even my best friend, Peggy, who worked there and got an employee discount, couldn't afford to buy their clothes straight out.

"Another thing," Susan said, and sipped from the good china cup my mother had used for the occasion, "I'll introduce you to the Young Wives' Club. You'll love it. There's always a project going, so you can get involved with that. We need volunteers for charity fund raisers. And we'll get you into the bridge club, of course."

"That's a wonderful idea, Lily," my mother said. "You'll meet some very good people in those clubs."

"It's nice of you to invite me," I said to Susan, thinking to myself that I would undoubtedly be blackballed on sight anyway, so it wouldn't hurt to go once. No one seemed to have noticed that I wasn't jumping at the chance to hobnob with the area's wealthier element. I remembered Keebe making fun of housewives like Susan, women who frittered away their time playing dress-up for each other and pretending their donations to the church flower fund made significant changes in the world.

"Too bad Jamie had to miss the party," Mom said. "I know it's no fun for you when you're on your own."

Susan had been glancing at her watch nervously all evening, probably waiting for Jamie to call or walk through the door. Now she looked at the time again and shrugged. "Must be one of those troublesome clients of his. People don't understand that a lawyer has a life outside the office. Still, I'd have thought he'd be here by now. Maybe he was tired and just went home."

"That may be," my mother said. "Call him, if you like. Ask if he'd like me to send a plate."

Susan stood up quickly, as if she'd only been waiting for permission to call home, and hurried to the hallway phone. My mother smiled at me as if we shared a secret, then said, "Aren't you glad it's only a few weeks now until you've got a husband to check up on?"

By this time Mom was so tangled in wedding plans that I didn't even have to answer. Whenever she talked about my wedding, her eyes would lose their focus, as if she'd turned away to look at a far-off world made of organza and taffeta and inhabited by the happy little couple from the top of a wedding cake.

"Manicure!" she said suddenly, and quickly added that to the List of Things to Do Before Wedding she had taped to the refrigerator door.

My nails were ragged and chewed off, and the summer heat had swollen my fingers, so that my engagement ring now fit so tightly it became a constant and uncomfortable reminder that time was slipping away while the list grew longer.

Mom returned to the table and plucked a dead leaf off the scrawny African violet she was killing. Several people had tried to tell her that violets needed more light than that one was getting, but Mom paid no attention. She wanted flowers to fit into her scheme, and she would put them where she wanted them, by golly, or else. In my entire life, I'd never seen a healthy one in our house.

"You'll have to make a hair appointment," she reminded me, still foggy eyed. "And when are you going to choose the music, Lily?"

I hadn't even begun to think about music, but fortunately Susan saved me the effort of lying. She pushed the swinging kitchen door open and came back to us with a weak smile and apologies. "Jamie's still at work," she said with a bitter little laugh. "Irene says he hasn't even called."

Irene. Irene was Susan's live-in housekeeper, and she also tended the children whenever Susan wanted to go out. On top of that, Irene's brother, Thad, did most of the yard work and repairs, because Jamie was so busy he had no time for it himself. It was no wonder that Jamie worked until all hours, I thought, with the expensive household he supports.

Naturally when the front doorbell rang at that precise moment, we all thought Jamie had made it to the party after all. Susan looked up nervously expectant, while Mom rose and pulled a plate down from the cabinet. "I'll fix him a bite to eat," she said, digging around the silverware drawer for utensils. "Susan, you go on out there and get Jamie to the kitchen. Otherwise those men will start him talking and he'll starve to death."

Obediently Susan started to do as she'd been told, but before she could leave the kitchen, the door swung open. My brother, Davey, was standing there, looking as good as ever in his policeman's uniform, and glancing around the room as if he'd come to perform a military inspection.

"Susan," Davey said, without even a glance for me, "I'd like you to sit down."

And that was how we learned that Jamie Milam had been murdered.

Death should not be this civilized, I thought. The church was cool and tidy, and all the mourners stood quietly in their places amid the arrangements of scentless plastic flowers, murmuring polite sympathy. I felt we should have howled and ripped our clothes and violently protested to heaven. Maybe some of the others felt the same way, but obviously none of us would break the solemn atmosphere with such honest grief.

Susan's doctor had given her tranquilizers to get her through the next few weeks. Even pale and drawn, she looked beautiful. She wore a navy suit that would have flattered her at any time, and since I knew she'd paid a fortune for it at Spengler's, it certainly should have looked good. For an instant, no longer than it took to shake the thought from my head, I wondered if she felt sick when she realized that she'd been in Spengler's adding to her wardrobe the afternoon that her husband died. It was an uncharitable idea, and I chided myself with my mother's voice.

Tommy and his dad looked as if they'd been tranquilized, too—both of them rigid and stone faced in matching suits, with Susan's two small children pressed between them. My heart broke for those little ones, still too young to understand what death meant but aware that a dreadful darkness had invaded their lives. I hoped that Susan would find a good father for them soon.

Once the service was over, and we'd all said our farewells at the gravesite, Tommy left his father and Susan for a minute to talk to me. "I'm taking them over to the house," he said, meaning to Susan's house. "The car'll be full. You ride with your parents and I'll see you there."

"Davey's going to drop me off," I said. "We'll be there soon."

Tommy's mouth set in a firm line, and I suspected he was about to disapprove of the plans I'd already made. Tommy had never been truly friendly with my brother, and I knew he didn't like the way Davey and I goofed off together, but he must have decided that a cemetery wasn't the place to bring it up again, because he just turned and went back to the other side of the crowd to herd Susan and her children into his car.

As soon as we pulled away from the cemetery and onto the blacktop highway, Davey slipped off his suit jacket and tie and tossed them into the back seat, turned up the radio (the only part of his old clunker that could be counted on to work every time), then lit two Chesterfields and offered one to me. I took a long draw and let it scrape my throat, already made raw by tears.

I peeled off my gloves, but there was nothing more I could do about my own comfort. My feet were pinched inside high heels and I hadn't thought to bring an extra pair of shoes, and my linen suit was not one I could modify without losing modesty.

"Just take off your shoes, then," Davey suggested. "We'll go to Bob's and eat in the car."

The heat of September was stifling, even with the windows wide open. There wasn't enough breeze to make the black interior of Davey's little Volkswagen comfortable. Martha and the Vandellas sang "Heat Wave," making it sound as if tropical weather could be a treat, but I wasn't convinced.

At least at Bob's we were able to park under the canopy and enjoy some shade. Curled up in the seat with a fiesta burger in one hand and a strawberry milkshake in the other, I waited for Davey to offer information. If the police department had known how much he told me about its cases, no doubt Davey would have been sacked right off the bat, but we'd shared secrets since we were children, and I don't think it ever occurred to him not to tell me about the investigation into Jamie's death.

"He returned to his office after lunch and left again right away," Davey started. "No one knows why or where he was going. They say." He gave me the look that meant he didn't quite believe what he'd been told. "No one saw him go into the motel, so we aren't sure when he arrived."

"But didn't he have to sign for the room?"

"Somebody had to," Davey told me. "But this is the Oasis Inn, you know."

He looked at me to be sure I understood. I did. The Oasis was a rundown motel on the outskirts of town. Some of the wilder students in my high school had bragged about going there on dates, leaving details to the imaginations of their listeners. In fact, their tales were so vague, I'd always assumed no one really went there at all.

"The room Jamie was in had been rented that afternoon, but the desk clerk does a lot of one-hour business. He couldn't remember faces, or said he couldn't. And the register says Mrs. Jane Jones was the only occupant. Of course, the register says Mrs. Jane Jones, or her relatives— Mrs. Jane Smith, Mrs. John Jones, and Mrs. Jane Brown— were in other rooms at the same time."

"Gee, they aren't very original, are they?" I said, truly amazed. What I knew about prostitutes I'd learned mostly from Davey, but Keebe had actually known one and I'd heard about that, too. Keebe's opinion did not agree with Davey's, but Keebe hardly ever agreed with anyone. "Wouldn't you think they could find better names for themselves?"

"At the Oasis, no one's interested." Davey offered me his french fries and I took them. The busy morning had not allowed time for a substantial meal, and I'd always been cursed with a hearty appetite that even catastrophe couldn't diminish.

"But I don't understand why Jamie was there," I said. "If one of those women needed a lawyer, why wouldn't she just go to his office?"

Davey ducked his head so I wouldn't see that he was laughing at me. "I don't think he was there to see a client. I think he *was* the client."

"No!" He had to be mistaken. "Jamie wouldn't. With a beautiful wife like Susan?"

"It has nothing to do with Susan," Davey told me. "Some men just want variety, or excitement." He blushed, embarrassed to be talking that way to his baby sister. "We found hair on the sheets—blond, brown, even some Negro hair. Could have been there for days. The sheets aren't changed too often at the Oasis."

"Cripes!" I said, and shuddered at the thought of sleeping on sheets where someone else had slept—or worse—and tried to think of another reason Jamie might have been in that motel room.

"You could be right, though," Davey added. "There was something fishy about it. Jamie had all his clothes on, and so far we haven't found any reason to believe he'd been doing anything. Which doesn't mean he hadn't intended to do it. Looks like somebody caught him just right with the base of a lamp." Davey pointed to a spot on his own head to indicate where Jamie had been hit. "His wallet wasn't gone. We can't figure out why he wasn't robbed, unless she got scared when she saw he was dead. Or maybe she was interrupted before she could take the money and didn't even realize he *was* dead."

"Will you be able to catch her?" I asked.

"Well, we're doing what we can." he said. "We're supposed to talk to everyone we can find who was in the motel that day. The manager didn't like the idea, but I guess he wants to stay in business, too, so he's given us the names of all the regular girls who work out of there, plus the names of a few regular customers. He even managed to figure out the real names of two couples who turned up there. Married, but not to each other, if you know what I mean."

"I know," I assured him. What a sordid conversation. There I was, on the verge of marrying my childhood sweetheart, and I just could not understand what made married people behave so badly. I asked myself if someday, far in the future when we'd both gotten old and fat, Tommy might be one of the men looking for excitement at the Oasis. I swirled the last french fry in catsup and decided that Tommy would never be caught dead in the Oasis. The phrase was unintended, but I couldn't help laughing even as my stomach did a tiny flip-flop. I didn't know why, but it bothered me that I couldn't imagine, try as I might, Tommy doing something so impulsive and wild and undignified.

"I'll get you over to Susan's," Davey said, turning the key in the ignition. "Unless you'd rather go home."

"No," I told him firmly, trying to fit my heat-swollen feet back into my shoes. Are you coming in for a while?"

"Not with Mom there."

I nodded. It had been weeks since Davey had even come to our house for a visit. "I used to think you were too touchy. But since I've been home from school it's been difficult. I guess I got used to living on my own. It seems like I can't do anything to please Mom. We fought for weeks while I was trying to pick out a wedding dress. I finally settled for the one that she liked, just to get her off my back. Now she's decided that my bouquet should be pink roses, and you know I hate pink."

"Just tell her you've decided not to get married at all. That'll scare her so much she'll go along with anything you say."

Davey knew me too well. When I didn't answer, he glanced sharply at me. "What? Having second thoughts?"

I squirmed in the seat, fully aware that I couldn't tell him the truth but knowing that he would recognize a lie. "You know I love Tommy. I always have."

"But," Davey prodded.

"I don't know. I guess I got used to not seeing him so much. When we were both at school and busy with classes or club meetings, I didn't spend a lot of time with him. Not like before and certainly not like now. It's taking a while to get used to going everywhere with him. Being with him. I feel like he's changed so much, I barely know what he's talking about sometimes."

The road to Susan's was coming up, but Davey drove past

without turning in. "Listen, sweetie. Don't let it get you down. No one's going to railroad you into marriage. You can back out any time."

"Good heavens! I don't want to call off the wedding. What would I do if I didn't marry Tommy? But you know what I think? I think going to college was a bad idea. If I'd stayed home and waited for Tommy to graduate, everything would have been fine."

"Yeah," Davey said, with that faraway look he got sometimes, "college can sure turn you around."

Susan's house was crowded with friends and family who kept Irene busy collecting dirty dishes, replenishing drinks, and cleaning up behind the thoughtless few who left their messes when they departed.

Susan seemed calm, but her movements were slow and plodding, as if she'd been enveloped in pudding. She sat in the corner, hands folded in her lap, eyes down as if praying for relief from pain, unaware of the ritual being performed by those around her. My mother hovered there, too, concerned for Susan but also relishing her important role as caretaker. Between them they managed to respond politely to the steady stream of mourners who passed by to express condolences before moving on to the bar and the food.

Without meaning to do it, I became the hostess. I circulated, chatting with this one and that one, offering to refill drinks or plates, keeping an eye on the table and informing Irene whenever the food needed replenishing. Irene's brother, Thad, had been pressed into service as dishwasher and occasionally he would make a pass through the room to collect plates or offer drinks. People kept arriving, bringing covered dishes and sympathetic words. I looked around the room, saw that all was well, and decided to remind Irene to bring in more ice for the bar.

Just as I was about to push open the kitchen door, voices from the other side caught my attention. I paused, hand in air, barely an inch from the door. The voices were low, whispering, but with such intensity they stood out from the deliberate monotones used throughout the rest of the house.

"If I go—" I heard Thad say.

"If you go, what you think's gonna happen? Keep your nose where it belongs."

I waited a few seconds until silence from the kitchen assured me that I would not walk in on a family argument before pushing the door open. While Thad and Irene had chosen the wrong time and place for their petty conflict, I did not want to reprimand either of them. I just wanted to get through the afternoon as quickly and smoothly as I possibly could. "Oh, Irene," I said, as if surprised to find her there. "Someone's spilled a drink on that little table in the hall. And the ice is getting low."

"Yes, m'am," Irene said cheerfully. "I take care o' that right now."

Moving through the house I caught bits of conversation drifting through the low hum of voices. Three of my mother's friends were still talking about the moving service that morning. I gave them the tight smile that is exchanged at such gatherings and moved on.

Others were less touched by the eulogy and already behaved as if the funeral had passed into distant memory and they were not standing in the widow's home. Two women who must have been friends of Tommy's family were hanging over the refreshment table, exchanging recipes for potato salad. I even heard some of the men speculating about Jamie's reason for being at the Oasis. I almost spoke to them, to point out how impolite that was, especially right there in Susan's house, but I didn't want to make the situation worse by causing a scene. Best to ignore it, I decided.

I realized to my great surprise that I was playing a role, gliding through the crowd, saying the right things, making the proper gestures, just as I'd watched my mother do for years. I'd always hated funerals and their aftermath, been uncertain and awkward in conversation, at a loss for words of comfort. Yet there I was, a perfect walking imitation of my mother and Susan and all the other women I'd admired for their grace under pressure. This is a wifely quality, I thought at first, a perfect appearance in spite of everything.

For an instant I was relieved and proud that I'd mastered it, but I couldn't remember *why* this skill was important.

It seemed to take days, but actually was only a couple of hours, before the crowd thinned out. By five o'clock, only Tommy and his father, Susan, Jamie's parents, and I remained. My parents had left moments earlier, rushing to a dinner engagement they'd arranged weeks before and couldn't, in good conscience, cancel.

Maybe it was the absence of my mother's tender care, or perhaps just the natural result of a long and wearing day. For whatever reason, Susan seemed to be coming apart. She hadn't moved from her corner perch all afternoon, but she looked as if she'd been standing at the edge of a twister. Her hair was mussed and going limp at the crown, her stockings had gathered around her ankles, and wriggling in that chair had hitched her skirt up until her garter belt was exposed.

Thad was collecting the final round of dirty dishes, and every time the china clinked, Susan's eyes would dart toward him as if accusing him of deliberately trying to disturb her.

I knelt beside her, patting her knee in a motherly fashion. "Susan," I said quietly, "Davey will be here soon to pick me up. Is there anything you need before I go?"

She nibbled at her nail polish and shook her head, but tears had welled up in her eyes.

"Susan, why don't you go upstairs and rest? You look exhausted."

Again, she shook her head, but this time she took her finger out of her mouth long enough to say, "I'm so keyed up, like I'm about to shatter." A flake of Pink Pearl polish was stuck to her lower lip.

"Have you taken a tranquilizer lately?" I asked. "Maybe you should."

"Yes," she said quickly, seizing the suggestion with almost feverish desperation. "Get them for me, Lily? In my purse. Upstairs."

I gave her knee another pat and left the room as quickly as I could without running, grateful for a chance to be useful.

It hadn't sounded like a difficult task: get a pill bottle from

Susan's purse. The rest of the house was immaculate as well as beautiful, since Susan had redecorated twice in five years and had Irene to keep it spotless, but the bedroom looked as if it had been ransacked. Clothes had been tossed across every surface, the vanity was covered with jars and pots and bottles, and through the open closet door I could see every imaginable wardrobe item spilling off the shelves and onto the floor. The bed had not been made, and in addition to the clothes left on it, the sheets and pillows were twisted and thrown as if Susan had fought to wake herself that morning. Or perhaps she'd struggled to sleep, to drift away into a small dark corner of herself, where Jamie still lived and her life had meaning. I felt hollow inside, imagining the bleak future ahead of her.

I tried to remember the purse she'd carried that day— small, I recalled, and navy blue. Clutched tightly in her gloved hands. I thought a purse that size might be buried under the clutter on the bedside table. Everything else was there—used handkerchiefs, the previous Sunday's society page, a couple of glasses half full of water, a Spengler's receipt, assorted recipes clipped from magazines. But no purse.

Automatically I started to straighten the table as I tried to think where Susan's purse might be. The Spengler's receipt caught my eye. It was for the pink sheath she'd worn the Friday night of my engagement party, purchased that afternoon, when Susan's world was still rosy and Jamie was still alive. The price she'd paid was outlandish, as I'd assumed it would be. But there was something else that grabbed my attention: the receipt was dated September fifth, Thursday. Susan hadn't been shopping while her husband was murdered, at least not for that dress. I felt doubly guilty about that stray thought I'd had earlier.

Stacking recipes neatly, with the receipt on top, I placed them toward the back of the table. I folded the newspaper, then removed the little piles of lace-edged hankies, thinking to put them in the bathroom hamper on my way downstairs. Underneath the linen I found Susan's purse and dug through the contents, searching for the pill bottle. What I found instead was a key, engraved with a room number and *Oasis Inn*.

Susan was behind me when I turned around, her eyes red and puffed. She snatched the key from my hand and stuffed it into the little pocket of her jacket. Then she grabbed the purse. Withdrawing the bottle of tranquilizers, she poured two or three tablets into her hand and popped them in her mouth.

"Should you take so many?"

She dropped the purse and pill bottle onto the bed and stepped in front of me to get one of the water glasses from the bedside table. "I don't care," she said stubbornly, like a pouting child. "I'm as nervous as a cat. I can't stand it, Lily." Tears started to roll down her cheeks and she reached for the pile of handkerchiefs I'd just removed. Not finding them, she opened the drawer and rummaged through it until she came up with one of Jamie's handkerchiefs.

"Lily, it's such a terrible mess," she said, scrubbing her face and in the process smearing mascara across one cheek. "It happened so fast. Jamie was just there, standing in the doorway, and I was with Thad. . . ." her voice trailed off.

I was stunned, speechless, afraid to think about what she was telling me, unable to choose a soothing platitude. I suppose I saw her reach into the drawer again, but I must have thought she was looking for another handkerchief. She had the gun pointed at me before I even saw it in her hand.

"I'm so sorry," she said. "I'm so sorry."

Susan had her left arm linked through my right, her right hand and the gun tucked inside my elbow, so that the gun nudged my ribs but wasn't easily visible to anyone who watched us walk down the stairs and through the living room to the kitchen. They probably thought I was support-ing her, but in fact my knees were so weak that Susan practically had to drag me with her.

Irene and Thad were still in the kitchen and I tried to catch their attention with my eyes, but after one quick glance at Susan, they went about the business of cleaning, studiously ignoring us. Skilled in the ways of colored domestics, they minded their own business.

Leading me to the door that led to the garage, Susan gave me a little shove, then pulled the door closed behind us.

She motioned to the car. "You get in first," she said.

I slid in from the driver's side, with Susan close behind me. She reached across and locked the passenger door before settling herself behind the wheel, the gun still clutched tightly in her hand.

The key was already in the ignition and Susan's car was an automatic, so she was able to hold the gun on me while she drove by sticking her left hand through the steering wheel to put the car in gear. When she slowed to check for traffic before pulling onto the highway, I saw Davey headed our way. He was there to pick me up, in a patrol car that had never looked so lovely before. I tried to unlock the door and jump out, but Susan had seen him, too, and the sight of Davey's patrol car sent her into a frenzy.

Sobbing and cursing, she stamped on the accelerator and tore out onto the highway, swerving dangerously for a few yards before finally getting control of the car.

"Susan! Susan, listen to me! It's only Davey." I glanced behind us and saw Davey following. I couldn't see his face, but I knew he'd be confused. Susan's car, swerving as if the roads were iced, breaking the speed limit by a good twenty miles an hour—what was he to make of that?

"Susan, please pull over," I begged. She was in no condition to drive and kept honking the horn angrily as other drivers attempted to pull onto the highway. I held on to the dashboard with one hand, to the door handle with the other, and still I was tossed about the seat as Susan zipped around the cars in front of us.

Davey had turned on his lights and siren and was trying his best to keep pace with us, but he couldn't, or wouldn't, match Susan's recklessness, and so lagged two or three cars behind. Oncoming traffic pulled to the shoulder in deference to Davey's emergency signals, and Susan took advantage of that to move into the left lane and pass several cars at once.

Davey followed suit, trying to catch up, but Susan continued in the left lane around a curve. Davey was not so daring and pulled back into the line of traffic until the straightaway.

I alternately held my breath and gasped for air, instinctively sliding as far down into the seat as I could. I would have curled up on the floor if I hadn't wanted to keep watch out the back window, as if seeing Davey there could somehow protect me.

Susan didn't seem to have a destination. She drove as if the route meant nothing, as if driving had become her only goal. Down Jackson Street, a left on Twenty-fifth, a right on Madison. We were headed toward downtown, and traffic increased steadily, making Susan's mood even more anxious and her driving more dangerous.

"I'm tired, Lily," she said weakly. "I've been tired for so long. It's like pushing a boulder uphill, with someone on the other side pushing it back down."

Glancing in the mirror, Susan saw what I'd already noticed—we'd lost Davey. I knew that he would have reported by radio and that other patrol cars would be on the lookout for us, but at the moment none seemed to be in the vicinity.

Susan relaxed a bit—maybe all those pills had started to take hold—and she slowed the car to blend in with other drivers. I almost wished she would do something insane, like run the car up onto the sidewalk, to draw attention so the police would spot us sooner.

"I am sorry, Lily," she said at last. Putting the gun in her lap, she made a leisurely right turn on Twenty-first. "I don't know how this happened. Someone told Jamie, I guess, but who? I was always so careful. Still, there's always an old busybody with nothing to do but interfere and spread tales."

"Told him about?" I asked cautiously.

"About Thad and me," She shrugged. "You don't know yet what it's like. Wait until you've been married a little while. You go from being a beautiful, precious angel to a piece of furniture. A vacuum cleaner with hair. Jamie used to be all over me and I felt—" she sighed and gave up trying to find the right word.

I didn't tell her that marriage was a responsibility and not one long date, nor did I remind her that a wife's job was to be what her husband needed, and to do it as efficiently and unobtrusively as possible. For one thing, although I didn't understand it, I sensed that her anger was caused by that very rule of life. For another, I knew in that instant that I was angry, too.

"You thought Jamie didn't love you anymore," I said, "so you took up with Thad."

Susan laughed, a sharp, unbecoming snort. "Love has nothing to do with it," she said. "It's survival. Do you have any idea how empty life is? No, probably not. Let me tell you, Lily, there are only so many club meetings you can attend. Only so many dress shops. So many luncheons and charity benefits. And men?" She dismissed them with a flick of her hand. "One's just like another. Even Thad—just like the rest. And when Jamie burst into that room . . . well, Thad was no knight on a white charger, I can tell you. He took off and left me there to explain to Jamie."

She'd turned left onto Irvin Cobb Drive without even glancing at the traffic. I heard horns blast and tires squeal as the other drivers braked to avoid hitting us. Susan didn't seem to notice.

"Jamie was furious, of course," she said matter-of-factly. "He grabbed me and he was shouting. I'm surprised the whole town didn't hear. And he said he was going to leave me. Take the children and leave me."

Susan glanced at me, her eyes asking for understanding or forgiveness, I wasn't sure which. "I waited to grow up, so I could wear lipstick and go out on dates. Then I waited to get married. I waited through all those months when I was carrying the children. I was waiting for something wonderful to happen. Waiting is like a prison cell, Lily. It's cold and hard and empty."

Picking up speed, she drove absently. I could see her eyes were losing fire, as if the mind behind them had started shutting itself off. They looked like my mother's eyes, as I imagined my eyes had looked back at Susan's, when I'd played the perfect hostess.

"There's nothing left, I suppose," Susan said. "I've had a hole inside me and everything has run out of it. Now there's nothing to fill it again."

We were on the Beltline when I noticed the siren coming up behind us. Susan noticed it, too, and hit the accelerator. This time I did slide down to the floor when I saw the bridge ahead of us—a long, narrow one across the Tennessee River. Susan slammed the brakes so hard the car spun around before stopping.

"You can get out now, Lily," she said calmly, but without looking at me.

I wasn't at all sure I could. My entire body had frozen in fear and shock, but Susan reached across the seat and unlocked my door.

"Get out," she repeated.

I stepped cautiously out onto the firm pavement, feeling the way sailors must when they first touch land after months at sea.

As the siren got louder and I slipped back away from the car, I heard Susan laugh. "I'm not waiting any more," she said, and took off before I'd had time to close the door.

The patrol car must have been in sight, but I was watching Susan as she reached the bridge, jerked hard to the right, and went through the guardrail. The car glided straight out, graceful and smooth, before diving nose first into the river.

Late in November, on what would have been my wedding day, I stood on the bridge at the exact spot where Susan had ended her waiting. Holding my wedding dress over the side, letting it blow and billow in the chill wind, I said good-bye. Even after I released it, the gown continued to float and dance on the air, like a precious taffeta bird set free at last.

Fannie's Back Fence Caper

Susan and Bill Albert

It was right at eleven o'clock on a bright and sunny Monday morning in June when Fannie Couch rolled her old red Ford into the parking lot. The witching hour, Fannie always thought, because eleven was when the magic started. Eleven to one, weekdays, two full hours of magic. Her favorite live radio call-in talk show.

And why not? Fannie asked herself. She leaned over and stretched her neck to see herself in the rearview mirror, patting her newly-rinsed silver curls and smoothing one eyebrow with the moistened tip of her little finger. Finding nothing more in the mirror to attend to, she got out of the car and reached for her floppy-brimmed purple straw hat (the one with the pretty pink roses). Settling it on her head, she started for the radio station. If the Back Fence wasn't her favorite show, she was in deep, serious trouble, because it was *her* show. "Fannie's Back Fence," beamed out over the airwaves on KPST-AM Radio, Pecan Springs, Texas, twenty-five kilowatts of power at 1290 kilohertz on your radio dial, Your Friendly Hill Country Family Station. For the last five years, "Fannie's Back Fence" had been sand-wiched between Harriet Osterberg's "Women's Hour" (which was really only a half hour and in Fannie's opinion pretty much a waste of good air time) and the agribusiness news that came on at one, with frequent breaks for the news, the weather, and paid advertising.

Everybody liked the Back Fence. The reason, somebody said, was that it was a combination of a Methodist potluck supper and the counter at the Doughnut Queen, where all you had to do was listen and pretty soon you'd know everything worth knowing about in Pecan Springs. There were Back Fence regulars as far south as Selma, which was almost to San Antonio on the Interstate, and as far north as Buda, which was practically a suburb of Austin. Not to mention traveling salesmen shuttling back and forth in between, ranchers riding fence in their four-wheel drives, and moms car-pooling to the local swimming pool—all equipped with car radios and car phones. It seemed that almost everybody in KPST's broadcast area tuned in to find out what was on the minds of Fannie and her friends.

Which was gratifying, if understandable, Fannie reflected as she walked down the hall. Looking through the control-room window, she waggled her fingers at Henry Morris, KPST's station manager, sound engineer, disc jockey, news-caster, and weather forecaster, as well as bookkeeper and lawn mower. Henry, who was reading the eleven o'clock news, shook his head and jabbed vigorously in the direction of the clock, indicating that it was three minutes to air time and she should forget about visiting the ladies' room.

It was gratifying because at the advanced age of seventy-eight, when so many of her acquaintances were being trundled off to the nursing home, Fannie had become something of a celebrity. She'd even been written up in *Texas Monthly*, right across from an article featuring the governor, whose white hair was almost as pretty and bouf-fant as Fannie's. Of course, it didn't quite put her in the same class as the governor, who was in a league of her own. But still, it was gratifying.

It was understandable, because Fannie had made up her mind in the very beginning that there wouldn't be any shilly-shallying around at the Back Fence. She wouldn't just air local gossip, which anybody could get at the Doughnut Queen or at Bernice's House of Beauty, if you didn't eat doughnuts. She would encourage listeners to tell their stories. (In Fannie's opinion, there wasn't enough story-telling going on in the world.) And she would air local controversy—the more controversial the better. Fannie knew which buttons to push to get her callers to give their opinions. Her radio personality was a cross between the acerbic Molly Ivins *(Molly Ivins Can't Say That, Can She?)* and the comedic Lily Tomlin ("Is this the party with whom I am speaking?") It was a potent mix.

Fannie went into her sound room, next door to the control room. Today's local controversy was already seated, resplendent in a fuchsia suit, neon-pink blouse and lips to match, in the visitor's chair across the desk from Fannie's own chair in the sound room. She was Pauline Perkins, who had recently won an unprecedented fourth term as mayor of Pecan Springs. The victory was, Pauline was fond of saying, an indication of the trust the fine citizens of Pecan Springs placed in her competence as a civic leader. Not, Fannie thought, as she blinked at Pauline, in her sartorial competence. (*Sartorial* had come up on Fannie's 365 New Words calendar yesterday. This was her first chance to use it.) But she shouldn't be too hard on Pauline. In Pecan Springs, pink was the color of this season's New Woman. The window of Doris's Dresses was draped with a plethora (day-before-yesterday's word) of pink suits, blouses, scarves, and accessories, which must have inspired Pauline's awful choice. It was a damn good thing they weren't on television.

On the other side of the glass window between the sound room and the control room, Henry gave Fannie a grin and a thumbs up. Fannie took off her hat, seated herself on the needlepoint pillow that brought her to the right height, and arranged her floral print dress over her knees, getting comfortable. She reached into her purse for the bottle of Gatorade she always drank during the show, and settled her earphones carefully onto her springy curls. Henry began running the prerecorded commercial and then Fannie's intro music, "The Eyes of Texas Are Upon You," while Fannie settled in for a lively show. Today's local controversy —growth versus no-growth—would make the switchboard light up like the courthouse square the week before Christmas. It was a hot topic, a topic that had been on the boil for months. A topic people seemed ready to kill over.

Fannie pulled the mike boom to bring it within reach, listened for Henry's countdown, and then spoke brightly, stretching her words to sound just a little more like Texas. "Good mornin', ever'body. Glad y'all could join us here at the Back Fence. Hope you've got your chores done for the mornin', but if you haven't, well, it's time to quit anyway. It's gettin' hot out there. But you'll have to turn on your fans an' get out that iced tea, 'cause it's goin' to be hot right here in a minute or two. Mayor Pauline Perkins is visitin' the Back Fence to tell us exactly why it is that Pecan Springs oughtta annex five hundred acres on the west side of town, below Sycamore Canyon. This five hundred acres, which right now is pretty much just cedar brake, scrub oak, and snakes, is called Oak Hills Estates. It's being developed by George Armstrong Autry, president of George Autry Real Estate Developers." Fannie paused and wiggled her eyebrows at Pauline to signal that it was her turn. "Pauline, why don't you take a minute or two to say how come you think Pecan Springs oughtta annex those snakes out there, and then we'll turn the mike over to the Back Fencers."

Pauline leaned nervously toward her mike, while Fannie fiddled with the knob of the VU meter, modulating the mayor's high-pitched voice. "Thank you, Fannie, and thanks for letting me talk about my favorite subject, Pecan Springs, the Friendliest Small Town in Texas! Of course, as we all know, growth isn't a newcomer to our fair town. Granted, it may have taken just about a hundred years to get going good, but since the nineteen sixties, we've been growing like a prairie fire." Pauline was speaking more easily now, warming to her task. "The college—Central Texas State University, of course—is up to twelve thousand. Tourism is booming—up seventeen percent in the last year alone. People from Dallas and Houston love to visit the

cool, clear Pecan River, as it flows over brilliant limestone
ledges between stately columns of hundred-year-old cy-
presses." Fannie sighed, wishing Pauline didn't sound as if
she were reading from a Chamber of Commerce pamphlet.
"Some of these visitors are settling down here. We need
places for them to live. That's why we need this development. And to be honest," she added confidentially, "we
need the revenue that property taxes bring in. It's a whole lot
more reliable source of income than sales taxes. I'm sure you
folks out there don't want us to have to hike the sales tax
another half cent, do you?"

Fannie winced. It sounded like political blackmail to her.
"But Pauline," she put in, playing her favorite role of devil's
advocate, "some people say that all this growth is bad for
Pecan Springs. They say you can't have a peaceful walk
down the Pecan River without runnin' into a tourist lookin'
for a historical marker. The new developments are ruinin'
bird habitats an' destroyin' the quiet life. The crowds are
lovin' this place to death. What's your answer to that?"

Pauline swung into her practiced rebuttal, which went on
for some time, while Fannie sat back and watched the phone
lines start blinking. When she'd first gone on the air, Henry
had wanted to install a delay so she could cut off an abusive
caller or somebody who used four-letter words. But Fannie
trusted her listeners, and she trusted herself. All the calls
that came in were live and real-time.

When Pauline took a breath from her peroration, Fannie
raised her hand and said, "Hold your horses, Pauline, we've
got a mobile-phone caller." She toggled a switch and said,
"Hey, there, you're on the Back Fence."

"Thanks, Fannie. I won't take much of your time." The
man's voice, educated if colloquial, was backgrounded by
the distinctive hiss of the mobile phone and the sound of the
car's motor, and Fannie adjusted the VU knob to compen-
sate. "This development you're talkin' about, Oak Hills
Estates, I don't think the City Council's got any idea what
it's goin' to cost. And I'm not just talkin' money, either. If
they knew what all's involved in developing that place out
there, they'd drop it like the hot end of a brandin' iron."

"But that's just not correct, sir," Pauline replied earnestly. "We *do* know what it will cost. According to the city planning office, the revenue projections from the expanded tax base look extremely good." Fannie always had to smile when Pauline talked about the city planning office, which consisted of Leota McKinney, a street map, and a calculator. "Mr. Autry has already committed to the capital improvements," Pauline added. "The roads, the sewer, the water—all that won't cost a dime in taxes."

"Yeah, sure," the caller said. "But there's somethin' you're not figurin' on, Pauline. Sycamore Creek runs through the middle of that five hundred acres, you know. I'm up here on Half-Mile Road right now, just south of Lookout Corner, and I can look down and see the creek. A coupla miles further on down, it runs into the Pecan River, and then on into town."

"Well, sure," Fannie put in. "I know Sycamore Creek. But it's a dry creek eleven months out of the year. What you're lookin' at is nothin' but snakes and runoff from the canyon up above." Her voice became brisk. It was time to move this one along. "So what's your point, caller?"

"My point," the caller replied, "is that there's somethin' up here that most of you folks don't know about." He dropped his voice as if what he was about to say was some sort of secret. "In fact, it's somethin' a few other folks don't *want* you to know about. I figure it's high time we got all this out in public. I'm ready to tell what I know, just to—"

Fannie's spine was shivered by a metallic screech. "Hey, what the shit!" the caller exclaimed. "Stop that, you asshole, stop—"

Fannie's hand went to the toggle switch to cut the caller off the air. But before she could flip it, the sound of a crash exploded into her headset and out onto the air waves. The needle on the VU meter bounced into the red and stayed there, because the crash was followed instantaneously by the high-pitched shriek of tires in a long slide, accompanied by a man's tremulous scream, then another crash, and then— disconnect. Eerie silence. The needle on the VU meter dropped back down into the normal range. Pauline's mouth had formed into a round O of horrified disbelief.

"Caller, are you there?" Stupid question. With a quick glance at Henry, Fannie followed it with "Whattya say, folks? Time for a commercial break, huh? Meantime, we'll check this out. You hang in there, okay? We'll be right back with Mayor Pauline Perkins and yours truly, Fannie Couch, on your favorite Back Fence." When she heard the commercial come on, she nodded to Pauline to stay put and slipped into the hall.

In the control room, Henry was already dialing. He began talking into the phone as she came in. "This is Henry Morris, at KPST. I'd like to report an accident. At least, that's what I think it was. One of our mobile-phone callers—" He paused, listening. "Yeah, right. Half-Mile Road, just south of Lookout Corner." He glanced at Fannie. "The dispatcher was listening to the show. She heard it. She's talking to the sheriff right now." A few seconds later, the dispatcher was back on the line. "Hey, no kidding?" A grin spread across Henry's face. "Would you ask him to let us know what they find? We'd like to put out the word. Half of central Texas is probably wondering what happened out there."

Henry put the phone down. "Turns out Sheriff Blackwell was listening, too. He said it sure sounded to him like a crack-up, bad one, too. He's sending the nearest patrol unit to check it out."

Fannie smiled, wondering if Blackie considered the Back Fence a good source of community intelligence or just a midday diversion. She'd known Blackie and liked him since he was a kid and used to ride shotgun with his father, who had been sheriff for goin' on twenty years until he died of emphysema. That was back when she and Claude had lived on the ranch, before Claude sold the stock and moved into town and retired to watching the Cowboys and the Oilers on TV. Retire! She snorted. She'd told Claude that he could become a Couch potato if he wanted to. It wasn't in *her* game plan.

Back in the sound studio, the commercial break was ending. Fannie slipped into her chair, put on her headset, and pulled the mike boom down. Pauline leaned forward to say something, but Fannie frowned and yanked her finger across her throat.

"Well, here we are again, folks," she said into the mike. "Fannie Couch, on this side of the Back Fence, with Mayor Pauline Perkins. Today, we're visitin' about the pros an' cons of annexin' Oak Hills Estates. You got an opinion on the subject? If you have, now's your time to speak up. The Back Fence is open for bid'ness." She said the word the way Claude and his cronies always said it, with an exaggerated *d*.

The incoming line was blinking. Fannie toggled the switch and moved her hand to the VU meter, ready to adjust the output. "Mornin', caller, you're on the Back Fence."

"Mornin', Fannie, this is Charlie Stubbs."

Charlie Stubbs was a regular. He had retired from the bank ten years ago, but he still used his eyes and ears. Back in his banking days, he'd learned a lot about certain prominent people in Pecan Springs—probably more than they wanted him to know—and he wasn't above mentioning it from time to time, especially after the person had passed on. He had a good memory, too. For instance, he remembered old Mrs. Peterson, who ran a boarding house behind the bank right after the Second World War and kept a thousand dollars in a savings account, which wasn't bad money for Pecan Springs in the forties. Mrs. Peterson also had a long memory. She remembered 1932, when Roosevelt closed the banks, and she was the type to worry. So she'd come in every once in a while to check on her money. Charlie would sit her down in the president's office while he went to the vault and counted out enough tens to make a thousand. Then he'd put them in an envelope with Mrs. Peterson's name on it, and let her count it. He always put a nice new ten on top, so she wouldn't suspect they weren't the same bills. He said he was just glad she didn't think to write down the serial numbers.

Fannie smiled. The only trouble with Charlie was that sometimes he remembered too much. He'd wander from his story, like a calf who'd get interested in a water hole when he was supposed to be heading home with the herd. "Well, hello, there, Charlie," she said. "What you got on your mind this mornin'?"

"I got a bad feelin', that's what," Charlie said somberly. "That last fella, the one called in before the break? Well, I think he bought it."

"Excuse me?" Fannie asked, not immediately comprehending.

"You know, bought it. Bought the farm, way we used to say in the navy. I was a fighter pilot in the Pacific, with Chester Nimitz, y'know. I was on an aircraft carrier. The *Yorktown,* before the Japs sank her at Midway." He paused reminiscently. "You ever been to Fredericksburg? That's his house there. Nimitz's house. Looks like a ship 'bout to sail across the street. They made it into a museum a few years back, with—"

Fannie nudged Charlie, like a recalcitrant dogie, back to the subject. "You were talkin' about gettin' a bad feelin'?"

"Yeah, well, like I was sayin', I was a fighter pilot. And it would happen just like that, just the way it happened just now. We'd get into it with a buncha Zeeks up in the clouds, y'know, and you'd be listenin' to your buddies shoutin' into the radio and then all of a sudden they wouldn't be there. I mean, you'd had bacon and eggs with 'em not two hours before and they'd be on the radio one minute and gone the next, just like that." He cleared his throat. "Anyway, that's what it was like for me, hearin' that guy just now. One minute he was there, next he wasn't. Ask me, he bought it."

"I think it's early to count anybody out," Fannie replied cautiously. "Henry says that the sheriff's got a car on the way. If they find anything, we'll let y'all know. But thanks, Charlie. You call again, y'hear?" She flipped the toggle again. "Caller, you're on the Back Fence."

The next two callers didn't have anything to say about the accident, but plenty to say, mostly negative, about growth. They put Pauline in a corner, but she didn't let that stop her. She swung away, bravely, while Fannie sat back and listened, wondering what was going on up on Half-Mile Road.

The third caller was Mrs. Powell, the president of the Northwest Middle School PTA, who was in favor of the annexation because it would mean more money in school taxes. It was the fourth caller, a woman whose voice was cracked and raspy with age, who got them back to the car wreck.

"Fannie, this is Miss Ima Mason. Miss Erma's here, too. She's got something to say about that young man who got cut off before he could spill the beans. She's got a theory."

Miss Ima and Miss Erma were in their early eighties. They had been twins once, although Fannie doubted that anybody would ever know it now, after the years had done their work. Miss Erma was frail and waifish looking, with wispy white hair, and she got around with a walker, murmuring vaguely to herself as she slid the contraption along in front of her, colliding with this and that. Miss Ima, on the other hand, was still nimble, with a quick temper, sharp eyes, and a fascinating past. She had spent most of the war as a WAC in France, where she was rumored to have Fallen into Sin with a Frenchman, although Fannie doubted that Miss Ima had ever fallen into anything. Jumped into it, more likely, with enthusiasm.

"A theory, huh? Well, good," Fannie said. "What is it?" She was glad that Ima had called in as an interpreter. When Erma herself called, it took all day to get anything out of her.

"Erma says she believes he was going to tell us about that old Indian burial ground up there in Sycamore Canyon."

"What burial ground?" Fannie asked. "Are you talking about a rock midden?" The hill country was full of two-thousand-year-old heaps of limestone rocks piled three or four feet high and fifteen or twenty feet across by ancient Americans. They were mostly located near the springs, where the mound-builders camped for lunch. These people ate a lot of acorn pudding, so clumps of live oaks grew around the springs, distant descendants of the acorns that didn't get eaten.

"Yes, there's a midden," Ima said. "Our papa did a lot of diggin' up there when he was a boy. He and his brother Pete. Do you remember Pete? He got to be a big shot in the U.S.

Department of the Interior, workin' for Albert Bacon Fall, who got into all that trouble with Teapot Dome in twenty-three. Mother always said that Pete would have turned out just fine if he hadn't fallen in with Fall."

Fannie cleared her throat. "What about that midden?"

"When Papa and Uncle Pete were boys," Ima said, "they'd ride their horses up the canyon and poke around, up where that old caliche pit is. Sometimes they found old bones and a skull or two, and every now and then they'd turn up an arrow point or some such thing. Erma says that maybe some of those old Indian spirits are still up there in the canyon, and they don't like the idea of houses. She says that if they took it into their heads to be troublesome, they might cause all kinds of mischief."

"Well, I suppose," Fannie said doubtfully.

There was a whispery sound on the line, then Ima's voice. "Erma says floods, for instance. They could cause floods."

"Well, now, that's something to think about," Fannie replied, "although I don't know about it being ghosts that makes it flood. When it rains up on the plateau, water can come down that creek five, ten feet high, roarin' like a steam locomotive."

Pauline had been listening. "I believe that George Autry is planning to channel the water," she said tactfully. "They're going to build a check dam at the mouth of Sycamore Canyon, just below the old caliche pit. The dam will impound the water and allow it to settle into the substrate so it will replenish the aquifer."

"Got that, Miss Ima?" Fannie asked. "For any of you who are new around here," she added, "caliche is the gravel and clay that's used to build roads. It's dug out of the hills."

There was a moment's pause, and some murmured conversation. "Erma says she's not too sure about substrate and aquifer," Miss Ima announced. "But she says to definitely mind those spirits."

"Thanks," Fannie said. "We'll pass the word along." She checked the clock. It was time for another commercial break and then the news. "Let's take another break," she said. "But don't go too far. There's more in store on the Back

Fence." She flipped off her mike switch, and cut Pauline's as well.

Pauline stood up. "Are you through with me for today?" she asked. "The Lions Club asked me to drop in at their barbecue luncheon and tell them how we're coming along with the termite treatment at City Hall." City Hall had broken into the news when it was discovered that there were termites in the baseboards in the City Council chambers. The Lions had volunteered to raise the money to eliminate the termites so that nobody had to put the bite on the taxpayers. In fact, Lamar Rhodes, this year's president of the Lions Club, had been on the program a couple of weeks ago to get people to send in money to pay the exterminator.

"I can handle it from here on out," Fannie said. "Thanks for coming." She reached under the counter and pulled out the gift she'd gotten Pauline as a present for being on the show. It was a basket with soap and bath things in it, trimmed with lavender, from China Bayles's herb shop. It was always good to give special guests a little something, Fannie thought. You never know when you might want them to come back. Pauline sniffed the lavender appreciatively, thanked her, and left.

Henry was at the mike in the control room, doing the news. Fannie sat back down and switched on her headset to see if there was anything on the accident. In a second, Henry's rich voice filled her ears.

"At the top of the noon news, the Adams County sheriff's office confirms a fatality in a one-car accident on Half-Mile Road, just below Lookout Corner. A man was killed when his late-model sports car missed a curve and crashed more than a hundred feet over the steep embankment into Sycamore Creek. The driver of the car was on the phone at the time of the accident with KPST talk-show personality Fannie Couch. Evidence in his conversation suggests the possible involvement of another vehicle. Sheriff's deputies continue to investigate. The name of the man is being withheld until his family can be notified. In other news, a White House spokesperson said . . ."

Fannie unscrewed the top from another bottle of

Gatorade, sat back, and waited for Henry to finish. It was chilling to think about the man who went over the cliff in his car at the very minute he was talking to her. A number of weird things had happened on Fannie's show—like the time a woman named Effie drove over from Dime Box (pop. 313) with her dog Maxwell. Maxwell was brown, with floppy ears and one blue and one brown eye. He could count. You'd hold up two fingers, and he'd bark twice. Or three fingers, and he'd bark three times. He could spell, too, as Effie demonstrated by unrolling some paper on which she had printed the alphabet. When she said "dog" or "cat," Maxwell would put his paw on the letters, *d-o-g* or *c-a-t,* one at a time. He was learning more words, too, like beer and taco, although Effie said she wasn't sure she wanted him to graduate to four-letter words. Her husband, Junior, wanted to put Maxwell on "Cheers," and he sent a video tape of Maxwell counting and spelling dog to the producers of the show. But when Effie found out that Maxwell would have to be on the set for weeks and weeks, she said no. She needed Maxwell at home, where he put in a good day's work every day at the Watering Hole, which Effie and Junior owned. Maxwell would deliver beer cans to customers, put the empties in the trash, and pick up his tip in his teeth. "It's like there's maybe a person inside that hide," Effie said, after Maxwell demonstrated his talents by taking a soda pop to Henry and bringing back a quarter. "You keep wantin' to pick him up and shake him to see who you can shake out."

But this was even weirder than Maxwell, Fannie thought, shivering as she remembered the crash. It was too bad the man hadn't finished his sentence before he died. She'd give a lot to know what it was he was ready to tell the instant before he went over that cliff. Henry signed off with the weather report—more hot and dry, no rain in sight except over in east Texas where they had no business with it—and punched up the commercial tape, while Fannie wondered what Maxwell would make of the guy driving over the cliff, still talking on the phone.

Fannie began her second hour the way she always did, with the list of current goings-on in Pecan Springs, starting with the garden club's bake sale and ending with a marimba recital at the First Evangelical Church. She was no sooner finished when the phone line began to light up. The first caller was from the Pecan Springs Merchants' Association in favor of the annexation. The second was Mrs. Caraway, who was staunchly anti everything. The third was a woman Fannie had never heard from. She had such a shrill soprano that Fannie had to reach fast for the VU dial to turn her down before Henry had a heart attack.

"Fannie, my name is May Humphrey. I live over on Alamo Street, a couple of houses down from Fourth."

"Glad to hear from you, May," Fannie said, watching the needle and giving the dial one more little twist. "What's happenin' on Alamo these days? Did the city ever get that cottonwood tree out of Mr. Petrie's front yard?" Struck by lightning one stormy night a few weeks before, the cotton-wood had posed an impending peril to the cars stopped for the light at Alamo and Fourth.

"Yes, that came down last week. But there's something else happening right now. I was listening to your show and watering my lemon geranium here in the dining-room window and thinking that if there *was* another car involved in that accident, like Henry Morris said, it could be driving around with a lot of damage." May paused, becoming confidential. "Just like this big white one with the front right fender all bashed in that's pulled up in the alley beside my house, not ten feet from my window."

"Hold on a sec, May," Fannie said. "The sheriff didn't say anything about what kind of car they're looking for, or what color. They just said . . ."

May's soprano voice became coloratura, decorated with trills and chirps. of excitement. "I know that, Fannie, but what I'm telling you is that there's a car out here in the alley, and this man is looking right through the window at— Oh, my goodness! Stop out there! Stop!"

There was a crash, and a long silence.

"May?" Fannie asked. "May? Where are you? What's going on? *May?*" She felt like an air traffic controller and

May was up there in the fog in a little single-engine Cessna. She hadn't lost another listener, had she?

But no, May was back on the line. "Sorry," she said. "I dropped the phone. I'm at the front window now."

"Where's the white car?"

"He just zoomed out onto Alamo," May replied excitedly. "And now he's zipping right through the red light at Fourth. Watch that bicycle! Watch—! Oh, my stars." May was panting. "Thank the good Lord, he missed Bertie."

"Bertie?"

"Bertie Bracewell. On that new red bicycle his uncle got him for his birthday last week. It's one of those racing bikes, and Bertie isn't too steady on it yet." She pulled in her breath. "I tell you, Fannie, it was eerie, watching that man! It was just like he could hear what I was saying to you!"

"Did you see which way the white car went after it missed Bertie Bracewell?"

"Well, no, not exactly," May admitted, "because the wisteria's in the way. But the last I saw, it was heading east down Fourth. Really, he ought to be arrested for running that red light."

"So there's a damaged white car, driving fast, east on Fourth," Fannie said. "I'm sure the Pecan Springs police will keep an eye out for him. Thanks, May." Quickly, she toggled the phone switch. "Caller, you're on the Back Fence."

The man's voice was rough and thick, with the trace of a German accent. That wasn't at all surprising, because Pecan Springs had been settled by Germans midway through the last century, and some of the families still preserved what they could of the Old Country in the way of crafts, foods, and language.

"Fannie, this is Gus Schwartzenhamer. That old caliche pit the mayor mentioned, up in Sycamore Canyon? Maybe you'd be interested to know that they dug that pit when the county was building Farm-to-Market 2316."

"FM 2316? That's a long time ago, Gus."

Gus sighed heavily. "Yeah, tell me about it. That was

when my son Willy was only seven or eight, and he's thirty now, and coaching football down in Alice. He had a winning season last year."

"Did he," Fannie said. "What else do you know about that pit?"

"Not much, actually, except that I doubt there are any Indian ghosts left in that area—too much heavy equipment. Willy and me, we used to go up there for target practice, but we had to stop. Somebody stuck No Trespassing signs all over the place, like it was all of a sudden off limits or something. I've always wondered why."

"Now, that's interestin'," Fannie said. "Any of you Back Fencers out there who know why that caliche pit went off limits, let us hear." She toggled the switch again. "Hi, you're on the air."

"Fannie, hi." The woman spoke crisply. "This is Hazel Jennings. I'm the secretary of the local chapter of the Audubon Society. That white car somebody phoned in about? Well, I can see it from here."

"Where's here, Hazel?" Fannie asked excitedly.

"My back porch, which looks out over the Pecan River on the opposite side from the park, just about even with the Josephine Gilbert Memorial Rose Garden. I sit out here every day about this time to watch birds. Anyway, that white car that lady phoned in about? It's a Lincoln. Right this very minute, it's sitting under the pecan trees on the other side of the rose garden. There's a man in the driver's seat."

Fannie frowned. "You can see across that river and clear to the other side of the rose garden? You must have pretty good eyes."

"I've got my binoculars." Hazel's voice tensed. "Fannie, that man in the car, he's bent over, like he's listening."

Fannie frowned. If the driver was listening now and he had been listening in the alley off Alamo Street, had he also been listening at the time of the wreck? Maybe he panicked when the first caller started to tell the world why Oak Hills Estates shouldn't be annexed, and on an impulse, ran the sports car off the road.

"Now he's straightening up," Hazel said. "He's starting the car. Now he's pulling out. He's coming up the dirt road."

Fannie was suddenly inspired. "Hazel," she said, "can you see his license plate?"

"Wait a minute, until he comes out from behind the rose garden. Yes, now I can see it! It's one of those plates with letters on it." Hazel was triumphant. "Got a pencil? Here goes. I-A-M-G-A-A. And there *he* goes! He's heading out of the park, up Anderson Avenue, in the direction of the square."

Henry's voice came over the earphones, telling Fannie it was time to take a commercial break. But the phone lights were blinking, the callers were stacked up like rush-hour on the Interstate, and Fannie had the feeling that things were happening out there that people ought to know about. She frowned at Henry, shaking her head and tapping her headset as if she couldn't quite make out what he was saying, and toggled the phone switch again.

It was Lester Mooney, whom she hadn't heard from in several months. For a while Lester would always call when somebody he knew was having a birthday so he could sing "Happy Birthday" over the radio. He said it was cheaper than buying a card, because cards had gone up to six bits for a good one, plus a first-class stamp, more if it was oversize.

"Hey, Fannie," Lester said. "Thought maybe I'd check in."

"If this is a birthday, Lester," Fannie said as tactfully as she could, "I'm afraid we don't have time this afternoon. We've got something cookin' here that—"

"I know, I know," Lester said. "That's why I called. Wife and I used to live just down the road a piece from that caliche pit, you know." Fannie didn't know. In fact, it always amazed her that some of her callers seemed to assume that she was party to the intimate details of their lives. "Anyway, what I was goin' to say was about those No Trespassing signs Gus Schwartzenhamer mentioned. I saw 'em too, and I wondered what the heck was happening. First there was the signs, and then there was this truck that would

57

come, usually around midnight. I told my wife, Annabelle, her name was, I said, 'If you ask me, Annabelle, somebody sure is dumb to be paying a driver overtime to haul stuff at night.' "

"What do you think?" Fannie asked. "Was it somebody stealing gravel, maybe? Hauling off caliche?" Lots of folks didn't know how valuable good caliche rock was until they left a pile alongside their lane, getting ready to mend potholes, and woke up one morning to find it gone.

"Nope, it weren't a caliche truck. It was a stake-bed with a green canvas tarp over it, tied down. Always wondered what it was that truck was haulin'. Come to think of it, there was something else odd, too."

"What was that?"

"Well, the afternoon before the truck would come, this tractor with a backhoe and a front-end loader would come up that road, and the morning after, it would leave. I put two and two together and figured they was buryin' somethin' up there."

"Is that right?" Fannie asked thoughtfully. "Do you happen to remember anything about that truck, Lester?"

"Well, yeah, matter of fact, I do. It had a kind of a funny sign painted on the side."

"Funny ha ha?"

"No, funny weird. It was the letters *A* and *E,* in red, kind of locked together with a black circle around it. Always remembered it because my wife's name was Annabelle Eloise. She was named after both her grandmothers. She died not long after that." He sighed. "It's lonesome, livin' on twenty years after your better half."

"I know, Lester. But listen, you call in any time, will you? Don't let yourself get too lonesome." Fannie toggled off and smiled up at Henry. "We're taking a commercial break, folks," she said. "But don't leave your radios. The Back Fence will be right back."

Fannie took the opportunity to go to the ladies'. She hadn't been since before eleven, and all that Gatorade made it necessary. When she was finished, and had washed and dried her hands and put on some of the Jergens lotion she kept on the shelf over the sink, she went back to the sound room and put on her headset.

Henry was cross. "I just wish you'd follow the rules, Fannie. You trying to make us lose our sponsors?"

"I'm sorry, Henry," Fannie said humbly. "I'll do better. I just got kind of interested in what people were sayin', that's all. Have you heard anything from the sheriff's office?"

"Yeah," Henry said, mollified. "There's a streak of white paint on the left side of the wrecked car. And Bubba's office called to say that they are on the lookout for that banged-up Lincoln, and will people please call in if they spot it." Bubba Harris was the chief of the Pecan Springs PD, not one of Fannie's favorite people. It was his cigar, mostly, although he never smoked it, just stuck it in one side of his face. But Fannie tried to make allowances. You couldn't like everybody.

"Thanks," Fannie said, and settled back in. The commercial over, she flipped the mike switch and passed on the word about the white paint on the wrecked car and Bubba's request for information regarding the whereabouts of a white Lincoln. Fannie consulted her notes and read off the license-plate number.

The first call came from another mobile phone. The caller was a salesman for an electrical supply company in New Braunfels, on the way to San Antonio.

"Been listening to your show," he said. "That logo on the side of that truck—*A* and *E* in a black circle? Well, as I recall, that was the logo for a company used to be located in San Antonio. Agerton's Electric, it was called. They made transformers for power companies."

Fannie chewed her lip, thinking about that stake-bed truck with the tarp tied down over its load, driving up Half-Mile Road at midnight to rendezvous with a tractor with a front-end loader. "Don't electrical companies use a lot of chemicals?" she asked.

"You bet they do. Some of it's pretty nasty, too. PCBs and even nastier waste products, like dioxin. Not the kind of stuff you want in your backyard."

Fannie hunched over the mike, thinking out loud. "What

if that truck was hauling chemicals up to the caliche pit for burial?"

The salesman laughed shortly. "What if? Listen, Fannie, that's such a bad what-if you don't even want to think about it. If somebody hauled barrels of PCBs up there twenty years ago, they're leaking like sieves by now."

"Leaking?" Fannie asked. "You mean, the chemicals could be polluting the soil?"

"Yeah," the salesman said, "that's exactly what I mean. Somebody oughta go up there and check. But not me. Not after what happened to that guy in the sports car. The one who went over the cliff."

"So you're thinking that he might have known what was in that caliche pit and somebody killed him to keep him from telling?" Maybe it wasn't deliberate, though. If the driver of the white car had been listening, he could have just panicked. Seeing the sports car ahead of him and knowing that the driver could put a stop to the annexation, he might have just lost his head. It could have been a crime of passion, of opportunity.

"Yeah, maybe that's what happened," the salesman said. "Hey, here's my exit. Ten-four."

Fannie ten-foured, still thinking about how the wreck might have happened, and fielded a call from Sara Oljewski, who had just tuned in and wanted a recipe for prickly pear jelly. Fannie, who kept a box of most-frequently-asked-for recipes under the counter, obliged, although she couldn't help wishing that people wouldn't interrupt with irrelevant questions. Where was that white Lincoln? Why didn't somebody call in and say it had been spotted?

The next call was back on track, although it had nothing to do with the white Lincoln. It was Jake Browne with the Texas Water Commission. Fannie was gratified to learn that Mr. Browne's state car wasn't equipped with a mobile phone. He'd stopped at the Dairy Queen up by Kyle to put in the call.

"I've been listening to your program," he said, "and I need somebody to give me directions to this caliche pit you've been talking about. I'm on my way back from an inspection in south Texas, and while I'm in the area, I was thinking I'd just drop in for a look at the site, maybe take a few samples."

"Good idea," Fannie said, and gave directions. "By the way," she added, "what do you think about that check dam they're fixin' to build up there at the foot of Sycamore Canyon?"

Mr. Browne was cautious. "Well, it's hard to say until we get up there and see what the situation is. But if there *are* any chemicals buried in that caliche pit, all I can say is, it had better not flood, which is what would happen if somebody puts in a dam down below. The way the substrate is around here—"

"By substrate," Fannie said quickly, mindful that some of her listeners—Miss Ima, for one—might need a little help, "you mean the underground limestone? And while you're at it," she added, "would you also say a little something about the aquifer?"

"The limestone is the substrate," Mr. Browne said. "It's like a layer of Swiss cheese, a couple hundred feet thick. It's full of holes, some of them as big as a house, and the holes are full of groundwater. This Swiss cheese is what we call the aquifer. It soaks up the water and anything that's dissolved in it and then delivers the water to the springs and the water wells."

"So if somebody built a dam that flooded the caliche pit where chemicals might be buried, we could end up drinking PCBs here in Pecan Springs?"

"Quite likely," Mr. Browne said. "I'm not saying for certain, mind you," he added hastily, "but there's a chance."

"And if that's true," Fannie said softly, "there's also the chance that somebody didn't want anybody else finding out about it."

"Stranger things have happened, I suppose."

"They sure have," Fannie said, brightening. "Have you ever heard of Maxwell, the Mathematical Wonder Dog?"

Mr. Browne said he hadn't, thanked her, and promised to let her know what the tests turned up.

"Well," Fannie told her listeners after Mr. Browne had said good-bye, "that must be about it, isn't it?"

But it wasn't, quite. There was another call, and as Fannie toggled the switch, she thought that her fingers were getting tired and she might just be glad to get home and join Claude on the couch. But when she heard the throatily familiar voice saying "This is Ruby Wilcox," she perked up.

"Ruby!" she said. "Welcome to the Back Fence!" Last fall, Fannie had done a very interesting phone interview with Ruby on the subject of cults in Pecan Springs. This had taken place after the deaths of Bob Godwin's black goat and Beatrice Bragg's chickens, and in the wake of a particularly nasty murder at Lake Winds Resort Village, out by Canyon Lake. For her listeners, she added, "Ruby owns the Crystal Cave, Pecan Springs's only New Age shop. She's an expert on weird things. What's going on at the Crystal Cave today, Ruby?"

"Lots!" Ruby exclaimed. "But it's what's going on in China Bayles's herb garden that's interesting right this minute."

"Why?" Fannie asked. "Is China growing some new kind of herb?" China Bayles, who at one time had been some sort of lawyer in Houston, was now the owner of Thyme and Seasons, a flourishing herb shop. China's and Ruby's shops were side by side in a big stone building on Crockett Street.

"It's not an herb," Ruby said. "It's a white Lincoln. The driver lost control as he came around the corner. He hit the front porch of the Craft Emporium and ended up in the tansy bed."

"A white Lincoln?" Fannie exclaimed eagerly.

"I can see it through the window. The driver's staggering out! Now he's falling over. No, he's getting up again, and he's looking all around. Fannie, he must be able to hear me on his car radio!"

"Well," Fannie said reasonably, "tell him to surrender."

"Hey, you, there," Ruby said loudly. "Put up your hands!" There was a moment's pause. "That's right. Now turn around and put those hands on the hood! No false moves. We've got you covered. The cops are on their way."

Fannie bounced up and down in her chair, punching the air with her fists. "We've got him, Ruby!" Over the phone, Fannie could hear the sound of a siren, then the screeching of tires and the slamming of doors. She could imagine Bubba Harris hoisting his bulk out of the police car, his gun at the ready.

"Bubba's here," Ruby announced breathlessly. "He's got a deputy with him. The deputy has her gun out. Now Bubba's patting the man down, looking for a gun or a knife. Now he's putting on the handcuffs, and the deputy is reading something off a little card."

"His rights," Fannie explained, to those of her listeners who didn't watch "Murder She Wrote." "It's the Miranda rule."

"And now Bubba's looking at the front right fender," Ruby reported. "And the deputy is putting the guy into the back seat of the patrol car." Ruby took a deep breath. In the background, a siren began to wail. "And there they go," she said.

Fannie glanced at the clock. "And here *we* go," she said. "It's nearly one o'clock and time for the agri-weather report. Thanks for that great wrap-up, Ruby. And thanks, too, to all you fine Back Fencers for a wonderful job."

It wasn't until she signed off that Fannie figured out that the license plate I AM GAA had to belong to George Armstrong Autry. She felt kind of foolish for not having realized it before. If Maxwell the Wonder Dog had been there, he probably would have put his paw on it immediately.

But that was all right. Her listeners were every bit as smart as Maxwell. They'd figure it out for themselves. And when they did, they'd be sure to call in and let her know.

His Tears

Marilyn Wallace

═══════════

The way I remember it, things started unraveling at Ralph Medina's funeral. Alex started crying then, and his tears eventually washed over all my suppositions about my husband and my marriage, and about ordinary life as I'd understood it.

At the memorial service, everyone cried. All the women, of course, but the men, too. Five days earlier, a truck carrying oranges from the Central Valley to the local Safeway spun out of control on a rain-slicked street and Ralph was killed instantly. His two little girls, aged eight and eleven, spent weeks in the hospital. I wondered what life would be like for them if their injuries never healed right, what it would be like to grow up with a permanent limp or a ragged white scar running down one of those beautiful cheeks.

The weather had turned cool and sunny for the memorial service and the coastal hills were still green. At first, Alex didn't cry. "It's strange," he whispered as we filed in to the empty pew in the middle of the chapel, "being here with all these people you know from some committee to improve street lighting, neighbors you talk to on line in the hardware store on Saturday morning. Ralph had so much to live for. It's hard to believe he's really dead."

I put my hand on his arm and whispered to him. "Those poor girls, losing a father. And Angie . . . We're so lucky. It's a good thing, I guess, that we all don't know when it's going to be our time." My eyes stung and my nose began to drip. I leaned over and gripped his hand. "One minute, you're just standing there, and the next . . . Bam!"

And then Alex cried, quietly, just for a little while, right along with everyone else. "Poor Ralph, taken by surprise like that. Didn't have any warning," he whispered hoarsely.

His voice and his manner were so strange, as though he felt personally guilty about not telling Ralph that his life was in danger. I put that thought out of my mind and started worrying about Angie Medina. She and Ralph had been poring over brochures for a summer camping trip to the Tetons. Now, she had only empty evenings in that house, wandering from room to room in search of a husband who would never go anywhere with her again. I didn't catch the real meaning behind Alex's words until months later.

When I did think about it, I assumed that Alex was just on an emotional edge, teetering and unsettled over the situation at work. It was no secret that his team's petroleum explorations might mean a partnership for him. He'd been preparing for that for sixteen years, maybe from the very first day of graduate school, certainly since he returned from the field trip for United Geotechnologies on which three of the new geologists earned the title Wylbur's Wonders.

Actually, there were four of them at first. They'd been a team in graduate school, Alex, George Stoddard, Dick Micelli, and Danny Forsythe. They spent so much time studying at our cramped married-students' apartment, I even fell a little bit in love with dark-eyed, quixotic Danny for a few weeks, shared two sweet, furtive kisses when we volunteered to get jelly doughnuts and coffee to fuel a late-night cram session. Those kisses made me so afraid I'd do something to jeopardize my marriage, I made myself fall out of love with Danny and never let myself be alone with him again.

They were among the nine men—in those days, there were no women on staff—hired when the company expanded. Charlie Wylbur must have told them fifty times that he expected them to do wonders for United Geo, and the name stuck: Wylbur's Wonders. They spent from summer into the late, almost snowy fall together, first in the sharp peaks of the Tetons and later at Nevada's echo-filled Paradise Mountain. Beery and grubby, they dug around extracting samples, trying to coax out the earth's secrets.

Poor Danny never made it back. In the very last week of the trip, the ledge on which Danny was standing gave way. He fell hundreds of feet to his death. When I heard the news, I cried for days, trying to drown the feeling that his death was some form of divine punishment for those stolen kisses. Eventually, my good sense won out. It had been an accident caused by bad judgment, nothing more.

Coming back to the home office in San Francisco was hard for the remaining three. They mourned Danny, and made light of my attempts to talk about field safety, as though that was all they could expect of a woman. Something about Alex, a way of disappearing in the middle of a conversation, marked a change in him that I feared would be permanent. He spent hours each week tramping through the thick stand of eucalyptus trees behind the house rather than join in the active—perhaps too active—social life of our suburban town. Life lived in buildings and on streets, he told me once as he was lacing up his hiking boots, seemed artificial, covered up.

But by the following winter, things had changed again. On a flight back from a conference in Boston, somewhere between the folds of the Appalachians and the Continental Divide, he accepted the fact that an increasing share of his time would be taken up with office work. He wanted to get somewhere, he said, for his family's sake.

He never spoke of Danny Forsythe again. He'd made the adjustment well, it seemed to me. Until he started crying.

A month after Ralph's funeral, Alex and I sat on the screened porch enjoying the night silence. I was lost in the velvet black sky, enchanted by stars that looked like Christmas lights resting in the tops of the trees. With as much emotion as he'd pack into a comment on the price of coffee, he delivered a story that pricked my curiosity and confirmed my wariness. He described sitting in an empty conference room on the sixteenth floor of United Geo, working on a presentation, but I knew he was trying to tell me something else. I had always been good at listening between the lines, but I couldn't quite decipher the meaning of his tale.

"All of a sudden, I realized that the project was going to be junked before the end of the week. All the calculations and projections, months of studying contour maps and analyzing core samples, all for nothing. The hotshot rockhounds on the new field team decided that there was no chance of finding oil in that quadrant unless a freighter sprang a leak."

Huge tears plopped out of his eyes. He waited, then said, "I thought I could talk about it without *this.*" He brushed at his eyes with the back of his hand. "At least then I was alone. I took the papers back to my office, told Irma to hold my calls, and cried."

I understood his tears at the memorial service. But this sounded like just another business situation. I found it hard to believe that the idea of young hotshot rockhounds baking in fellowship and the Arizona sun and finding no sign of oil had reduced him to tears. When I asked, Alex only mumbled something about tension at the office.

It worried me. I tried five or six times to get him to open up to me, but he brushed away my questions with a joke or a shake of his graying head. We had always been partners, sharing our thoughts and feelings, and the responsibilities of earning money, taking care of Janet and Jeffrey, and running our four-bedroom, three-bath house. Alex puttered in the yard, tending the tidy border of flowers and seeing that the white latticed gazebo was kept painted and sturdy. I did the stuff women have done forever—shopping, cooking, chauffeuring the kids. The arrangement had suited us for years. I wondered whether his job had become too stressful, whether I should start working full time instead of the thirty hours a week I was putting in at the real estate office. To take some of the pressure off him. Even, to start shifting my life around so that when Janet and Jeff went off to college in the next several years, I wouldn't have huge gaps to fill.

The next morning, Alex was sullen and withdrawn, staring out the window, not even hearing the children call out to him.

I suggested a trip. We piled into the car and went down to the marina to work on *No One's Fault,* the thirty-five foot sailboat the Wonders had bought.

There were only two Wonders now. Right after Ralph's funeral, Dick Micelli decided to try his luck in a new place. He moved to Minnesota so quickly I hardly realized what had happened. But he really wasn't making it in San Francisco. The change would be good for him, we agreed. Poor Dick, so embarrassed that he took off without anyone having a chance to say a proper good-bye. One day he was at United Geo and the next it was as though he'd fled for his life. Alex and George bought out his share of the boat; it was the least they could do, they decided.

We clambered onto the deck and the kids got busy up near the prow. A wind surfer, a speck far out on the water, caught my eye. Alex spotted him too, and he stumbled and his keys went over the side. It was only a clumsy accident but he stood there, stone still, and watched the keys sink into the oily water. A little tear formed in the inner corner of each eye. The wind surfer made a great sloping turn toward the shore, and Alex began to cry in earnest.

"Dick always wanted to take wind surfing lessons." He said something else but his words were lost in the soft sobs.

His tears didn't last very long, but for the first time, I started putting pieces together. Danny Forsythe's death sixteen years ago, the failure of a geology field team, Dick Micelli's hasty departure: they were all triggers. I eased away from Alex and studied his tanned and frowning face. What was he hiding from me? Why was my husband crying?

I wasn't sure I really wanted to know.

Then I began to wonder whether it would ever stop.

He cried when the Giants lost an eleven-inning heart-stopper.

He cried when the kids took their new rollerblades for a test ride and whooped and hollered all way down the street.

He cried when he watched Steve McQueen jump that fence in *The Great Escape*. It was two A.M. and he thought I was asleep, but I heard him sniffling.

I crept back into bed without telling him I'd seen him. I added the notions of losing, of risk-taking, to my list of things that made Alex cry. But it still didn't make sense. He finally had most of what he'd always said he wanted—his family well cared for, a good job. Maybe he was worried that the Arizona project would cost him points with United Geo. If that was it, he was keeping it to himself, shutting me off from his fears. Protecting me, perhaps, but this silence was harder on me than whatever he might be hiding. Missing out on a partnership wouldn't be the end of the world. Actually, he wasn't planning on it until he was forty-five, so he still had six years to go.

We were in the garage, wrestling with the patio furniture, and Alex stepped on something. He bent down and peered at the battered old canteen he used to carry dangling from a strap on his pack when he worked the Tetons and the Bighorns. A canteen, and it made him cry. Before I could say anything, we heard George Stoddard in the yard, talking to Janet. Alex pulled on his sunglasses and carried the lounge chair cushions out.

"How about it, old man," George said heartily—everything about George has always been hearty, even when he was twenty. "Want to come by this afternoon and watch the fights? Meredith and the kids are off to get outfitted for summer camp and I've got some cold Beck's and some warm Guinness."

Saturday afternoon boxing. Alex and George used to watch those bouts together years ago. I'd forgotten about that.

"Love to, George, but I have too much to do. Why don't you and Meredith come by later for happy hour? Maybe we can decide on the paint for *No One's Fault.*"

George put his arm around Alex's shoulder. "Sounds great, old buddy," he said brightly, and turned back to his yard.

"I can finish up here," I told Alex, anticipating a quiet afternoon spraying down the patio furniture with a hose, letting the water mist my skin as the wind blew it back to me. "If you want to go over to George's, don't worry about the chores."

"And watch two men hit each other until one falls down?"

I looked at him and wondered whether I'd rather be the one to fall down or the one to knock the other guy down. Either way, I never could watch boxing matches because I couldn't stand the thought that I was taking pleasure in seeing someone else's pain. But my husband used to love those afternoons.

Another piece to the puzzle named Alex? Or further proof that something terrible had happened that first year, that Danny Forsythe's death wasn't really an accident? My husband was behaving like a man with a dark secret. Perhaps his crying was his way of releasing inner stresses, the way small earthquakes are said to relieve larger subterranean ones.

He wiped at his eyes under the lower rim of his dark glasses and turned away from me, but I caught his arm.

"What's going on, Alex? You haven't been this upset since Danny died." Breathless, I waited for his response.

He yanked his arm out of my grasp. "What are you talking about? Danny Forsythe? Why did you bring that up now?" His eyes filled not with tears but with a dark, heavy curtain that dropped from somewhere inside and let me see nothing. He stalked into the house, and I was left in the cool and dark of the garage to do battle with the facts.

This wasn't going to go away on its own. I wanted the Alex I'd married to come back. Steady, loving, absorbed in his work and his family. Always the good friend. More than anything, I wanted our life to unfold the way we'd planned it, right down to Janet going to medical school, Jeff coaching baseball at some Ivy League university, and Alex and me taking pleasure from our garden, our friends, and an occasional trip to Europe as we enjoyed our golden years.

That earthquake image, though, made me look at Alex with new eyes. It set me at a distance to be watching him that way, but I convinced myself that maybe Alex needed to be left alone a little while, so that he could work out whatever was eating at him. He seemed to be feeling better. A whole week, and he didn't cry; not in my presence.

The next Saturday, we took our coffee out back into the yard. The sun bounced off a quartz crystal Alex had put on the kitchen windowsill last year, making dazzling patterns on the soft, dewy grass. The quiet was restful. Then, we heard the children's voices.

Jeff was sitting on the bench in the gazebo with his hands balled into tight fists on his knees. Janet was crosslegged on the floor, looking up at him, her hair held behind her ears with two red clips that look like hearts.

"I should have been the starting pitcher," Jeff said. "I worked for it. I'm just as good as Timmy."

Alex's jaw tightened, and I was sure he was preparing to tell Jeff that he'd talk to the coach, rush to his car, and go off to champion Jeff's cause. But he sat still, eyes fixed on the two kids enclosed by their bond in an invisible circle of shared secrets. There was no room for Alex or for me.

"You're angry, huh?" Janet toyed with the laces of her Nikes.

"Yeah. I feel like smashing Timmy in the face." Jeff's fists opened and clenched shut again.

"I bet you feel sad, too." My daughter's voice was steady. Jeff didn't answer, and when she looked up at him he lowered his gaze. "You know," she said slowly, "it's okay to cry when you feel sad. I've seen Daddy do it. Lots. Yesterday in the car, this morning, when he was reading the newspaper."

"I don't believe you!" Jeff stared at her. Then he jumped down from the deck of the gazebo and ran up the path toward the house, not even seeing us as he pounded toward the door. When he reached the steps he whirled around. "You're a liar!" he shouted.

Janet's mouth fell open and she clutched her stomach.

Alex turned deathly pale, pushed himself out of the chair, and fled in the direction of the house.

This escalation was a signal to me. Whatever was bothering Alex, it had caused a rift between the children. Alex's tears were ripping the family apart. Too much was at stake, and I couldn't let it go on.

If I couldn't get this new and strange Alex to talk to me, I could at least get the voice of the old Alex to share some insight into the situation. The old Alex. Did he know something about Danny Forsythe's death that was just now rising to the surface of his memory?

The house pulsed with tension as I hustled the kids to collect all their gear—lunch money, sneakers, science projects, sweaters—so that Alex could drive them to school. He tapped his foot against the chair leg, drummed his fingers on the table, then rose slowly, kissed me distractedly on the cheek, and went out to the garage.

The sound of the car starting up sent an eerie chill through me. He had never forgotten the kids before. But by the time I reached the door, Jeff and Janet zipped past me, hollering their good-byes as they piled into the car. I waited until they rolled away into the bright morning sunshine and then I climbed the stairs.

The tiny room at the end of the hall used to be a dressing room off the master bedroom, but Alex had claimed it and converted it into an office. I stepped over the threshold, certain that I would find something in his ancient field notebooks that would bring me closer to unearthing the truth.

Alex's drafting table stared at me blankly, its white surface gleaming in the river of sun spilling down from the skylight. Each specimen on the shelves recalled an outing, some even before the children were born: glittery pyrite from Tennessee, books of pearly mica we'd found in South Dakota, a chunk of Staten Island serpentine, a perfect trilobite. But it was the notebook that would serve up Alex's secret, and it wasn't right there on the bottom shelf, where it had been every day of the ten years we'd lived in this house.

Calm and suddenly cold with the potential meaning of its disappearance, I sat in the oak chair and made a swiveling sweep of the room. Alex had chosen this room as his office because he said he could reach everything he needed without ever having to get out of the chair.

Two-thirds of the way around the circle, I stopped; my heart banged noisily in my chest. A new cardboard file box sat against the wall, and I leaned forward and touched it lightly, then lifted the lid and pushed aside six rolled up tubes of stratigraphic drawings. The battered gray-green cover of that first journal, the one he'd kept on the trip that had begun with *four* Wylbur's Wonders, drew my hand like a magnet. I lifted it out and riffled the pages.

Each one bore a heading, Alex's precise, draftsman's letters recording the date, the location, and the weather. The entries seemed to follow a pattern: general topography, followed by a description of some unusual structure or mineral, and then notations of the samples collected that day. The bottom third of the page was reserved for questions, theories, ideas to follow up on.

I scanned ten or twelve entries, struggling to make sense of the synclines, the anticlines, the rhombohedral brucite from the flanks of Paradise Mountain. Nothing about how Alex felt, how the four of them were getting along, only rocks and formations and fossils and slip faults and thrust faults, until halfway through the journal, my name appeared in a penciled note at the bottom of the page.

> Lisa's letters keep me attached to that other world. I can almost hear her voice. God, I miss her. Wish we could get our mail more than once a week.

Instantly, I was transported to the snug little yellow-and-white room in our student apartment, to the yearning in that much younger me to share everything with the rugged, smiling, meticulous young man in whose sunburned arms I imagined myself to be as I wrote those long, chatty letters. The effort to be cheerful for him, it appeared, had succeeded.

But that wasn't what I was here for, and I turned pages frantically, looking for names, stopping to read a note about George telling the story of making the college wrestling team (Alex even then had pegged George as supercompetitive), and one brief reference to Dick Micelli's tendency to want to quit for the day before they'd reached their destination. *Plus ça change.* But what about Danny? Not a word, not a sign that he was even there with the rest of them.

Again, my heart did its trip-hammer tattoo. Was that Alex's secret—that whatever befell Danny happened very early in that trip? I flipped faster, my eyes flying down each page in search of Danny's name.

And then, finally, there it was.

Danny asked if I'm worried about Lisa being alone so long. He says

The entry ended there.

I conjured up a scene around a campfire, Danny knocking back a couple of beers and explaining why he doubted that I'd wait, patient and faithful, for Alex to come home, telling my young, trusting husband about those kisses. Was Alex crying now because of something he'd done then, in response to Danny's confession? I tossed the journal back in the box, laid the tubes of drawings over them, and invented a pressing need to get in the car and hunt down some fresh shark steaks for dinner.

None of my options appealed to me. If I confronted Alex, he might tell me something that would forever alter our lives. But if I didn't and he continued to cry, wasn't that

74

bound to have the same effect? I waited until the children were asleep and Alex was settled into his chair in the living room. Vivaldi drifted softly from the speakers.

"Did you ever talk about real-life stuff on your field trips?" I asked.

The book fell out of Alex's hands; his face was hidden from me as he bent forward to pick it up. Give me the right answer, my heart urged, but I sat calm and still in the corner of the sofa.

"What in the world are you talking about? Where did that question come from, Lisa? Of course we did. How do you spend months with two, three other guys in the wilderness and not talk about real-life stuff?" Alex frowned at me, then smiled the kind of indulgent what's-she-thinking-up-now smile that usually greets one of my outlandish decorating ideas.

I wanted to strangle him, but I smiled back, my it's-not-nice-to-underestimate-your-wife grin that always put him on his guard. "I was vacuuming in your study, and I had to move that box, and the cover came off and a bunch of stuff spilled out. The journal was . . . it was lying open, and I just looked at one of the entries and it made me think about what you guys talked about out there. You know what I mean?"

Alex stared down at his hands. "What entry was that?" he asked.

I took a deep breath. "The one about Danny wondering if I was going to be all right alone for so long." Despite my misgivings, a strange inner calm filled me. This is transcendence, I thought, and realized that I had somehow become detached from the scene, as though I were a camera floating near the ceiling in the far corner of the room.

Alex frowned but he didn't respond. I forged ahead. "Did that ledge really just crumble out from under Danny? Is that honestly how he died?" There. I'd said it, or at least come as close as I could without actually accusing my husband.

Alex stared at me. The look was cool at first, but gradually it simmered until everything boiled over at once. "Stay out of that room. Those are my things. That's my life in that box. Danny's, too. God, we were too young, too stupid. He never looked, just stepped out onto the ledge. If only we could go back and learn some of those lessons before the mistakes that cost us—" A sob choked off his words, and he hid his tears behind his large, smooth-skinned hands.

My floating camera came crashing to the ground. I wanted to shake him. I *did* shake him, grabbing his shoulders, looking into his startled face, shouting that I couldn't take it any more. "You have to tell me what this crying is about. I can't live with your secret, with whatever is it that's eating away at you. Erosion, right? You study wind erosion and water erosion. Well, something is wearing away pieces of you. So I'm going to ask you straight out. Tell me about how you *really* feel about Danny Forsythe. Tell me why all these tears started after I mentioned his name. Tell me why you cry whenever someone does something physically risky, tell me why you sob when Steve McQueen jumps fences on his motorcycle. Tell me, dammit!"

I sank into my own chair, trembling with confusion and even relief, almost not caring anymore what would happen. But what Alex did next was the last thing I expected.

He laughed. A great, bellowing guffaw that rolled on and on. A huge, rollicking belly laugh that ebbed into giggles. He wiped at his eyes with his hand and then, when he'd caught his breath, said, "You're wonderful. You have such a wild imagination, honey. I swear, it sounds as if you think I killed Danny or something. Maybe you should take up fiction writing. God, it's so classic, and I couldn't even see it until you let go like that."

Thoroughly confused, even a little insulted, I started to defend myself. "But the things that made you cry, it seemed as if some awful memory was breaking through, something you—"

Alex held out his hand to stop me. "Here's what's going on. I can't stand the thought that I'm not the brave, young explorer any more. That I'm just another pencil-pushing number cruncher. I'm mourning my youth is what it is, saying good-bye to the past, and not without regrets. Don't get me wrong. I'm glad we're here, together, with the kids. But I never admitted until now, at least not consciously, that I'll never do some of those things again. Your fantasy that I'm hiding something about Danny's death is way wrong," he said, reaching for my hand. "Why would I want to do *that?*"

His sigh was more like a shudder, and for a moment, I thought the floodgates would burst open again, but he shook his head and said quietly, "What you've witnessed these past few months is my very own mid-life crisis."

Mid-life crisis or memories of murder—whatever had started Alex crying, with that admission the tears stopped.

I felt foolish. I should have realized that Alex's fortieth birthday was only two months away.

For weeks afterward, as the big day approached, we took long walks and talked endlessly about the pleasures we anticipated as the kids grew up and we had more freedom. Gradually, Danny Forsythe's ghost faded, and I accepted Alex's explanation for his tears. I was glad to have my husband back in his place in my life. And I let myself believe that Danny had never told Alex about those kisses, convinced myself that they couldn't have been the cause of Danny's death, that the pages I hadn't read in Alex's field notebook held no new surprises.

Until yesterday.

I hadn't been in Alex's study since I'd read the journal, and I pictured the dust forming a new layer, clinging like sedimentary deposit to everything in the room. But when I hauled out the vacuum cleaner and pushed the door open, I noticed immediately that the file box was gone. The notebook wasn't on the shelf, wasn't on his desk, wasn't anywhere.

When I asked Alex about it after dinner, he told me he'd taken all that stuff down to the office. "I wanted to show some drawings and notations to the new guys. Now, what do you say we take a walk? I'm in the mood for some jelly doughnuts and coffee."

At once, I flashed back to that other, long-ago walk to retrieve jelly doughnuts. But Alex had referred so many times in the past few days to my fantasies that I laughed at myself and pulled on my moccasins.

As we ambled down the street, he pressed me against a tree. "You're not going to let anything come between us anymore, are you?" Then he kissed me. Twice. Two sweet, lingering kisses. "Even Danny said you had an overactive imagination."

Right then, I made up my mind to get hold of myself. That story I'd concocted about Alex and Danny shouldn't be confused with reality. Besides, whatever had happened couldn't be changed, could it?

With Alex's tears dried and his mid-life crisis weathered, the past seemed much less significant. It was our future I had to consider.

Sign of the Times

Nancy Pickard

Gentleman Joe had worked with some gorillas in his time, but this was ridiculous. This one was three hundred pounds of ugly and her name was Bubba.

"Good evening, dear," Joe said politely as he stepped into her house trailer that Friday night. "How's my girl?"

The nine-year-old lowland gorilla raised her massive head from the comfy nest of blankets where she slept in her cage. She opened one intelligent black eye, lifted the rubbery fingers of one hand and greeted Joe with an easily identifiable and definitely obscene gesture.

Joe's companion stared.

"Did that monkey just do what I think she did?" Melvin asked. His own blue, but not nearly so intelligent eyes widened. "I don't think she likes you, G.J."

"Nonsense." Joe entered his initials and the exact time in the logbook in which the university professors kept minute-by-minute track of the care and feeding of Bubba. She was rarely left alone or unguarded; a gap of only thirty seconds appeared between the time the last graduate student, a woman named Carole, had signed out and Joe signed in. He stepped over to the refrigerator, opened the door and looked

79

over the tasty assortment of gorilla treats and vitamins.
"Here, have a banana."

"Thanks." Melvin caught the fruit Joe tossed to him, but
paused before he peeled it. "She's looking at me funny, Joe.
Is this her banana?"

"Melvin." Joe spoke with the exaggerated patience one
uses with the lower orders. "Try to remember she's just an
animal. Try to remember who's boss." He grabbed an apple
for himself. Bubba's eyes fastened on its shiny red beauty;
the thick fingers of her left hand moved in her right palm.

"Yeah, but ain't this the one what can talk?"

"She has a vocabulary, yes," Joe said loftily. "The professors have taught her sign language and she knows about six
hundred-fifty words."

"Do any of them include get your hands off my banana or
I'll kill you?"

Joe chuckled. He fastidiously picked gorilla hairs off the
seat of Bubba's favorite easy chair and sat down. In her cage,
Bubba's brows came down over her eyes. "You have the
wrong idea about gorillas," Joe explained to Melvin.
"They're strong, of course, but they're not mean. Bubba
won't hurt you."

"If you say so." Melvin put the uneaten banana on the
coffee table. He offered the gorilla a tense, but conciliatory
grin. She drew back her lips in a wide grin, too, showing off
large teeth that were rather more white than Melvin's.

"See?" Gentleman Joe crunched down on the apple.
"Now go back to sleep, Bubba, it's past your bedtime."

The gorilla obediently lowered her eyelids, though a glint
of white continued to show between her lashes. She was
accustomed to Joe's presence as her night guardian now that
he'd been on the job a month. It was his probation officer
who'd convinced the university to hire him based on the
facts of his college degree and his reputation for having a
peaceable—albeit greedy—nature.

"She's amazing, really," Joe lectured. "Or so the good
professors say. Her 'talk' is not just a simple matter of saying
yes, no, and feed me; any dog can communicate that much.
Bubba's use of language extends even to abstractions."

He automatically answered the blank look on Melvin's face.

"I mean she can understand concepts like right and wrong, good and bad, happy and sad. You've just seen her insult me. She can also make jokes and even play games of pretend. She actually seems to *think*. She makes up words, she asks simple questions, and answers others correctly. What I find most astonishing is that she has a sense of time—past, present, and future. She can refer back to events and emotions that took place in the past, for instance."

Melvin looked dumbfounded.

"Do you mean to say," he demanded, "that tomorrow she'll remember we was here tonight?"

"Correct factually if not grammatically."

"And she'd be able to tell somebody that?"

"Very good, Melvin. You're nearly as perceptive as Bubba."

Melvin ignored the sarcasm. He grinned broadly and, this time, genuinely. "Well, my God, G.J., that there gives me an idea."

Joe grimaced at the solecism.

"Your last idea got me five years in Leavenworth, Melvin. Don't talk to me about your ideas."

"But you got out for good behavior."

"I *always* get out for good behavior." Joe crossed one leg of his crisply clean jeans over the other. He always had his jeans dry cleaned—hung, no starch—and his shirts professionally pressed, even if the luxury entailed other sacrifices. "A gentleman," as he frequently remarked, "has his priorities." His immaculate appearance was one reason for his nickname. Joe might be a thief, but he always looked the part of a gentleman. He said determinedly, "And now I'm going to stay out on good behavior."

Melvin's small eyes shifted.

"But G.J.," he said in syrupy tones, "there's a charity ball tonight."

"Do not tell me. I do not want to know." His specialty was robbing the kitty at charity fund-raising events; in his trademark tuxedo, Joe moved easily among the rich from whose burdened shoulders he liked to remove the worry of wealth.

"It's a fund raiser for the preservation of English opera. . . ."

"Dear God, who'd want to preserve that?"

". . . And they're having a money tree, Joe."

"You are a manipulative and despicable person, Melvin."

"This money tree is going to be seven feet high and the guests will stick their cash gifts onto it."

"Cash?"

"Yeah, no checks. It's a gimmick for publicity pictures. All that beautiful green cash, like a tree budding leaves in the spring."

Joe rolled his eyes at Melvin's flight of poetic fancy. He took the neatly nibbled core of his apple and deposited it in the garbage disposal. From the cage in the corner came a low growl.

"You imply it is harvest time," Joe inquired of Melvin, "and I the happy reaper?"

"No." His companion grinned and sprang his idea. *"I'm* the reaper this time. Listen, G.J., we've got the opportunity here for the world's most unusual alibi. I'll put on a tux and pull the job while you stay here with Bubba. I'll make sure the job has all the earmarks of one of your heists, so the cops will naturally assume it was you."

"Are you *crazy?"* Gentleman Joe's carefully cultivated aplomb shattered for a moment, revealing a hint of pure, unadulterated Bronx.

"Then when the cops come to question you, you'll have a witness to prove you was here all the time." Melvin leaned back in his chair in a most irritatingly superior way.

"Bubba?"

"You said she remembers the past, right? And she answers questions, right? And the professors will back up whatever their monkey says 'cause their scientific reputations are at stake, right? What have we got to lose? They'll never connect this job to me, and you'll have an alibi that's so weird it's got to be true."

Joe picked up Bubba's favorite red ball from the floor and bounced it thoughtfully from hand to hand. The gorilla's eyes followed the ball, back and forth, back and forth. "I really loathe English opera," Joe said finally. "Sixty-fifty split?"

"Agreed." Melvin grinned hugely. "Guess I'd better go climb into my monkey suit."

They laughed uproariously.

In her cozy nest, Bubba grinned, too.

"We know you did it, Joe." Approximately twenty-four hours later, the police detective was squeezed into the house trailer with Joe and two university professors, Dr. Andy Kline and Dr. LouAnn Frasier. They'd come quickly in the middle of the night at Joe's request. "This job has your name all over it in capital letters. Not much of a challenge, frankly. You're not as much fun as you used to be, G.J."

The professors stared.

"I was here the whole time," Joe said calmly. He smiled reassuringly at his employers, who smiled uneasily back at him. "I could not possibly have robbed a charity ball."

The detective also smiled. "Prove it."

"I have a witness."

"Who?"

Joe pointed at the gorilla in the cage.

At the cop's incredulous look, the professors hastened to provide a short course on language development and intelligence in the lowland gorilla. They were very convincing.

"Nobody could make this up," the detective said finally. He shook his head. "If that gorilla says you were here, it's just so damned weird, it's got to be true."

"Ask her," Joe said confidently.

"Doctor?" The detective turned to Dr. Kline. "Would you please grill your gorilla?"

"Certainly, officer." The professor sat down on the floor facing Bubba, who glanced alertly at each human in turn, lingering a moment on Joe.

"I'm asking her to identify that man," the professor explained as he began signing.

"Joe," was Bubba's reply, through the professor's translation. The cop looked impressed.

"She's crazy about me," Joe assured the detective.

"I'm asking her if she remembers last night," Dr. Kline continued.

"Yes," Bubba signed, "Bubba sleep."

"I'm asking who she saw last night."

"Carole," Bubba signed, and the professor explained that Carole was the graduate student who had the duty before Joe.

"Who else, Bubba?"

The moving, rubbery fingers paused. Then they signed. "Nobody."

Gentleman Joe's heart began to pound to strange African rhythms.

"Nobody, Bubba?" Dr. Frasier broke in. "Joe was here last night, wasn't he?"

"No. Bubba alone. Bubba sad."

The professors and the detective stared accusingly at Joe. "I was here!" he protested desperately. "She's lying!"

The cop turned a skeptical face to the professors. "Is that possible? Can gorillas lie?"

"Oh, yes," Dr. Kline said. Joe's heart settled back into a normal rhythm. "Interestingly enough, the ability to lie is proof of advanced capability in language and thought. I'm afraid Bubba can fib with the best—or worst—of us."

"However . . ." Something in Dr. Frasier's tone set Joe's palms to sweating again. ". . . gorillas are individuals, just as humans are, with distinct personality traits. Bubba, for instance, always tells the truth about people she likes."

"Oh, my God," Joe said weakly. An image of a certain obscene gesture floated through his mind, followed by an image of Melvin basking on a beach in Acapulco, followed by an image of a neatly wrapped parcel containing thousands of dollars in cash that was sitting on a shelf in Joe's apartment.

The cop's grin was as wide as Bubba's.

"You said it yourself, Joe." He smirked. "She's crazy about me, you said. So much for this monkey business of an alibi! Let's mosey on down to the station, shall we? And have a nice gentlemanly conversation about all those incriminating clues you left scattered around the scene of the crime."

He led a stumbling Gentleman Joe out the door to the waiting police car.

In the trailer, black rubbery fingers moved quietly in a palm.

"Bye, bye, Joe," they said.

The Family Jewels
A Moral Tale

Dorothy Cannell

Emmalina Woodcroft, handsome, healthy, and by no means unmodishly clever, had attained the age of one and twenty with much to vex and distress her. She was the only child of a most indifferent father and a mother who, upon her wedding night, had succumbed to a fit of the vapors from which she had yet to recover. The affections of a powdered and painted maiden aunt, whose days were spent pounding away on the Tudor breakfront in belief that it was a pianoforte, did little to alleviate Emmalina's natural turn toward melancholy. Her one reliance was upon Jim, the youthful coachman, and she lived in hourly dread that his sanguine companionship would be lost to her, were the family fortunes to plummet to new lows.

Hartshorn Hall, having at its inception combined the best blessings of nature and architectural curiosity, had long since adopted the dissolute appearance of its male inhabitants past and present. The chimney pots were angled, one and all, at an inebriated tilt, and candlelight invariably transformed the windows into a multitude of liverish eyes, peering blearily out into the night. It may truly be said that a young lady of sound moral constitution might have rejoiced in the deprivations that were her appointed portion, but, as has already has been intimated, Emmalina was of that singular turn of mind that finds no delight in the absence of cotillions and liveried footmen.

It was on a raw March morning that she entered the winter parlor and arrived at a realization of the true evils of her situation. Squire Woodcroft stood before the window, which looked out upon the ruined rose garden, a pistol directed to his graying temple.

"Why, Papa," Emmalina's golden ringlets trembled as she pressed a hand to her muslin bosom, "is something amiss?"

"You do well to ask, Daughter," he said, taking a firmer grip on the trigger and squeezing his eyes shut.

"Were the breakfast ham and eggs perhaps not to your liking, sir?" Emmalina roused herself from a contemplation of her fingernails to make this inquiry.

"Do you women never think of ought but such fripperies as food?" The squire's face turned puce to match his smoking jacket.

"Unjust, Papa!" Emmalina's magnificent magenta eyes flashed. Her thoughts were indeed presently fastened upon coachman Jim, who could be glimpsed, flexing his muscles, if not his scythe, out on the ill kempt lawn. On his days off Jim made a very shapely gardener.

"Forgive me, my child." The squire's shoulders drooped. "I have ever been a sad excuse for a father, but I am not beyond remorse and my heart quakes when I tell you that last evening I lost at cards again in this very room." He waved a weary hand toward the table strewn with bottles, and in so doing shot a couple of bullets into one of his ancestors hanging upon the wainscotted wall.

"You always lose, Papa." Emmalina gave a wan smile. "It is a time-honored tradition."

A scowl darkened her parent's physiognomy. "Have you no maidenly sense of outrage, my girl? Must I go from excess to excess to rouse in you a sense of what is fitting? Tush! Let us see if this will ruffle your petticoats. At the break of day, I gambled away your hand in marriage to the Earl of Witherington."

"No!" Emmalina felt a constriction of her person that had nothing to do with the tightness of her stays. "You cannot mean it!" Perversity, her most winning characteristic, forbade her taking pleasure in this change of fortune. "His lordship is known throughout the county to be insufferably handsome and fiendishly plump in the pocket. I could never in a million years give my heart to such a monster."

"Me! Me! Let him take me!" Until that moment Emmalina had failed to notice that her Aunt Jane was seated at the breakfront pounding away on the knives and forks, which she had laid out to do duty as pianoforte keys.

"Silence!" Mr. Woodcroft bellowed, rounding on the older woman and shooting down a flurry of plaster doves from the ceiling in the process. "I can't take Mozart at this hour of the morning."

Oblivious, Aunt Jane, who had possessed a fondness for foot soldiers and law clerks in her youth, threw off her shawls with vulgar abandon and continued to shout, "Why does she get to marry him? Why am I always the bridesmaid?" before breaking down into discordant sobs.

Unable to bear more, Emmalina fled up the stairs to her mamma's bedchamber, where she found Mrs. Woodcroft reclining, as was her wont, upon her couch, a bottle of laudanum to hand and a glass of medicinal ratafia to her lips.

"I might have known," sighed the good lady. "Your papa has spilled the beans. And upon my word there was no need of so wanton a haste, for you are not to marry the earl until tomorrow morn."

"So soon!" Emmalina sank, in a graceful swirl of skirts, beside the chaise. "Dearest Mamma, you must know that my heart sinks at the thought of marriage to such a rake."

"All men are rakes when the bedroom door closes." Mrs. Woodcroft took a sip of ratafia, before bravely setting her glass down and fixing her maternal gaze upon her daughter's pale visage. "Distasteful as it is for me to speak of such matters and for you to hear the revelations from my lips, the moment I have dreaded these long years is upon us. The bleak truth, my dear child, is that a husband views as his entitlement certain encroachments upon the person of his wife, which, while repellent to the female sex . . ."

Emmalina's mind, never her best feature, was in a whirl. What Mamma was describing sounded uncommonly like the ministrations Jim Coachman had provided after she, Emmalina, fell from her horse in the home wood. He had insisted that such was the most efficacious way of preventing deep bruising. Fie upon the man! She had looked up from the bracken into his eyes—one of midnight blue, the other emerald green—and assured him that this was better than any of Nanny's heat poultices any day. There had been no sense of horror or revulsion, but that might be explained by the fact that Emmalina—not usually one to pay homage to Mother Nature—had found herself, for those spine-tingling moments, transported by the glories of earth and tree, sun and sky to a rainbow of delight unlike anything she had ever experienced, which left her gasping and moaning in wonderment at the pretty little flowers that she had crushed to purple pulp in her hands.

An awareness of deep betrayal seized poor Emmalina. For years her mamma had warned her never to let a member of the susceptible male sex glimpse her creamy ankles. Therefore, being of a biddable nature, she had dutifully arranged her garments over those tempting regions while Jim Coachman ministered to other parts of her person. And now she must discover such circumspection had all been for naught. She was deflowered. Worse, if she correctly comprehended the epilogue to her mother's narrative, she might even now be with child.

Wearied at having performed her maternal duty, Mrs. Woodcroft drifted into a doze, which prevented her from witnessing Emmalina's left hand fluttering sideways to appropriate the laudanum bottle and pocket it, even as she dipped into a dutiful curtsy. A nunnery being denied her—the good ladies of the cloth being unlikely to welcome an unmarried woman expecting shortly to be confined— Emmalina set her heart upon putting a period to her existence the moment she reached the seclusion of her own chamber.

She was hindered in this object because she had failed to place the map delineating the maze of Hartshorn's corridors in her reticule and thus, by taking three false turns, found herself in the stables. There she encountered the errant Jim Coachman and, upon signally failing to sweep him aside with her muslins, found herself seized and crushed to his manly breast. Wondering if she would ever more inhale the sweet scent of ripe manure without a rememberance of grievous ill usage, Emmalina pictured Jim weeping copious tears over her tombstone. Yes, he must be made to repine, and at once.

"Have you heard, my dear one?" Emmalina lowered her lashes and smiled her most wayward smile. "This morning the Earl of Witherington waited upon dearest Papa and solicited my hand in marriage."

The coachman dutifully touched his forelock before planting an impassioned kiss upon her inclement lips. "Aye! The devil in his many caped riding cloak made boast of his good fortune. T'was as much as I could do not to send him off upon his horse with a flea in his ear, along of . . ." holding her closer, ". . . along of a burr under his saddle."

"Avail yourself of no false hopes," Emmalina cried archly, "for the bridal documents are signed and sealed. His lordship and I wed tomorrow daybreak and depart immediately thereafter for his estate in the wilds of Yorkshire."

An anguished "Nay," broke from coachman Jim's lips, to be echoed by an equally gusty "Neigh," from the brood mare in the third stall. "Be of stout heart, my pretty peahen. What say we take this night by the coattails and elope to Gretna Green?"

"My dear one, I would like it of all things," Emmalina tossed her golden ringlets, "but you must know we have not a ladder tall enough to reach my chamber window."

A frown furrowed the coachman's brow as the truth of her words struck him most forcibly. Then a gleam appeared in his blue eye, or it may have been the green, and his lips thinned into a thoughtful smile. "I do be forgetting," he looked across the ebb and flow of the manor's park land, "that the bridal path do not always run smooth, and there do be many a slip twix . . ."

Desirous as she might be to harden her sensibilities against Jim, Emmalina could not but avail herself of the temptation to ease his suffering by offering a parting glimpse of both her ankles as she gathered up her skirts and returned to the house. There, in the confines of her chamber, she did savor the evils of her situation.

No benevolence intruding to prevent the coming of the morrow, Emmalina awakened at first light to the less-than-sanguine realization that in a few short hours she would be inexorably wed to a nobleman on whom she had yet to fasten her magenta eyes. Her dependence must be on the bottle of laudanum, for the elegance of her mind determined her against succumbing to her bridegroom's broad shoulders and well molded calves.

"Are you awake, my love?" Aunt Jane drifted into the room, her red wig as askew as any of Hartshorn's chimney pots, and her painted face atwitch with trepidation. "You are not about to throw a candlestick at me, are you dear one? For I should not like that above half." Receiving no response but a lachrymose look from Emmalina, the good lady proceeded to bustle about, fetching forth stays and petticoats, all the while rattling on about the sad affliction of nerves that prevented Mrs. Woodcroft's attending the nuptials.

"But you must not think her unmindful of the felicity of the occasion, for she has instructed Cook to serve only a strengthening gruel at the breakfast. Rich food, my dear Emmalina, does not adjust well to the rigors of travel. And the earl's estates are sufficiently removed as to require several changes of horses."

"Are you then acquainted with his lordship's place in Yorkshire?" Emmalina permitted her tears to flow unchecked because they dampened her muslin gown so that it clung to her bosom as was the daring mode. Being absorbed in the perusal of her fair face in the looking glass, she failed to see Aunt Jane's face turn as waxen as the bedside candle.

"Indeed, I know that accursed place well. I visited at the time the late earl's wife was brought to bed with the son and heir."

"How vastly dull."

"Evil was in that house. I was threatened with the lunatic asylum if I e'er revealed to a living soul what untoward doings I witnessed at dead of night through a crack in the master bedroom door."

Emmalina, with her bridal night looming, had no inclination to reflect upon the untoward doings between men and women. She was still of a mind that it was the delights of Mother Nature which had imparted a degree of complacency to Jim's impositions in the woodland glade. A blue sky and the singing of a lark must always bid fair to banish the most grievous of ills, but doubtless a gentleman, most particularly an earl, would not choose to take his ease outside the bedchamber.

Happily, Aunt Jane said no more to vex her, removing instead to pound away madly on the invisible keys of the Henry VII breakfront, whose carved spindles were highly evocative of the pipes of the organ at St. Egret's church, whither Emmalina was shortly destined to direct her lagging steps. She found, on descending to the hall, that Mr. Woodcroft's paternal sensibilities, while not prevailing upon him to attend her to church, had led him to write a most affectionate benediction, informing her he was gone hunting.

Upon traversing the path alongside the stables Emmalina permitted herself the hope of one last sight of Jim, but this was not to be, and perchance it was as well. During her sleepless night she had reached an understanding of her own heart. While neither pride nor prejudice might preclude the bestowing of her affections upon her father's coachman, she mostly certainly was not so far unmindful of what was owing a young lady of her quality as to wed such a lowbrow.

A soft rain having molded her muslins even more closely to her dainty bosom, Emmalina entered the chill gloom of the Norman church, to the swell of organ music and a weary acceptance of her fate. It would have been folly indeed, when she could not find the way to her own bedchamber without aid of a map, to attempt a flight to parts unknown. And surely in time she would learn to endure the earl's insufferable good looks and oppressive wealth. As she wended her way up the flagstone aisle, she made out his shadowy form, and it did not seem to her timorous gaze that he was excessively tall. Indeed he would appear to be a head shorter than the vicar, who was not known for his commanding presence. The earl was also, she realized upon drawing ever closer to the altar, decidedly stout and what gray hair he had was combed over a mostly bald head.

"Dear beloved . . ." The clergyman's voice went shivering out into the farthest reaches of the church, but Emmalina failed to bestow on him so much as a glance. She beheld only her bridegroom, whose fat purple cheeks spilled over his cravat and whose gooseberry eyes bulged with terror.

"You, Sir, are not the Earl of Witherington!" Emmalina, mindful of where she was, gave her satin-shod foot the demurest of stamps.

"But I am, dear lady." The gentleman endeavored to control his apoplexy before he burst forth from his corsets. "Your mistake perhaps was in expecting the fifth earl, and I am the sixth. Pray accept my assurances that I find myself almost as afflicted by this truth as your gentle self, having come into the title only yesterday, upon the lamentable demise of my cousin Hugh."

"Who?"

"Hugh, who suffered a fatal riding accident before reaching the outskirts of your father's park."

"How exceedingly provoking," said Emmalina seriously. "And how kind of you, My Lord, to avail yourself of this opportunity to advise me I am widowed before being wed. Now if you and the revered vicar will permit," she picked up her skirts in readiness to quit the scene, "I must hasten to convey the intelligence to Papa that he has lost a son-in-law and gained back a daughter."

"You misapprehend the situation, Miss Emmalina," The earl was now wringing his plump hands and his complexion had paled from puce to lavender. "The Witherington code of honor demands that I fulfill my cousin's matrimonial obligations. Besides which, your devoted Papa threatened to call me out if I endeavored to slip the noose."

Emmalina, who neither played the pianoforte nor painted in watercolors, was known to swoon divinely. The moment was not entirely propitious—she preferred a larger audience—but telling herself that when needs must . . . she slipped into delicious oblivion, punctuated only by a distant rattle, which might have been the rain beating on the stained-glass windows or the murmur of voices.

When she awoke, after what seemed a sennight, Emmalina still felt decidedly unsteady, as if the ground were moving beneath her person. A ground, she discovered on pressing down with her hand, which was uncommonly soft and well sprung. Never plagued by quickness of mind, it was some moments after she raised her beleaguered lids and perceived the earl seated beside her before she came to an awareness that she was in a coach traveling across a landscape fast fading into dusk.

Leaning back against the squabs Emmalina fixed her fine magenta eyes on the wedding ring encircling her finger and opined that she was, willy-nilly, a married woman. She did recollect having murmured the word *yes* in response to that distant rattle of voices, but she had thought she was being offered a reviving whiff of smelling salts.

"Feeling more the thing, m'dear?" The earl pursed his lips until they appeared ready to pop.

Emmalina, heedless of the proprieties, bared her pearly teeth at him.

His lordship looked ready to leap out the door, but mindful of his manners, if not his manhood, said with some energy, "If your ladyship and I are to deal comfortably together you should be aware that mine is a sadly delicate constitution."

"Indeed?" Emmalina brightened.

"A war injury." The earl coughed behind a pudgy hand and stared hard out the window.

"Your leg?" His wife looked almost fondly at the gouty member propped upon a footstool.

"No, no! That comes from a fondness for port wine. Deuce take m'doctor! The old sawbones has made me swear off the stuff. As if a man ain't entitled to enjoy what pleasures are left him." The earl hacked out another of his coughs leaving Emmalina to conclude that his ailment was in all probability that angel of death, consumption, incurred from sleeping in tents with the doors and windows not properly closed to keep out drafts from horrid old battle fields. Unaccountably cheered, she realized the horses had slowed to a clop and between one breath and the next the carriage swayed to a halt. Rubbing a peephole in the fogged window she made out a house with many battlements jutting ominously against the sky.

"Here we are, m'dear!" the earl said as a groom leaped out of the night to open the door. "Welcome to Withering Heights."

Shivering in her bridal muslins, Emmalina followed her husband across the courtyard and up a flight of steps to a heavily carved door, whose forbidding aspect was reflected in the countenance of the black-garbed woman who admitted them.

"So this be the new mistress." A smile, thin as a scythe, sliced the face in two. "Do step in out of night, Your Ladyship, before the house takes the ague." Sound advice, for the hall in which Emmalina found herself already appeared to be suffering from a malaise. The walls were dark and dank, the ceilings low and moldering, and every time someone breathed, something creaked.

"And you must be . . . ?" Emmalina's heart quaked at the thought she might be addressing her mamma-in-law, for the widow's cap was as sallow as the face beneath it, and the ebony eyes as glassy as those of the fox heads on the wall.

"I'm the housekeeper," the woman ducked a belated curtsy, "Mrs. McMurky."

"Her ladyship is wishful to retire." The Earl of Witherington spoke from behind them in a voice plump with pride.

"I'm none surprised, on this night of nights." Mrs. McMurky raised a threadbare eyebrow. "I have the bridal

chamber all ready, if you do be so good as to follow me."
Her ghoulish chuckle caused the flame of the candle she held
aloft to tremble as she trailed her black skirts up the stairs to
a gallery haunted by the painted faces of long-dead
Witheringtons in gilded frames.

Emmalina's gaze met that of a bewigged gentleman
possessed of one blue eye and one green, putting her forcibly
in mind of Jim Coachman. Taking the coincidence as a good
omen, she experienced an elevation of the spirits.

"Here we be!" Mrs. McMurky flung back a door opening
into a wainscotted apartment dominated by a bed, whose
tapestry curtains depicted scenes from every battle fought
during the Hundred Years War.

"How sweetly pretty!" Emmalina exclaimed. She was in
truth not beyond being pleased. The night was young and so
was she, and not even the realization that the earl had
followed her into the chamber could quite subdue her
vivacity. Thanks to the novels of Mrs. Radcliffe, the gothic
was all the rage, and Emmalina desired above all things to
be in the mode.

"I went and set out a decanter of your favorite port, my
lord." The housekeeper gave a murky smile from the
doorway.

The earl inclined his head.

"Shall I be off, then?"

"You are a gem beyond price, Mrs. McMurky."

At the closing of the door, a silence, thick as the fog which
blanketed the windows, descended upon the room.
Emmalina could not but experience a certain sympathy for
the earl, for while it was inconceivable that she return the
ardent affection which must have assailed his breast upon
first beholding her golden ringlets and alabaster curves, she
was not insensible to the good breeding which caused him to
refrain from prostrating himself at her feet.

"M'lady," he puffed around the room in circles, "there is
a matter of a most urgent, not to say delicate nature, which I
must in all justice impart without delay."

"Yes, my lord?"

He ceased his perambulations to stand with his hands folded upon his formidable stomach, his coat buttons straining and appearing to watch her with the same shiny bright intensity as that of his protuberant eyes.

"I beseech you to be brave, my dear."

Emmalina did not have to feign incomprehension; it was something at which she had always excelled.

"You are a young and healthy woman and I most earnestly feel for the bitterness of your disappointment. Indeed, I attempted to give you a hint in the carriage as to the nature of my infirmity."

"But I guessed, truly I did!" Emmalina clapped her hands. "You have the silly old consumption."

Blushing painfully, the earl strove for speech. "South, m'lady. What ails me is south of the lungs."

Never had Emmalina regretted more acutely her failure to master the rudiments of geography, especially where they applied to human anatomy. She was not entirely certain if the heart was east or west, or perhaps it was a matter of whether one was left or right handed. As for the other internal organs, she pictured them now as a number of unnamed continents, adrift in an uncharted black sea. Her magenta eyes blurred and a tear trickled gracefully down her ivory cheek.

Much moved, the earl constrained his own embarrassment, cleared his throat, and said, "M'dear, tax your pretty little head no further. When I fought for Mother England against old Boney I sustained an injury to my male person which prevents . . . ahem . . . my rising to the occasion as your husband."

"Oh!" A memory came, clear and pure as a blue sky above a woodland glade, and Emmalina was back amid the buttercups with Jim the coachman and she grasped the full import of her situation. That mysterious member with which gentlemen were beset would seem, in the earl's case, not to be in proper working order. At first she was elated at the prospect of being spared the necessity of fulfilling her wifely obligations, but, swift as a bird of prey, came a darker realization. Having permitted Jim to avail himself of certain felicities, she must assuredly be with child. And, were she were not to be afforded the opportunity of passing it off as the earl's own, she was ruined. Never again would she be permitted to wear white, which was far and away her favorite color.

Desperation, which is the grandmother of invention, made Emmalina do something contrary to her nature. She came up with an idea. Hidden in her reticule was her mother's bottle of laudanum. Rather than doing away with herself, which now seemed excessive, she would add a few drops to his lordship's glass of port, and when he awakened from his drugged state she would be entangled with him amid the sheets, eager to impart the glad tidings that he had miraculously mastered his infirmity to make her the happiest woman alive. For certain he would moan that he could not remember, but she would assure him that she had liked it of all things.

The difficulty was in persuading the earl to overcome his fear of the gout and indulge his taste for port wine, but Emmalina pouted prettily and entwined a golden ringlet about one finger.

"Surely, my lord, we would not wish to disappoint Mrs. McMurky. She did most particularly fetch up the decanter."

"You are right m'dear. But I suspect she did so for your benefit, for she supports the doctor's dictum that I not partake of anything stronger than beef tea."

"La, sir! This is surely a night for uncommon revelry."

When the earl, appearing ready to succumb to a fit of the vapors, buried his face in his silk handkerchief, Emmalina whipped out the laudanum and poured several drops surreptitiously into a glass, before topping it up with gentlemen's ruin.

"Will you take your refreshment upon retirement, sir?" Emmalina dipped a wifely curtsy. It was a most happy thought. The earl disappeared into his dressing chamber and returned after a short interval, cozily attired in his nightshirt and cap. Ascending the mounting block he drew back the bed's tapestry curtains and plunged, as nimbly as a man of his considerable corpulence could do, beneath the bedclothes.

"Here you are, my lord," Emmalina proffered the glass with much trembling of her eyelashes.

"Are you not to join me, m'dear?" The earl looked sadly out of countenance.

"Pray accept my excuses, sir, but spiritous liquor does most seriously disagree with me."

"Fiddledeedee!" His lordship took a mighty swig to show how palatable was the stuff.

"It gives me the convulsions." Emmalina watched his majestic cheeks pale, before begging permission to retreat and disrobe. Within the sanctuary of the dressing chamber, she took a moment, while removing her petticoats and stays, to congratulate herself. All would come about with the utmost harmony. Her child would be born heir to Withering Heights. And with a measure of good fortune and a great many beefsteaks and suet puddings the earl would not live to a ripe old age. Meanwhile, as befitting her youthful charms, her life might yet be solaced if she fetched Jim Coachman into service at Withering Heights. Surely even the most prattle-tongued persons would have little to say if she were to occasionally enter the stables and be found with him amid the hay.

Garbed in a tucked and pleated bedgown, Emmalina returned to the nuptial chamber and upon climbing into bed was much struck by the earl's appearing to be deeply asleep with his eyes wide open. Happily, Mrs. Woodcroft having instructed her that gentlemen were in all ways so very different from females in their habits, she concluded this to be but one more trial of the married state and not to be blamed particularly on the laudanum, any more than was his leaving the wineglass sprawled in slovenly fashion upon the coverlet. She was cheerfully engaged in unbuttoning his lordship's nightshirt, so as to create the necessary state of dishabille to which he would awaken, when the door was peremptorily thrust open to reveal the beaky nosed Mrs. McMurky in her nightmare black.

"You rang, Madam?"

"No!" Emmalina cowered against the capacious pillows as the housekeeper advanced with the unrelenting tread of an army of foot soldiers to stand by the bed.

"What ails his lordship?"

"Nothing!" Emmalina rallied to smile demurely and avow with a peachy blush. "He is but somewhat fatigued, which is surely not a wonderment after asserting his husbandly rights."

"Fatigued!" Mrs. McMurky's eyes burned like coals in her sallow visage. "My master is dead!"

"You must be funning!" For the moment Emmalina was sadly discommoded, then her mood lifted. She would so enjoy being a widow and there could be no doubt her child's future was ensured. For would it not readily be decided that the earl had succumbed to the apoplexy due to certain exertions? The only puzzlement must be that whole kingdoms of gentlemen did not routinely meet the same fate. Emmalina would have liked above all things to dance upon the bed sheets, but she knew she must be at pains to repine.

"Oh, woe is me!" She assumed a doleful mien. "I killed him!"

Mrs. McMurky's eyes shone with a strange, gloating light, as without a word she moved to the window, drawing back the curtain so that the moon stared balefully into the chamber, probing and pointing its silver fingers at the young woman who stepped from the bed to stand shivering in her bridal night attire.

"Providence be praised!" the housekeeper exclaimed, "I do be seeing Dr. Leech riding his piebald mare Polly up to the door."

"What a happy chance."

"That it is." A smile strayed across Mrs. McMurky's stark features, but before more could be said, the doorbell pealed and she departed with a rustle of black skirts to admit the doctor. Voices in the hall, followed by footsteps mounting the stairs. Their sound echoed the beating of Emmalina's heart. She told herself it was not unreasonable to be anxious; she had never before been widowed and was thus uncertain as to the social niceties. Would she be expected to wear black bedgowns?

She was occupied in reaching for a shawl when Dr. Leech entered the chamber, with Mrs. McMurky hovering like a shadow behind him. He was tall and spare as a long-case clock. Indeed, his head almost scraped the ceiling as he advanced upon the bed, and his countenance was too long and bony to be immediately pleasing. But Emmalina, having determined not to remarry upon encountering the first man to cross her path, did not hold his looming presence or unpruned eyebrows against him. Thinking he might need something to steady his nerves, she offered him a glass of port.

"No, I thank you." He exchanged a look with the housekeeper before bending over the earl. "My lady, I have been your husband's physician these many years and know him to have enjoyed the most robust health."

"Doctor, I did be telling you as how she confessed to . . ." At the lift of his knobby hand, Mrs. McMurky fell silent.

"My husband died with honor, in the performance of his manly duty." Emmalina squeezed out a tear. "Indeed, it would seem to me he should be posthumously awarded a medal, as are other gallant men who fall upon the field of battle."

"Balderdash!" The doctor whipped off the bedclothes to leave the late earl exposed to the chill that had descended upon the room. "His lordship was incapable of such action. The last time he saw battle he lost the family jewels."

"I hardly see what that has to say to anything!" Emmalina responded roundly. But when she turned her magnificent orbs to where his lordship's nightshirt was lifted to reveal those most private parts of his person, she perceived with much lowering of spirits that he was missing certain baubles which, if all men are created equal, might not be of any great rarity, but which must needs have been present for her story to have possessed the ring of truth.

"But I thought him to have meant . . ." Delicacy forbade Emmalina's endeavoring to explain further, that she had understood his lordship to mean that the necessary equipment was present if not operational. What a wet goose she was! So this was what was meant by missing in action!

"Murderess!" The housekeeper was hugging the bedpost and dancing a jig in venomous ecstasy. "Couldn't content yourself with being a hussy, could you."

"I do declare, Mrs. McMurky, I have not a notion what you are talking about!"

"Don't make me laugh!" The unearthly cackle blew out a couple of candles. "You poisoned the old goa . . . dear's port!"

"No!" Emmalina had never mastered the art of talking and swooning at the same time. Was it possible that she had been too unstinting with the laudanum?

"And if I b'ain't missing the mark, you did away with Hugh."

"Who?"

"The fifth earl. Very peculiar it was him having that riding accident, and him jumping before he was out of leading strings."

"Hanging's too good for her!" The doctor's lips flapped with fury.

Vastly cheered by this reasonable approach, Emmalina would have embraced a lifetime diet of bread and water, but before she could bat her eyelashes, Mrs. McMurky had drawn a coil of rope from the bowels of her skirt pocket and was tying her to the bedpost in the manner of one who would have enjoyed watching her burn at the stake like Joan of Arc. There was, alas, no appealing to Dr. Leech, for he was off into the night gloom to seek the assistance of the Justice of the Peace, a crusty gentleman of the old school who had never been known to get out of bed on the right side in forty years.

It was with a melancholy hope of any continuance, that Emmalina awakened the next morning in one of the dungeons of Foulwell Castle, which served the county as a makeshift prison until such time as a habitation even more incommodious could be built. After waiting in vain for the arrival of her morning chocolate, she determined to bear her misfortunes bravely. But the prospect from her barred window, being a wall that even the ivy seemed loath to climb, was not conducive to merriment. And the wretchedness of the room she shared with at least forty of the great unwashed soon made itself felt. There were no portraits upon the walls nor any carpets upon the floor. When she went in search of the bell rope in order to summon the butler that he might have a word with the upstairs maid about the chamber pots that appeared not to have been emptied in a sennight, she discovered there was no bell rope.

"What do you think this is, Hampton Court?" A toothless crone, swatched in rags, broke into gales of mirth.

"You leave 'er be." A younger woman with frowzy red hair sidled up to Emmalina and stroked her ringlets. "The good fing about being 'anged is that they don't chop of your 'air, like what they do when they use the ax."

Emmalina stopped squealing only when she felt someone picking through the folds of her gown. "Don't let me bother you, love," an urchin faced girl of about her own age said. "I'm just lookin' for fleas. We have races with them, don't you know. Helps pass the time."

"'Ush up, everyone," bellowed another voice. "'Ere comes Mr. 'Orrible with our grub."

The fellow who brought in the bowls of slop did not resemble any butler Emmalina had ever encountered. There was a fiendish look to his eye and she was forced to speak sharply to him about his failure to shave the pirate's stubble from his chin. Time, alas, did not compose her. The uncertainty of her situation weighed heavily upon her spirits and she found herself looking forward with utmost eagerness to the day of her trial. Her youth and beauty must surely touch the heart of judge and jury and she could not fail to believe her father, however heretofore indifferent, would be in the court, eager to attest to her having been well tutored in the minuet.

How melancholy it was for Emmalina to discover, when guided into that chamber of justice by her wardens, that the spectators' gallery was unoccupied save for an elderly woman in dark bonnet and cloak and a man in rough country tweeds seated, with head bent, beside her. Mrs. McMurky and Dr. Leech were installed where their presence could not be missed, and indeed, Judge Blackstone Smyte, when he finally deigned to put in his velvet and ermine appearance, seemed to be very much taken with the pair.

"Tell me, Madam," he sat with ponderous chin resting on his palm, his wig sliding over one ear, as he addressed the housekeeper, "did Her Ladyship confess to the murder of her sainted husband."

"Yes, M'Lud!" The denouncement bubbled from Mrs. McMurky's lips. "As true as I'm standing here, and strike me down if I tell a lie, the prisoner's very words was 'I killed him.'"

"But I meant only . . ." Emmalina cried out.

Frowning, the judge rebuked her. "My lady, did you, or did you not secret a drug in his lordship's port wine?"

"I . . ." The golden head hung low.

"A bottle of laudanum was found in her reticule." Slick as an eel, Dr. Leech rose to his monstrous height in proffering this contribution to justice.

"Tut, tut!" the judge said, more in sorrow than anger.

Most bitterly did Emmalina regret her imprudence in being caught out in a crime she had not committed. "But, Sir! I have witnessed my mamma partake of the entire bottle to no ill effect, save for the occasional fall from her boudoir balcony."

"Silence!" The judge had bethought himself of his dinner, which today was to be his favorite braised kidneys and buttered cabbage. "In the name of mad King George, I find you Emmalina, Countess of Witherington, guilty of murder most foul. It is my sorry duty to sentence you to be hanged by your comely neck until you are quite dead. And may God have no mercy upon your soul." Rising in a flurry of velvet he made to quit the room, but was forestalled by a voice floating down from the spectators' gallery.

"Not so fast, my love!"

The judge's face turned first the color of his crimson robe, then white as its ermine trim. The speaker had removed her black bonnet to reveal a powdered wig above a painted face. At the instant Emmalina recognized her spinster aunt, his lordship cried aloud in thrilling accents, "Jane! My lovely lost Jane! In the days when I worshipped at the shrine of your loveliness I was a lowly law clerk. But on the day your father forbade me pay you my addresses, I determined to rise in my profession so as to be worthy at last of making you mine. Then came the day when I knew I was no longer young, and could not trust that you would even remember me."

"I would not have done so." Aunt Jane drummed her fingers upon the gallery rail as if it were a pianoforte keyboard. "I have been afflicted in my mind these many years. The physicians spoke of shock treatment as the only hope of cure, but the thought of being dipped in scalding water did not vastly appeal. However, all is well that ends well. For the news of my niece's tribulations brought me back to full possession of my powers. So sit yourself back down on that throne of yours, Blackstone, while I tell you a thing or two."

"Yes, my dove! At once, my dove!"

"Forget all this twaddle about my niece murdering her husband. I was engaged in reading my teacup this early morn and beheld the face of the real villain floating in the murky . . ." she drew out the word, ". . . murky depths. And I can tell you, Blackstone, you need not resort to your eye glass in searching out the true villain." Aunt Jane stopped drumming to point her finger. "The earl's death lies at your door, Mrs. McMurky."

"You are mad, quite mad!" Hollow laughter.

"No, it is you, Minerva McMurky, who don't have both oars in the water. I ascertained there was something not quite nice about you when I was staying at Withering Heights, many years since, and discovered you had made fate your accomplice when you and the countess both gave birth to boys on the very same day. At dead of night you switched the infants so that your son would be heir to an earldom, leaving the rightful scion to grow up a hireling."

As was Emmalina's wont, she could make neither head nor tail of what she was hearing.

"It was your son," Aunt Jane pressed on inexorably, "your son, Hugh—"

"Who?" the judge inquired with a seraphic smile.

"Hugh, who was killed yesterday on his return from Hartshorn Hall. In one terrible stroke all your plans had come to naught, Minerva. It was then, I believe, that your evil took a nasty turn. You blamed my poor Emmalina for your son's demise. And it was she, not the sixth earl, you determined to kill. He was known to abstain from port wine on account of his gout. But you shrewdly suspected that a young woman married off to a man with whom she had established but a day's acquaintance might be anxious to steady her wedding-night nerves with a glass of something stronger than ratafia."

"Lies! All lies!" Mrs. McMurky's screams tore through the court with the force of a hurricane. Dr. Leech could not quiet her, even as she babbled that he was the father of her child and that he had been all for the murder plot when he thought it would leave her mistress of Withering Heights. The judge cried "Guilty," but instead of pounding out the verdict with his gavel, he tossed it aside, knocking out one of the wardens in the process, so as to be free to hold out his arms to Aunt Jane, who ran into them with mature squeals of joy and promises of giving up the pianoforte.

As for Emmalina, she did feel that somewhat more fuss might have been made of her who had so narrowly escaped the hangman's noose. Mrs. McMurky did not have the grace to offer one word of congratulation as she was dragged screaming from the court. And Dr. Leech was no better. Sighing, Emmalina doubted that even swooning could alleviate the tedium of this day, and her magenta eyes blurred with tears so that the man in rough country clothes, who had been with Aunt Jane in the spectators' gallery, came toward her out of a fog. And it was not until he was within a hand's breadth that she recognized him.

"Why Jim Coachman!" Emmalina cried.

"The Earl of Witherington, to you, my lass. I was the true

heir, switched at birth." The lofty tone was belied by his kneeling at her feet, and Emmalina most ardently hoped that after they were wed he would continue to touch his forelock before taking those liberties which gentlemen would seem to hold so dear.

"Beloved," he rose to clasp her to his breast, "there is a dark and mordid revelation I must make before you pledge your love and life to me."

Emmalina shook her golden head, unable to hazard a guess as to what could make him look so melancholy. Pray heaven he was not about to confess a dislike of turnips, for they were of all things her passion.

"I tried to tell you at our last meeting, but mayhap did not make myself clear, that I put a burr under the saddle of the earl."

"Who?"

"Hugh. The one what was me when I was him. I was determined that he should not marry you. So you see, my angel, his death was no mishap. I . . ."

"Hush!" Emmalina pressed a finger to Jim's lips, lest the judge have ears in the back of his wig. She was by no means unmindful of the compliment her love had paid her in removing a rival suitor from the bridal path. But she could not but think wistfully back to her former husband; for surely a tendency to gout might more readily be accepted in one's lord and master than an inclination to murder should the breakfast ham and eggs perhaps not be to his liking.

Another young lady might have quaked at the prospect before her, but Emmalina, perceiving many opportunities in the coming years to indulge her natural inclination to melancholy, gave him her most droll smile and said, "I will marry you, my lord Jim, and I do most dutifully suggest that given the perilous state of the world you arrange with Mr. Lloyd of London for the insuring of the family jewels."

The Trouble with the Shoot

Camilla T. Crespi

"Sorry, you beautiful people out there. I'm tied up with life right now and can't come to the phone so—"

I hung up and walked back half a block to a barred basement flat in a fancy townhouse just off Madison Avenue on Sixty-seventh Street. The doughnut in my mouth kept me from screaming.

"No luck?" asked the security guard I'd hired. He was sitting on the stoop, smoking.

I shook my head. Above the guard, the townhouse shutters were closed, as if the owners had gone off for the summer season. It was eight o'clock in the morning on a sunny June Tuesday and HH&H Advertising expected me to shoot a magazine ad in Central Park. The guard's name was Mike and mine's Simona Griffo. I've been working for HH&H Advertising since I came to this country from Rome, four years ago.

"Maybe he slept in some chick's place," Mike offered.

"He" was Clive Hayden, a snooty fashion stylist in his late twenties with a heavy lock of brown hair he liked to shake over his forehead, a cellular phone in his Versace breast pocket, and a Filofax as thick as the arm it was under. In the fashion business he was considered hot, and usually accessorized clothes on ads for top designers like Bill Blass or Geoffrey Beene. Today he was supposed to work for our client, a manufacturer of middle-priced dresses—the Christine Renée line—that cloned the high-end designers.

Now Clive hadn't shown up at the shoot site, wasn't answering his doorbell, or our pounding, or the phone, and he had the evening dress we needed—a sample that hadn't gone into production yet—plus seventy-five thousand dollars' worth of jewelry which a Madison Avenue jeweler had loaned us for the price of a mention in our ad.

"You think he got the stuff inside?" The guard was a thin, man in his forties, with a sweet face that made him look as if he'd have a hard time squashing a cockroach. At least he had a gun, even though we still didn't have the jewelry he'd been hired to protect. The reason I'd shown up at Clive's apartment was because shoot days get me *un poco poco* tense.

At the last Renée photo session, two months earlier, a gold-and-sapphire necklace had been stolen right under all our noses. The insurance company paid, but my boss had a few hysterics. Lynn Crimmins, the advertising director for Renée, cooly accused Steve, who had styled Renée ads for the past five years, during which nothing else had been stolen. Lynn admitted she had no proof, but she fired Steve anyway. When I protested, she almost fired us. But we lowered our price and won her back on a trial basis. I was all for dumping the client, since I liked Steve and didn't think him a thief, but money wins out over justice, at least at HH&H. And I needed my job. Hiring Clive had been Lynn's idea.

"He better have the stuff inside," I said. I'd gotten an insurance rider to cover the jewelry while it stayed in Clive's apartment overnight. It was not a highly unusual procedure. Fashion stylists sometimes take charge of expensive clothes and jewelry. It's part of their job. In this case Clive had wanted the dress the day before so that he could get it ironed, and the jewelry came from a store three blocks away from Clive's apartment. He also happened to live six blocks from our shoot site. Yesterday the arrangement had made sense. Now it was pure *puzza,* otherwise known as stink.

"Maybe you're right," I told Mike, licking sugar from a corner of my mouth. "He's dangling diamonds to tempt some innocent woman." Clive had plenty of girlfriends, I heard. Last night I'd bumped into him in front of the Gotham Bar and Grill in Greenwich Village, where I live. He'd been in a very good mood, telling me how great I was, what fun we were going to have today. I'd asked him if the accessories were safe. In reply I got a kiss I didn't want and a whispered "you need a mood adjuster." Then he'd swept his date inside the restaurant.

"Or maybe he's asleep with a hangover." I jiggled the doorknob of the metal gate for the thousandth time. His date hadn't looked innocent and she wasn't wearing diamonds. In fact, she wasn't wearing much of anything.

"I've got to get in that apartment." I gulped the last of the doughnut and tried to give Mike one of my intense looks. "Don't you sometimes pick locks in your business?"

He considered that for a moment, carefully stubbing out his cigarette on the step. "Not in my current one, no."

"Cavolo!" That's Italian for cabbage, which is a euphemism for what men think is their most precious possession. I don't mean brains. "Now what?" I sat on a wooden planter next to Clive's step and let the juniper prickle my back. The look on my face must have been desperate.

"I've had several jobs," Mike said, with an encouraging grin. His teeth weren't the bright little gems sported by most Americans. They were long and uneven, a fact that endeared him to me. Mine are slightly buck. He stood up, hand on his hip holster, and stepped down to the gate. Clive's entrance was under the stairs to the townhouse's main entrance.

I smiled as I saw him looking at the lock. "You'll shoot your way in?" I didn't stop to think what his old jobs might have been. I wanted dress and jewelry. And Clive, if I could wake him from his stupor.

"Hell, no. Could you take a walk down the block? I don't want witnesses." I backed off and saw him push the planter next to the door. From the sidewalk, which had only an occasional passerby, it looked as if Mike were relieving himself behind the juniper bush. I discreetly looked the other way.

It took him less than five minutes. Gate and door. I motioned for him to go in first.

Mike did a slow shake of his head. "We're splitting fifty-fifty. I do the breaking, you do the entering."

"Fair enough." I stepped inside and called Clive's name. His apartment was small, painted a taupe gray with striped burgundy and beige silk drapes and creamy damask upholstery. His living room looked like a decorator's showcase. I walked into the narrow bedroom, which was overpowered by a king-size bed. Crisp linen sheets. Fluffed out shams. The banana-yellow silk bedspread was wrinkled on the closet side. Clive hadn't slept here, but he had sat on the bed.

The sliding door of the closet was open. I peeked. No blue evening dress in its Christine Renée garment bag, but Clive's suits had been pushed to one side as if to make room for a dress that shouldn't be crushed. I sat on the bed and reached down to the double row of drawers at the bottom of the closet. I opened the top one, feeling guilty that an ad shoot had me acting like a thief, but then I remembered the stolen gold-and-sapphire necklace and plunged in with both my hands.

There was no jewelry nor folded dress. Just more handkerchiefs, socks, and black Jockey shorts than any one man could possibly want in a lifetime. Then incongruously, in one corner, a rectangular space. I thought of a cufflink box with the missing jewelry and immediately had visions of a real thief sitting in my exact spot on the bed, lifting the box carefully, hand sheathed in a black glove. Just like in the movies. But Clive's cufflink box was square. Brown Florentine leather sitting right on top of the drawer, full of studs, cufflinks, change. No earrings or pin.

I tried the bottom drawer. I got three piles of bright Turnbull and Asser shirts. I nudged between shirts with my fingers. Nothing else. Pushing the drawer back I heard a crinkly sound. I reached to the back of the drawer, felt paper between my fingers and tugged. It was an airmail letter addressed to Clive, with no return address. Just right, I thought, opening the top drawer again, to fit into that empty corner. I dropped the letter back in its appointed space. It looked a little lonely there, but I found myself oddly happy that at least something was back where it should be.

I left the bedroom and glanced at the shower-size kitchen just off the living room. Everything neat, spotless, unlike my own closet kitchen which, because I love to cook, always looks as if it feeds a family of twenty at hourly intervals. Clive favored elegant Chinese food, judging by the bulletin board where an Auntie Yuan menu shared the same tack as a plane ticket. On the counter a half-dozen ivory chopsticks protruded from a flamingo-pink South Miami mug, the only garish note in the apartment. I checked the freezer for diamonds. I got ice, the kind that cools drinks and gets stuck to poking fingers. There was nothing else in there except for a tempting single Bacio Perugina, the little mound of chocolate and nuts wrapped in silver paper. Would he mind? I asked myself, my tongue twitching. No! I slammed the freezer door shut. That would be theft!

The rest of the refrigerator yielded nothing, and I moved on to a closed door opposite the bedroom. The bathroom! The dress was probably hanging on the shower bar. That's where I put my clothes when I wanted them to hang out. Except it wasn't a bathroom. Another closet, this one shelved full of white linen sheets, beige and burgundy towels, toilet paper, and other bare necessities of life. No dress. No jewelry. The last door had to be it.

What I first noticed, after opening the door, was dozens of Simonas. In front of me, to the side, on the ceiling. Mirrored panels covered the entire bathroom, even the floor, reflecting me back until I became almost a dot. I thought I looked pretty awful, but Clive looked worse. He was sitting on the floor behind the door, in his black Jockey shorts, his head stiff against the toilet bowl. He was quite dead. Shot in the chest. The dress, needless to say, wasn't there. Neither was the jewelry as far as I could see. I don't think of myself as heartless, but in moments of horror I do focus on superficialities as a way to keep my heart quiet, to stop my knees from folding. This time it didn't work so I quickly walked back to the kitchen, opened the freezer compartment and swiped the Bacio.

"Clive's dead. He's been shot," I told the guard once I was back outside. Mike was his name, I managed to remember.

He spread his blue eyes. "The stuff's gone?"

"I don't know." I munched on chocolate and marched Mike by the elbow to the twin phones on the street corner. "The police will look. You call them. I'm calling the client."

"Man, I gotta call my company first."

I was already dialing. "The police, please. You're still on the job."

I got Lynn's answering machine, but she picked up after I said "something terrible has happened."

"Clive's dead with a bullet hole in his chest." I couldn't go on. I thought my breath had been snatched from me forever. Actually I was choking on the nuts.

There was a moment of silence, then Lynn asked about the dress, then the jewelry. I told her the police might find the jewelry, but the dress was gone.

She told me to meet her at the shoot. She was going to her office for another dress. "A red stunner we were saving for a December spread. And call Steve, I'm rehiring him."

"You can't do that!" I sputtered. Mike had hung up and was hovering nervously.

"I need diamonds," Lynn said. "Fake ones so he doesn't get tempted. Besides, he won't be able to get real ones in an hour. That's all he's got. Sixty minutes." Her voice stayed calm.

"He's not going to do it, Lynn!" I overlapped her, but she heard me.

"Of course he is. I'll call him. I'll pay him double and don't stay around for the police. They'll keep you tied up all day. Talk to them after the shoot. We should be through by two P.M. I have a five o'clock plane to Miami." She hung up. Lynn was having a great romance in Florida with a man who "thrills my heart." I'd never have thought she had one.

"You don't need me no more, right?" Mike asked, doing a

little dance on his sneakers, as if getting ready to streak away.

I grabbed his arm. "No, please wait for the police. I have to go." I told him where the shoot was, gave him the photographer's cellular phone number. "They can reach me there."

Mike didn't like it. "How we gonna explain you gettin' in?"

"I had the key." There was no sense in his losing his job.

"Man! You don't!"

"I'll come up with something. Don't worry. I won't give you away. Thanks." I gave him a kiss, which he probably didn't want, but I was grateful and couldn't help myself. He was a sweet man, I decided.

I ran all the way to the pond off Seventy-second Street and Fifth Avenue and had second thoughts. I got more change from the boathouse cafe and used the graffiti-clad pay phone by the ladies' room to call the security company. It was now eight forty-three. I hoped someone would answer. The phone rang; I looked out at the pond shaded green by the surrounding trees, at the three ducks leaving a wake of Vs. A large, unclipped poodle lay on the bench nearest me, looking at me from under gray fluff. A woman finally answered.

"It's not nine o'clock yet," she bellowed. I apologized, introduced myself, and asked her how long Mike had worked for the company.

"What? He done something wrong?"

"No, he's perfect. The insurance company wants to know." She grudgingly told me to hold on. A starling, its summer coat streaked with beige, pecked at my feet.

"Six years," the woman yelled. The starling flew away; the dog cocked his ears. "He's the best we got."

"Thanks." I hung up happy.

Fifty feet north of the pond was our shoot site, the Margarita Delacorte Memorial, a haven for children of all ages. In front of a towering willow tree, a bronze Alice sat smiling on a table-size mushroom, her hands outspread as if to include all of us in her wonderland. Cheshire Cat & Co.

surrounded her in eternal attendance. The evening dress we had to advertise was fairy-tale-blue tulle. Alice and her friends represented a world of fantasy, a journey that led to excitement, the thrill of the unknown. Wear a Christine Renée gown and who knows what new possibilities lie ahead, we wanted to imply.

"Find him?" The photographer, Michele Stuart, looked up from her Leica. She was a big, good-looking brunette with thick black eyebrows and a smile permanently glued to her soul. She took great pictures and was on her way to the big league of fashion photography.

"I'm for calling off the shoot." I ran my hand over the dormouse ears, shiny from being constantly touched.

"Why?" Hannah said, her German accent strong. She'd been the exclusive Renée model for seven years. "I have the dress. It is in the van."

It took me two seconds to reach the park bench where she was sitting. "Why do *you* have the dress?"

Hannah twitched at the force of my voice. But then, in the last year Hannah had often twitched at the Renée shoots. Her career was going downhill. She was twenty-seven and showing it. Despite the recent talk in the media about older models getting a second chance, in modeling years twenty-seven still meant sixty. Hannah was also big boned and big chested. The current look was the waif, borderline anorexic type exemplified by Kate Moss. There were rumors that even the super-famous model Linda Evangelista was on her way out. Hannah had reason to be nervous.

She tightened her grip on the lapels of a worn chenille bathrobe she always insisted on wearing, a memento from her Berlin home. "Last night Clive gave me the dress."

"Clive is dead."

Hannah cried out, then burst into tears. Everyone huddled around me—everyone being the photographer, her assistant, the hair and makeup men. They wanted details. I kept it at a minimum, saying only that I found him in the bathroom. Hannah tried to stop crying.

"I will be ugly." She closed her red eyes and patted them

with her fingertips. *"Furchtbar!"* With her blond hair wrapped around gigantic curlers and without makeup, she looked like a harassed housewife who'd just been dumped.

I sat on my haunches and asked as gently as I could. "Why did Clive give you the dress? Did he plan not to show up?"

She opened her mouth, said something in German, then tried again. "That dress, it is my job." She pointed at the willow tree as if it held her dress. "No dress, no job."

"When did he give it to you? Why?"

"Last night," she said, looking up at the clustered crew. They were hanging on her every word.

That's when Steve popped up from behind the White Rabbit.

"It's late, it's late for a very important ad?"

I stood, glad to see his narrow, pointed face despite the circumstances. The crew welcomed him loudly. Michele, the photographer, slapped him a high five.

"I love Alice in Wonderland!" Steve declared, giving the White Rabbit a hug. He swung a battered suitcase onto the mushroom. "Hannah, *meine Liebe,* I'm going to have you dripping diamonds. Faux, of course, as per instructions from Morticia." Lynn dressed only in black.

"Looks Tiffany real to me," Michele said, peeking in the suitcase. Steve laughed. "Hey, Michele, I forgot to ask. How was Belgium?"

Michele punched a thumb in the air. "Fab." She'd gone to Brussels last month on her second *Vogue* assignment. As I said, she was on the way up.

"How did you get that jewelry so fast?" Hannah asked from her bench, her almond-shaped eyes narrowing suspiciously.

"I sleep with it, how else?" He saw my face. "Sorry. A death, I forgot." He turned to Hannah. "I used it on a shoot yesterday. Thanks to Morticia I don't do shoots with the real thing anymore. It's a miracle I work at all." Michele patted his back. The crew got busy shuffling feet, kicking dirt.

"I've never understood why she did that," I said, sitting back down next to Hannah. "I'm glad you're back."

Steve smiled and started to say something. I raised my hand. "Later. I need a few minutes with Hannah."

That didn't stop him. "Lynn wanted Clive. A big coup for her, getting hot, hot Clive to style her Renée rags. You're next to go, Hannah. It'll be catalog ads for you, honey. Maybe she'll even try to pin Clive's death . . ."

"Stop it, Steve!" I said. "What's the matter with you?"

"I didn't take that necklace! I hate that woman!"

"Then why did you come? Tell Lynn to stuff it. Come on, you can't take it out on Hannah. Walk out on this job."

Steve looked at me with a sad, tired face. "I need the money, Simona," he said quietly.

"Clive wasn't hot," Michele said with a flat voice. She was standing on one of the smaller mushrooms that children used to step up to Alice. "He's been fired from his last three jobs. I thought the whole world knew."

"Why?" Steve asked. He looked pleased.

"Why were you fired? He wore the wrong shirt, kissed the wrong cheek. Who knows?" She spread her arms out like Alice behind her.

"And now he's dead," Steve said.

"You killed him," Hannah said suddenly, shooting up from the bench. Michele jumped down.

"God, not you too, Hannah!" I tugged her bathrobe.

"I saw you across the street this morning." She was looking at Steve.

I tugged harder. "What street? When? What are you talking about?"

Hannah pushed my hand away. "Where Clive lives. He was waiting to kill him. I saw him. At seven this morning." She quivered.

"Yes, I was there," Steve said. He draped a zircon necklace around the brim of the Mad Hatter's hat. "I met Michele yesterday for a drink. She told me the shoot was today." He looked over at the photographer.

"No sin in that," Michele said, leaning against the tree, arms crossed. Her assistant was munching nachos. Makeup was testing colors on his hand. Hair was cleaning brushes. If they listened any harder the White Rabbit was going to envy their ears.

"You killed him," Hannah insisted.

Steve pocketed a hand. "No, Hannah, I wanted to talk to Clive. I couldn't get him on the phone. I figured on the street he couldn't avoid me. I was going to ask Clive to pass some jobs my way, ones he didn't want. Since Morticia fired me two months ago, I've done two shoots." His gaze shifted from Hannah to me.

"I waited, saw Hannah go in and out in five minutes. Then you, Simona, showed up with the security guard and I chickened out. I didn't want you to know."

"I'm sorry, Steve." I wanted to believe him because I'd always liked him, but I wasn't sure. Sentimentality has tripped me up too often, and now I could see Lynn sweeping around the far end of the pond, the "red stunner" in its garment bag held high, ducks waddling after her for food. The sight was enough to freeze one's heart.

"And what were you doing in Clive's apartment, Hannah?" I asked.

"The dress, I told you. Clive gave me the dress." A curler had come undone, releasing a strand that twisted around one large, scared eye.

"Sit down, Hannah, and get your story straight."

Surprisingly she did sit down. "First you said Clive gave you the dress last night, now it's the morning." She looked bewildered, as if she had forgotten what had actually happened. I took her hands in mine. "Steve saw you go into Clive's apartment this morning." Maybe she was a great actress.

"I saw her, all right. Seven ten, seven fifteen, around that time."

"Please shut up, Steve." I didn't like his ratting tone, even if Hannah had been the one to start it. "How did you get in? The gate was locked when I tried it."

"I did not kill him."

She hadn't killed him at seven this morning, an hour before I found him. Clive's head and neck had been stiff, and rigor mortis usually took three to five hours to set in, starting with the face and jaw. But that didn't mean she hadn't killed him last night and maybe gone back this morning to remove some incriminating evidence.

"How did you get in?" I was whispering. Out of the corner of my eye, I could see Michele gathering everyone and marching them toward the pond. I'd forgotten about Lynn. I shook Hannah's hands. "Lynn's coming. The police are right behind her. Quick, Hannah, tell me. Why did you go to him?"

She looked at her chenille lap, then at me, and started to cry again. *"Ich liebe Clive."*

"You love him?"

"Ja. Clive gave me a key. He said it means 'I love you.' Look." She fished in the pocket of her bathrobe and showed me two keys on a Gucci green-leather key chain. She closed fingers over the keys. "He loved me no more, but I kept the keys. Lost them, I told him." There was a note of triumph in her voice.

"If your affair was over, why did you go to him this morning?"

"What are those two doing?" Lynn asked from somewhere behind me, her voice like a Frisbee aimed at the back of my neck.

"Simona's calming her down," Michele said. "Hannah took it hard."

Hannah looked at them in panic. "To see who was in bed with him," she whispered to me. "I did not see him dead, I promise." She blinked her eyes wide, as if to get rid of any leftover tears. "No one had been in the bed so I took the dress from the closet. No dress, no job. I do not want to do catalogs."

I stood up. "When the police come, tell them the truth. They'll believe you." Somehow I was sure that if she'd shot Clive, she would have been too scared and upset to think about taking the dress.

"What do you mean she's got the blue dress!" That was Lynn again. This time her stiletto voice aimed at heaven.

"But do me a favor," I said quickly, "and tell the police that you lent me the keys, okay? I don't want a nice man to get in trouble."

She smiled, looking lovely and sweet.

I turned around, hiding her behind me. "Shall we get on with this shoot, Lynn? Hannah's going to the van to get made up." I kicked her shin lightly. Hannah took the hint and fled as Lynn came at me, swinging her garment bag. I half expected her to exclaim, "Off with her head!"

"What's going on here?" she asked instead, elegant in wide, floppy black silk pants, a tight-fitting matching black jacket, and a black straw hat circling her head. Her skin was vampire white.

Steve was behind her. "Do cats eat bats? Do bats eat cats?" he quoted from *Alice in Wonderland.*

I tried to sound efficient. "What's going on here is the shooting of a double-page spread ad scheduled to appear in the September issue of *Glamour* and *Cosmopolitan.* We have a week to make the deadline. There is no, I repeat, no time to reschedule. And then there's Miami at five P.M. today. How long a vacation is it going to be this time?"

Reminding Lynn of her Florida lover did the trick. She pursed her red lips for a moment, then broke into a smile. "I think we'll go back to the blue dress." She shoved the red dress in Steve's face and looked at her watch. "Let's get going. I want my first shot. We'll use a fan to blow hair across Hannah's face. I don't want puffy eyes in a Christine Renée ad." She turned around, reflections of trees swinging across her sunglasses. "Michele?"

As everyone got busy, I wondered what had happened to the police. I'd found the body. They had to question me. Forty-five minutes had passed since Mike had called. Or had he called?

"Michele, can I use your phone?" I ran over to her L.L. Bean tote by the willow tree. My stomach was doing a Heimlich maneuver all on its own.

"Go ahead," Michele's assistant said. "She's gone to the john." She gestured toward the boathouse.

Lynn made an impatient noise.

I reached in, picked up the phone. Its antenna, which hadn't been pushed back in, got caught in the straps. I tugged to free the phone and turned over the bag, spilling everything. I cursed, dropping on my knees to stuff the contents back in. That's when I noticed the letters. Six or seven of them. Airmail. Exact replicas of the one I had found in Clive's drawer. For a moment I looked around, too surprised to think. Cheshire Cat grinned maliciously. White Rabbit showed me his big brass pocket watch, reminding me not to waste time. I grabbed the letters and ran to the boathouse.

Michele was just coming out of one of the stalls. No one else was in the dank green bathroom.

"What are these?" I waved the letters in her face. She grabbed them and pushed past me.

"It's none of your business, Simona."

"There's one letter left in Clive's drawer. The police are going to find it."

Michele slammed her fist against the tile.

"Please tell me you didn't kill him." I really liked her.

"That jerk wasn't worth the effort. I'm the one who should be shot for falling for him. We lasted five months together. I went to Rio for *Vogue* and wrote to him. Wrote from Brussels, too. And when I came back," she snapped her fingers, "I was yesterday's leftover." Michele tucked her love letters under her T-shirt. "Clive was onto some Miami lady."

Something clicked. The bathroom door. Lynn stuck the rim of her hat inside. "Ladies, I have a plane to catch." She said it almost nicely. Michele and I walked out.

And then, in a Spielberg-like special effect, the pieces swirled together. Steve being fired with no proof. Lynn telling the world about her stupendous man in Miami. Elegance-conscious Clive sporting a flamingo pink cup in his immaculate kitchen. The picture was as clear as the blue sky.

The gray poodle scratched his ear as I passed by, his tags

jingling. Which made me think of keys. I leaned into Michele. Lynn was setting the pace on her black platform shoes a few feet ahead of us.

"You also have Clive's keys," I whispered. "That's how you got the letters?"

A homeless man looked up from his bench bed as Lynn approached. "Death be not proud!" he shouted at her as she hurried past.

"Keys on a blue Gucci leather key chain," Michele said. "I was going to give them back today. Hannah has green. I think he color coded his women." Lynn had black for sure.

"Did you see him dead?"

"I couldn't have gotten into his place if I'd wanted to. I lost the keys. Hannah found the letters snooping around this morning. She took them, along with the dress, and gave them to me. She said she wants to protect her career. Then she asked to see my keys. I couldn't find them in my bag."

We were back with Alice and friends. Hannah looked shimmering in the blue tulle dress, a subdued Romeo Gigli knock-off. She leaned over to nuzzle the White Rabbit's nose, her hair cascading to her shoulder. Michele's assistant clicked. The fake jewelry glittered as brightly as the real. Puffy eyes weren't in sight.

Lynn murmured approval. Steve exclaimed, "Oh, my fur and whiskers!" I had to call the police.

Lynn spun around. "Thanks, Steve. You've done a good job under the circumstances." Steve looked nonplussed.

I went over to the bench and started dialing. If Mike had called the police, I thought, one of them would already be here, asking questions. Or maybe he'd called, and then legged it out of the fancy neighborhood without telling the police where to find me. He probably hadn't believed me when I said I would take the blame for breaking and entering.

Lynn was standing by a Rat Poison warning. Seemed fitting. Clive was her Miami man. She'd fired Steve to give Clive the job. He'd probably just ditched her. She'd killed him, then taken the jewels just to confuse the issue. God, why didn't the police answer?

Steve hunched down next to me. "You look bushed," he said while I waited. I nodded, sadness finally coming down on me.

Someone picked up. Lynn looked at me.

"I'd like to report a murder." I hesitated, wanting to add, "I know who did it." Instead I gave Clive's address and told the man on the phone where to find me. "Send someone right away." He asked if I could wait on the phone.

"No," I answered too late for him to hear. Lynn turned to watch Hannah move from one fluid pose to another while Michele shot. Playing with her oversized onyx earrings, she uttered approvals and disapprovals in the same even tone. Lynn's aplomb was remarkable. I had trouble keeping my lips from trembling.

"Clive doesn't deserve any feeling," Steve said. "The toilet bowl was a fit place for him to die on."

The policeman came back. "That death's already been reported, ma'am. Our men are on the scene."

I clicked the phone shut. Wrong again, Simona. On two counts. "How do you know that, Steve?"

"What? Clive used women like they were Kleenex!"

"I didn't mention the position of the body to anyone."

Steve tried laughing, then stopped. His eyes seemed to blank out for a second, then he whispered, "I can't explain myself, I'm afraid, sir, because I'm not myself, you see."

He bolted, knocking the tripod down as he ran past Alice toward the pond. Hannah cried out, Michele cursed, Lynn shouted. I went after him, yelling, "Stop him!" The poodle heard me and shot off the bench. Steve twisted back to see what distance he had on me. The dog caught Steve's pant cuff. Steve kicked to free himself. That's when he smashed into the broad blue chest of one of New York City's finest.

All I could manage to say between heaving breaths, was, *"Era ora!"* It's about time!

Now it's Saturday night. Greenhouse, my detective boy-friend, is coming to my Greenwich Village studio for dinner. We haven't seen each other in a week. He's been up in Maine with his son, Willy. I've changed my makeup three times in the last half hour.

The police found the real diamond earrings and pin in Steve's apartment along with Michele's missing keys. He'd snitched them while they were having drinks together. There was no trace of the missing gold-and-sapphire necklace that had gotten him fired. Steve's in jail. He couldn't make bail.

We did finish the shoot and we'll make our deadline with the magazines. Lynn's boss thinks it's our best yet. "Electrifying," he called it. I think we could all use fewer jolts.

Yesterday Oscar de la Renta's agency called and told Michele she was on for the spring campaign. Tonight she's out on a date with a Belgian she met in Brussels. "I like the way he says my name," she said on the phone. "It's sexy."

Lynn reassured Hannah she had no intention of firing her. "My boss would fire me first. You're the image of his wife when she was young." Hannah thinks she might open up a bistro with some model friends. "Just in case the boss gets a divorce," she says with Teutonic practicality.

After the shoot Lynn kept her plane date to Miami. She never dated Clive. Her man's name is Doug. "Red hair, pink face that gets lobster red in the sun," she said as she tried to flag down a cab. "With a brain the size of Manhattan. I adore him." The cab cut across two lanes to screech at her feet. As she got in, she looked up, her black hat hitting the top of the door.

"That's why I rehired Steve for this shoot, you know," she said. "My intuition told me he was the killer." She looked smug as the car drove away.

I missed Greenhouse and Willy when I went to pick them up at Newark yesterday. Their plane was early. Not expecting me to be there, they'd taken a cab into town. I was so disappointed I ordered two hot dogs. I'd even brought a camera along to record their surprised faces. Well, the surprise is on me, I thought, as mustard drops graced my brand-new shirt. And then I saw her, walking down that long corridor, with a black crocodile knapsack hitched over one shoulder. She was swinging a different garment bag this time. I dropped my hot dog and snapped a picture of her. Lynn wasn't at all pleased. But that gold-and-sapphire necklace looked so good against that white neck of hers, how could I stop myself? She lunged at me. The airport police took it from there.

I hear Greenhouse coming up the stairs. I have to raise the flame under my pasta pot. We're having Relax Pasta tonight. It's easy to make and perfect for a summer meal for two. If you're as hungry as I am, take two large, very ripe tomatoes, dice them and scrape them into a large bowl. Add a minced garlic clove, six basil leaves torn with your fingers, a couple of shakes of red-pepper flakes, the leaves of four stems of fresh thyme, and lots of pepper and salt. Add two table-spoons of olive oil and let the mixture marinate at room temperature for at least an hour. Cook your favorite short pasta, toss it in the bowl, and mix well. *Buon appetito!*

Ah! I almost forgot. My hero, the thief-catching poodle, made NBC news the night of the shoot. He's going to be shooting his own ads, for a renowned brand of—what else? Sneakers that can outrun dogs.

Double Delight

L. B. Greenwood

Alicia's expression as she contemplated the uneven surface of the casserole was courteously curious. "Does it have a name?"

"Why not Maria's Broken Leg," Maggie returned sharply, "since that's the reason for its existence." She broke the lava-like surface with a resolute spoon. "Or perhaps Double Delight. The contents are all the leftovers I could find in the fridge. If I'd thought, I'd have cut a bouquet to match."

"No," Alicia said quickly, "cut some irises or something. Don't cut the roses."

"Why not? You can hardly see that urn, with all those forsythias taking over the patio. And anyway the irises have been finished for two months and more."

"Ted gave me that rose bush," Alicia observed dreamily.

"I know, I was here, remember?" And the bush would have died ten times over if I hadn't carefully tended it ever since, Maggie thought. Roses really don't do well in containers.

"I think I might give him a call."

"What?"

As far as Maggie knew, Alicia and Ted hadn't as much as laid eyes on each other since he'd walked out of this very house three years ago. Maggie had, of course, since in driving into Victoria to do the shopping it was very little out of the way to go by his apartment, and sometimes he'd be out on the balcony. Once she'd even seen him climbing into his car, and he'd waved. Nothing like that had happened with Alicia, as far as Maggie knew, and on this subject she knew quite far indeed.

"Why," she asked bluntly, "do you think you should call Ted?"

"Oh, I just feel I should. Ask him over for a drink." Alicia ate a dainty forkful of casserole. "Return his call."

"Ted called you? When?"

"A couple of days ago. Something to do with Samantha."

Maggie, as the sometimes-paid-poor-relation-companion, did her duty, if with somewhat tightened lips. "Who is Samantha?"

"Not *who,* darling, *what.* It's a mine. I don't mean *mine,* you know. Though I suppose in a way I do. My mine—how funny." Alicia gave a tiny giggle. "Samantha would be a mine if one had ever been built. Or dug, or whatever it is you do with mines. One of Wes's projects, and Ted's, of course, and they were supposed to leave their shares to each other. Only somehow Wes never got around to doing that. So when the dear passed on, of course as his wife I inherited, and now there's some kind of legal bother about it."

"And Ted phoned to explain."

Alicia nodded. Her expression was airy, yet she had managed to finish most of her casserole. "Only, naturally, I didn't understand. I never do. So I thought I'd better have him over. Denny, too, of course." This was at least understandable since Wes's nephew was the notary who handled such small business as there still was with the old firm.

"In fact," Alicia rose, "they'd better come for supper."

"Alicia—"

"And stay the weekend. If there's any dessert, I don't want it."

"There isn't, and—Alicia, wait! Maria only got out of hospital this afternoon! She's on *crutches,* for heaven's sake!"

"Oh, we'll have something simple." Alicia was already half way across the living room. "I know. Chili. Ted always liked Maria's chili."

"Alicia, Maria has—"

"And don't cut the roses. Those Double Delights."

"Why not?" Maggie demanded, momentarily diverted from the main problem.

"I want them for my balcony."

The balcony off her bedroom, with Ted in his old room next door.

Surely Alicia couldn't be seriously interested in her ex, an ex who had left her because of her open flirtation with the firm's young engineer, Andy. Of course there hadn't been anything in it—at least probably not—until Ted walked out. Then, as a matter of principle, Alicia had invited Andy to walk in. Which he had promptly done, being the type who believed in taking what you could while it was available.

He still drifted by occasionally, seeming on the best of terms with Alicia, a situation Maggie found as beyond her as she was sure it would be for Ted.

On a more steady basis, there'd been Johnny and George and Harold. And Mike, though he hardly counted: a few weekends and no more.

Could Alicia be realizing at last that she was past the come-hither game, and did she indeed hope to renew old times with Ted? With simple, honest, quiet Ted?

Ted won't, Maggie told herself firmly. Not Ted. Alicia is spoiled goods to him now.

Isn't she?

"So! My chili is simple!"

Maggie had to step hastily back from the arc of one of Maria's flailing crutches. "Of course your chili isn't simple, Maria. Unless it's simply delicious."

Maria was not placated. "It be so simple, let her make it."

"You know you wouldn't wish such a disaster on poor Mr. Ted."

"Poor Mr. Ted." Maria smacked the can of coffee on the counter. "He like all men—stupid."

From the adjacent dining room, as if on cue, came Alicia's deliberately raised voice. "Ted? Of *course* it's me. Why don't you come for supper tomorrow night so you can tell me all about that dumb ol' Samantha?" A pause, a trilling laugh. "Oh, nonsense, Teddie, it's no trouble. Better still, stay the weekend. You know what a silly I am over papers and things. It'll take me ages to understand." Another pause. "Oh, of course, Denny too. Then we can tidy it all up." Another pause, this one very brief. "That's a good boy, sweetie. See you tomorrow."

With at least four other phones in the house, Maggie assessed the situation, Alicia chose to use the one in the dining room, knowing Maria and I are in the kitchen. Point made and taken.

Maria broke the silence. "Miz Smith . . ."

"I've already called her. She'll come next Wednesday as usual and doesn't want any more hours, thank you."

"Her daughter?"

"Pregnant."

"Fool."

"Maybe I could help you," Maggie offered helplessly.

"What you put in that cass'role?"

"Yes, well . . . There'll be the two rooms to get ready—the extra bathroom too—and the spare hasn't been used for ages. And all the shopping . . . Something easy, Alicia says! Why, whoever is that out there?"

"Where?" Maria swung around so fast one crutch crashed to the floor.

Maggie picked it up. "Oh, *do* be careful, Maria. It's just a girl, a tall, thin girl, coming up the back path. Selling something, I suppose. Though she hasn't any bag or anything. . . ."

Jan had left her knapsack and bedroll under the bushes by the gate. Three months ago she'd had a ticket from London to Toronto, where her boyfriend was to meet her. What she found waiting was one short line of apology, one even shorter of good wishes, and a very definite period.

Her first job, as nanny to a menagerie of children, had taken her to Winnipeg, the next to Regina. With nothing to go back to, she'd continued to head west, until she was nearly as far west as she could get without swimming for her life. Which was more or less what she felt she *was* doing.

"The tourist season's over," the girl on the ferry from Vancouver had told her, "so the hotel and bus and cafs aren't good prospects. There're Help Wanted notice boards and agencies and stuff, but the good places are always gone before you even phone, and you can waste more bus money running around than it's worth. Victoria isn't really big, but it's spread out.

"What I'd do," the girl had suggested over the hamburger they'd split (the ferry hamburgers were reportedly famous, and were at least pretty good, at least when you were as hungry as Jan), "is head to the suburbs. To the kind of place that really ought to have full-time help, but can't quite afford it—get by on weekly cleaning and a half-a-day gardener. Wouldn't answer an ad, much less run one themselves, but if you're on the spot . . ."

She'd given Jan a calculating stare and then grinned. "You *are* clean, look decent, and have an English accent. That should get you something in Oak Hill."

Jan had, of necessity, left the Oak Hill bus at the bottom and quested from house to house up the winding road. So far she'd had three no answers and four refusals, one of them snippy. Now she'd reached the crest of the hill, with the autumn dusk deepening around her. Just this one house left, half buried in growth. She'd pushed her knapsack and bedroll under the hedge in order to keep her forlorn state at least a momentary secret, and had stepped inside the gate when—

What was that? Over there, behind those bushes on the far side of the garage. A man? Bare headed, dark haired, tan jacket. Gone, swallowed up by the undergrowth. What was he doing, prowling around a neighborhood like this?

Jan thought of the long walk back down the winding road, with houses carefully staggered to remain discreetly hidden, and of the very lean state of both her belly and her money belt.

If this last house wouldn't hire her, perhaps they'd let her bunk down in the yard for the night. The place had a rather friendly English look, with its ivy-covered back and a flagged walk bordered by yellow mums and red snapdragons. A border that needed weeding, flags that had overgrown edges. She could tidy up both, if given the chance.

Anyway, there was no backing down now. She abruptly realized that she was under the scrutiny of two women, one sitting, one standing by the kitchen window. One short, plump, and dark, in a bibbed apron; the other tall and angular, with brown hair waved back into a bun, light blouse with open collar, pale sweater, dark skirt.

It'll be the plump one who comes to the door, Jan thought, giving them what she hoped was an equal and sufficiently subservient smile. She was wrong: her first barrier was the level gaze of the thin woman.

Jan had long ceased verbose niceties. "Good evening. I'm looking for work. Any kind of work."

The gray eyes widened and the door did, too. "Why, you're English!"

"Been working my way west from Toronto," Jan said (she'd learned that this was a wise thing to say, though she hadn't yet figured out why) with forced cheer, "seeing the country."

"Well, good for you. What sort of work have you done?"

"Caring for children, gardening, clerking, chambermaid, waitress, cleaning—"

"Any cooking?"

The undertone of eagerness gave Jan the key. "I'm very good at following orders."

"Who's that, Maggie? Is the coffee ready?"

She was tiny, surely too small to have as much bust as the ivory cashmere sweater delicately hinted at. The slim hips were certainly real, though the thighs probably owed some of their firmness to the perfect tailoring of the beige cords. Blond, multiple shades so cleverly mixed that no one would ever be able to find either dark roots or telltale gray.

Hasty introductions were made. "This girl has been working her way across the country from Toronto," Maggie ended, with a meaningful tilt to her head. "In fact, she's looking for a job right now."

Blue eyes surveyed Jan, with quite as much shrewdness as mascara in evidence, and then joined the pale rose lips in a disarming smile. "Whatever you all think best, my dears. Bring coffee to my room, will you? I must look over my clothes." And out she floated.

Light footsteps sounded from the stairs, and a soprano voice equally light, telling the world what seemed to be an obvious truth: that the singer enjoyed being a girl.

"Where she sleep?" Maria demanded, scowling.

"Why . . ." Maggie paused. "There's that little garage room—"

"No," Maria fairly shouted her objection. "It dirty."

"I can clean it," Jan offered quickly.

Apparently too quickly. Maria's scowl turned in her direction, and her dark head shook an unyielding negative.

"Well . . ." Obviously overruling Maria was not in Maggie's programming. "There is the old storeroom, off the kitchen here, only there's no furniture in it. And it'll be a bit dirty, too, I'm afraid. Maybe even spiders."

"Give me a mop and I'll face any spider," Jan promised. "And I've got a sleeping bag. I really don't need anything else."

The revealed space was indeed dusty, small for a room, big for a cupboard, with bare shelves along one end. There was a shuttered window on the opposite wall and a toilet-shower between the room and the kitchen. Maggie rounded up not only a chair but a lamp, and Maria stomped in with sandwiches, a mug of coffee, and a slice of chocolate cake.

Out of gratitude, and the sense of duty that generated, Jan blurted out, "Earlier, just as I turned in at the gate, I saw a man—"

"What?" Maria had swung back, crutches and all.

"A man. Sort of . . . running off into those bushes on the far side of the garage."

Maria shook her head, firmly. "No man. Dog. New neighbors have dog."

"A man," Jan insisted. "In a tan jacket and—"

"Dog." Maria was on her way out, pausing to throw over her shoulder, "Not nice, girl alone, dark. *You stay in.*"

Jan assured her, with the utmost truthfulness, of her total desire to stay in, and Maria clomped out. She apparently had her own quarters on the other side of the kitchen and neither needed nor wanted any assistance from Jan tonight.

Jan had seized on the chance to wash her hair, and was standing in the dark by the window, fluffing it dry in the mild evening breeze, when she caught a slow and jerky movement on the path: Maria, with something very like a plate in one hand. And under her arm, tucked against the crutch, a thermos.

So the dog not only wears a tan jacket, he drinks from a thermos. And sleeps in that garage room? I wouldn't be surprised, in fact I'd be surprised at anything else. How old is Maria, forty? At least. Well, well. We never learn, we women, do we?

Jan slipped into her sleeping bag and stretched out, wrapped in the security of knowing where she'd be tomorrow: in a house where even the leftovers would be good and abundant.

In that assumption she was only partly right. For breakfast Maria made a batter for pancakes so light they could have qualified as crêpes, and Jan was permitted to do the frying. She took Alicia and Maggie's plates into the dining room, with a bowl of blueberries and a jug of thick cream, and then continued making pancakes until all the batter was used up.

This created an awfully big stack, far more than she and Maria finished. Yet by the time Jan had taken fresh coffee into the dining room and cleared, the pile had completely vanished. As had the remaining berries and cream, and Maria was herself washing the coffee pot.

If it were any of my business, which it certainly is not, Jan thought, I'd have a look at that garage room. Or at least try to, because I'll warrant it's locked.

As it was, she dutifully followed Maggie upstairs to take orders for the day's work. Alicia passed them, all sleek navy and white, and with only "into town" named as destination or purpose. Maggie, obviously expecting nothing else, merely mentioned to Jan that Alicia's room was at the side of the house over the living room, and her own at the front. Each had a bathroom, and, being in constant use, received a weekly cleaning from Mrs. Smith, and could therefore be ignored.

Ted's old room, next to Alicia's, had also been used and cleaned not too long ago. The bathroom next to that was likewise not a major task. Bit of washing up, fresh linen, not much more.

In the back corner, though, was what was to be assigned to Denny: small, furnished with mismatched leftovers, dusty, even cobwebby, with the closed smell of windows shut for months. Jan spent most of her morning there.

She returned downstairs just in time to help Maggie in with the shopping. Supper, she informed Maria, would be broccoli soup, almond-lemon sole, cress salad, fresh rolls from the German bakery, and custard with raspberry sauce. Maria gave a short nod and continued making sandwiches for lunch, rather a lot of sandwiches for three women. The remainder again disappeared while Jan was taking fresh coffee in to Maggie. Uh-uh, she thought, virtuously refraining from even a glance in the direction of the garage.

Maggie had rounded up a few stray flowers, mostly daisies of various kinds, from the decidedly neglected garden and was struggling to create a table center. Jan was doing her best to follow Maria's directions for supper preparations (these were seldom more explicit than a pointed finger at food or dish and a "You—do") when Alicia returned. She tripped in from the front hall, pausing just inside the kitchen door. No more was necessary.

Her hair was now a mass of tiny ringlets, her makeup English to the extreme, and a boutique box, rather a large box, was under one arm.

She met Maggie's wide-eyed stare with a complacent smile and a preening pat at the coiffure. "Thought I'd try a change," she explained smugly. "Like it?"

"Very nice," Maggie replied, distantly. Her addition—"for a sixteen-year-old"—was too *sotto voce* for anyone except Jan to hear, though Maggie's mouth and shoulders held comments of their own.

Now what, Jan thought with frank curiosity as she set the dining-room table, is in that boutique box? A new frock, of course, but what *kind* of frock? Something sleek and black, with one bare shoulder, guaranteed to make this Ted's eyes pop? Probably. For between what Maggie and Maria had and had not said to each other during the day, Jan was pretty well abreast with what was going on this evening. And with what had gone on during Alicia's previous event-filled years.

Certainly nothing of the whole performance was meant for Denny. In theory he was coming because, as notary, he might be needed to deal with the Samantha papers. In practice he was to partner Maggie at supper, leaving Alicia with a clean aim at Ted.

"Uh . . ." The voice that came from the open patio doors was masculine, youngish, and diffident. Its owner was tall, thinner than he ought to be, with straight hair that flopped and then hesitated, as if waiting for the hand that would automatically push it back. Like now.

"You must be Denny." Jan had said it before she thought of her manners, so she simply explained her presence and added, tentatively, the location of Denny's room upstairs.

He grinned. "Known as the spare room, and my invariable quarters. I'll go up, then. Unless there's something I can do to help?"

Jan was quite astonished to find how much she appreciated that. It seemed so genuine, and to have no hint of attached strings, unlike so many offers in her life of late.

"Denny!" Alicia, in a dressing gown that was far dressier than most gowns, floated in from the hall. *"Just* who I've been waiting for. Come and move this heavy ol' urn thing for me. I've cut all the blooms for my room." So she had, Jan realized. The mass of ivory and pink blossoms had gone. "And now the bush does look . . . well, it's not pretty, is it? So I thought if it was pulled to the back it wouldn't show much, only it's so heavy I'm sure I could never budge it."

Not that there was any sign that she'd tried, and indeed, Denny had to exert himself before he had maneuvered the concrete container to the back of the sunken patio, right against the steps.

"Thank you so much, dear boy." Alicia gave Denny his obvious dismissal with a pat on the arm. "Now," heading briskly back into the living room and summoning Jan with a corner glance, "let's have a look at the drinks, shall we?

"Not cocktails—too tacky, don't you think? Just wine at supper. The Chateau Chambre, I think. We just opened that bottle a couple of days ago, and there's another, that should do. The liquor's on the bottom shelf. Whiskey—oh dear, not much left, is there? Oh, there's a fresh bottle, good. And brandy—yes, nearly full. And crème d', if Maggie wants it. Gin, yes. Tonic water, soda. Ice in the fridge, of course. And the glasses—you understand the glasses? Wonderful.

"Oh, and Jan, you *do* have a dress of some kind, don't you? Lovely." Leaving a brilliant smile as reward, she sailed out.

Other women might have had some difficulty in managing so much floating drapery. Not Alicia. She whisked around the corner and up the stairs with the billowing yards following her like a well trained lapdog.

She knew how to make an impression, did our Alicia.

After all this buildup, Ted was somewhat of a disappointment—well, he had to be, really, Jan told herself. The reality was middle sized and middle aged, half bald, bifocaled, clean shaven, quiet mannered, and . . . nice. A nice chap. One could understand why Alicia had wanted him. Unfortunately, one could also understand why she had developed a roving eye soon after the acquisition.

As for Ted himself, he was clinging quite openly to the idea that he had come on business. He was quite prepared, standing in the center of the living room with his shoulders back and his head up, to be courteous, pleasant, gentlemanly.

He should have known that those qualities wouldn't keep Alicia at bay if she didn't wish to stay there. She floated into the room in a low-cut gown of ivory chiffon that managed to both cling and flutter, with a wide satin belt of deep pink. On it was pinned a full rose, and in Alicia's ringlets half a dozen tiny rosebuds nestled, each the exact same combination of ivory and pink. No wonder Alicia had been late in returning from shopping.

She paused for a moment just inside the door to receive universal homage, and then whirled right to Ted, rose scent a veritable cloud around her, high, ivory heels twinkling. She put her hands on his shoulders and stretched up with such open intent that he had to stoop to meet the kiss.

Thereafter the evening was all Alicia. Though the table was round, that made not a particle of difference. Alicia was at the head, Ted was her audience, Denny was very soon reduced to amused watching from the wings, and Maggie to overly crisp and generally unneeded directions to Jan.

Once back in the living room, Jan served coffee, and Ted, under Alicia's orders, the drinks. That done, he positioned himself by the hearth (out of the immediate danger zone, Jan labelled it), and attempted to bring up the topic of the Samantha mine.

"Oh, Teddie," Alicia wailed, "not that boring ol' thing."

Ted persisted. Not that there was anything that sounded very complicated to Jan as she came and went, clearing the dining room.

Alicia's late husband, Wes, had been a promoter, Ted an engineer, and they had gone into partnership on the Samantha mineral rights. Wes, having financial troubles at the time (which may or may not have had something to do with his recent marriage to Alicia), Ted had loaned him the money to buy his share, each supposedly willing their half to

137

the other. This, somehow, had never been done by Wes, and at his death, Alicia, as his wife, had inherited his half of Samantha.

"Wes never paid a penny for it, Alicia," Ted said earnestly. "Not a penny. I loaned the money to him, and I've the papers to—"

Alicia waved that aside with a flip of a rosebud. "Don't be so silly, Teddie. Of *course* I believe you."

"Well, good. Now the Samantha didn't turn out to be worth what we thought, at least not at the time. Plenty of ore, just low of quality. But now, with this new technology, there's a company interested—very interested, except I've got to own the rights unconditionally in order to be able to deal with them." He paused. "You do understand, don't you, Alicia?"

She shook her silken curls. "No, honey, I don't. I told you I'm an awful goose about papers and things. I always was, remember?"

"What don't you understand?"

"Oh, I don't know. Why is the dumb ol' place called Samantha?"

You might as well give up, Ted, Jan silently advised him. Alicia doesn't intend understanding anything as long as not doing so is keeping you here.

So it proved, Ted patiently persisting, Alicia as steadily dodging. Finally she said, with a positive pout, "I don't see why that mean ol' company can't leave things as they are, anyway. We both own the property now, or the rights, or whatever all the fuss is about, don't we? We *are* husband and wife, and—"

"*Were* husband and wife," Maggie interjected coldly.

Alicia patted her multiple rosebuds. "Uh-uh. We never divorced, did we, honey? Just sort of . . . separated."

"That's right," Ted agreed, awkwardly, "and you could buy Wes's share outright by paying me back the loan, but I don't suppose . . ."

"Oh, I haven't any money," Alicia charmingly conceded, quite as if money were an utterly unfeminine matter to possess.

"So you see this is the only way, really, of—"

"Oh dear!" Alicia cried, rising in a graceful sway of chiffon. "Better make us fresh drinks, honey, and come up to my balcony. Maybe if you explain it all again . . ."

"Well . . . all right. You'll stay around, won't you?" he asked Denny. "In case we need those papers witnessed?"

"I'll stay around," Denny agreed, his lips twitching as he watched his aunt lead Ted on a tripping pace upstairs.

Jan, collecting cups and glasses, found herself looking down at Maggie. She was wearing a sea-green plain silk with a matching shawl over her shoulders, and was now sitting very still, thin ankles neatly crossed in their low-heeled sandals, hair in its precise waved wings and tight bun, eyes unreadable and fixed on the retreating pair, hands locked on the stem of her untouched glass.

"Ah . . ." Denny made a hesitant throat clearing. "There's a movie on TV I'd kind of like to watch. *A Taste of Honey.* Remember it?"

"What?" Maggie seemed to return from a great distance. "Oh. No, I never saw it, and don't want to. A *taste* of honey doesn't have much appeal for me, I'm afraid." She drained her glass in one swallow and rose. "So I'll say good night."

Jan had thought she was tired enough to sleep, yet didn't. Too many questions circled around her head.

Just how vital was it to Ted to have this Samantha paper signed?

How long would he and Denny stay?

How long would her job last?

Would Alicia pay her anything when she left, or was she on board wages? That matter had never been raised.

Who *is* in that garage room? I hope he appreciated his supper tonight. It was fit for Teddie-boy, so it should do for garage interlopers. Who didn't get any wine. Bet he got some coffee, though.

Does Alicia really want Ted back? And would she be a better wife, second time around? Might be, I suppose. Though I doubt it. Not in her nature. Might Ted be more tolerant? I doubt that very, very much, I doubt that. Definitely not in *his* nature.

Oh dear, why can't I sleep?

What was that? That sort of light, sneaky sound. And there was no lock on her door, as Jan all too abruptly realized. She came out of her sleeping bag, crouching, hands outstretched, before she even paused to think.

Feeling a trifle ridiculous, she paused, holding her breath. Yes, something, though not as close as it had first sounded. Yet still there, too quiet, too careful, too furtive, for a respectable household.

Jan eased her door open and, pausing every couple of yards to listen, edged down the back hall. Tiny, intermittent noises continued from somewhere ahead, from out of the general dark that had enveloped the whole downstairs.

From the front hall she could see through the open door into the living room. Across it—surely by the liquor cabinet?—was a shape, distinguishable only by its solidity and slight movements.

Someone making a last drink? Nonsense, not in the dark. Someone, though, certainly that. Someone now moving across the room right toward her.

Jan froze where she was, desperately hoping that the deep shadows of the angled hall would be enough. Nearer and nearer the soft sounds came, and then, just when her heart seemed ready to leap from her throat, changed to a slight creak, another and another. The person was feeling his or her way upstairs.

Drawn by a curiosity as senseless as it was strong, Jan dropped to her hands and knees, crept to the bottom of the stairwell, and cautiously peered up. She could hear breathing shorter and heavier than normal. In the faint and indirect light from above she could discern a shape. A man's? Probably. And the faint smell of sweat that drifted down was surely also a man's. Whoever, he or she had reached the upper landing and had disappeared into its shadows.

What could—should Jan, the stranger, the temporary servant, do? There were, after all, two men by legitimate right in the house, Ted and Denny. Whatever they might be up to, wherever they were, was no business of hers. More, since the whole downstairs was now in darkness, the mistress and her companion-housekeeper were presumably both upstairs themselves.

Yet Jan waited, irresolute, until she became aware of a chill on her bare feet—of a draft, apparently coming from across the living room, from the direction of the patio. Now that, Jan thought, *is* well within my province to investigate.

She felt her way across the unlit room. With each step she became more conscious that the sliding panels were indeed open a couple of inches, and that she faced a new dilemma. Presumably someone from the house had gone out. Well, that was their privilege, and it was certainly not Jan's duty to bolt them out. And yet . . . The dark, to have everything happening in the dark—that was what was so bothersome.

Staring out into the deep shadows of the garden, she could make out the white cement urn where Denny had wrestled it, at the edge of the sunken patio. All else was merely shades of blackness.

Sounds, though. Jan was catching sounds, distant yet very different from those she had followed from her room. These were careless and bright and from above, a woman's giggle, a man's laugh. Alicia and Ted on the balcony?

Jan eased open the sliding doors and stepped down to the sunken patio. As she did so, a star fell from the sky—so incredibly near that she jumped—and landed even more incredibly in the tangled leaves of the rose bush.

"Bull's eye, Teddie-boy!" Alicia, loud and clear and merry. The star had become a cigarette butt, dying in the greenery of the urn.

"Oh, *must* you go, honey?" Alicia again, pleading. "Well, until tomorrow, then. Say nightie-night nicely." Another giggle.

Jan stepped back into the house, leaving the patio doors as she had found them, and headed back to her little room. As she passed through the hall she paused, looking up the long staircase, but all was silent above now.

* * *

Jan had that traveler's friend in her pack, wax earplugs, and this time put them to use. It seemed to take ages before the stuff was soft enough to be wedged into place, and she was thoroughly chilly. *Sleep*, she ordered firmly, and scrunched low in her bag, head well inside the opening.

But she wasn't asleep when the woman screamed.

Jan wasted countless seconds, each seeming a minute long, in freeing herself from her earplugs and bedding, more in pulling on her shoes and jacket and fishing out her small torch. Yet she did all that. Those screams were making it abundantly clear that she wouldn't soon be back in the comforts of her little room and sleeping bag.

Guided by the beam of her torch, Jan ran down the hall. No doubt at all that the uproar was coming from upstairs—a woman sobbing, "Ted! Oh, Ted!" and a man replying, "There, there," a response that so far seemed totally ineffective—and Jan had one hand on the banister when she felt it again.

This time on her bare ankles, that draft, cutting across the living room from the patio doors, apparently still open. And there was . . . movement of some kind beyond, on the patio itself.

For inexplicable reasons she extinguished her torch, crossing the living room apparently by memory, certainly without hesitation or mishap. Someone had covered the urn, as if it were going to freeze. Which it certainly wasn't. Covered it with something very light colored and rather . . . billowy. Covered it with—with Alicia. Sprawled across an urn that had been toppled onto its side. And bending over her, for the moment seeming as still as she, was Denny.

They were all still there, tableau figures in the dark, when the hall light burst forth, jumbled footsteps staggered down the stairs, a living-room lamp came on. The sounds became Maggie, in blue Viyella, still babbling hysterically, and Ted, in maroon terrycloth and striped pajamas, repeating, "Hush, hush now," mechanically, as if he no longer had any expectations of being obeyed. He reached for the wall with his free hand, and the patio lights blazed out, removing any possible doubts.

Alicia's form lay where it had been, unmoving, half on its right side across the toppled urn. Rising to his feet was Denny. "She's dead," he said simply.

At that Maggie buried her head on Ted's shoulder. "She must have leaned over too far. Oh, how could she be so silly!"

Of course, Jan thought unavoidably, silly was exactly the way Alicia had been acting all evening. But that created its own problem, because she *had* been acting. She hadn't been out of control at all, far from it.

"The police?" Denny asked quietly, and Ted nodded.

"Oh no!" Maggie wailed from his arms. "Poor Alicia!"

Denny had already disappeared into the dining room.

"Shall I," Jan hesitated, "wake Maria? Or make coffee?"

"Both," Ted answered, sounding relieved that some assistance was available, no matter how slight. "Come on, Maggie, hush now." He was trying to push her gently into a chair, without much success.

In the kitchen, Maria was already emerging from her quarters, an old coat over her long, white nightgown, a crutch under each arm. Jan explained, tersely. Maria's face had been expressionless and remained so. Only the mention of coffee brought her into motion, and silently Jan proceeded to help.

The police had arrived before the coffee was ready. Two men, then three, then four or five—Jan couldn't keep track, nor of what they were doing, outside, upstairs, back, and front. As from a great distance she watched and listened and served coffee, and only came somewhat to herself when they were all gathered in the living room.

The patio lights were still on, but the curtains were now tactfully drawn, and a tall man, with a comfortable, though no doubt unregulation, tummy, was asking plain, kind questions and making short notes.

Ted said that when he and Alicia had left for upstairs, they had gone at once out to her balcony and stayed there, finishing their drinks and talking about the Samantha property (which he briefly explained). Alicia still professing herself bewildered, Ted had agreed that they'd better talk about it again tomorrow, had said good-night, and gone to his room. He'd undressed and decided to shave to save time in the morning, in case he slept late. First thing he knew of anything's being wrong was Maggie's calling out. Startled him so much he'd spilled aftershave all over himself. Afraid he still reeked of it, he added apologetically. (Did he? Jan wondered. She hadn't noticed.)

Maggie said she had been nearly asleep when she'd heard . . . something. No, she couldn't say what, only that it was . . . a *heavy* kind of noise, unusual. She'd opened her door, seen that Ted's light was on, as was Alicia's, so she'd tapped on Alicia's and called, had no answer. Pushed the door open, saw no one, only the balcony door was open and that light on, too. So she'd gone out there and found no one, and, bewildered, had looked over, and . . . Here Maggie buried her face in her hands, Ted patted her arm, and she dropped her head onto his shoulder again.

Denny said he'd watched TV in the den, off the living room, until the movie was over, didn't feel sleepy, and had gone for a walk, leaving by way of the patio doors. He'd strolled all the way out the front gate and down the road to the next house, which was in darkness, and then returned. As he'd rounded the hedge into the grounds, he'd heard . . . well, a noise near the house, and could make out something pale and sort of collapsing like an umbrella over the urn. He'd done no more than lift Alicia's hand to know the truth. No, he hadn't moved her.

Jan didn't mention her earlier expedition. It seemed so silly to have done as much and no more. So she had been wakened suddenly by the upstairs noises, she said, had run out, felt the coolness from the patio door, investigated, and seen Denny. That was all.

Maria had heard nothing until she heard something, and had met Jan in her kitchen. To which she then returned.

"That balcony," the policeman now commented, "has rather a low top railing, but the poor lady was short, wasn't she? She wouldn't have fallen unless she'd been leaning out very far, or possibly had climbed up onto the lower railing. Would she have been apt to have done either of those things, do you think?" No one answered. "You said you each had a last drink, sir," the policeman now addressed Ted pointedly.

"We did," Ted answered steadily, "and if you're asking how much Alicia'd had to drink during the evening, I don't know, I didn't notice. I made her first drink—gin and tonic—and the one I took upstairs. Couple of ounces of gin in each. I'm not sure if she had anything else—"

"No," Denny interjected. "I'm virtually positive that she didn't."

"Before supper?" the policeman suggested.

"No," Maggie said shortly. "Wine at the meal, a white Chateau Chambre, nothing more. We emptied one bottle that had been a bit over half full and finished another, between the four of us. Alicia probably had her share."

The policeman raised an eyebrow at Jan. She mutely nodded agreement.

"You'll be able to tell from your tests, anyway, won't you?" Denny asked bluntly. "The blood alcohol—"

"Denny." Maggie moaned.

"Don't be foolish, Mags," Ted urged tersely. "Of course there'll be blood tests. Others, too, no doubt. And what the officer is really asking us is whether or not Alicia seemed . . . tipsy. Right?"

"Alcohol does affect people in different ways," the officer tactfully agreed.

"With Alicia," Ted paused, "I'm not sure. You'd have to have known her to understand. She was very . . . buoyant all evening."

"Alicia," Maggie sat up abruptly and spoke equally so, "enjoyed playing the fool. No, no, Ted, we might as well say it. She was quite capable of climbing up on that lower railing, or of leaning way out over the top one, to look at the moon—"

"There wasn't one," Denny interposed.

"Maybe she saw you coming back and was waving."

"She couldn't have seen me until I came around the corner of the hedge, and by then . . ."

"Well, anything," Maggie returned, impatiently. "Maybe she was wondering if she'd leave that urn where it is and was gazing down at it. All I mean is that whatever she thought she'd do, she would. That was Alicia."

"It's a good thirty feet from the balcony to that sunken patio," the policeman observed sympathetically, "and the poor lady seems to have hit her head against the urn's side hard enough to topple it." He paused, looking at Denny. "You weren't close enough to have heard if she cried out as she lost her balance, sir?"

"I didn't hear anything," Denny said shortly. "Just that . . . thud."

Maggie began moaning again, loudly, and the policeman, offering general condolences, left.

Only when Jan was at last back in her little room did her thoughts fix on that nearly silent figure whom she'd seen first at the liquor cabinet and then going upstairs. It didn't seem that he or she could have been either Denny or Ted, nor yet Maggie. Might as well suppose it could have been Alicia herself, and, putting all else aside, the cloud of scent in which she had chosen to have her existence that evening ruled that out.

As for her being slightly under the influence, no matter what she'd had to drink before, during, or after supper, she had certainly tripped gaily up the stairs in her high-heeled sandals without missing a step. Jan very much doubted if a gin and tonic would have turned her into a mad gymnast an hour later.

Besides, something was wrong about the whole picture. Something (or things?) didn't fit. What?

And what was *that* sound? Right now, outside, at the back of the house?

In shoes and jacket once more, electric torch in hand, Jan tiptoed out. The kitchen was in darkness, though a faint glow came from outside. From, as Jan discovered by peeking through the curtains, under the door of that mysterious garage room, the one that was too dirty for her to use.

She stepped outside, quietly. As she reached the bottom of the steps, the light under the door went out. The door opened, jerkily, and Maria, leaning heavily on her crutches, filled the space.

For a long moment the two women stared at each other through the deep gloom. Then Maria, sagging against the jamb, jabbed her stick at the darkness behind her.

"Look," she challenged, "look. He gone."

"Who was he?"

Maria's face was shadowed and sagging dough. "You marry, ever?"

"No."

"Then what you know, young fool?" The tears were trickling unheeded from one wrinkle to another. She reminded Jan of a wooden Pietà she'd seen somewhere in Spain.

"He was your son."

Maria nodded, heavily. "My son. My no-good son. The work I find for him, the work everybody find for him. He keep, he do hard, he please? No. No, never. Never. Bad friends, trouble, police, run. Come here. Mama, mama, what I do? Not stay, I say. Got to, he say. Little while, I say, little while only. Then you come. Tomorrow, I tell him, you go. At night, he say. I go at night. I wait, I not sleep, he not come, say good-bye. Then noise, shouting, police . . . he gone, *her*," a jerk of her head at the house that loomed over them both, "dead."

Jan crossed the dark path and took the older woman's arm. "Go back to bed. And have a brandy, hot, with lemon and sugar. I'll make it for you."

"*Their* brandy?" Maria's tone expressed her shock.

"*Their* brandy," Jan promised firmly. One hand on Maria's elbow, she guided her in and then headed for the liquor cabinet, boldly put the light on.

The liquor was on the bottom shelf: the crème de menthe,

the nearly empty whiskey bottle, the unopened one—no, that bottle was the brandy. Where was the unopened whiskey? Nowhere.

That's what Maria's son had been after: what he could steal without giving himself away. And that's why he'd gone upstairs: to steal. He'd seen the light under Alicia's door, probably heard her and Ted too, and would have given that room a wide berth. But Ted's: bet he went in there. Wonder if he took anything? He'd leave Maggie's room alone: she could still be awake. Denny's, though: Maria's son had quite likely seen or heard Denny go off for his walk, and would certainly go into that room.

In fact, he probably ended trapped in Denny's room— first by Ted's leaving Alicia's, no doubt stopping to go to the bathroom, then going into his own; next by Maggie's popping out and starting the uproar. What would the fellow do? Leave by way of the window and the ivy growing so thickly below it?

Jan took the hot toddy to Maria and told her not to bother about breakfast. She'd see to it. And not to worry about her son, at least not as far as this evening's events went.

"You sure?" Maria asked, pathetically eager.

"Positive," Jan replied. Though she wasn't quite, for still that elusive something was bothering her.

She slept little and, with making breakfast her excuse, was up and out as soon as the late sun was on the eastern side of the house. She didn't need to be Sherlock Holmes to see that the ivy had indeed been pulled away from the wall in places, nor that one heavily descending foot had landed on a patch of soft earth.

"Hi," Denny, leaning out of his window. "Awful night, wasn't it? I don't suppose you happened to notice my navy sweater anywhere, the one I was wearing yesterday? I could have sworn I left it on the chair here, but it seems to have vanished."

No doubt it had, being of good quality and nearly new. "I haven't seen it," Jan replied all too truthfully. She retreated to the kitchen, wondering if Ted had also lost anything.

That was answered at breakfast. In the middle of the silent and largely uneaten meal, Ted murmured that he'd have to run into town. "I don't know how I contrived to be so careless, but I seem to have come with hardly a dollar in my wallet."

Which of course he'd left in his room, being in a dinner jacket for supper. Well, that tidied that up.

Ted had left, Denny had gone back to his room to try for a nap, Jan had finished the breakfast dishes and was wandering around, feeling both lost and bothered. She found Maggie out on the patio, with shears and garden gloves, clipping back the damaged rose bush.

"Those kind policemen set the urn upright again," she told Jan, "but somehow that just made the poor thing look worse. All the blooms gone, and the branches crushed."

"It'll live, won't it?" As Alicia won't, Jan's mind unwillingly reminded her.

"Oh yes." Maggie snipped busily. "It'll take a while to bush out again, but the main stem is firm." She was putting the clippings in a little box. "I thought that perhaps Ted would like it for his place. He has a condo, you know, with quite a nice patio."

"This house isn't his?" Jan asked in surprise.

"Oh no, it wasn't even Alicia's. Wes left her a life interest—it was his family's home, you know—and it reverts to Denny's mother, his sister. And since she's dead now, too, I suppose . . ." Maggie paused for a moment. "Well, I suppose the house is Denny's. He was an only child. And it'll be such a good thing for him because he can't make much as a notary. It's a very small firm, the one he's with."

"And that Samantha property, or mineral rights, or whatever it is—who will have that now?"

"Oh, that'll be Ted's." Maggie was positive. "After all, not only were he and Alicia still married—though I'm sure they were the only ones who . . . I mean, everyone assumed that there'd been a divorce. Anyway, Ted had loaned Wes the money originally, so one way or another it's Ted's now. As it should be.

"There, that looks much better, doesn't it? Now I'll just take this box around to the back—it's garbage pickup today. Oh, thank you, my dear. Just put it by the can."

Jan did, though first she emptied the little box stem by stem, for she'd remembered at least one of the problems that was stuck at the back of her mind. That cigarette butt that Ted had thrown from Alicia's balcony, which had landed right on the rose bush, had originated in a household that, as far as Jan had seen, contained not a single smoker.

The butt wasn't among the clippings, nor was it still in the rose bush, or on the patio. Jan looked, very carefully.

Denny had been first on the scene last night, and had knelt by his aunt's body. Had, he'd said, touched her hand and known she was dead. No doubt he'd been shocked. Had he also thought that now the house and grounds—the really very nice house and grounds, even if they were rather neglected—were now his?

And Ted. Ted who would now, one way or another, have clear title to the Samantha property. He had said he'd been shaving when Maggie had come flying to his room, and had been so startled that he'd spilled aftershave all over himself. He'd even apologized for reeking of it. But he hadn't. Jan had served him coffee and might have caught a little whiff of something like aftershave, no more than that.

No doubt making up Ted's room was one of Jan's tasks. At any rate, she headed there. There *was* a kind of pervading aroma of masculine cologne, but it didn't come from Ted's robe or pajamas. In fact, it didn't seem to come from anywhere, exactly. Only by sniffing as industriously as a bloodhound did Jan finally locate the source: the window-sill. A patch about the size of her palm, roughly in the middle of the bottom sill of a window that was, as she had left it yesterday, half open.

There was neither smell nor sight of cigarettes, though, stifling pangs of guilt, Jan ruthlessly searched for both.

She heard Denny go into the bathroom and the shower start, and made a resolute dash for his room. Maid service, she told herself, that's what I'm doing, and searched quickly. An easy enough task, the room being scantily furnished and holding no more of Denny's possessions than had come in one old gray plastic suitcase.

Nothing, until she pressed her nose to the dinner jacket, hanging so innocently in the closet. The one pocket, though now bare of even lint, held in its folds the distinctive essence of flower child: grass, marijuana.

Jan made the bed, left the room, and paused. The shower ceased; she had to go somewhere or meet Denny. So she kept on down the hall to Alicia's room.

Nothing had been changed or, as far as she knew, even touched since the police had left, and they hadn't been here long. Certainly Alicia's presence was still strong, the furnishings all pink and white luxury, and the atmosphere that of a perfume shop. Scents of all kinds, rose dominant, though only just. Jasmine here, something spicy and exotic there, lavender—*lavender?* Yes, lavender. Apparently Alicia had had her old-fashioned moments, too. Or at least moments when she had liked to pretend she did.

Jan undid the balcony door and stepped out. Two comfortable lounge chairs by a low table, and on it a bouquet of Ted's roses, the very air still sweet with their aroma, their perfect ivory centers and deep pink edges reminders of Alicia's deliberately chosen color scheme.

She'd certainly set the scene last night, no doubt sure she could entice Ted up here with little enough trouble. In that she had succeeded, though apparently in little else. He really was only interested in that Samantha business. And she hadn't really seemed to mind, either. Of course she would intend renewing her campaign today, sure no man could resist her long. "Say nightie-night nicely." Of course by then she was a bit high. . . .

Had she given Ted that roach, or had he given it to her? It was more the sort of thing Alicia would do. And he'd thrown the butt away—really more than a butt, half the cigarette. He'd taken it because he was trying to please her. Then, knowing his breath would carry the aroma, he had hastily rinsed his mouth with aftershave, attempting to spit it out the window.

Where did Alicia get the stuff? Through Andy and his

crowd? According to Maggie's terse references, they were a decidedly lively gang. That would also explain why the young engineer still dropped by now and then, and seemed on excellent terms with the older woman he'd (to put it bluntly) dumped?

Where would Alicia keep her stock? Somewhere easy of access, yet innocuous. Somewhere no one would stumble on by chance . . .

Why was that padded stool by that corner whatnot? Jan surveyed the room from the balcony door. The stool surely belonged in front of the dressing table, which looked nude without it. Alicia had been short, Jan was not. By standing on tiptoe, she could reach the top shelf and its small row of books. The only books in the room, though magazines abounded.

Several paperback romances, a couple of Jack Londons with Wes's name scrawled inside. And an old and cheap edition of *Vanity Fair*.

So Andy had at least a sense of humor, Jan thought, pulling it out. "To A from A" in neat gold printing, with the whole center of the book cut out and the space taken up by a foil-wrapped package whose fragrance told a tale unknown to Becky Sharp.

Denny had removed the butt from the rose bush and hidden it in his dinner jacket, trying to cover what he could of his dead aunt's folly. Well, bully for Denny. Probably he thought that Alicia had been high enough to have somehow fallen.

Why didn't Jan agree?

Because she'd heard her, only moments before, certainly happy—happy enough to take merry farewell of Ted—but not at all out of reality. Why would she then do something as daft as climbing on that bottom rail, or leaning over the top one until she toppled? A short person would have to be practically doubled over to fall.

Yet she *had* fallen. Most certainly she had done that.

Without crying out. At least without crying out loudly enough for Denny to have heard her as he rounded the hedge. At least according to Denny.

Jan had solved quite a few of the little mysteries surrounding Alicia's death, only not the main one. And she was still bothered by what it was she knew and couldn't remember. Something that was becoming more and more important.

From far down the hill she could hear the sound of a heavy vehicle starting on its way up. Of course. Maggie had said this was pickup day for the garbage.

The garbage. Jan had taken out last night's garbage this morning. A plastic bag of kitchen waste, an empty whiskey bottle, an empty wine bottle . . . *An* empty wine bottle? Yes. Only one. Yet two had been finished at supper.

What could anyone do with an empty wine bottle?

Use it as a club. Hit a dreamy Alicia, leaning on the balcony rail and smiling off into the night, hit her on the temple and then topple her over to fall onto the urn. Then hide the bottle—no, wash it first, then hide it, somewhere easy of access. This morning put it . . . Not in the dustbin: it wasn't there. It wasn't there because someone might notice that it was too clean. So where had it gone?

The garbage truck was grinding up the hill.

The neighbor's dustbin. The neighbor who was quite a long way by road, but was probably reached quite easily through that wild tangle of garden.

Jan ran down the stairs, in and out of the kitchen, around the house. Yes, there was a path, an overgrown path through the shrubbery. She plunged into it, recklessly running, yet noting, too, that someone else had indeed come this way recently. Twigs of overhanging branches were broken, a footstep showed in a loamy patch, things to be examined later, only not now, not now.

She caught sight of the neighbor's dustbin, set neatly on the side of the road, and nearly burst out from the last clump of bushes. She just caught herself in time, for there was Maggie, walking briskly along, headed back toward the house, a few bits of leaves caught on the back of her tweed skirt, with the green shawl she'd had over her shoulders last night now tossed over her arm.

Rather a bulky shawl. You really wouldn't notice if there

was anything under it. Which there was not, now. And as Maggie passed by she was humming, humming something that Jan knew. Oh yes: "Lucy in the sky with diamonds."

Now Jan ran, lifted the lid of the dustbin by the outside edges, set it aside, pulled out another plastic bag of miscellaneous garbage (very tidy people, these Oak Hillers), and found what by now she knew she would—the wine bottle. The very clean wine bottle, which she removed by inserting her finger in the top.

She had no time to do more than hide the bottle behind her and appear to be idling about as the garbage truck rounded the corner. The driver was young and gave her a cheerful grin. She managed a wave of her free hand.

Now what? She had the bottle, she had her story. There was evidence of a kind on Maggie's skirt and no doubt on the path, perhaps even on the dustbin lid. But how did she deliver it all to the police? Because she definitely was not going back to the house.

A car was coming from that direction. Denny. And he had his old suitcase in the back. He stopped by her, and they considered each other. Slowly Jan brought her hand with its bottle addition to the front. Denny frowned, thoughtfully.

"So that's how she did it," he said, and leaned to open the passenger door.

"Maggie always wanted Ted," he said as they drove away, "and I guess she had a few renewed hopes during the time she thought he and Alicia were divorced. Once she knew they were not, and that Alicia was on the hunt again as well . . ."

"How did you guess?" Jan asked. "That it was Maggie?"

Denny hesitated. "Alicia was dead by the time I reached her, so she couldn't have just fallen. A few minutes had to have gone by."

"But you heard the . . . thud."

"I heard *a* thud," Denny agreed. "Of the urn's being pushed over, before Alicia's body was pulled over it. As I ran across the lawn, I seemed to see . . . I don't know, something like movement by the patio doors. But I couldn't be sure. It might have been nothing."

"It was Maggie, on her way back upstairs."

"Yes."

They had reached the bottom of the hill and turned toward Victoria.

"I head right to the police station?" Denny asked.

"I think so. There's nothing else we can do, is there?"

"No. I guess not."

They drove on in silence. Then, as the city's lights mounted around them, Denny hesitantly observed, "I know a guy who runs a sort of coffee house. His wife has a sort of gift shop at the back. They just might have a sort of job for you."

I like Canada, Jan felt suddenly. It's . . . friendly. "That'd be great," she agreed. "Sort of," and found Denny's grin very comforting.

High Heels in the Headliner

Wendy Hornsby

"Exquisite prose, charming story. A nice read." Thea tossed the stack of reviews her editor had sent into the file drawer and slammed it shut. The reviews were always the same, exquisite, charming, nice. What she wanted to hear was, "Tough, gritty, compelling, real. Hardest of the hard-boiled."

Thea had honestly tried to break away from writing bestselling fluff. What she wanted more than anything was to be taken seriously as a writer among writers. To do that, she knew she had to achieve tough, gritty, and real. The problem was, her whole damn life was exquisite, charming, nice.

Thea wrote from her own real-life experience, such as it was. One day, when she was about halfway through the first draft of *Lord Rimrock, L.A.P.D.*, a homeless man with one of those grubby cardboard signs—Will Work for Food—jumped out at her from his spot on the median strip up on Pacific Coast Highway. Nearly scared her to death. She used that raw emotion, the fear like a cold dagger in her gut, to write a wonderful scene for Officer Lord Rimrock. But her editor scrapped it because it was out of tone with the rest of the book. Over drawn, the editor said.

Fucking over drawn, Thea muttered and walked up to the corner shop for a bottle of wine to take the edge off her ennui.

In her mind, while she waited in line to pay, she rethought her detective. She chucked Lord Rimrock and replaced him with a Harvard man who preferred the action of big-city police work to law school. He was tall and muscular with a streak of gray at the temple. She was working on a name for him when she noticed that the man behind her in line had a detective's shield hanging on his belt.

She gawked. Here in the flesh was a real detective, her first sighting. He was also a major disappointment. His cheap suit needed pressing, he had a little paunch, and he was sweating. Lord Rimrock never sweated. Harvard men don't sweat.

"Excuse me," she said when he caught her staring.

"Don't worry about it." His world-weary scowl changed to a smarmy smile and she realized that he had mistaken her curiosity for a come on. She went for it.

"What division do you work from?" That much she knew to ask.

"Homicide. Major crimes." *He smiled out of the side of his mouth, not giving up much, not telling her to go away, either. She raised her beautiful eyes to meet his.* No. Beautiful was the wrong tone. Too charming.

"Must be interesting work," Thea said.

"Not very." *She knew he was flattered and played him like a . . .* She'd work out the simile later.

"What you do is interesting to me," she said. "I write mystery novels."

"Oh yeah?" He was intrigued.

"I suppose you're always bothered by writers looking for help with procedural details."

"I never met a writer," he said. "Unless you count asshole reporters."

She laughed, scratching the Harvard man from her

thoughts, dumping the gray streak at the temple. This detective had almost no hair at all.

Thea paid for her bottle of Chardonnay. The detective put his six-pack on the counter, brushing her hand in passing. Before she could decide on an exit line, he said, "Have you ever been on a ride-along? You know, go out with the police and observe."

"I never have," she said. "It would be helpful. How does one arrange a ride-along?"

"I don't know any more." *The gravel in his voice told her he'd seen too much of life.* "Used to do it all the time. Damned liability shit now, though. Department has really pulled back. Too bad. I think what most taxpayers need is a dose of reality. If they saw what we deal with all day, they'd get off our backs."

Thea did actually raise her beautiful eyes to him. "I think the average person is fascinated by what you do. That's why they read mysteries. That's why I write them. I would love to sit down with you some time, talk about your experiences."

"Oh yeah?" He responded by pulling in his paunch. "I just finished up at a crime scene in the neighborhood. I'm on my way home. Maybe you'd like to go for a drink."

"Indeed, I would." Thea gripped the neck of the wine bottle, hesitating before she spoke. "Tell you what. If you take me by the crime scene and show me around, we can go to my place after, have some wine and discuss the details."

Bostitch was his name. He paid for his beer and took her out to his city car, awkward in his eagerness to get on with things.

The crime scene was a good one, an old lady stabbed in her bedroom. Bostitch walked Thea right into the apartment past the forensics people who were still sifting for evidence. He explained how the blood spatter patterns on the walls were like a map of the stabbing, showed her a long arterial spray. *On the carpet where the body was found, she could trace the contours of the woman's head and outstretched arms. Like a snow angel made in blood.*

The victim's family arrived. They had come to look through the house to determine what, if anything, was missing, but all they could do was stand around, numbed by grief. Numbed? Was that it?

Thea walked up to the daughter and said, "How do you feel?"

"Oh, it's awful," the woman sobbed. "Mom was the sweetest woman on earth. Who would do this to her?"

Thea patted the daughter's back, her question still unanswered. How did she feel? Scorched, hollow, riven, shredded, iced in the gut? What?

"Seen enough?" Bostitch asked, taking Thea's arm.

She hadn't seen enough, but she smiled compliantly up into his face. She didn't want him to think she was a ghoul. Or a wimp. To her surprise, she was not bothered by the gore or the smell or any of it. She was the totally objective observer, seeing everything through the eyes of her fictional detective character.

Bostitch showed her the homicide kit he kept in the trunk of his car, mostly forms, rubber gloves, plastic bags. She was more impressed by the name than the contents, but she took a copy of everything for future reference to make him happy.

By the time Bostitch drove her back to her house, Thea's detective had evolved. He was the son of alcoholics, grew up in Wilmington in the shadow of the oil refineries. He would have an ethnic name similar to Bostitch. The sort of man who wouldn't know where Harvard was.

In her exquisite living room, they drank the thirty-dollar Chardonnay. Bostitch told stories, Thea listened. All the time she was smiling or laughing or pretending shock, she was making mental notes. *He sat with his arm draped on the back of the couch, the front of his jacket open, an invitation to come closer. He slugged down the fine old wine like soda pop. When it was gone, he reached for the warm six-pack he had brought in with him and flipped one open.*

By that point, Bostitch was telling war stories about the old days when he was in uniform. The good old days. He had worked morning watch, the shift from midnight to seven. He liked being on patrol in the middle of the night because everything that went down at oh-dark-thirty had an edge.

After work he and his partners would hit the early opening bars. They would get blasted and take women down to a cul-de-sac under the freeway and screw off the booze before they went home. Not beer, he told her. Hard stuff.

"Your girlfriend would meet you?" Thea asked.

"Girlfriend? Shit no. I'd never take a girlfriend down there. There are certain women who just wet themselves for a cop in uniform. We'd go, they'd show."

"I can't imagine," Thea said, wide eyed, her worldly mien slipping. She couldn't imagine it. She had never had casual sex with anyone. Well, just once actually, with an English professor her freshman year. It had been pretty dull stuff and not worth counting.

"What sort of girls were they?" she asked him.

"All kinds. There was one—she was big, I mean big— we'd go pick her up on the way. She'd say, 'I won't do more than ten of you, and I won't take it in the rear.' She was a secretary or something."

"You made that up," Thea said.

"Swear to God," he said.

"I won't believe you unless you show me," Thea said. She knew where in the book she would use this gem, her raggedy old detective joining the young cowboys in uniform for one last blow out with young women. No. He'd have a young female partner and take her there to shock her. A rite of passage for a rookie female detective.

The problem was, Thea still couldn't visualize it, and she had to get it just right. "Take me to this place."

She knew that Bostitch completely misunderstood that she was only interested for research purposes. Explaining this might not have gotten him up off the couch so fast. They stopped for another bottle on the way—a pint of scotch.

It was just dusk when Bostitch pulled up onto the hard-packed dirt of a vacant lot at the end of the cul-de-sac and parked. A small encampment of homeless people scurried away under the freeway when they recognized the city-issue car.

The cul-de-sac was at the end of a street to nowhere, a despoiled landscape of discarded furniture, cars, and human-

ity. Even weeds couldn't thrive. She thought humanity wouldn't get past the editor—over drawn—but that was the idea. She would find the right word later.

Bostitch skewed around in his seat to face her.

"We used to have bonfires here," he said. "Until the city got froggy about it. Screwed up traffic on the freeway. All the smoke."

"Spoiled your fun?" she said.

"It would take more than that." He smiled out the window. "One night, my partner talked me into coming out here before the shift was over. It wasn't even daylight yet. Some babe promised to meet him. I sat inside here and wrote reports while they did it on the hood. God, I'll never forget it. I'm working away in my seat with this naked white ass pumping against the windshield in front of my face— bump, bump, bump. Funny as hell. Bet that messed up freeway traffic."

Thea laughed, not at his story, but at her own prose version of it.

"You ever get naked on the hood of the car?" she asked. She'd had enough booze to ask it easily. For research.

"I like it inside better," he said.

"In the car?" she asked. She moved closer, *leaning near enough to smell the beer on his breath. During his twenty-five years with the police, he must have had half the women in the city. She wanted to know what they had taught him. What he might teach her.*

She lapped her tongue lightly along the inner curve of his lips. Thea said, with a throaty chuckle, "I won't do more than ten of you. And I won't take it in the rear."

When he took her in his arms he wasn't as rough as she had hoped he would be. She set the pace by the eager, almost violent way she tore loose his tie, ripped open his shirt. His five-o'clock shadow sanded a layer of skin off her chin.

They ended up in the back seat, their clothes as wrinkled and shredded as the crime scene report under them. At the moment of her ecstasy the heel of Thea's shoe thrust up through the velour headliner. She looked at the long tear. *The sound of the rip was like cymbals crashing at the peak of a symphony, except the only music was the rhythmic grunting and groaning from the tangle of bodies in the back seat. She jammed her foot through the hole, bracing it against the hard metal roof of the car to get some leverage to meet his thrusting, giving him a more solid base to bang against.*

Bostitch seemed to stop breathing altogether. His face grew a dangerous red and drew up into an agonized sort of grimace that stretched every sinew in his neck. Thea was beginning to worry that she might have killed him when he finally exhaled.

"Oh Jesus," he moaned. "Oh sweet, sweet Jesus."

She untangled her foot from the torn headliner and wrapped her bare legs around him, trapping him inside her until the pulsing ceased. Maybe not, she thought. Pulsing, throbbing were definitely overused.

After the afterglow, what would she feel? Not shame or anything akin to it. She smiled with pride in her prowess. She had whipped his ass and left him gasping. Thea buried her face against his chest and bit his small, hard nipple.

"You're amazing," he said, still breathing hard.

She said nothing. That moment was definitely not the time to explain that it was her female detective, Ricky, or maybe Marty Tenwolde, who was amazing. Thea herself was far too inhibited to have initiated the wild sex that had left their automobile nest in serious need of repair.

When they had pulled their clothes back together, he said, "Now what?"

"Skid Row," she said. "I've always been afraid to go down there, but I need to see it for the book I'm working on."

"Good reason to be afraid." *The cop spoke with a different voice than the lover, a deep, weary growl that* something or other. "You don't really want to go down there."

"I do, though. With you. You're armed. You're the law. We'll be safe."

She batted her big, beautiful eyes again. Flattery and some purring were enough to sway him. He drove her downtown to Skid Row.

Thea had never seen anything as squalid and depraved. Toothless, stoned hookers running down the middle of the street. Men dry heaving in the gutter. *The smell alone made him wish she hadn't come along. He was embarrassed that she saw the old wino defecate openly on the sidewalk. But she only smiled that wry smile that always made the front of his slacks feel tight.*

There was a six- or seven-person brawl in progress on one corner. Thea loved it when Bostitch merely honked his horn to make them scatter like so many cockroaches.

"Seen enough?" he asked.

"Yes. Thank you."

Bostitch held her hand all the way back to her house.

"Will you come in?" she asked him.

"I'll come in. But don't expect much more out of my sorry old carcass. I haven't been that fired up since . . ."

"I thought for a minute you had died," she said. "I didn't know where to send the body."

"Felt like I was on my way to heaven." He slid a business card with a gold detective's shield from behind his visor and handed it to her. "You ever need anything, page me through the office."

So, he had a wife. A lot of men do. Thea hadn't considered a wife in the equation. She liked it—nice characterization. Bostitch called home from the phone on Thea's desk and told the wife he'd be out late on a case. Maybe all night.

"No wonder you fool around," Thea said when he turned his attention back to her. "It's too easy. Does your wife believe you?"

He shrugged. "She doesn't much bother anymore believing or not believing."

"Good line," Thea said. More than anything, she wanted to turn on her computer and get some of what she had learned on disk before she forgot anything. She had a whole new vocabulary: boot the door meant to kick it down, elwopp was life without possibility of parole, fifty-one-fifty was a mental incompetent. So many things to catalog.

"Where's your favorite place to make love?" she asked him.

"In a bed."

That's where they did it next. At least, that's where they

163

began. Bostitch was stunned, pleased, by the performance Thea coaxed from him. He gave Thea a whole chapter.

All the next week she was his shadow. She stood beside him during the autopsy of the stabbing victim, professional and detached because female detective Marty Tenwolde would be. The top of the old lady's skull made a pop like a champagne cork when the coroner sawed it off, but she wasn't even startled. She was as tough and gritty as any man on the force. She was tender, too. After a long day of detecting, she took the old guy home and screwed him until he begged for mercy. Detective Tenwolde felt . . .

That feeling stuff was the hard part. Tenwolde would feel attached to her old married partner. Be intrigued by him. She couldn't help mothering him a bit, but she could by no stretch describe her feelings as maternal. Love was going too far.

Thea watched Bostitch testify in court one day. A murder case, but not a particularly interesting one. It was a garden-variety family shootout, drunk husband takes off after estranged wife and her boyfriend. Thea added to her new vocabulary, learning that dead bang meant a case with an almost guaranteed conviction.

Bostitch looked sharper than usual and Thea was impressed by his professionalism. Of course, he winked at her when he thought the jury wasn't looking, checked for her reaction whenever he scored a point against the defense attorney. She always smiled back at him, but she was really more interested in the defendant, a pathetic little man who professed profound grief when he took the stand in his defense. He cried. *Without his wife, he was only a shell occupying space in this universe. His wife had defined his existence, made him complete. Killing her had only been a crude way to kill himself.* If he had any style, he would beg for the death sentence and let the state finish the job for him. Thea wondered what it felt like to lose a loved one in such a violent fashion.

Detective Tenwolde cradled her partner's bleeding head in her lap, knowing he was dying. She pressed her face close to his ear and whispered, "My only regret is I'll never be able to fuck you again, big guy. I love your ragged old ass." Needed something, but it was a good farewell line. Tough, gritty, yet tender.

Out in the corridor after court, the deputy district attorney complimented Bostitch's testimony. Thea, holding his hand, felt proud. No, she thought, she felt lustful. *If he had asked her to, for his reward in getting the kid convicted, she would gladly have blown Bostitch right there on the escalator.* Maybe she did love him. Something to think about.

After court, Thea talked Bostitch into taking her to a Hungarian restaurant he had told her about. He had had a run-in with a lunatic there a year or so earlier. Shot the man dead. Thea wanted to see where.

"There's nothing to see," he said as he pulled into the hillside parking lot. "But the food's okay. Mostly goulash. You know, like stew. We might as well eat."

They walked inside with their arms around each other. The owner knew Bostitch and showed them to a quiet booth in a far-back corner. It was very dark.

"I haven't seen Laszlo's brother for four or five months," the owner said, setting big plates of steaming goulash in front of them. He had a slight accent. "He was plenty mad at you, Bostitch, I tell you. Everybody knows Laszlo was a crazy man, always carrying those guns around. What could you do but shoot him? He shot first. I think maybe his brother is a little nuts, too."

"Show me where he died," Thea said, her lips against Bostitch's jug-like ear. He turned his face to her and kissed her.

"Let's eat and get out of here," he said. "We shouldn't have come."

There was a sudden commotion at the door and a big, fiery-eyed man burst in. The first thing Thea noticed was the shotgun he held at his side. The owner rushed up to him, distracted his attention away from Thea's side of the restaurant.

"Shh, Thea." Bostitch, keeping his eyes on the man with the shotgun, pulled his automatic from his belt holster. "That's Laszlo's brother. Someone must have called him, told him I was here. We're going to slip out the back way while they have him distracted."

"But he has a gun. He'll shoot someone."

"No he won't. He's looking for me. Once I'm out of here, they'll calm him down. Let me get out the door, then you follow me. Whatever you do, don't get close to me, and for chrissake stay quiet. Don't attract his attention." Bostitch slipped out of the booth.

She felt *alive. Adrenaline wakened every primitive instinct for survival. Every instinct to protect her man. If the asshole with the gun made so much as a move toward Bostitch, Tenwolde would grind him into dogmeat. Bostitch was only one step from safety when Tenwolde saw the gunman turn and spot him.*

Dogmeat was good, Thea thought. The rest she was still unclear about. That's when she stood up and screamed, "Don't shoot him. I love him."

Bostitch would have made it out the door, but Thea's outburst caused him to look back. That instant's pause was just long enough for the befuddled gunman to find Bostitch in his sights and fire a double-aught load into his abdomen. Bostitch managed to fire off a round of his own. The gunman was dead before he fell.

Thea ran to Bostitch and caught him as he slid to the floor, leaving a wide red smear on the wall.

His head was heavy in her arms.

"Why?" he sighed. His eyes went dull.

Tenwolde watched the light fade from her partner's eyes, felt his last breath escape from his shattered chest. She couldn't let him see her cry; he'd tease her forever. That's when she lost it. Bostitch had used up his forever.

"It's not fair, big guy," she said, smoothing his sparse hair. She felt a hole open in her chest as big as the gaping wound through his. Without him, she was incomplete. "You promised me one more academy-award fuck. You're not going back on your promise, are you?"

He was gone. Still, she held on to him, her cheek against his, his blood on her lips. "I never told you, Bostitch. I love your raggedy old ass."

Make Yourselves
at Home

Joan Hess

═══════

It was the summer of her discontent. This particular moment on this particular morning had just become its zenith;
its epiphany, if you will; its culmination of simmering
animosity and precariously constrained urges to scream
curses at the heavens while flinging herself off a precipice,
presuming there was such a thing within five hundred miles.
There was not. Florida is many things; one of them is flat.

Thus thwarted by geographical realities, Wilma Chadley
could do no more than gaze sullenly out the kitchen window
at the bleached grass and limp, dying shrubs. Fierce white
sunlight baked the concrete patio. In one corner of the yard
remained the stubbles of what had never been a flourishing
vegetable garden, but merely an impotent endeavor to
economize on groceries. Beyond the fence, tractor-trailers
blustered down the interstate. Cars topped with luggage
racks darted between them like brightly colored cockroaches. The motionless air was laden with noxious exhaust
fumes and the miasma from the swampy expanse on the far
side of the highway.

Wilma poured a glass of iced tea and sat down at the
dinette to reread the letter for the fifth time since she'd

taken it from the mailbox only half an hour ago. When she finished, her bony body quivered with resentment. Her breath came out in ragged grunts. A bead of sweat formed on the tip of her narrow nose, hung delicately, and then splattered on the page. More sweat trickled down the harshly angular creases of her face as the words blurred before her eyes.

From the living room she could hear the drone of the announcer's voice as he listed a batter's statistics. As usual, her husband, George, was sprawled on the recliner, drifting between the game and damp, uneasy naps, the fan whirring at his face, his sparse white hair plastered to his head. If she were to step between him and his precious game in order to read the letter, he would wait woodenly until she was done, then ask her to get him another beer. She had no doubt his response would be identical if she announced the house was on fire (although she was decidedly not in the mood to conduct whimsical experiments in behavioral psychology).

Finally, when she could no longer suffer in silence, she snatched the leash from a hook behind the door and tracked Popsie down in the bathroom, where he lay behind the toilet. "It's time for Popsie's lunchie walk," she said in a wheedling voice, aware that the obese and grizzled basset hound resented attempts to drag him away from the cool porcelain. "Come on, my sweetums," she continued, "and we'll have a nice walk and then a nice visit with our neighbor next door. Maybe she'll have a doggie biscuit just for you."

Popsie expressed his skepticism with a growl before wiggling further into the recess. Sighing, Wilma left him and went through the living room. George had not moved in over an hour, but she felt no optimism that she might be cashing a check from the life insurance company any time soon. Since his retirement from an insignificant managerial position at a factory five years ago, he had perfected the art of inertia. He could go for hours without saying a word, without turning his head when she entered the room, without so much as flickering when she spoke to him. He bathed irregularly, at best. In the infrequent instances in which she failed to harangue him, he donned sweat-stained clothes from the previous day. Only that morning he'd made a futile attempt to leave his dentures in the glass beside the bed, citing swollen gums. Wilma had made it clear that was not acceptable.

She headed for the house next door. It was indistinguishable from its neighbors, each being a flimsy box with three small bedrooms, one bathroom, a poorly arranged kitchen, and an airless living room. At some point in the distant past the houses had been painted in an array of pastels, but by now the paint was gone and the weathered wood was uniformly drab. Some carports were empty, others filled with cartons of yellowed newspapers and broken appliances. There were no bicycles in the carports or toys scattered in the yards. Silver Beach was a retirement community. The nearest beach was twenty miles away. There may have been silverfish and silver fillings, but everything else was gray. During the day, the streets were empty. Cemetery salesmen stalked the sidewalks each evening, armed with glossy brochures and trustworthy faces.

Polly Simps was struggling with a warped screen as Wilma cut across the yard. She wore a housedress and slippers, and her brassy orange hair was wrapped around pink foam curlers. There was little reason to dress properly in Silver Beach since the air conditioner had broken down at the so-called club house. For the last three years the building had been used solely by drug dealers and shaky old alcoholics with unshaven cheeks and unfocused eyes. Only a month ago a man of indeterminate age had been found in the empty swimming pool behind the club house. The bloodstains were still visible on the cracked concrete.

"Damn this thing," Polly muttered in greeting. "I don't know why I bother. The mosquitoes get in all the same." She dropped the screen to scratch at one of the welts on her flabby, freckled arm. "Every year they seem to get bigger and hungrier. One of these days they're gonna carry me off to the swamp."

Wilma had no interest in anyone else's problems. "Listen to this," she said as she unfolded the letter. When she was done, she wadded it up, stuffed it in her pocket, and waited for a response from one of the very few residents of Silver Beach with whom she was on speaking terms. Back in Brooklyn, she wouldn't have bothered to share the time of day with the likes of someone as ignorant and opinionated as Polly Simps. That was then.

"I never heard of such a thing," Polly said at last. "The idea of allowing strangers into your own home is appalling. The fact that they're foreigners makes it all the worse. Who knows what kind of germs they might carry? I'd be obliged to boil the sheets and towels, and I'd feel funny every time I used my silverware."

"The point is that Jewel Jacoby and her sister spent three weeks in an apartment in Paris. Jewel was a bookkeeper just like I was, and I know for a fact her social security and pension checks can't add up to more than mine. Her husband passed away at least ten years ago. Whatever she gets as a widow can't be near as much as we get from George's retirement." Wilma rumbled in frustration as she considered Jewel's limited financial resources. "And she went to Paris in April for three weeks! You know where George and I went on vacation last year? Do you?"

Polly blinked nervously as she tried to think. "Did you and George take a vacation last year?"

"No," Wilma snapped, "and that's the issue. We talked about driving across the country to visit Louisa and her loutish husband in Oregon, but George was afraid that the car wouldn't make it and we'd end up stranded in a Kansas cornfield. He's perfectly happy to sit in his chair and stare at that infernal television set. We've never once had a proper vacation. Now I get this letter from Jewel Jacoby about how she went to France and saw museums and cathedrals and drank coffee at sidewalk cafes. All it cost her was airfare and whatever she and her sister spent on groceries. It's not fair."

"But the French people stayed in her apartment," Polly countered. "They slept in her bed and used her things just like they owned them."

"While she slept in their bed and sat on their balcony, watching the boats on the Seine! I've never set foot in

Europe, but Jewel had the time of her life—all because the French people agreed to this foolish exchange. I'll bet they were sorry. I've never been in Jewel's apartment, but she was the worst slob in the entire office. I'd be real surprised if her apartment wasn't filthier than a pig sty."

Polly held her peace while Wilma made further derogatory remarks about her ex-coworker back in Brooklyn. Wilma's tirades were infamous throughout Silver Beach. She'd been kicked out of the Wednesday bridge club after an especially eloquent one, and was rarely included in the occasional coffee-and-gossip sessions in someone's kitchen. It was just as well, since she was often the topic.

Wilma finally ran out of venom. Polly took a breath and said, "I still don't like the idea of foreigners in my house. What was the name of the organization?"

"Traveler's Vacation Exchange or something like that." Wilma took out the letter and forced herself to scan the pertinent paragraph. "She paid fifty dollars and sent in her ad in the fall. Then in January she got a catalog filled with other people's ads and letters started coming from all over Europe, and even one from Hawaii. She says she picked Paris because she'd taken French in high school forty years ago. What a stupid reason to make such an important decision! I must say I'm not surprised, though. Jewel was a very stupid woman, and no doubt still is."

Wilma went home and dedicated herself to making George utterly and totally miserable for the rest of the summer. Since she had had more than forty years of practice, this was not challenging.

Florida/Orlando X 3–6wks O
George & Wilma Chadley 2/0 A, 4, 2 GB
122 Palmetto Rd, Silver Beach FL 34101
(407) 521-7357
ac bb bc cf cl cs dr fi fn gd gg go hh mk ns o pk pl
pv ro rt sba se sk ss tv uz wa wf wm wv yd

"Here's one," Wilma said, jabbing her finger at an ad. "They live in a village called Cobbet, but it's only an hour away from London by train. They have three children and want to come to Florida in July or August for a month."

"I reckon they don't know how hot it gets," Polly said, shaking her head. "I'd sooner spend the summer in Hades than in Silver Beach."

"That's their problem, not mine." Wilma consulted the list of abbreviations, although by this time she'd memorized most of them. "No air conditioning, but a washer and dryer, modern kitchen with dishwasher and microwave, garden, domestic help, and a quiet neighborhood. They want to exchange cars, too. I do believe I'll write them first."

"What does George think about this?"

Wilma carefully copied the name and address, then closed the catalog and gave Polly a beady look. "Not that it's any of your business, but I haven't discussed it with him. I don't see any reason to do it until I've reached an agreement and found out exactly how much the airfare will be."

Polly decided it was too risky to ask about the finances of this crazy scheme. "Let me see your ad."

Wilma flipped open the catalog and pointed to the appropriate box. While Polly tried to make sense of the abbreviations, she sat back and dreamily imagined herself in a lush garden, sipping tea and enjoying a cool, British breeze.

Polly looked up in bewilderment. "According to what this says, the nearest airport is Orlando. Isn't Miami a sight closer?"

"The main reason people with children come to Florida is to go to Disneyworld. I want them to think it's convenient."

"Oh," Polly murmured. She consulted the list several more times. "This says you have four bedrooms and two bathrooms, Wilma. I haven't been out in your back yard lately, but last time I was there I didn't notice any swimming pool or deck with a barbecue grill. We ain't on the beach, either. The nearest one is a half-hour's drive and it's been closed for two years because of the pollution. It takes a good two hours to get to an open beach."

"The couch in the living room makes into a bed, so they

can consider it a bedroom. One bathroom's plenty. I'll be the one paying the water bill at the end of the month, after all."

"Your air conditioner doesn't work any more than mine, and if you've got a microwave and a clothes dryer, you sure hide 'em well. I suppose there's golf and skiing and playgrounds and scuba diving and boating and hiking, but not anywhere around these parts. You got one thing right, though. It's a quiet neighborhood now that everyone's afraid to set foot outside because of those hoodlums. Mr. Hodkins heard gunfire just the other night."

Wilma did not respond, having returned to her fantasy. It was now replete with crumpets.

122 Palmetto Road
Silver Beach, FL 34101

Dear Sandra,

I received your letter this morning and I don't want to waste a single minute in responding. You and your husband sound like a charming couple. I shall always treasure the photograph of you and your three beautiful children. I was particularly taken with little Dorothy's dimples and angelic smile.

As I mentioned in my earlier letter, you will find our home quite comfortable and adequate for your needs. Our car is somewhat older than yours, but it will get you to Disneyworld in no time at all.

You have voiced concern about your children and the swimming pool, but you need not worry. The ad was set incorrectly. The pool is a block away at our neighborhood club house. There is no lifeguard, however.

I fully intended to enclose photographs of ourselves and our house, but my husband forgot to pick up the prints at the drug store on his way home from the golf course. I'll do my best to remember to put them in the next letter.

I believe we'll follow your advice and take the train from Gatwick to Cobbet. Train travel is much more limited here, so we will leave our car at the Orlando airport for your convenience.

In the meantime, start stocking up on suntan oil for your wonderful days on the beach. I wouldn't want Dorothy's dimples to turn red.

Your dear friend in Florida,
Wilma

"Have you told George?" Polly whispered, glancing at the doorway. Noises from the television set indicated that basketball had been replaced with baseball, although it was impossible to determine if George had noticed. His only concession to the blistering resurgence of summer was a pair of stained plaid shorts.

Wilma snorted. "Yes, Polly, I have told George. Did you think I crept into the living room and took his passport photographs without him noticing?"

"Is he excited?"

"He will be when the time comes," she said firmly. "In any case, it really doesn't matter. The Millingfords are coming on the first of July whether he likes it or not. I find it hard to imagine he would enjoy sharing this house with three snotty-nosed children. Look at the photograph if you don't believe me. They look like gargoyles, especially the baby. The two older ones have the same squinty eyes as their father."

"The house looks nice."

"It does, doesn't it? If it's half as decent as that insufferably smug woman claims, we should be comfortable. The flowerbeds are pretentious, but I'm not surprised. She made a point of mentioning that they have a gardener twice a week. I was tempted to write back and say ours comes three times a week, but I let it go." She tapped the photograph. "Look at that structure near the garden wall. It's a hutch, of all things. It seems that Lucinda and Charles keep pet rabbits. Because little Dorothy has asthma and all kinds of allergies, the rabbits are not allowed in the house. The idea of stepping on a dropping makes my stomach turn."

"Will that cause a problem with Popsie?"

Wilma leaned down to stroke Popsie's satiny ears. He'd been lured away from the toilet with chocolate-chip cookies, and now crumb-flecked droplets of saliva were sprinkled beneath the table. She felt a prick of remorse at the idea of leaving him for a month, but it couldn't be helped, not if she was to have a vacation that would outshine Jewel Jacoby's. "I haven't mentioned Popsie in my letters. The boarding kennel wants twenty-five dollars a day. I've had to set aside every penny for our airfare, which is why the washing machine is still leaking. The tires on the car are bald and the engine makes such a terrible rattle that I literally hold my breath every time I drive to the store. There's absolutely no way I can get anything repaired until we build up some cash in the fall. Besides that, my Popsie is very delicate and would be miserable in a strange place. If there are any disruptions in his schedule, he begins piddling on the floor and passing wind." She looked thoughtfully at Polly and decided not to even hint that Popsie would enjoy a lengthy visit in his neighbor's home. Not after what Popsie had done to Polly's cat.

"I do want to ask a small favor of you," she continued with a conspiratorial wink. "I'm worried about the children damaging the house. I'm going to lock away all the good dinnerware, but they're quite capable of leaving muddy footprints all over the furniture and handprints on the walls. I'm hoping you'll drop by at least once a day. Just ask if they're having a pleasant vacation or something."

Polly flinched. "Won't they think I'm spying on them?"

"That's exactly what I want them to think. They need to be reminded they're guests in my home."

"Is there anything else?"

"One other favor. I'm going to leave a note in the car for them to come by your house to pick up the house key and a letter regarding their stay. If you don't mind, of course?"

As dim as she was, Polly suspected the British family might be disgruntled by the time they arrived in Silver Beach. However, nothing interesting had taken place since the knifing by the club house several weeks ago. Shrugging, she said, "I'll make a point of being here when they arrive."

Dear Sandra,

Welcome to Florida! I'm writing this while we pack, but I'll try very hard not to forget anything. I hope you and the family enjoyed the flight to Orlando. I was a tiny bit muddled about the distance from the airport to the house, but George insisted that it was no more than an hour's drive. How embarrassing to have discovered only the other day that it's nearly three times that far! In any case, I shall assume my map and directions were clear and you successfully arrived at my dear friend Polly Simps's house. She is excited about your visit, and will come by often to check on you.

I must apologize for the air conditioner. The repairman has assured me that the part will arrive within a matter of days and he will be there to put it in working order. Please be very careful with the washing machine. Last night I received a nasty shock that flung me across the room and left my body throbbing most painfully. I was almost convinced my heart had received enough of a jolt to kill me! You might prefer to use the launderette in town. I had a similar experience with the dishwasher —why do these things go haywire on such short notice???

I am so sorry to tell you that our cleaning woman was diagnosed with terminal liver cancer three days ago. She immediately left to spend her last few weeks with her family in Atlanta. Her son, who works as our gardener, went with her. I was so stricken that all I could do was offer her a generous sum and wish them both the best. The lawn mower is in the carport storage area. It's balky, but will start with encouragement. You can buy gas (or petrol, as you say) for it at any service station.

And now I must mention dearest Popsie, whom

you've surely discovered by now. We've had him for twelve years and he's become as beloved to us as a child. I had a long and unpleasant conversation with the brutes at the boarding kennel. They made it clear that Popsie would be treated with nothing short of cruelty. He is much too delicate to withstand such abuse and estrangement from his familiar surroundings. You will find him to be only the most minor nuisance, and I implore you to behave like decent Christians and treat him with kindness.

He must be taken for a walk (in order to do his duty) three times a day, at eight in the morning, noon, and five in the afternoon. His feeding instructions, along with those for the vitamin and mineral supplements and details regarding his eye drops and insulin shots, are taped on the refrigerator. Once he becomes accustomed to the children, he will stop snapping and allow them to enter the bathroom. Until he does so, I strongly suggest that he be approached with caution. I should feel dreadful if dear little Dorothy's rosy cheeks were savaged.

The Silverado Community Beach is closed because of an overflow from a sewage disposal facility. You'll find Miami Beach, although a bit farther, to be lovely. The presence of a lifeguard should be reassuring, in that you've obviously neglected to teach your children how to swim. You might consider lessons in the future.

The refrigerator has been emptied for your convenience. I left bread and eggs for your first night's supper. Milk would have spoiled, but you'll find a packet of powdered lemonade mix for the children. Polly will give you directions to the supermarket.

The car started making a curious clanking sound only yesterday. I would have taken it to the garage had time permitted, but it was impossible to schedule an appointment. George suspects a problem with the transmission. I will leave the telephone numbers of several towing services should you experience any problems. All of them accept credit cards.

But above all, make yourselves at home!

Wilma

Ferncliffe House
Willow Springs Lane
Cobbet, Lincs LN2 3AB
15 July (as they say)

Dear Polly,

We're having an absolutely wonderful time. The house is much nicer than I expected. Everything works properly, and even the children's room were left tidy.

I spend a great deal of time in the garden with a cup of tea and a novel, while George pops over to the pub to shoot billiards and play darts with his cronies. Last Sunday our lovely neighbors invited us to a picnic at the local cricket field. The game itself is incredibly stupid, but I suffered through it for the sake of cucumber sandwiches and cakes with clotted cream and jam.

I must say things are primitive. The washing machine is so small that our cleaning woman has to run it continually all three mornings every week when she's here. Her accent is droll, to put it kindly, and she is forever fixing us mysterious yet tasty casseroles. If I knew what was in them, I doubt I could choke down a single bite. The village shops are pathetically small, poorly stocked, and close at odd hours of the day. I don't know how these people have survived without a decent supermarket. And as for their spelling, you'd think the whole population was illiterate. I wonder if I'm the first person who's mentioned that they drive on the wrong side of the road.

I had reservations about the lack of air conditioning, but the days are mild and the nights cool. Sandra "conveniently" forgot to mention how often it rains; I suppose she was willing to lie simply to trick us into the exchange. She was certainly less than honest about the train ride from London. It takes a good seventy minutes.

I've searched every drawer and closet in the entire house and have yet to find a Bible. It does make one wonder what kind of people they really are. In the note I left, I begged them to treat Popsie with a Christian attitude, but now I wonder if they're even familiar with the term. Everyone is so backward in this country. For all I know, the Millingfords are Catholics—or Druids!

I must stop now. Tonight we're being treated to dinner at a local restaurant, where I shall become queasy just reading the menu. And I'm dreading tomorrow morning. Someone failed to shut the door of the hutch and the rabbits have escaped. No doubt the gardener will be upset in his amusing guttural way, since they were his responsibility. I honestly think it's for the best. The animals are filthy and one of them scratched my arm so viciously that I can still see a mark. What kind of parents would allow their children to have pets like those? Dogs are so much cleaner and more intelligent. I do believe I shall leave a note to that effect for Sandra to read when the family returns home.

Wilma

Polly was waiting on her porch when George and Wilma pulled into the driveway. She would have preferred to cower inside her house, blinds drawn and doors locked, but she knew this would only add to Wilma's impending fury. "Welcome home," she called bravely.

Wilma told George to unload the luggage, then crossed into the adjoining yard. "I feel like we've been traveling for days and days. It would have been so much easier to fly into the Miami airport, but the Millingfords had to go to Disneyworld, didn't they?"

"And they did," Polly began, then faltered as the words seemed to stick in her mouth like cotton balls (or, perhaps, clumps of rabbit fur similar to the ones the gardener had found in the meadow behind Ferncliffe House).

"So what?"

"They left two weeks ago."

"Just what are you saying, Polly Simps? I'm exhausted from the trip, and I have no desire to stand here while you make cryptic remarks about these whiny people. I'm not the least bit interested at the moment, although I suppose in a day or two when I'm rested you can tell me about them." She looked back at George, who was struggling toward the house with suitcases. "Be careful! I have several jars of jam in that bag."

Florida was still flat, so Polly's desperate desire to disappear into a gaping hole in the yard was foiled. "I think you'd better listen to me, Wilma. There were . . . some problems."

"I'm beginning to feel faint. If there's something you need to say, spit it out so I can go into my own home and give Popsie the very expensive milk biscuits I bought for him in England."

"Come inside and I'll fix you a glass of iced tea."

Wilma's nostrils flared as if she were a winded racehorse. "All I can say is this had better be good," she muttered as she followed her neighbor across the porch and through the living room. "Did the Millingfords snivel about everything? Are you going to present me with a list of all their petty complaints?"

"They didn't complain," Polly said as she put glasses on the table. "They were a little disappointed when they arrived, I think. Five minutes after I'd given them the key and your letter, Sandra came back to ask if it was indeed the right house. I said it was. Later that afternoon David came over and asked if I could take him to the grocery store, since your car wouldn't start."

"What colossal nerve! Did he think you were the local taxi service?"

Polly shrugged. "I told him I didn't have one, but I arranged for him to borrow Mr. Hodkins's car for an hour. The next morning a tow truck came for the car, and within a week or so it was repaired. During that time, they stayed inside the house for the most part. At one point the two older children came to ask me about the swimming pool, but that was the last time any of them knocked on my door."

"I'd like to think they were brought up not to pester people all the time. But as I hinted in my letter to you, they seem to be growing up in a heathen environment. You did go over there every day, didn't you?"

"I tried, Wilma, but I finally stopped. I'd ring the bell and ask how they were enjoying their visit, but whichever parent opened the door just stared at me and then closed the door without saying a word. Once I heard the baby wailing in one of the bedrooms, but other than that it was so quiet over there that I wondered what on earth they were doing."

Wilma entertained images of primitive rituals, embellishing them with her limited knowledge of Druíds and gleanings from Errol Flynn movies. "Poor Popsie," she said at last. "How hideous for him. Did they walk him three times a day?"

"For the few days. Then the baby had an asthma attack and had to be taken to the hospital in an ambulance. After that, they left Popsie in the backyard, where he howled all night. The misery in that dog's voice was almost more than I could bear."

"Those barbarians! I'm going to write a letter to Mrs. Snooty Millingford and remind her that she was supposed to treat poor Popsie in a civilized, if not Christian, fashion. Your instincts were right, Polly. It's very dangerous to allow foreigners in your home."

"There's more. Once they got the car back, they took some day trips, but then two weeks ago they upped and left. It must have been late at night, because I never saw them loading the car and I made sure I kept an eye on them from my bedroom window during the day. Anyway, the key was in my mailbox one morning. I rushed over, but their luggage was gone. Everything was nice and neat, and they put a letter addressed to you on the kitchen counter."

Wilma started to comment on the unreliability of foreigners, then realized Polly was so nervous that her eyelid was twitching and her chin trembling. "What about Popsie?" she asked shrewdly, if also anxiously.

"Gone."

"Gone? What do you mean?"

"I organized a search party and we hunted for him for three days straight. I put an ad in that shopping circular and called the dog pound so many times that they promised they'd call me if they picked him up."

Wilma clasped the edge of the table and bared her teeth in a comical (at least from Polly's perspective) parody of a wild beast. "They must have stolen Popsie! What did the police say? You did call the police, didn't you? All they'd have to do is stop the car and drag those wicked Millingfords off to jail."

"They wouldn't have taken him, Wilma. When the ambulance men came to the house, I heard the father say that the baby's asthma attack was brought on by dog hairs. The last thing they'd do is put Popsie right there in the car with them and risk another attack."

"Well, I'm calling the police now," Wilma snarled as she shoved back her chair and started for the front door. "And you can forget about your jar of jam, Polly Simps. I asked you to do one little favor for me. Look what I get in return!"

George was sound asleep on the recliner as she marched through the living room, intent on the telephone in the kitchen. Of course it was too late for the police to take action. The Millingfords had safely escaped across the Atlantic Ocean, where they could ignore official demands concerning Popsie's disappearance. She could imagine the smugness on Sandra's face and her syrupy avowals of innocence. Perhaps she would feel differently when her children discovered the empty hutch.

The envelope was on the counter. Wilma ripped it open, and with an unsteady hand, took out the letter.

Dear Mrs. Chadley,

Thank you so very much for making your home available to us this last fortnight. It was not precisely what we'd anticipated, but after a bit we accepted your invitation to "make ourselves at home."

Tucked under the telephone you will find invoices from the towing service, auto repair shop, and tire shop. They were all quite gracious about awaiting your payment. The chap from the air conditioner service never came. My husband called all shops listed in the back pages of the telephone directory, but none seemed to have been the one with which you trade. He tried to have a look at it himself, but became leery that he inadvertently might damage some of the rustier parts.

After he checked the wiring, I had a go at the washing machine, but I must have done something improperly because water gushed everywhere. It made for quite a mopping.

We've changed our plans and have decided to spend the remaining fortnight touring the northern part of the state. Lucinda and Charles are frightfully keen about space technology and are exceedingly eager to visit the Kennedy Center. Dorothy adores building sand castles on the beach. Also, this will make it easier for us to leave your car at the Orlando airport as we'd arranged.

I hope you enjoyed your stay in Cobbet. Our neighbors are quite friendly in an unobtrusive way, and several of them promised to entertain you. I also hope you enjoyed Mrs. Bitney's cooking. She is such a treasure.

In honour of your return, I adapted one of Mrs. Bitney's family recipes for steak and kidney pie. It's in the freezer in an oblong pan. When you and your husband eat it, I do so hope you'll remember our exchange.

Yours truly,
Sandra Millingford

Wilma numbly put down the letter and went to the back door. Popsie's water and food bowls were aligned neatly in one corner of the patio. A gnawed rubber ball lay in the grass. The three pages of instructions were no longer taped to the door of the refrigerator, but several cans of dog food were lined up beside the toaster.

She went into the bathroom and peered behind the toilet as if Popsie had been hiding there all this time, too wily to show himself to Polly while he awaited their return. Not so much as a hair marred the vinyl.

At last, when she could no longer avoid it, she returned to the kitchen and sat down. As her eyes were drawn toward the door of the freezer, they began to fill with tears.

Sandra Millingford had made herself at home. What else had she made?

Cara's Turn

Marlys Millhiser

Ed Hornsby could smell the closing before he and his client stepped out of his car. This property had certainly been good to him.

The house sat up close to the street, an updated Victorian on the outside with clear-stained cedar siding and bay windows, teal colored trim, and picket fence. Inside it was modern, quality all the way, and unique even for Boulder. Ed should know: he'd built it for himself.

But Cara Williams pulled up short before she reached the tiny front porch. "You're beginning to remind me of a used car salesman, Mr. Hornsby." She'd called him Ed until he'd sold her house out from under her. "You promised to show me only houses in my price range. I told you we can't afford much debt right now with Jay due to retire. And he's not going to move twice."

Cara was middle-aged, plump, and taking on that vagueness older married women use to fight stress. Ed had noticed how divorce or widowhood resharpened them fast. His ex, Sharon, for one. She'd turned into a veritable stiletto after only a few months of shock.

"This is in your price range. And notice it has a small yard so your husband won't have to spend all his time mowing. And the double garage he wanted."

"It's almost sitting in the street." But she rolled her head back to look up at the peaked roof above the porch that matched the peaked roof of the house above the upstairs bays.

"Hey, you don't have to mow street." Ed had talked the Williamses into putting their house up for sale because it was on an acre with a buildable lot behind it. Well, he'd talked Cara into it. That was the only house the couple had ever owned, an old fifties ranch. They'd raised a family and now had extra rooms in a rundown seventies decor, but in an upscale Boulder where deserting Californians were infilling the little available space left. Ed had set the price low and turned that sucker over before Jay Williams had the chance to pout and scowl long enough to make his wife give up the idea.

"So what's wrong with it?" The sky was gray, her hair was gray, her eyes were gray, and so was the lone snowflake that glided down to rest on the top edge of her rimless glasses. Why didn't she take hormones, color her hair, lose weight, fix herself up? Sharon had, but not until he'd dumped her. Bitch.

"You said you wanted a change at this point in your life." He rang the bell and waited until it appeared Custler wasn't home before he went to the lock box attached to the garage door handle, spun the combination, and extracted the house key.

Ed had planned all along to move the Williamses out of town. Boulder was getting too upscale for them and they were afraid of debt. They could afford a real upgrade out in the county with the money he'd sold their property for. But they refused to budge and on that he hadn't been able to out-maneuver them, even with the closing date on their house days away.

This house was, frankly, the only choice they had unless they wanted to risk renting until something else turned up. California money was driving everything sky high and Real

Realty was raking it in. And the Williamses were definitely not risk takers. He reached for the front door hoping she wouldn't notice the scratches where a workman had been careless the last time the locks were changed. And he remembered to turn off the alarm system just inside the front door without her noticing it. It was embarrassing to have the police arrive while you were showing a house.

"Well, welcome home, Cara."

Cara Williams had heard those words before and from the same mouth. She'd seen other doors open with the same flourish by the same hand. She wasn't impressed. But she was panicked. Jay was going to be hell to live with for being forced to move at all. He wouldn't stand for it twice if they had to rent. He did not appreciate anything ruffling his routine. Flat and placid is how he liked his life and made hers. Sometimes she appreciated that and sometimes it suffocated her.

At first glance, Cara couldn't tell what was wrong with the house.

The door opened to stairs climbing the wall to the second floor. Next to them was a long room serving as both living and dining room. The carpet was a lighter teal than the trim and the picket fence outside, rather than the cheap sterile neutral color that coated every other house Ed Hornsby had shown her. The small kitchen and family room combination had golden hardwood flooring Jay would never have allowed in their huge country kitchen. The two combination main-floor rooms formed an L around the attached garage.

A grand piano. An elegant glass-topped dining-room table. Shiny gas fireplaces with marble hearths in living and family rooms. Small sculptures and large paintings of hunting scenes or couples copulating. Jenn-Air appliances and ceramic tile counter tops in the kitchen.

Everything was of a fineness Jay would consider ostentatious and nonessential. Pipes and insulation and furnaces and wiring were what mattered.

"So what's wrong with this place, Mr. Hornsby?" But Cara, once she figured out all the locking mechanisms and lifted the floor bar, opened the sliding glass doors to step out onto a back deck and discovered what was wrong with this place for herself.

A deck crowded with a covered hot tub Jay would never pay to keep heated. Tiny backyard with a circle of grass around a circle of sandstone with a charming fluted-edged birdbath at its center. Two little wrought-iron chairs on the sandstone suggested morning coffee in your bathrobe in summer, watching a frisky robin bathe.

But what was wrong with this place was what put the front porch almost on the street, not unusual in Boston and San Francisco maybe but damn strange in Boulder, Colorado. An eight-foot (at least) solid wood fence, not at all in keeping with the ornamental teal picket decorating the tiny front and side yards, enclosed the one in back. Great slashes of white and gray and bluish bird droppings streaked the upper portions of the inside of the fence in spite of rows of barbed wire affixed to its top edge. And right up next to it was a low roof with heat fumes rising out of a pipe chimney.

Ed Hornsby took her elbow and walked her down the steps of the deck to the birdbath, gesturing around him at the incredible barrier. "Keep the deer out, that fence."

Boulder's resident deer population would soon outnumber its human.

Ed reminded Cara of a rotund and balding Elvis (whom she'd personally dubbed "old blubber lips" when she and Jay and Ed and Elvis were young.) She pulled her elbow out of the realtor's hand and swallowed back a lurch of distaste. From down here you couldn't see the roof. "So who lives on the other side of the fence? I didn't know zoning would allow that kind of thing."

"Nice people. Keep to themselves. You can get variances if you know how to go about it. But what I wanted you to see was the upstairs."

Upstairs were a lavish master bathroom and bedroom of equal size. A guest room and another full bath. Cara had wanted to look down from the back windows at the house behind the fence but Ed Hornsby whisked her into the remaining upstairs room and she forgot all about the other house.

Bookshelves lining two walls. A desk twice the size of her crowded one at home. A padded window seat with a view of the mountains.

Mountain views were fast becoming the prerogative of doctors, lawyers, drug dealers, CEOs, Arab sheiks, university administrators, and other wealthy life forms. But this house was situated directly across from a side street that would never grow trees or houses to block the view. The window faced south and sparse gray snowflakes still fell. The flatiron-shaped mountains on the edge of town were lost in weather murk halfway to their knees. But the winter sun, slanting low at this time of year, stabbed a hole through the gloom to light a swath through Boulder. It spread gold across the window seat. It was like a religious experience. Cara sat down in the desk chair. She could see the view from there, too.

"Merry Christmas, Cara Williams," Ed Hornsby said as if he were Santa Claus himself. He had her and he knew it. "Know who's selling this house? Warwick Custler, the writer. He sits right there where you are now and looks at that view and gets his inspirations. And in the basement there's a laundry room, three more finished rooms, and plenty of storage."

Cara caressed the desk top in front of her. She'd raised four children and then worked low-paying jobs to help educate them. Jay was about to retire from work that had interested him. Now it was her turn. Cara'd written some articles for the local newspaper. She'd always wanted to write novels. She wasn't interested in the basement.

She should have been.

The sun rays caressing Cara and her fantasies did not reach Wilma in the house behind the fence. The only light piercing the gloom in that house came from the television in the living-dining-kitchen-family room which was also her father's bedroom. He moved grudgingly from the daybed to the tiny bathroom next to Wilma's equally tiny bedroom to the La-Z-Boy lounge in front of the mammoth television where Wilma brought his food.

He ordered it over the telephone and had Wilma store most of it in a freezer that took up half the kitchen space and made nearly as much noise as the television. He selected it from a catalog sent to them each month. Food (mostly beefsteak even Wilma could fry and frozen pies she could pop in the oven), but also toilet paper and things anybody would normally need. Unless they were fancy folk who lived in the house that blocked Wilma's sun. Or Wilma's friends who came to visit.

Wilma was "retarded," her father never tired of telling her. She'd come to know it meant there were many things she didn't know that other people did. But Wilma knew she knew things other people didn't.

She knew critters—deer, squirrel, raccoon, skunk, and all the lovely whimsical birds. Wilma especially liked the birds. She had been to a special school as a child, before her mother died, and could read some, if laboriously. She found a flier from a wild bird store in the house in her front yard once. Wilma discovered that deer, squirrel, skunk, and coon liked the black oil sunflower seeds as much as the birds. She stole money from her father's secret horde in the root cellar. Then she convinced whoever lived in the front yard at the time to fetch the bags home for her.

Raymond Jorgenson would have her bring him a handful of bills out of which he'd pay their expenses by mail, wrapping the money in plain paper before putting it in the envelope and sending Wilma with it out along the pretty blue-green fence to the mailbox on the street.

Raymond rarely left the house these days. The old Chevy sat on flattened tires in the shed by the back door. His joints were knotting up on him. The knuckles in his skinny fingers looked like unshelled walnuts Wilma had found in the house in the front yard last year at this time. That was when her enemy had brought her a box of chocolates and wished her a Merry Christmas.

It had been a long while since her father had called for a cab and taken Wilma on an excursion for some new item they needed. But Wilma had a way of convincing the people in her front yard to run errands for them, so the Jorgensons and Wilma's friends didn't do without for long.

Wilma knew lots of things. One of them was how to bide her time.

Wilma stepped outside to rest from the television/freezer noise and to check the feeders. She found a patch of sunlight on the side of the house that wasn't facing fence. High privacy fences surrounded the little house and its shed. But, like a cat, Wilma knew every spot of warm sunlight left to her and where it would move with the seasons. She could remember when the farmhouse was surrounded by orchard and pasture land and she could roam for sunspots. Little by little, as her father sold off the land to build the horde in the fruit cellar, bulldozers had destroyed Wilma's world and fences her freedom.

But, like the deer and raccoons and birds, she'd learned to cope with change and turn it to her advantage. The city deer had learned to look both ways before crossing streets and to turn around and kick the crap out of loose dogs instead of running. Wilma had learned to use the people in her front yard.

And, like her critter friends, she sensed things she couldn't verbalize. Wilma sensed, for instance, that the one thing her enemy would hate more than death would be the loss of his own flamboyant freedom.

The Real Realty sign had gone up next to the mailboxes again. Wilma saw the man who'd persuaded her father to sell off the last piece of house yard talking to Mr. Custler while he pounded the sign into the dirt edging the road. He'd used a mallet that was the same color as the sign. They were yelling at each other, he and Mr. Custler, and had become so engrossed in their mean words that the Real Realty man left the mallet leaning against the picket fence when he drove off.

Mr. Custler was not a good neighbor. He didn't leave the

house to go off to work like the others. Wilma liked to sit on the upstairs window seats in the sun and look at the pretty mountains and sky.

Wilma decided she'd bided her time long enough.

"This is one hell of a time in our lives to start having to deal with stairs," Jay Williams said the minute Ed Hornsby opened the front door on the house Cara had decided was to be their new home. Jay was a Republican and knew there was no purpose in change for its own sake. But the older the woman got the less she would listen to reason.

He'd made the mistake of taking off work early and met the two in his driveway. Instead of a cold beer and a warm dinner, he had to look at another goddamned house. Jay was an engineer at a government research lab where he'd spent his entire working life and would soon be forced into early retirement. Too many changes coming at him too fast.

But his wife took his arm and pulled him up the stairs to a room with a massive desk and with bookshelves reaching to a ceiling that sported one of those silly fans. A bay window with a seat in it. His wife looked at him expectantly.

"What the hell am I going to need with all this?"

"This is for me, Jay. This is where I'm going to write my novel. This is where Warwick Custler writes his."

"Aw Jesus, not that again." He stalked out to inspect bed and bathrooms. Hornsby followed him.

The master bathroom was huge, carpeted, with a skylight, mirrored walls so you could watch yourself pee, a glass chandelier to bang your head on in the middle of the night, and two sinks for chrissake.

"You can damn near trade even up for this one, Jay," Hornsby said. "You have to go some place and fast. Everything's quality here."

"This isn't a house. It's a pad." Jay had signed the Real Realty contract, thinking their property wouldn't bring enough to replace itself now that all the rich were moving in to jack up prices and that his wife would get over this latest whim when she realized that. He'd made the mistake of assuming the sale was contingent on finding a replacement home first, could have sworn Hornsby had assured him of that. He was so pissed off at the whole idea he hadn't read through the contract carefully enough. Jay would love to wring Hornsby's neck.

Instead, he looked out one of the three bathroom windows. A giant of a woman, wearing overalls and with a thin spot at the crown of stringy gray-yellow hair, bent down in the drive of a tiny house built hard up against the solid back fence of this one. A magpie ate something from her hand, a deer licked at a pile of something on the ground, and behind her a squirrel impatiently scratched his ass.

"Only in Boulder, huh?" Ed stood next to Jay. "You're right, though. This was going to be a bachelor pad. I built it myself after my divorce. But you know realtors. Got such good offers I was forced to sell it."

No, Jay didn't know realtors but he was fascinated with the size of the woman below and the fence enclosing the nothing backyard his wife was about to sentence him to in retirement. The fence was well decorated with bird excrement. This was a hell of a strange house and he'd seen only the top floor.

"I don't think 'only in Boulder' is going to cover this one, Ed. I can handle Bambi and the birdshit, but why is that tiny house slap up to the fence? I can handle you manipulating my wife into all this glamor stuff, but who's that down there and why is this yuppie finery so cheap? Tell me that, Ed." It was then Jay realized his wife had joined them.

She watched him in the mirrored walls that were really sliding closet doors. The disappointed tears spoke all she'd probably have to say to him for awhile. Why couldn't she ever be satisfied with what they had?

Jay passed her to walk into the master bedroom, which also sported a bay window and seat. He could already tell by the furniture that their comfortable, lived-in trappings would be out of place here. How could Cara have lived with him all these years and learned nothing about the built-in waste of extravagant living? "Where in hell would we put the kids when they come home to visit?"

Hornsby led him down the stairs to the living-dining

room, replete with costly furnishings, pornographic art, two tall narrow windows on either side of the fireplace that looked onto the side yard, and another bay window with a view to the front. Jay thought he saw a movement or shadow edging out of one of the side windows but Hornsby drew him into the tiniest kitchen he'd ever seen and he forgot all about movement or shadows.

Great. Just great. Cara was going to start being a novelist and stop being a cook.

There was even that icon of yuppiedom, a hot tub, on the deck. And an intricate set of locks on the sliding-glass door leading to it, wires from a security system along its edge.

Ed Hornsby shrugged. "California people can't sleep at night without security systems. You know how they are."

"I still want to know who lives on the other side of the fence. Is it a rental? Who's the monster?"

"Owner. Nice quiet people. She's the owner's daughter. But what I wanted to show you was the space for a workshop in the garage. And the full finished basement where you can stick the kids when they come home to visit. Cara barely glanced at it but I knew you'd want to inspect the furnace, pipes, washer-dryer hookups, storage, hot-water heater." He closed the door to the garage and opened the one to the basement stairs.

Ed Hornsby had given up trying to figure out how the huge vacant Wilma Jorgenson managed to get in and out of the house at will no matter what kind of locks and security devices various owners had tried. Why they rarely called the police on her he couldn't figure out either. One had resorted to trained guard dogs but Wilma tamed them to feed out of her hand in a few days. One owner explained she'd felt sorry for the retarded woman. But by the time she put the house up for sale a month later she'd looked more frightened than sorry.

Custler had actually called the cops when he first moved in but they took one look at Wilma and decided no way could she outsmart that security system. Besides, her father claimed she'd been watching a football game on TV with him at the time. Boulder police were getting fed up with paranoid refugees.

Jay Williams studied the floor drain in front of the washer and dryer, the insulation behind the water heater and furnace. "Forced air. Isn't as good as the hot-water heat we got."

"You don't got it anymore," Ed reminded him. Jay Williams's house belonged to the Baggleys, who would gut it, build on top of it and around it. And Jay's kids were all planning to come home from three states to help the folks move over the holidays. Ed had been in sales most of his life and he knew a man like Jay Williams would have a tough time passing up a freebee like that. Moving costs, like everything else in Boulder, had gone ballistic.

Cara wandered down the hall and peered into rooms without entering as she'd done earlier that afternoon and with about as much interest. She did straighten up, blink, furrow her brow, and step inside the game room this time though. Custler had installed a wet bar and a fancy pool table. A big stuffed Santa'd been lying on it and a partially decorated tree stood in the corner when they'd glanced in before. The writer was apparently getting ready for some Christmas entertaining despite his angst at having to list with Real Realty.

Whenever this house was listed with another realtor weird Wilma would make herself too apparent and scare off the customers. So old Warwick had been forced to call Ed, like all the rest. But he sure hadn't been happy about it. Ed didn't know why Wilma favored him, but he was thinking he ought to give her another box of candy this Christmas, when Cara Williams shot out of the game room with her hand over her mouth. She didn't make it to the floor drain before she lost her cookies.

"That's what all them sirens was about," Raymond Jorgenson repeated with a particular glee, struggling to sit up in his La-Z-Boy. "I'll be damned." He gave his old-man cackle. His daughter had grown fond of it. Which was fortunate for him. This is exactly what he'd said when the nice policemen left. Now he and Wilma sat enraptured by the ten o'clock news, watching the stretcher being carried out to the ambulance past the Real Realty sign.

"There's our mailbox." Raymond raised gnarled fists. "See? See?"

The voice on the television explained that famed Boulder novelist, Warwick Custler, had been found murdered on his pool table in the basement of his home, stuffed into a Santa Claus suit and bludgeoned with a mallet striped in red, white, and blue with Real Realty written across it. The camera zoomed in on the For Sale sign again.

"Witnesses report the novelist and his realtor, Edward B. Hornsby, had a shouting match in the street. Custler's head and face were almost totally destroyed. The bloodied mallet was found in the trunk of Hornsby's automobile. He is the president of Real Realty in Boulder. When asked why the alleged murderer would dress his victim in a Santa Claus suit, his ex-wife, Sharon, said she wasn't surprised, that she'd always thought of him as Weird Ed."

Next, the man talked to a graying couple who had found the body while Weird Ed was showing them the house. He tall and thin and scowling, she short and plump and bewildered. Wilma took a closer look at "she" and decided she'd be a lot easier to handle than the previous tenant.

So when the "he" came to the door to check out the Jorgensons, Wilma was on her best behavior. She was repaid by seeing the couple move in. It was like a present.

But it wasn't until after Easter that the man on television told Wilma that the president of Real Realty had been convicted of the murder of Boulder author, Warwick Custler. His were the only fingerprints on the death mallet. His ex-wife, Sharon, testified to his violent nature. Passing walkers, runners, cyclists, and homeless had come forward to recount witnessing the ferocity of the argument he'd had with Custler out on the street. The murder weapon had been found in his car.

Defense lawyers argued that Hornsby wouldn't have shown the house if he'd killed the victim and left him on the pool table.

The prosecution, however, pointed out that he'd have done exactly that to avert suspicion. And the jury brought in a guilty verdict.

"Merry Christmas, Mr. Real Realty," Wilma said softly and left her father napping in front of the giant flickering screen. She slipped out the back door and around the shed where she hoisted up the doors to the root cellar.

She flicked on the switch to the overhead lights—two bare bulbs, one at the front of the cellar and one in the middle— and picked her way through the debris of her father's treasures, mostly old papers and tools. He was sure they were safe from thieves down here. They weren't safe from raccoons and damp, but Wilma didn't bother him with that, couldn't remember the last time he'd been to the cellar.

The ghost smells of the fruits, jellies, and vegetables her mother had stored here years ago when there'd been more on the table than beefsteak and pie always saddened her.

To protect the metal boxes filled with money from the masked bandits, Wilma had devised a grid over a ledge at the back of the cellar. The mischievous critters didn't mean any harm, had in fact shown her how to reclaim her front yard.

It was a long, narrow cellar and when she found the raccoons had pulled out loose bricks and then dug the dirt away to try to reach Raymond Jorgenson's money from behind, Wilma began to think the cellar of the new house wasn't all that far from hers. It was still in the process of being built and she could hear the building sounds. And, since her father dozed off more than he didn't, she had ample time to use his tools to continue the digging once the builders left. Hammering through the hard wall of the other cellar took longer. But behind it had been a piece of wooden paneling Wilma pushed out now and, slipping through the hole it left, replaced it. If you didn't know what to look for you couldn't see where she'd come in.

Once inside, Wilma brushed off the seat of her overalls and went up to see how Mrs. Williams's writing was coming along. She sure hoped the woman wasn't going to be any trouble.

Highwater

D. R. Meredith

Time had moved on and left Highwater, Texas, drowsing in the shade of its own history. Even its responsibilities as county seat of Bonham County did little to disturb the town's slumber. Cowboys still rode over the flat plains, but they no longer rode for the giant XIT brand that once encompassed Bonham and nine other counties of the Texas Panhandle. Instead they hired out to smaller ranches carved from the dead carcass of the XIT. Cattle still grazed the sweet grass on the semi-arid land, but in much smaller numbers, and cowboys no longer drove them into Highwater for shipping to meat packers in the east. Trains still ran through the town, but they only stopped at the grain elevator on its outskirts and then only during wheat harvest. The giant XIT ranch was a memory, a legend born during the last quarter of the nineteenth century and dead by the end of the first quarter of the twentieth century. For the most part, the same was true of Highwater and its four hundred fifty-five residents.

Nothing much ever happened to rouse the town from its sleep.

Most of the oldtimers in their cracked boots, sweat-stained hats, and worn Levis who sipped strong black coffee at Buddy's Cafe every morning at ten o'clock swore that Highwater's long nap began when the XIT sold up. Others pointed to World War II, when so many young Bonham County men marched off to war and never bothered coming home. Buddy himself pointed to 1956 as the beginning of the town's descent into sleepiness. That was the year the hitching rails around the courthouse were finally torn down.

"Them hitching rails were a symbol, you see," insisted Buddy, wiping his hands on the long white apron he wore over his Levis and checkered shirt. "When Highwater torn them down, it was like the town was wiping out its whole history and starting over, 'cept there wasn't nothing to start over with. We ain't got nothing but ranchers and cowboys and a few farmers thrown in here and there. Highwater's always been a cattle town, and where you got cattle, you got horses, and where you got horses, you got hitching rails." Buddy folded his arms above the overhang of his belly and nodded his head for emphasis.

Elizabeth Walker sipped her coffee and smiled to herself. The men argued at least once a week over the reason for Highwater's demise as a town of consequence in the Texas Panhandle. The argument was as pointless as her two sons' squabbles over whose girlfriend was prettiest, but she didn't see any harm in it as long as tempers didn't get out of hand. The town was too small for a man to carry a grudge for long. He might need his neighbors' help, and there were too few neighbors to risk offending even one. Living in a place as tiny as Highwater was an exercise in tact and diplomacy, with unwritten but clearly understood rules. Don't cast doubt on a man's legitimacy, honesty, or his wife's fidelity; keep your insults general, such as cussing the weather or the Department of Agriculture, both likely targets for discontent; and leave your disagreements at Buddy's door to be parceled out again over coffee the next day.

It was a social system that had worked nearly as long as Highwater had been a town, which was coming up on a hundred years.

"What's this we hear about you running for justice of the

peace, Elizabeth?" asked Buddy, who apparently thought the argument over the hitching rails had run its course for one day.

Elizabeth wrapped her fingers around her coffee mug to hide their tremor. She'd filed for the office only the day before and was a little nervous over the idea of being a political candidate, but she didn't think any of the men watching her needed to know that. They might not vote for a woman with shaking hands. Not that they wouldn't think twice about it anyway. No woman had ever run for public office in Highwater, and the town's menfolks might be uncomfortable with her breaking tradition.

"I figure I'm as qualified as the next person," said Elizabeth, leaving unspoken the thought that any possible opponent was likely to be a man.

"Ain't a justice of the peace supposed to poke around dead bodies?" asked one of the farmers.

A justice of the peace also officiated at marriages, thought Elizabeth, but decided not to mention it. Marrying anywhere but in church was not a Highwater tradition either. "I won't poke dead bodies," she said. "That's what the pathologist in Amarillo does. I just look at them, investigate the circumstances, and try to determine if the death is natural or unnatural."

"Hell's bells, Elizabeth, there ain't been an unnatural death in Highwater in, oh, maybe forty or fifty years," said Buddy, scratching his head. "Leastwise, none that I can remember."

"What about Tommy Hatcher?" demanded Ed Hays, a grizzled rancher whose sour disposition hadn't been sweetened any by his wife's running off with the Hi-Pro seed salesman ten years before.

"There wasn't nothing unnatural about that," retorted Buddy. "It was the most natural end in the world for a man with no more sense than Tommy Hatcher had. He ought to have knowed better than to curl up with the hired girl in Mrs. Hatcher's own feather bed while she was in town buying groceries. Or else he ought to have filled up the car before Mrs. Hatcher left so she wouldn't run out of gas and have to walk a mile back to the house in the hot sun. Nadine Hatcher said later at her trial that if Tommy had fixed the gas gauge in the car when she told him to, he might have lived another twenty years."

"Tommy Hatcher always was as worthless as a milk bucket under a bull," agreed Hays. "If you get right down to it pure laziness killed him."

"The shotgun Nadine Hatcher was firing at the time had something to do with it," Elizabeth pointed out. "Double-aught buckshot generally makes for an unnatural death."

"It sure makes for a messy one," said Buddy. "I was a sheriff's deputy when it happened, and there was blood and feathers all over that bedroom. Nadine was fit to be tied. She was awful fond of that feather bed."

"The jury had no business sending Nadine to jail for something Tommy brought on himself," continued Hays, staring at Elizabeth from shiny gray eyes that always reminded her of melting ice. "He wronged her and there ain't no two ways about it."

"If every woman shot every man who wronged her, there would be a lot fewer men in the world," said Elizabeth. "She should have thrown him out and his clothes after him, then filed for divorce. That's what I would have done."

Ed Hays shoved his chair back and stood up. "You forgetting that Texas is a community-property state, Elizabeth? Tommy Hatcher would have gotten half the ranch and the hired girl to boot. Nadine's mistake wasn't filling Tommy full of buckshot, it was trusting her neighbors to see things her way."

The old rancher grabbed his Stetson off the hat rack and stomped out the cafe's front door, leaving the other men and Elizabeth staring into their coffee mugs and feeling uncomfortable.

Buddy cleared his throat. "I guess I shouldn't have said so much about Tommy Hatcher. Talking about fornicating always puts Ed's nose out of joint. He's got strong views on the subject."

"I always thought it was a good thing Ed's wife run off like she did," said Carl Dean, a sunburned man with jug-handle ears and a kind nature, whose ranch shared a common fence line with Hays's. "Considering how Ed feels about his ranch, I don't think he'd have taken kindly to losing half of it in a divorce. He just might have taken his shotgun to her the way Nadine did to Tommy."

Buddy shook his head. "I don't think so. If I remember right, Jenny Hays run off right after Nadine Hatcher went to jail. I reckon Ed wouldn't have gambled on the same thing happening to him. Ed ain't never been much of a gambler, won't even play poker for matchsticks. Just stays out on that ranch and works like the devil's after him. To tell the truth, I'm always surprised when he joins us for coffee. I figure he only does it when he gets so lonely for other people's company that he can't stand it no longer. If you want to know, I feel sorry for the man."

"I don't know about feeling sorry for Ed," said Carl. "I'd have to chew that one over and I suspect it would stick in my craw. The wife and I liked little Jenny Hays and we watched her try so hard to make something likeable out of Ed, but he was just like one of them black holes in space that my youngest son's been studying in school. They just suck up light and never give any back just like Ed Hays used to suck up all the caring Jenny Hays give him, but never gave any in return. I always figured her running off with that seed salesman was self defense 'cause living with Ed was killing her by inches. I never thought badly of her at all."

Carl's eloquent defense of Jenny Hays surprised Elizabeth. Carl Dean wasn't known for bucking public opinion. Of course, Jenny Hays was a special case. She wasn't from Highwater and folks naturally didn't expect as much in the way of decent behavior from strangers as they did from their own. Still, Carl's words made her uneasy, conjuring up as they did an image of a pale young woman with odd, peach-colored hair and round hazel eyes. Elizabeth hadn't thought of Jenny Hays in years, and wondered why the memory of her was so clear. And why she felt she owed the woman a defense.

"I never blamed Jenny, either," said Elizabeth, surprised to realize it was true.

In the silence that followed she heard the loud ticking of the old wall clock hanging behind the red vinyl counter along the cafe's east wall. It was the same clock that hung there when the building had been a filling station, before Buddy converted it into Highwater's only eating establishment. The old gasoline pumps still stood out front as though waiting for time to run backward and cars to stop for a tank of 20.9-cents-a-gallon regular instead of a chicken-fried steak. Past and present overlapped in Highwater and change, when it came, altered the purpose of what already existed. Change adapted to Highwater rather than the other way around.

But opinions seldom changed and Highwater, particularly its men, didn't approve of wives running off. Elizabeth suspected she had just lost the votes of every man seated around the crowded little table in Buddy's Cafe.

She cleared her throat and prepared to redeem herself as much as she could without stretching the truth too far. She didn't like backing off an opinion, but she didn't have a lot of choice. She had to win the election. "That doesn't mean that I approve of what she did, exactly, just that it would take a stronger woman than Jenny Hays to face up to Ed. We can't blame a woman for being weaker than we think she ought to be. And maybe she was scared. Maybe Carl's right. Maybe she was afraid Ed would shoot her just like Nadine Hatcher shot Tommy."

Several of the men looked thoughtful and Buddy nodded his head. "Never thought of it like that, but it's probably true. Jenny was just a little bit of a thing and there wasn't much that didn't scare her about the country, her being from the east and all. She reminded me of a kid sometimes the way she'd nearly jump out of her shoes if a strange dog barked at her, or if the wind got up high, she'd be sure a tornado was coming. I used to wonder how she lived out on that ranch with horses and cattle all around and coyotes howling at night and nobody to comfort her but Ed, and Ed ain't what I'd call a man much given to comforting any critters but nervous cows."

Buddy slapped his dish towel against his leg. "I think

you're probably right, Elizabeth. I think Jenny Hays took the only way out she could."

Elizabeth felt the tightness in her chest relax. If Buddy thought she was right, then Highwater would, too. The town gave a lot of consideration to Buddy's opinion.

"Does that mean you'll vote for me?" asked Elizabeth.

Buddy rubbed his chin. "I reckon so. It ain't as if there's a man running, and I figure you can handle whatever comes as long as you don't have to mess with any dead bodies. That ain't no kind of job for a woman."

Given what she knew of Highwater's code of the old West, which said a woman could give birth, ride a horse, herd cattle, plow a furrow, and drive a grain truck, but was in need of a man's protection when faced with life's harsher realities, Elizabeth supposed Buddy had just endorsed her candidacy.

She paid for her coffee and left while she was ahead.

After taping up campaign signs in the front windows of Highwater Grocery, the hardware store—which also sold boots, overalls, longjohns, dishes, toasters, and plows—the seed store, the barber shop, and Sue's beauty salon, Elizabeth drove the twelve miles home to what was left of her ranch. Except for twenty sections around her headquarters, most of her land was leased and had been since her husband died two years ago and she discovered that she owed more to the government in inheritance taxes than the ranch earned in five good years. The lease money went directly to the IRS, and Elizabeth and her two sons lived on whatever they made on the small herd of cattle she hadn't already sold. It wasn't much. Which was why she let Sheriff Jim Hayworth talk her into running for justice of the peace. She needed the paltry salary the job paid.

Otherwise she wouldn't have eaten crow at Buddy's Cafe this morning.

Elizabeth smelled the smokey scent of tobacco the instant she stepped inside the old, sprawling ranch house built nearly eighty years before. She followed the scent into the kitchen. "I didn't see your patrol car parked out front, Jim."

Sheriff Jim Hayworth put his cigar in an ashtray sitting next to the cup of coffee and pushed his chair away from Elizabeth's kitchen table. Gentlemen always rose when ladies entered a room, and Jim was a gentleman. Elizabeth supposed she was a lady. At least she didn't do any cussing when men were around.

"I didn't think it would do your campaign much good for the neighbors to count how many evenings I come to supper. Don't want you to get a reputation you haven't earned," said Jim.

"I don't have any neighbors closer than five miles and you can't see the house from the road, anyway. Besides, it's nobody's business what I do. I'm forty-three years old and a widow with two grown boys. If I want to invite an old friend to dinner, I will, and if I want to invite him to stay over for breakfast, I'll do that, too."

Jim grinned at her, the skin crinkling up around his eyes. As nearly as Elizabeth could remember he was pushing fifty. He had a flat belly and hard muscles, but was of an age that his skin was loosening up around his eyes and neck. The same could be said of her, though. She'd noticed a few lines she'd swear hadn't been there last year.

"You interested in my staying for breakfast, Elizabeth?" He saw her hesitate and reached out to catch her hands. "I shouldn't have asked that. I'm sorry. I reckon when the right time comes, if it does, you'll let me know in no uncertain terms. And if it don't ever come, then we'll go along the way we always have. I'm not such a young buck that I can't enjoy a woman's company without asking for more than good conversation."

She smiled and squeezed his hands. Jim had never hid his interest in her—at least not since she was widowed—just stated it and let it lie. What she did with it was up to her. Elizabeth knew Jim Hayworth would never push harder than she let him. He was a throwback to the days in the old West when a woman was respected just because she was a woman and scarce on the Texas frontier. As scarce as jobs in Highwater.

She abruptly let go of Jim and sank into a chair at the old

round table. She hooked her boot heels on the front rung of her chair and sighed, closing her eyes for a moment.

"Would you rather I left, Elizabeth?"

She opened her eyes and turned her head to watch Jim pour her a cup of coffee from the dented old pot her grandfather had used when he was a cowboy for the old XIT. "No, I don't want you to leave. I'm feeling down and I need your company."

He served her coffee and sat down across from her. "Drink it, Elizabeth. It ain't been sitting long. I made myself to home while I was waiting and put on a fresh pot." He tilted his chair back and watched her while she drank, puffing on his cigar. "I hear you made a stir at Buddy's Cafe this morning."

She set her cup down and looked at him. "Where did you hear that?"

He shrugged. "Three or four of the ranchers who were there happened to drop by the office and mention it. You knocked them off kilter."

"But they agreed with me!" Elizabeth protested.

He scratched his head to give himself time to think, a gesture Elizabeth recognized. Her own husband had done the same thing. Men around Highwater weren't given to running off at the mouth without thinking, another hold-over from pioneer days, when a man was expected to stand by his word and it behooved him to be sure his word wasn't careless.

"I never said they didn't. They never said they didn't," said Jim. "What they were was uncomfortable. You ripped off their blinders and they looked at the whole picture of Jenny Hays running off, top and bottom and all the corners, that they hadn't seen before. The other side of that coin is that now they're looking at you without blinders, too, and wondering what might be in your corners that they might not have noticed before."

"I explained myself."

Jim tipped his chair forward and the front two legs landed on the faded linoleum floor with a hard thump. He reached across the table and clasped her hands. "That must have been a sight to see, Elizabeth Walker trying to persuade a bunch of men that you're right and they're wrong, or at least, mistaken."

"Carl Dean said the same thing, but I bet nobody mentioned him."

"I don't recall his name coming up, but Carl Dean ain't running for justice of the peace."

Elizabeth pulled her hands out of Jim's warm grip rubbed her temples. She felt a headache coming on and she never had headaches, but she suspected this might be the first of many. "Are folks going to root through everything I say from now on like a pig at the trough, looking for something they disagree with?"

"I suppose they will, Elizabeth, people being contrary the way they are. Damn it all, I should have warned you to watch what you say."

"Why didn't you?"

Jim shook his head. "You were skittish as a colt about running for office anyway. Like a lot of folks in Highwater, you think a politician and a liar are two names for the same skunk. I was afraid you wouldn't see the difference between keeping your opinions to yourself and out-and-out lying so I didn't say anything for fear you'd refuse to run. And I wanted you to make the race, Elizabeth, and not just because you're my best friend's widow. You'll be a good justice of the peace. You're a sensible woman, a God-fearing woman, and you're the third generation of your family to live in Highwater. You know the folks in this end of the county. You'll know when to push and when to hold off. In a town this small that's as important as the letter of the law."

Elizabeth pushed her cup away. She had a bad taste in her mouth that hot coffee wouldn't chase away. Bitterness always soured the stomach and left the taste of bile on the tongue. "I wouldn't have refused to run, Jim, because I need the job too badly, but I don't like talking out of both sides of my mouth. It galls me to find out that I'm so good at it."

Jim mashed out his cigar. "And it galls me that you had to find out by arguing over Jenny Hays."

Elizabeth gave him a sharp look. "And you didn't think

much of her, I suppose? Like the rest of the men in Highwater except for Carl Dean and Buddy, you think she was a slut."

He looked startled, then thoughtful, rubbing his chin as he stared at her. "That's not what I meant, Elizabeth. As a matter of fact I liked Jenny Hays. Most of the men in Highwater did. She had a way of bringing out the best in a man. She'd smile and tilt her head to one side and really listen to what a man was saying even if he was just remarking on how dry the weather had been lately. We'd open doors for her and carry packages out to her car and she'd thank us like we'd done something really fine. She was a kind person and I think we all lost sight of that fact when she ran away until you and Carl Dean reminded us. I think those men at Buddy's were ashamed of forgetting what Jenny Hays was really like, and like most men, they didn't like being reminded by a woman."

"But I didn't say she was kind. I said she was weak and too scared of Ed Hays to tell him face to face she wanted a divorce. She had to run off and do it from a distance."

"She never divorced him, Elizabeth, and I'd know, because I'd be the one to serve the papers on Ed. That's part of a sheriff's job."

"But Ed never divorced her either, Jim, because there's no way he could file the papers in Bonham County without everybody finding out," said Elizabeth slowly. "The county clerk's got a tongue that wags at both ends."

They sat looking at each other, the silence in the old kitchen seeming to wrap around them until Jim broke it by clearing his throat. "Stubbornness on Ed's part, I guess. He doesn't want to be the first to admit he made a mistake."

Elizabeth thought of Ed Hays's cold gray eyes. "I don't think so. I think it comes down to money. Ed would have to split his ranch with Jenny, or at least pay her half its value, and most ranchers can't raise that kind of money without borrowing or selling off some land. I don't think Ed would sell his land to pay off Jenny any more than I did to pay off the IRS."

"That doesn't make good sense, Elizabeth. Ed ought to

file first so the hearing will be here in Bonham County where the judge knows the circumstances. There's no hard-and-fast rule that says Jenny gets half of everything. The judge has a lot of discretion and is likely to be sympathetic to Ed."

"Then why didn't Ed file? Why hasn't he filed yet? Good heavens, it's been ten years! What's he waiting for? The Second Coming?"

"Why are you getting so worked up over a ten-year-old scandal, Elizabeth? If Ed Hays wants to roll the dice and gamble that Jenny never files for divorce, that's his business."

Elizabeth gripped the edge of the table and leaned toward Jim. "Ed Hays doesn't gamble."

This time the silence stretched out while Jim scratched his head, looked out the window at the endless flat prairie, then finally met her eyes. "What exactly are you saying?"

Elizabeth took a deep breath before she spoke. "How do we know Jenny Hays ran off with the seed salesman? Everyone says she did, but how do we know?"

"Because Ed Hays got a letter from Jenny—mailed from Clovis, New Mexico, as I recall."

"Did you see the letter, Jim?"

"As a matter of fact, I did. Ed reported her missing around noon a couple of days after she ran off—I guess he waited a while, thinking she'd come home—and by the time I rounded up my deputies and we drove back out to his ranch, the letter was waiting in his mailbox. Ed ripped it open and started reading it. I'll never forget the look on his face when he realized he was reading it out loud. He cut his words off short, but it was too late by then. Every man there heard the important part. 'I'm not cut out to be a ranch wife,' she wrote, 'and I'm going with the Hi-Pro seed salesman. I believe I'm better suited to him."

Jim shifted in his chair as if the memory made him uncomfortable and lit another cigar. He peered through the smoke at Elizabeth. "There was more, of course, but I'm the only one besides Ed who read it, about her waiting until he was asleep and packing a bag and walking to the highway to meet the seed salesman, and about how sorry she was. I felt like a peeping Tom, looking in on a couple's private life like that, but as sheriff I had to be sure Jenny was safe before I called off the search."

"Are you sure it was her handwriting?"

"Damn it, Elizabeth, of course I was sure! I even compared it to her signature on their marriage license."

"Then you weren't sure you believed Ed at the time?"

Jim carefully placed his cigar in the ashtray, then leaned over and grasped her shoulders. "Elizabeth, listen to me. I read the letter, I investigated . . ."

"I never heard of any investigation," interrupted Elizabeth.

Jim drew a deep breath and expelled it. "That's because I was real careful. This is a small town, Elizabeth. Have you forgotten that? I wasn't about to blacken a man's reputation by accusing him of doing away with his wife if it turned out I didn't have any cause to. In other words, I kept my opinion to myself until I knew if that opinion was worth a damn. And I'm glad I did because it wasn't. Ed Hays might not be my favorite person in Highwater, but he's not a murderer."

"Then why hasn't Jenny Hays divorced Ed?"

"I don't know, Elizabeth, and it's none of my business, anyway. It's none of yours either and I'd advise you to put it out of your mind. Stirring up an old scandal won't help you get elected if that's what you're thinking."

Elizabeth twisted out of his hold and got up to stand behind her chair. "That's not what I'm thinking, Jim Hayworth, and I'll thank you not to accuse me of it."

"Then what is on your mind? Why are you asking all these questions?"

She traced the carving of a Texas longhorn on the back of her chair, done by her grandfather when he grew too old and his back too twisted to ride a horse and work cattle. She supposed the carving was as much a symbol of the old Panhandle as the hitching rails around the courthouse had been. But nobody raised longhorns anymore and the hitching rails were gone, and with them the danger of the frontier where a man slept with one eye open so no one could sneak up on him in the dark. Now Highwater slept with both eyes closed and didn't much appreciate it when somebody disturbed that slumber.

"I woke up, Jim," Elizabeth finally said. "Or I ought to say that Carl Dean woke me up with his talk of Jenny Hays. She wasn't a particular friend of mine and I didn't like Ed Hays at all, still don't for that matter, so I went along with everybody else condemning Jenny to perdition. I was always uneasy about it, but not enough to stir myself and ask why, not till Carl shamed me into it."

Jim's eyes held a solemn expression. "Why were you uneasy, Elizabeth?"

She felt her face grow hot. She never liked confessing to being small minded, and she especially didn't like confessing it to Jim. She valued his opinion too much. "Because condemning Jenny Hays is like kicking a dog, and I've known it for years, just never admitted it. She wasn't as strong as I was, was scared of everything in sight, and I didn't have enough human charity in me to defend her until today. And even today I did a wishy-washy job of it, calling her weak instead of agreeing with Carl Dean that her running away from that marriage was self-preservation, because I was afraid I'd lose votes. I didn't like myself very much this morning, Jim."

"Blaming Ed Hays isn't any way to soothe your conscience, Elizabeth."

His gentle tone didn't hide the faint disapproval Elizabeth could hear in his voice. "It's not my conscience that needs soothing, Jim. It's my common sense. You said yourself that I'm a sensible woman and there's nothing about the Jenny Hays case that makes sense. And I'm not blaming Ed Hays for killing her, because I don't know for sure that he did. He's just the most likely suspect."

Jim shoved his chair back so hard it fell over when he stood up. "There's no Jenny Hays case, Elizabeth, because Ed didn't kill her. Nobody killed her because she isn't dead! She just ran off."

Elizabeth took a deep breath, blew it out, and took another before she spoke. She was about to dive into water over her head and she wasn't certain she wouldn't sink like a stone. "Then why didn't she divorce Ed Hays? You said she was a kind person and so did Carl Dean. A kind person wouldn't leave a man in limbo."

"Maybe she figured Ed would do the divorcing. He didn't even have to know where she was. In Texas you can get a divorce by publication in the newspaper, a sort of leftover law from frontier days when people disappeared on a regular basis."

"But he hasn't done that, Jim, and that doesn't make sense. Ed Hays has a lot of land and as long as she's legally his wife Jenny has an interest in it. And that land keeps growing more valuable all the time. If Jenny suddenly turns up Ed's going to pay through the nose and I don't care how sympathetic the judge is to him. A wife can't be thrown out with nothing—not in a community-property state. Ed knows that. He even mentioned that Nadine Hatcher was right to shoot Tommy full of holes because that way she wouldn't have to split the ranch."

Jim frowned. "Nobody mentioned that to me."

"Of course, they didn't. They were too busy telling on me and worrying about whether I was turning into one of those feminists who hates men and thinks a few less of them would improve the world," said Elizabeth. "And another thing, Jim, that letter that Jenny supposedly wrote, the words are all wrong."

"What are you talking about?"

"If you're remembering the words right . . ."

"I am," interrupted Jim.

". . . then Jenny Hays never wrote it. She wasn't from Highwater and she didn't talk like we do. 'I'm not cut out to be a ranch wife,'" quoted Elizabeth. "That's western talk, and Jenny was from the east. Somebody else dictated the words and Jenny wrote them down, but she never thought them up. And something else that Jenny would never do and that's walk to the highway in the dark. I don't think she would have even done it in the daylight. She was terrified of anything that crawled, hopped, galloped, loped, or flew. I saw her freeze crossing Main Street one day when a dog suddenly jumped out of a pickup on the other side. Ed's house is two miles from the highway. Two miles! Jenny Hays would never have walked it. If anybody met the Hi-Pro seed salesman, it was Ed, not Jenny, and he met him with a double-barreled shotgun."

"For God's sake, Elizabeth! Now you've got Ed killing everybody in sight!"

"No, just the two he thinks wronged him."

Jim grabbed his hat off the table and clapped it on his head. "I don't think I'll stay for supper after all, Elizabeth. You're gonna worry this thing like a dog worries a bone and I've heard enough."

"But I'm not through talking," Elizabeth began.

Jim's chin jutted out the way it always did when he made up his mind. "Yes, you are, too. Now you listen close because this is the sheriff of Bonham County talking, not your friend Jim Hayworth. You're talking libel and that's against the law. Furthermore, you're endangering the peace and dignity of this county by your talk because you're liable to stir folks up and when folks get stirred up, they get to taking sides and fighting and somebody gets hurt. I won't have that happen in Highwater. You stay out of Ed Hays's business and keep your opinions to yourself, Elizabeth Walker, or I'll throw you in jail and you'll lose the election and then where the hell will you be? Flat broke and accepting donations from the charity jar Buddy keeps next to his cash register."

Elizabeth felt her hands start to shake again but not because she was nervous. She was mad clear through. "You get out of my house, Jim Hayworth. I don't let any man talk to me like that."

For just a second she thought she saw his shoulders slump and regret dull his eyes, but decided it was wishful thinking. Jim Hayworth wasn't a man given to careless talk he might regret. He meant every word he said. But so did she.

He slammed the back door when he left.

Elizabeth drove up to Ed Hays's ranch house the next morning at sunrise, campaign cards in one pocket and milk bones in the other. Like everyone who lived in the country

Ed Hays had dogs and dogs barked at strangers but didn't kick up near the fuss at folks they identified as friends. Elizabeth hoped a few pats on furry heads and a generous helping of milk bones would change her from stranger to enough of a friend that she could poke around Ed's place after dark without the dogs raising Cain when they smelled her. Jenny and her lover had to be somewhere close to the house so Ed could his eye on them. Too risky otherwise. Bury a body out in a pasture and the coyotes might dig it up and carry off pieces and nobody from cattle country would mistake a human femur for a cow bone.

She waited in the pickup until Ed Hays stepped out of his house. "Hey, you dogs, shut up now," he shouted, his hand shading his eyes as he looked into the rising sun toward her. "Elizabeth, what do you want so dern early?"

Not hello or get out and sit a spell, thought Elizabeth, but what do you want. Ed Hays always figured people wanted something from him and wasn't about to give it. And this was the man Jim Hayworth thought would let a seed salesman take his wife. Not if hell froze over. Jim was wrong and Elizabeth was going to prove it and prove to Highwater at the same time that she could handle investigating unnatural deaths, even ones ten years old.

She slid out of her pickup and let the three long-haired dogs engulf her while she patted and passed out milk bones.

"Kick them dogs away, Elizabeth," said Hays, walking across the yard toward her. "They'll wart you to death if you let them."

"They're not hurting me, Ed," she said, not adding that she wanted to smell like the dogs. One more way to confuse the issue of stranger or friend.

Ed Hays grabbed the dogs' collars and pulled them off, giving each a shove toward the barn. "So what do you want?" he repeated.

Elizabeth handed him a card. "Just your vote, Ed. I'm out campaigning early so I can catch all the ranchers before they head for the pastures. I don't want to trespass on anybody's land. They might shoot first and ask questions later."

Ed took the card and squinted at it. Like most men

Elizabeth knew, he was more used to focusing on a calf a half mile away than looking at something close up. "Any reason why I should vote for you?" he asked, tucking her card in his pocket.

"Besides the fact that I'm the only one running?"

"That ain't a good enough reason. I can always write in somebody else's name."

"Because I'm honest and tough and not afraid of anybody and I won't play favorites."

He studied her face with those hard gray eyes, then abruptly nodded. "That's good enough. I don't favor weaklings."

Elizabeth had a few questions of her own and tried to think of some way to ask them without giving herself away. "Those are mighty fine roses you got climbing up the side of the house, Ed. I guess Jenny must have planted them. She had a real green thumb, didn't she? Do you ever hear from her?"

"If you don't have anything else to say, I got work to do," said Hays, an expression on his face that Elizabeth thought would sour milk.

"I'd sure like a cutting if you don't mind. I'd like to plant some roses along the front of the ranch and I don't want the hybrid kind. They just can't take the heat and the wind like these old-fashioned roses can," continued Elizabeth, walking toward the ranch house with its wall of scarlet blooms. "My, but Jenny must have spent hours tending these plants so they would get a good start. She might have wronged you, Ed, but she left you something beautiful. I've never seen roses do so well in this country. What kind of fertilizer did she use? Cow manure?"

Ed Hays grabbed her arm without any warning. One minute Elizabeth was walking toward the house and the next Ed had twirled her around and was marching her back in the direction of her pickup.

"You got what you came for which was my vote. Now you get off my property before I change my mind."

"You can't manhandle me like this, Ed Hays!" shouted Elizabeth. "I won't stand for it."

He opened the driver's door and boosted her into the pickup. She sprawled across the seat. "I reckon you will. You come on my place without my permission, caused me pain and suffering by asking about Jenny, who's been gone these ten years and none of your concern anyway, and then you try to steal my roses."

Elizabeth scrambled up and rubbed her wrist which was turning purple from Hays's grip. She glared at Ed. "I never tried to steal your roses!" She froze and felt a chill run up her spine. "Your roses? You planted those flowers, not Jenny?"

"She was useless as teats on a boar hog around green things or anything else for that matter. Everything that blows and grows gave her hay fever and that included roses and cows. I planted them flowers after she was gone. Went to Clovis, New Mexico, to the greenhouse for the plants. Worked most of two days getting the ground worked."

Elizabeth's head jerked up. "Clovis? Where Jenny's letter was mailed from? My God, she's under the roses, isn't she?"

Too late she remembered Jim's advice to keep her opinions to herself and grabbed for the pickup's door to slam it shut.

Ed Hays got to it first and reached in the truck for Elizabeth. "You always was too big for your britches, thinking you're as tough as any man and sticking your nose where it doesn't belong."

Elizabeth scrambled across the seat and out the passenger door, hitting the ground at a run. "Leave me alone, Ed Hays! You'll only get in worse trouble. Jim Hayworth knows I'm suspicious of Jenny's running off. If I disappear too, Jim will turn you every way but loose."

She looked around, desperate for a place to hide, but the flat prairie didn't offer much. Ed Hays could keep her in sight for miles, climb in his pickup and run her down. Her only chance was the barn. If she barricaded herself in the hayloft, she might live long enough for her sons to miss her and call Jim. Maybe Jim would think to come out to Ed's. Surely to God he knew her well enough to guess that his threats wouldn't scare her off.

She ran for the barn.

"You ain't gonna disappear," called Hays, his boots thudding on the hard ground behind her. "Your truck is going off the bridge over that dry ravine a few miles down the road and your head's going through the windshield. Everybody knows you never wear a seat belt."

Elizabeth felt her stomach turn over at his threat, but she didn't waste the breath to answer as she darted into the barn. Empty horse stalls lined one side, with tack rooms, storage rooms, and a machine shed on the other. Seeing the ladder to the hayloft at one end of the building, she scrambled up it, sprawling through the trapdoor at the top. Twisting around, she grabbed the top rung of the ladder and pulled it up after her, then slammed the trapdoor and shoved a bale of hay on top. Panting, her heart pounding, and sweat rolling down her sides under her shirt, she crawled away from the opening and collapsed on the dusty floor.

A roar and a hole appeared in the floor less than a foot away. She wasn't a woman who squealed much, but she came close to it this time. A shotgun blast was liable to startle most anybody.

"Elizabeth, you ain't got no way out and I'll be waiting down here. You're smart enough to know there won't be but one end to this. You can make it as hard or as easy as you want to. You come down and I'll wring your neck like I would a chicken—like I did to Jenny after I made her write that letter. You won't have time to know you're hurt before you're dead. That's the merciful way. Or you can make me find another ladder and come up after you. I reckon I'll have to shoot you then, and if you're running I might not make a clean shot. It'll hurt some and maybe a lot. Then I'd have to pluck out the buckshot and set fire to the truck after I wrecked it so your body will be too burned for any doctor to know you've been shot. Have to have a closed casket at the funeral, Elizabeth, and your boys won't be able to view the body."

Elizabeth clapped her hands over her mouth to hold in a hysterical laugh. Ed Hays might be a murderer, but he believed in tradition and an open casket was a tradition in Highwater. His first mistake was thinking she cared. She didn't intend to occupy a casket, open or shut, not if she could help it. Ed's second mistake was confusing her with Jenny. Elizabeth Walker had no intention of meekly offering up her neck to be wrung or her body to be ventilated with buckshot. Ed Hays might kill her, but he'd have a fight on his hands first.

"You listening to me?" Hays asked, his voice coming through the floor directly below her. She barely had time to crawl on top of a bale of hay before another blast shattered the spot where she'd been sitting.

"Jenny was a lot more gullible than you, I guess. She thought I was just gonna let her and that seed salesman drive off once she wrote that letter. I told her I needed the letter to save face in front of the neighbors. If it hadn't been for Nadine Hatcher going to prison for shooting her husband, I'd have killed Jenny and that damn salesman the minute they told me what they was planning instead of burying them and planting those roses. Took me most of one day just to dig the graves what with the ground being so hard. Nobody suspected a thing, Elizabeth, not even Jim Hayworth, once he read the letter."

The sound of his voice moved off and she heard the rattle of a metal ladder. She clenched her teeth together and looked around the loft one more time for a weapon—any kind of a weapon. And found one.

"I guess you picked the hard way, didn't you, Elizabeth? You always was a stubborn woman."

She listened for the sound of his movements as she shoved one end of the rope she found under the tight baling wire that bound up the bale of hay. She tied a knot and hoped that the weight of the hay didn't pull it loose. If it did, she'd blame the Boy Scouts, since that's where she learned to tie knots. She always knew she'd get some benefit out of spending all those years as a den mother. No experience is ever wasted.

"This is the quietest I've ever seen you, Elizabeth,"

remarked Ed, his voice louder now as he climbed the ladder. "That's one thing about Jenny. She never talked much until that last night when she was telling me how what she was doing was best for both of us. How the hell she could figure her taking half my land was best for me was something I never did understand."

Elizabeth threw the other end of the rope over a rafter and threw all her weight into hoisting the hay bale up until it hung directly over the trapdoor. For once she was grateful for the few extra pounds she had gained when she passed forty. A hay bale might weigh sixty or more pounds, and this one weighed every bit of that. She figured when she let go of the rope, that bale would drop like a lead weight right down on Ed Hays's head. If she was lucky, it would break his neck. If she wasn't, maybe he would at least drop his shotgun and she could grab it. If neither one happened—well, she'd cross that bridge when she came to it. She generally liked to plan ahead, but then she'd never planned to kill a man before and to some extent was feeling her way.

Elizabeth heard Ed grunt as he pushed up on the trapdoor. Ed was going to have his fill of hay bales she thought. First the one she'd shoved on top of the trapdoor, then the one hanging suspended over it. She took a firm grip on the end of the rope and waited.

Ed gave a final heave and the trapdoor flipped open and his head and shoulders poked through the opening. It was just as Elizabeth hoped. The metal ladder supporting Ed's weight was a little short and she figured he was braced on its very top rung. With everything that had happened this morning, she figured she was due at least that much luck.

"Hey, Ed, look up!" she shouted and let go of her rope at the same time.

She barely had time to see the startled expression on his face before the hay bale hit him square on the forehead. She had been right about his being off balance as he tumbled backward off the ladder. She was right about his neck, too, but she figured that was as much because he was looking up at a forty-five-degree angle when the bale hit him than anything she did. Sixty or more pounds of hay just increased that angle a little more than a man's neck was designed to bend.

Elizabeth really didn't feel she deserved all the praise for being so clever that Jim Hayworth heaped on her when he drove up Ed Hays's road a few minutes later, not when luck had so much to do with it. His apology was a horse of a different color. She figured she had earned that.

"I swear to God, Elizabeth," said Jim, bandaging her hands where the coarse rope had left huge blisters. "I took you seriously when you told me why you suspected Ed Hays of killing Jenny, but a sheriff can't go bulling his way onto a man's property and accusing him of murder without any kind of proof. I had to investigate and I had to be quiet about it so Ed wouldn't get wind of it and cover his tracks, what were left of them after ten years. But I couldn't have you saying anything. I knew Ed Hays made a bad enemy even if it turned out he wasn't a murderer, and if he was, then he wouldn't think twice about hurting you. I didn't want you in any danger. That's why I was so mean and threatened to throw you in jail. I'm damn sorry if I hurt your feelings, but I'm not sorry for trying to protect you."

"You ought to have told me what you had in mind. I'm a sensible woman. I'd have kept my nose out of your business," said Elizabeth.

"And your opinions to yourself?" asked Jim, raising one eyebrow. "What if I hadn't found any proof one way or the other against Ed Hays? Would you have let it lie?"

Elizabeth debated using her new-found talent of talking out of both sides of her mouth, but decided against it. Say one thing and mean another often enough, and a body wasn't any better than a liar. "Probably not. I don't like the idea of a man like him getting away with murder for no better reason than money, and that's all it was. He wasn't even jealous of the seed salesman. I would have poked around looking for something that said he killed them, but probably come up short if he hadn't tried to keep me out of his roses."

A sweaty and very dirty Buddy wearing a paper star that said deputy walked up to Elizabeth and Jim. The cafe owner was an on-again-off-again deputy depending on the crime rate in Highwater at a given time. Since the crime rate was mostly nonexistent, Buddy never remembered from time to time where he left his badge.

"We found them, Sheriff," said Buddy, "or rather what was left of them. It's Jenny all right. I recognized that funny peach-colored hair of hers, and I reckon the other one's the seed salesman. Kind of fitting when you think about it, him buried in a flower bed." He reached over and patted Elizabeth's shoulder. "I sure am glad you didn't try digging up them bodies yourself. It wasn't no job for a woman."

Elizabeth smiled. Nothing much ever changed in Highwater.

Gentle Reader

Sharyn McCrumb

———————

367 Calabria Road
Passaic, New Jersey 10543

Dear Laurie Gunsel:

I hope you don't mind me writing to you via your publishers. It says on the book jacket that you live in the Atlanta area, but that's a big place, so I figured this was the best way to make sure that you got my letter.

I have just finished reading your new book, *Bullet Proof,* and I had to write and tell you how much I enjoyed it. Since finding that book, I have been looking for the rest of the Cass Cairncross detective series. I located your first book (*Dead in the Water*) in a used-book store, and I hope to acquire first editions of all your works. In hard cover yet, which is something I don't do for many authors.

I especially liked the scene in *Bullet Proof* in which Cass's preppy boyfriend Bradley turns out to be the killer, and, as he's attacking our heroine, he falls out the window of the apartment when he trips over Cass's cat Diesel. Nice touch!

Anyhow, Ms. Gunsel, you do good work. So I wanted to write and tell you that you have a satisfied customer, and that I'm looking forward to Cass's next adventure, which I'm sure you're working on even as I write.

Here's wishing you the best of luck and continued success.

Sincerely,
Monty Vincent

Laurie Gunsel

Mr. Monty Vincent
367 Calabria Road
Passaic, New Jersey 10543

Dear Mr. Vincent:

Thank you very much for your kind letter about my books. It's always nice to hear from readers. It's nice to *have* readers.

I'm glad you liked *Bullet Proof.* It's one of my favorites, not only because it went book club, but also because I got some rage out of my system toward an old ... acquaintance, shall we say? I don't think libel comes into it, because unfortunately, he *didn't* trip over a cat and fall out a window. But I certainly enjoyed writing the scene and picturing him taking the plunge. Getting paid for it was just a bonus.

Thanks again for writing!

Feloniously yours,
Laurie Gunsel

367 Calabria Road
Passaic, New Jersey 10543

Dear Laurie Gunsel:

I can't tell you what a kick it was to get your letter! Wow! A busy lady like yourself answering fan mail. I'm amazed.

Since I last wrote, I've finished the superb *Dead in the Water,* and started *The Gang's All Here,* in which the intrepid Cass goes up against the Mafia on Martha's Vineyard. An interesting choice of locales, and, having never been there myself, I certainly enjoyed all the New England seaside ambience with which you highlighted your story. I'd never have thought to set a Mafia story on Martha's Vineyard. What creativity and contrast! A great read.

A question, though: in the scene in which Enzio Lombardi is pushed out of the lobster boat by Sewell, gets entangled in the lobster traps, and is left to drown and be eaten by lobsters, I thought I detected a note of satisfaction—dare I say glee?—in the narration, which would be the voice of you personally, I gather. So then I had to wonder. I went back and looked at the window scene in *Bullet Proof* again, and, to my unliterary eye, there seems to be a marked resemblance between the preppy boyfriend in that book and Enzio the mob guy in *The Gang's All Here*. They don't look alike, but I notice that they're both "pretentious dressers" and that they have prominent ears. An interesting coincidence, I say to myself. Either the talented Ms. Gunsel has a thing about ears, or else we are seeing the same guy meet his demise yet again. So I decided to presume upon your good nature and ask.

Congratulations on making the B. Dalton bestseller list. I noticed your name on the list on my last visit to the mall, and cheered you silently as I passed the mystery section.

Sincerely yours,
Monty Vincent

Laurie Gunsel

Mr. Monty Vincent
367 Calabria Road
Passaic, New Jersey 10543

Dear Mr. Vincent:

Thanks for writing. I'm glad the Cass Cairncross series has kept you interested. I'm fond of her myself. After all, I suppose she makes my house payments. She's certainly fictional (I should be so sylph like!) but at times, she seems quite real—like a roommate who has gone on vacation, but may be back any time now. Not that I've ever had a roommate—not another woman, that is. And judging from my one unfortunate experience with a live-in guy, maybe I'll just stick to cats. Diesel is quite agreeable, and never wants to watch pro football when "Murphy Brown" is on, so we get along fine. I wonder if Cass would be a good roommate. She's obsessively neat, and having a detective around the house would certainly diminish one's privacy.

You are quite a detective yourself, Mr. Vincent. Not even my editor, Joni, who has known me for *years,* spotted the resemblance between Enzio in *The Gang's All Here* and Bradley, the preppy boyfriend in *Bullet Proof.* But then, she received the manuscripts several years apart, whereas you are speeding through the books at the rate I wish I could write them! Okay, Monty, you got me. I confess. Bradley and Enzio are the same guy. He's not in the earlier books, because I didn't know I hated him back then.

So how come he's real? There are many ways to create characters—one is to take hostages from life, because people never recognize themselves. Of course you change most of the details about the person, but you leave the one little mannerism that drives you crazy, so that deep inside, you (the author) know who the character is, and it makes the narrative so much more—sincere, I guess. (I am never more sincere than when I am plotting the demise of Bradley/Enzio in a novel.)

I used to worry that he might read my books and know which character was him, but apparently that hasn't happened. He probably doesn't even bother to buy my books—when did he ever care what I thought? And I assure you that a conceited lout like him wouldn't see himself as a gangster, or even as the preppy boyfriend. (That window scene was appropriate. He and Diesel cordially loathed each other. I think I kept the right one.) He probably *likes* his "Windsor" ears.

Sorry. I didn't mean to burble on to you about the fine points of characterization. I'm so used to being interviewed that sometimes I go on automatic pilot. Anyhow, if you ever do a book review for a fanzine, please don't mention that Bradley/Enzio have roots in real life. That's something I *don't* tell interviewers. Besides, the last thing I need is for *him* to come after me with a subpoena.

As to setting the Mafia book on Martha's Vineyard—I'm not sure that was terribly creative of me, except in terms of tax management. You see, I took a vacation that year at the Cape, and if I set the book there, the whole thing was deductible. And I didn't see any guys there wearing white ties and answering to the name of Vinnie, so maybe the Mob doesn't vacation there after all, but it made a good setting, and I knew I could describe it accurately. Glad you approved.

So, tell me something about *you*, Mr. Vincent. Writers always wonder who we're talking to when we send a book out into the world. It's nice to know someone out there is listening.

> With all best wishes,
> Laurie Gunsel
> and
> Cass Cairncross

> 367 Calabria Road
> Passaic, New Jersey 10543

Dear Ms. Gunsel:

What a great letter! Thank you so much for taking the time to answer my foolish questions. I was absolutely delighted with your explanations about the characters and the Martha's Vineyard setting. Knowing little facts like that adds a whole new dimension to the book. I reread both books and enjoyed them all over again. Paperback, of course. My first editions are in plastic covers, stored safely away like the treasures they are.

So Enzio and the Preppy are based on a real guy. This explains what a ring of truth there is in your characterization. But how sad that such a gracious and talented lady like yourself should have to put up with a jerk like that. But you show admirable spunk in getting the rage out of your system, instead of weeping quietly into a lace hankie about how wronged you were. Cass must get her style from you.

Great line about Martha's Vineyard! I'm not surprised you didn't see any "Vinnies" in white ties. Those are strictly the leg men in the operation, and I think Martha's Vineyard is a little beyond them in taste, if not in price. They'd be happier in Atlantic City, I think. But your big shots in the Armani suits and the Italian silk ties, *them* you would find on Martha's Vineyard, but you'd never notice them, because they have money and they know how to fit in with the society types. When you have to hob-nob with senators and company presidents, it doesn't pay to look like a cheap hood. Of course, in fiction we have to be able to spot the bad guys, so you very rightly gave your readers the gangsters they expected. What a storyteller!

I was also impressed with your knowledge of medical matters in *The Gang's All Here.* The scene of poor Enzio in the lobster trap still makes me shudder. One thing you might look into, though, is the bit about the Kevlar body armor. Remember when Cass gets shot in the back, and it doesn't even slow her down because she's wearing the Kevlar vest? Actually, she'd feel a little more discomfort than that. Depending on the distance and the caliber of the weapon, the impact would probably knock her down, and she'd have anything from a bad bruise to a cracked rib to show for the experience. Check with some of your Atlanta policemen on this. I'm sure they'd be honored to help you with your literary research.

You asked me to tell you a little about myself. There's not much to tell, I'm afraid. I'm a grandfather—got two beautiful little grandkids living in Rockaway, but alas, I don't get to see them very often. I'm retired now, and maybe I miss the old business a little bit, but I have my garden to tend to, and my collection of books. It's terrific to finally have time to read anything I want, and not have to cram in a chapter here and there on a plane or waiting around for my next appointment. My copy of *Free Lance Murder* just arrived in the mail from *Murder by the Book,* and that will be my evening's entertainment. So, Ms. Gunsel, I want to thank you for being the highlight of my "golden years." I'm enjoying my armchair adventures with the intrepid Cass Cairncross. Keep 'em coming!

Sincerely yours,
Monty Vincent

Laurie Gunsel

Mr. Monty Vincent
367 Calabria Road
Passaic, New Jersey 10543

Dear Mr. Vincent:

You've already got *Free Lance Murder?* They haven't even sent me my author's copies yet! That was quick work on your part. At least I know it's out in stores now. Can the autographings be far behind? Which reminds me: since you're spending your hard-earned pension buying my books and keeping Diesel in cat food via my royalty statements, wouldn't you like to have your copies signed? I wouldn't mind at all, really. All you do is put the books in a mailer, and enclose another stamped mailer in with them, and I'll sign the books and ship them right back to you. Book collectors tell me they're more valuable if I just sign and date them, but if you want them personalized to you (or the grandchildren?), I'd be happy to.

Thanks for pointing out my mistake with the Kevlar vest. I guess I took the term *bulletproof* a little too literally. Actually, I'm kind of shy about asking the local police to proof my work, because the ones I know were *his* buddies. You know how cops and lawyers stick together. (I hope I didn't just offend you. You sound knowledgeable enough to be a retired policeman. Just put me down as a victim of a legal shark attack.) I suppose I ought to find a new source somewhere, like downtown Atlanta, especially since I need some technical advice for the new plot. I need to know how my professional hit man can smuggle his .44 Magnum onto

S0-ASH-097

RECIPE FOR ROMANCE

Terri Fields

SCHOLASTIC INC.
New York Toronto London Auckland Sydney

One

Holly Hanson stood on the doorstep of the large white stucco house and stared up at the big gold Greek words Kappa Omega Epsilon. Her knees were shaking and she wondered how her courage could be deserting her now just when she needed it most. Her whole plan had seemed so logically simple when she'd explained it to her best friend Lani.

Now she was really here on the Arizona State University campus in front of a big house filled with college guys, and nothing seemed simple any longer. Stalling for time before she actually entered the fraternity house, Holly mentally replayed her conversation with Lani. Maybe it would bolster her courage again. Holly smiled, thinking of the way she'd boldly announced her plan to Lani and of Lani's amazed response: "You mean you're really going to march into a college fraternity house and demand that they give you a job as assistant cook?"

How easy it had been then for Holly to vehemently toss off, "Why not? They advertised for one; I'm qualified and I'd be good. Besides, I really want the job."

Lani had remained doubtful. "Aren't you going to die, having to just walk in uninvited to a whole house of fantastic-looking college guys?"

"I'm not even going to think about that part," Holly had replied, feeling sure she knew what she was doing. "You've got to look at the whole situation. I mean, you know how much I want to be a great chef one day. You know that I want to go to the Cordon Bleu Cooking School in France." She sighed. "And you and I both know that Mom and Dad's school teacher salaries are never going to get me there."

So far the only money Holly had been able to save was from baby-sitting. It was almost impossible for a high school student to get a job in Tempe, Arizona. With a big university right in the middle of town, there were tons of college kids for every available opening. She'd been so convincing when she'd told Lani, "This is the perfect job for me. It's right in my field. I've got past experience; in fact, I can probably even get a recommendation from Chef Shand. Besides, the hours fit in with school perfectly, and it pays great. I'd be nuts not to want it." She'd looked at Lani with a grimace. "But we both know that even though I spent an hour filling out an application for the job, I'll never get it. And we both know it's because in spite of all the time I spent on my application, it'll get tossed out." Holly sighed deeply. "And why? Because I'm just a high school kid and everyone else who applies will be older. But I'm not giving up so easily. I'm going to that fraternity house in person and convince the cook that I'm the right one for the job."

It had all sounded great when she was explaining it to Lani, except that now that she was actually here, she couldn't make herself walk in the door. She'd never even been inside a fraternity house and had no idea what to expect.

Holly felt a hand tap her on the shoulder and her thoughts were immediately broken as a tall, broad-shouldered boy said, with a smirk, "Excuse me. I've been watching you standing here ever since I got to the corner. I'm Greg, and I live here. What I want to know is, are you going in or did we hire someone to guard the front door?"

Holly could feel herself blushing. "I, uh, I came about the assistant cook's job." She hated herself for the hesitation in her voice. After all, she'd promised herself to be so forceful that everyone would be impressed, but she hadn't thought about having to contend with a guy who looked like a movie hunk before she even got in the door.

"Ah-ha." Greg continued smirking. "Well,

the cook usually is in the kitchen, not the front doorstep." He thought a moment. "Come to think of it, I didn't even know she was interviewing anyone yet." Greg shrugged and opened the door. "Well, you coming in or you planning on having her meet you out here?"

Holly's temper overcame her nervousness. This guy, regardless of how terrific he looked, wasn't going to get her so shook that she didn't get the job. After all, she'd come for the first step in achieving her career, not for a date.

That resolved, Holly didn't bother to answer his question; she just followed him inside the fraternity house. With Holly right behind him, he walked across a huge living room filled with an assortment of furniture. A big fraternity crest that read Kappa Omega Epsilon hung on one wall, and there was even a piano over in the corner. The fraternity living room looked more like a hotel lobby than the bigger version of her older cousin's apartment that she'd imagined. Greg reached a big staircase and, turning toward Holly, he said, "Well, I'm going to my room. You planning to follow me up there, too?"

Her blue eyes flashed with anger. People who knew her well saw that look and stayed away. "Could you just tell me where the kitchen is?"

He grinned and pointed. "It's over that way. Say, I don't think I caught your name."

It was on the tip of her tongue to say that she hadn't given it and she didn't plan to give it to him, but then she decided that if she did get the job, there was no point in having an absolute enemy. "It's Holly," she replied.

"Yeah, well good luck, Holly. Glad I could help you. But frankly, I don't think you're going to get the job." With that terrific send-off, Greg bounded up the stairs. Holly's legs suddenly felt like wood, but she dragged them toward the kitchen. Several fraternity boys passed through the living room and regarded her curiously, heightening her apprehension. In a way, she wished that stupid Greg were still here. He was so infuriating that when he was around, she forgot to be scared.

Pushing the door open to the fraternity kitchen, Holly felt somewhat reassured. This kitchen wasn't nearly as big as the one at camp. Then she saw the cook. A large woman in a white dress and white apron was practically up to her elbows in some kind of dough. Holly's first impression was that the woman must have eaten a lot of that dough. Her round arms almost looked like big loaves of bread, but her fingers expertly kneaded the dough in front of her. She glanced at the clock, then at the dough, and then frowned at Holly. "What do you want?" she asked in a deep voice that sounded as if it brooked no nonsense.

Holly had the feeling that she'd definitely

come at the wrong time, but it was too late to do anything about that now. She tried to put on her most assured voice. "I came about the job." She'd planned to really impress the cook, but before she got a chance to say anything further, the cook motioned her to stop.

"Honey, I'm sorry you came all this way, but you're just not what I'm looking for at all."

The smells of the evening meal filled the kitchen, and Holly desperately wanted the cook to at least give her a chance. She just knew that the job was right for her and that she was right for the job. Why did people think she was a baby just because she was short? No one ever thought she was sixteen, and because she was small, no one ever thought she was very strong. Maybe that's why she was such a fighter; she was always having to prove to people that she wasn't what they'd expected.

Holly evaluated for a minute and made a quick decision. This woman didn't look as if she liked to be argued with and Holly had the feeling that once the cook made up her mind, it would be hard to get her to change it. Holly mentally crossed her fingers and hoped she was taking the right approach. "You really handle that dough beautifully," she said. "What kind of rolls are you making?"

"Cinnamon rolls," replied the cook, continuing to work. "A hundred of 'em." She sighed. "I try to tell these boys that I can't keep up at this pace and they can't expect baking until I get a new assistant, but they look so upset that I give in and do it anyway."

"Have you ever thought about those pullapart cakes that you can let rise overnight?" Holly chose her words carefully. "Of course, I'm sure that they're not as good as your rolls, but I've got a recipe that makes fifteen cakes of eight rolls each."

The cook seemed intrigued. "Now why would a little thing like you have a recipe to make so much food?"

Holly smiled. "Oh, I've worked as an assistant cook at a children's camp for the last three summers." It wasn't exactly a lie, it just wasn't exactly a perfect description of the truth. What she'd neglected to include was that her parents had summer jobs as the codirectors of Peaceful Pines Summer Camp in Prescott, Arizona. Holly had spent every summer there that she could ever remember, and while it had been really fun when she was young, by the time she was thirteen, she'd pretty much had it with the camp routine. Her parents had told her that she no longer had to be one of the campers, but then it was up to her to keep herself busy and out of trouble. That was how one day she'd stumbled into the kitchen, looking for something to do, and one of the cooks had asked her if she'd like to help.

Finding it great fun, she'd spent most of the rest of the summer working in the kitchen.

Her parents thought her fascination would fade, but it hadn't. She'd told them that she planned to grow up and become a great chef, and at first, they'd been inclined to dismiss that as much as they had when she was five and had told them she planned to be a firefighter. But Holly's interest in cooking for large groups of people hadn't subsided. Her home economics teacher had told her that she was very good and very creative, and by last summer, the camp head cook had remarked to her parents that he'd really come to count on Holly. In fact, he'd implied that next summer, her parents might want to hire her on as an assistant cook for the camp.

A young man ran into the fraternity kitchen. "Mrs. Clausen, I forgot to sign up a guest for dinner. Can I still bring him tonight?"

The cook looked at him sternly. "Alan, you know the rules." But then, seeing the dejected look on the young man's face, she continued, "Okay, go ahead. But from now on, remember, you've got to sign up two days ahead if you're bringing a guest."

The cook then turned her attention to Holly. "Listen dear, I really don't have time to chat right now. It's been nice meeting you, but I really can't use you."

Holly bit her lip. "I'd do a good job. I'm sixteen. I'm not as young as I look, and I'm really strong. I've lifted big pots of boiling water from the stove and I've never spilled a drop, and — "

Mrs. Clausen cut her off. "I'm sure that's true, and you seem like a nice enough girl, but I have to work with the assistant cook every day, and I know what qualifications I want the person to have, and you don't have them. Now, I've got to get back to work. Thanks for stopping."

Holly knew when she was defeated. Fighting the tears, she started out the door. "Well, thanks for talking to me," she tried to get out without crying.

Mrs. Clausen's face softened. "I'm really sorry," she said. It was clear that she was only sorry to have hurt Holly's feelings, not sorry that she wasn't going to give her the job.

Holly walked quickly through the living room back toward the front door of the fraternity house. She hoped that she wouldn't meet Greg again; she was in no mood for his teasing. Fortunately, she escaped the fraternity house with no one even noticing her. She pulled the big white door closed behind her and walked slowly back down the walk. So much for her brave speeches to Lani. So much for her great plans to get this job. It was all so unfair. She was good; she was responsible. Mrs. Clausen wouldn't even give her a chance and she wouldn't even tell her why not.

She kicked a pebble and watched it fly

down the rest of the walkway. "Ouch," said a voice, and Holly looked up.

"I'm sorry," she started, and then she stopped. "Jeff, is that you?" It was, and he seemed delighted to have run into her. Though Jeff had been a year ahead of Holly at Tempe High, they'd been in the same Spanish class together. They'd done lots of skits and dialogues together and had always hit it off very well. Holly had always thought Jeff was nice and for a while she was sure he was going to ask her out. But he never had and she hadn't seen him since graduation.

"What on earth are you doing here?" he asked.

"Well, I . . . it's a long story. Do you live here?"

"Yeah," Jeff said. "I went back and forth trying to decide about pledging a fraternity. On the whole, I'm glad I did. Most of the guys are great and the house is a fun place to live." He paused a moment. "But that still doesn't answer what you're doing here," he said.

Much to her absolute horror, Holly began to cry. "Hey," said Jeff, looking alarmed, "don't do that. Let's go over to the Student Union. I'll buy you a soda and you can tell me all about it."

She nodded, and they walked the block and a half in silence as Holly tried to stifle her sobs. Sitting across from Holly in the Student Union cafeteria, Jeff insisted that she tell him what was going on.

At first, she had planned to say it was nothing, but then the story began to spill out. It felt so good to tell someone the whole thing. "And I feel like such a jerk. My friends told me that this was a stupid idea and that I didn't have a chance for the job, but I informed them that I really wanted it and I'd figure out a way to get it." She took a sip of her Pepsi. "I don't know why I ever thought I could just go to the fraternity house and convince the cook, but I really did think so." Jeff was listening attentively. "You know what's worst of all?" Holly said sadly. "She wouldn't even tell me what was wrong about me."

"Well, I can help you there," Jeff said. "That's easy. What's wrong with you is that you're a pretty teenage girl."

Holly smiled at the compliment. It was really sweet of Jeff to try to make her feel better. "Thanks, Jeff, but really, why won't she even consider me? Is it because I look so young?"

Jeff shook his head. "Aren't you listening? I just told you the reason." With that he began a detailed explanation. Mr. and Mrs. Clausen had become Kappa Omega Epsilon's cooks ten years ago, and since then all the sororities and fraternities had tried luring them away because they made the best food on campus. But the Clausens had remained loyal to KOE and had been given complete control over the kitchen, including all the menu planning. Jeff said that from what he'd been told, everyone was very pleased with the situation. "Then last year, Mr. Clausen had a heart attack and died. At first, Mrs. Clausen tried to do everything herself which, I guess, was a complete disaster."

Jeff went on to say that the housemother had finally convinced her that she had to have some help in the kitchen and had hired one of the guy's girl friends who said she was a home economics major. But instead of helping, the girl was either sneaking off to be with her boyfriend or fighting with him and too upset to be of any use.

"This year, Mrs. Clausen came out of the kitchen one night at the beginning of the semester. She made an announcement that meals would be simple for a couple of weeks until she had time to hire an assistant, and that *she* would pick the assistant and she didn't want any help. So you see, there's just no way she's ever going to give you a chance."

Jeff and Holly talked for a while longer and then Jeff said that it looked as if Holly was feeling better and he really had to get some studying done. She thanked him appreciatively for all his help, but Jeff waved away her thanks, saying that it had been terrific to see her. Still, Holly couldn't help but notice that he'd made no mention of getting together again.

Watching him leave, Holly decided she couldn't worry about that now. Jeff was a nice guy, but he was just a friend; if he never asked her out, she'd survive. Besides, somewhere in the back of her mind a plan for getting the job was developing. For now, that was going to take all of her attention.

Two

It was a long walk back to her house and by the time Holly arrived, both her parents had come home from school. Mrs. Hanson was sitting at the kitchen table with a stack of papers in front of her, but as soon as Holly walked in, she put down her red pen, and asked, "How'd it go, honey? Did you wow them with your cooking skills?"

" 'Fraid not, Mom; the cook wouldn't even give me a chance."

With that, Holly poured herself a glass of milk and in spite of her mother's frown took three chocolate chip cookies. Then, sitting down at the table across from her mother, she told her the whole story. "At first, I just felt so mad and so defeated, but now, I still think I might have a chance."

Her mother's forehead wrinkled in the crease that Holly knew meant she was worried. "Well, Holly, you can't change what you are, and from what you've said, I think you're fooling yourself if you think that cook is going to give you any chance at all. Hon, sometimes life just isn't fair. She shouldn't judge you by that other girl's actions, but I'm afraid that's what she's done. I'm sorry it didn't work out, and I want you to know that both Dad and I are proud of you for trying."

But Holly refused to give up. "Mom, could I call Mr. Shand at the ski resort where he's working? I want to get his recipe for pull-apart rolls." When Mrs. Hanson looked perplexed, Holly continued, "You know, the ones he made on Saturday mornings for the kids at camp last summer?"

"What's that got to do with anything?" asked Mrs. Hanson.

"Well, I've got this idea. It's probably dumb, but it's worth a try. Please, Mom, I'll pay you and Dad back for the call." Holly winced at her persuasive promise and hoped the long distance call wouldn't cost too much. Her mother still looked unconvinced so Holly, eyes glowing with excitement, explained her plan. When she'd finished, she again asked, "Please, Mom? Now, can I call?"

Mrs. Hanson smiled at her daughter. She really was very proud of Holly's determination and positive attitude. They were what made her successful in most of her projects, and Mrs. Hanson really admired Holly's stick-to-it-iveness. But she was afraid that this time Holly's hopes had gone beyond the realm of possibility. She sighed. It was hard to protect a child like Holly from being hurt. "Okay, Holly, but you better call after nine tonight. You don't want to bother Adam while he's cooking dinner for the guests at that ski lodge. And don't worry about paying Dad and me back, unless you start getting chatty. How's this? We'll pay for the first five minutes. You pay for anything over that."

Holly hugged her mom in thanks. It would sure be nice if some day they had enough money so that everything didn't have to be budgeted for so carefully. If she ever got to be a great chef, she was definitely going to share her wealth with her parents.

Holly walked back into her room, thinking as she entered that she loved her bedroom, although it was totally unlike most of her friends' rooms. It didn't have a single rainbow, unicorn, or heart in it. Sunny yellow walls and a yellow patchwork quilt on the bed made the room bright and cheerful. Holly flopped on her bed, turned on an Elton John cassette, and began to daydream. . . .

. . . KOE's cook had suddenly been called out of town, and the evening meal was all Holly's responsibility. In a panic, she realized that Mrs. Clausen had forgotten to leave an evening menu, but somehow, after surveying the kitchen and using her cooking skills, she'd managed to make a seven-course meal. Just as she'd put the finishing garnishes on all the salads, the fraternity president rushed through the kitchen door, looking white-faced. "Where's Mrs. Clausen?"

"She's gone. She had to rush out of town, but it's okay. I've got dinner all ready."

The fraternity president scowled. "I certainly hope so, because I just found out that Elton John used to be a KOE and he's here on campus and coming to this fraternity house for dinner!"

Holly gasped, and although she couldn't quite see in her mind what she'd made, she could hear the oohs and ahhs after she brought out each dish. At the end of the meal, Elton John himself walked back into the kitchen, asking her if she'd made this delicious dinner. When she blushingly admitted that she had, Elton John asked her to come be his personal cook!

"Well, Holly, what do you say?" he asked. "Holly, Holly?" She was simply too tonguetied to answer him, but he persisted in calling her name louder and louder.

Snapped from her daydream, she realized that her name really was being called, but it wasn't by Elton John, it was by her father and he wanted her to come to dinner.

"I'm coming," she called, and then sat thinking for a moment about what an amazing daydream it had been; it had seemed so real. She shook her head at her own craziness; in reality she couldn't even get the job, but in her mind, she already had Elton John arriving for dinner.

Lani called for an update after dinner, and when Holly told her that she'd been summarily dismissed, Lani seemed as disappointed as Holly. The evening dragged slowly by as Holly struggled through Spanish and algebra homework and tried to wait until it was nine-thirty so she could call Mr. Shand. The numbers of the digital clock on her desk were changing agonizingly slowly, and by nine twenty-six she could stand it no longer. She looked at the phone number her dad had printed in his typical block style and swallowed hard. Not really superstitious, she crossed her fingers anyway. If Mr. Shand wasn't there or didn't remember the recipe, her whole plan wouldn't work. Holly took a deep breath and picked up the kitchen phone. Unfortunately, her mother was on another extension.

It took another lifetime of fifteen minutes before her mother finally finished her call. Holly knew how nervous she was after the first time she called and found that the call hadn't gone through because she'd forgotten to dial the one before starting the area code. Finally, a voice answered. "Telluride Ski Lodge. May I help you?"

"Adam Shand, please." Holly's voice sounded hollow and childlike even to herself.

"Hold on a sec," said the voice. Holly waited for what seemed like forever. In the background she could hear what sounded like a party and she hoped that the man who'd answered hadn't put the phone down and forgotten about her. Why couldn't anything just be simple!

"Hello," said a voice.

"Mr. Shand?"

"That's me, who's this?"

Delighted to have finally reached him, she practically shouted, "Mr. Shand, this is Holly Hanson."

He sounded pleased, asking if she and her family were in Telluride. Holly explained as quickly as she could that she was still back in Tempe, she just needed to get a recipe from him.

Mr. Shand seemed perplexed. "Well, goodness, Holly, couldn't you have just dropped me a note?"

Holly explained that she needed it right away, that it was a long story, but that it might make the difference between her getting a job or not. "It's the recipe for the multiple pull-apart cakes. You know, the ones you made for Saturday breakfasts."

Mr. Strand said he had the recipe, but he didn't know it by heart. "Do you want to wait while I find it or should I just send it to you?"

Holly took a deep breath as the long distance minutes ticked away. "I'll wait, if you don't mind."

Waiting for him to return to the phone,

she nervously doodled a whole page of circles. Finally, he said, "Okay, I've got it. You have a pen?"

She wrote as quickly as she could. Actually, she hadn't remembered the recipe as being quite this long or complicated. She finished reading it back to Mr. Shand to make certain that it was right and then he said, "Okay, it's my turn now. What on earth does this recipe have to do with getting your job?"

Holly didn't want to be rude, but she didn't want to stay on the phone, either. As briefly as she could, she told Mr. Shand about the job. He listened carefully and then told her that he thought she should certainly get it, and he'd be glad to send her a letter of recommendation or more recipes if she thought it would help. As she was ready to hang up, Mr. Shand asked her to give his best to her parents and warned, "Holly, don't get your hopes too high. We chefs are pretty temperamental, and if the karma isn't right, we just won't work with someone. It doesn't mean you aren't good. Besides, Holly, I know you're going to make it to Cordon Bleu either way."

Holly thanked him for his help and hung up. Staring at the quickly written mess, she began to recopy it on recipe cards, using her best handwriting. As she wrote, she thought fondly of Mr. Shand. He'd been a chef at a fancy hotel in Europe for a couple of years and he'd told her all about it. It had all seemed very glamorous and exciting, and she could never see why he'd come back to the United States and taken a winter job at a ski lodge and a summer job at a kids' camp. He could have been working at some fine resort. Once she'd asked him, but Mr. Shand had just shrugged and said that he liked the lack of pressure and change of climate that his current winter and summer jobs provided.

Holly stared at the completed recipe card. It certainly looked fine. She sighed. If only she were going to present it to a kind, easy-going chef like Mr. Shand instead of the fraternity cook who had made it clear that she never wanted to see her again.

Carrying the recipe card back to her room with her, Holly stopped in her mother's room to let her see it. "Well," she said, half to her mother and half to herself, "here's step one. Now I just hope I have the nerve to carry out step two."

Back in her room, Holly stared in the mirror over her dresser. If only there were some way to make herself look older. If her dark hair were long, she could sweep it up into a bun and look both taller and older, but since it was wavy, she kept it short. That made it easy to manage, but it left her no way to ever change the style. Maybe she could put on more makeup. Of course it couldn't age her twenty years, and that's what she needed.

She giggled in spite of her aggravation,

remembering one of the plans she'd considered. After Jeff had first told her that Mrs. Clausen wanted to hire someone older, she'd had the idea of having Lani's friend in theater make her up like a little old lady and reapplying for the job, but then in a flash, she knew that she could never carry that kind of acting job off. She knew that even if she somehow managed to get the job, there was no way she could keep it unless somehow she could get Mrs. Clausen to accept Holly Hanson for herself. Tomorrow she was determined to give that her best try.

Three

At lunch the next day, Holly's "almost job" was her whole group's topic of discussion. "What a dream it would have been!" exclaimed Marlene. "Imagine having a reason to be in a whole house full of fraternity guys every single day and not having any other girls around at all. Talk about heaven on earth! I mean, even I'd have applied and I hate to cook." Lani, Holly, and Becky laughed. Marlene was by far the most boy-crazy of the crowd, although most any of the girls at Tempe High would have agreed with Marlene's assessment of the job.

The four girls ate pizza that they were sure had been made from left-over boxes, and the conversation turned to jobs in general. Becky said that her cousin in Denver actually had to choose which of three jobs she was going to take. "They're so desperate there that the fast food places have been calling her high school to leave messages saying they have jobs for teens who want them." The girls sighed collectively as they agreed for the hundredth time about their bad luck of having to live in Tempe. With over 30,000 college kids around, no one in high school ever had a chance at any of the jobs that opened. Becky sighed. "In her last letter, my cousin said that she was trying to decide whether to spend some of the money she was earning on a ski trip or a new spring wardrobe. Can you imagine that? In the last three weeks, I've made exactly $7.50, and that was only by baby-sitting that awful Johnson brat."

On that unhappy note the bell rang and the girls split up to head to their afternoon classes. Holly hadn't told any of them that she was still going after this job at the fraternity house. If she got it, she could always tell her friends, and if she didn't, no one had to know that she'd made a fool of herself twice.

The afternoon passed slowly until finally the three o'clock bell screamed release, and hordes of students began streaming through the halls. Not wanting to run into Lani and explain why she couldn't stop for a Coke, Holly hurried out the front door of Tempe High and began heading for the university. The walk was long enough to give ample time for the small butterflies in her stomach to become monstrouly big waves of nausea. Finally she passed the Sigma Chi house and the Sig Ep house. Down the block, she could see the large white stucco KOE house. Marlene had said that it was the best fraternity on campus.

Not wanting to get caught standing on the doorstep again, Holly stopped before she reached the house and checked her purse for the hundredth time to make certain that the recipe was still there. "Come on, Holly," she told herself in a pep talk, "it's got to be easier today. At least you know where the kitchen is." But in spite of what her voice was telling her, her insides were saying that they weren't one bit more relaxed today. Reaching the KOE house, she crossed her fingers and hoped she wouldn't see Greg; her confidence level definitely wasn't up to dealing with him.

Her shaking hand pushed open the heavy front door, and once again, Holly found herself in the living room of the KOE fraternity house. Shakily, she smiled to herself. Well, she joked silently, the place hasn't changed much since yesterday. And with that she forced her unwilling legs toward the kitchen.

Shoving open the door to the kitchen, she wasn't sure who was more surprised, herself or Mrs. Clausen. This scene wasn't developing at all the way it was supposed to. In her mind, Holly was sure that when she arrived, she'd find Mrs. Clausen shorthanded and hurrying to get dinner ready. Instead, she was sitting with a coffee cup talking to a middle-aged man. The speech Holly had rehearsed a million times was of no use now, and with a sinking heart she wondered whether this man was the new cook's assistant.

For a moment the three of them looked at each other uncomfortably. "I — I brought you the recipe I told you about yesterday."

Mrs. Clausen looked at Holly suspiciously. "I thought I explained to you then that I couldn't give you the job. And no recipe will change that."

"Oh, I know that," Holly said. "It's just that it really is an easy way to make good breakfast rolls for a lot of people, and I was nearby and thought you might like to have it."

At this point the middle-aged man broke in, "Ah, Helen, don't be so hard-hearted. It was a nice thing for the kid to do."

Mrs. Clausen looked a little sheepish. "Okay, excuse my manners. I'd like to see the recipe." But as Holly began to take it from her purse, Mrs. Clausen's guard again went up. "Remember, it doesn't have anything to do with my giving you the job."

Holly tried but couldn't smile as she handed Mrs. Clausen the magical recipe that was supposed to open the door to her career. It was now perfectly obvious that it wasn't going to do any such thing. The balding man said, "Well, I'll leave you women to discussing recipes. Helen, consider budgeting for those new knives I was showing you. You'll really like them."

The man left without Holly ever knowing for sure who he was, but one thing was definite: He certainly wasn't the assistant cook. In spite of everything that had gone wrong, Holly felt a ray of hope that, at least, maybe the job hadn't been filled.

Mrs. Clausen put on a pair of reading glasses and considered the recipe carefully. "You say you've tried this for a hundred people?"

At last, it was the opening she'd hoped for. Holly explained again that she'd worked in the kitchen of the Peaceful Pines Summer Camp for years. Intrigued, Mrs. Clausen talked to her for a few minutes about quantity cooking, and thanks to Mr. Shand's careful explanations every summer, Holly could converse with ease with Mrs. Clausen. In fact, Mrs. Clausen seemed almost nice now. Come on, thought Holly, if things could just keep rolling like this for a little while longer. . . .

But almost as soon as the thought had entered Holly's mind, Mrs. Clausen's chatty tone changed. "It was kind of you to bring me this recipe, and I will try it. Now you'll have to excuse me; I've got a whole dinner to prepare, and I'm afraid that between interviewing for the assistant's job, chatting with you about recipes and with Bill from Kitchen Products about knives, I'm running way behind."

"That's okay," Holly rushed in. "I'd be glad to help you. You wouldn't be hiring me or anything. I wouldn't even have to come back. It's just that I'm here, and it would be fun to help you get dinner ready tonight. I'm sure I'd learn a lot." She saw a pile of potatoes on the drainboard. Peeling potatoes was her least favorite chore, but before Mrs. Clausen could say anything, Holly walked over to the drainboard. "Why don't I just peel these for you?"

Looking a little stunned, Mrs. Clausen said, "Well, okay, if you're sure you want to, it would really be a help. But remember, I want to be fair. No job."

Holly nodded and picked up the potato peeler. She thought that mentioning she was planning to be a chef someday might help her cause, but then she remembered that Jeff had said the girl last year who'd been such a disaster had been a college home economics major with a specialty in cooking. At first, Holly decided that it would probably be best not to say anything, and then as she watched Mrs. Clausen work, she became so fascinated, she forgot about making conversation at all. How could Mrs. Clausen be making so many things at the same time, and still keep track of the exact stage everything was in? It was amazing.

Holly moved from one small task to another; none of them were things that Mrs. Clausen couldn't have done herself, but there was no doubt that having an extra pair of hands was helpful. When the dinner was fully prepared, Holly was genuinely sorry.

The experience had been exhilarating and filled with enthusiasm, and she told Mrs. Clausen so.

"You know, Holly, I don't know why you think so, but you're either a great actress or you really enjoyed it. It was fun to have you here, and I hope you find a good job somewhere. It just can't be here. I'm sorry, but I made myself a promise and I'm going to stick to it. I'm sure the boys will enjoy your rolls. Maybe you could come as one of their guests one day when I make them." Very casually, she added, "Now, let's see, which of the boys is it you're seeing, and I'll remind him to invite you."

"Oh, I'm not seeing any of them. I don't even really know these guys." Much to her surprise, Holly heard herself continue to blurt, "Listen, couldn't I just come back after school and help you with the evening meal until you do hire someone? You wouldn't have to pay me or anything."

"Why would you want to do that?"

"I already told you, it's really fun." By now Holly sounded childish even to herself. No adult asked for a job and then said she didn't need to be paid. Knowing how she must have sounded, Holly began to wash her hands, and hang up the apron she'd borrowed.

Mrs. Clausen regarded her carefully. "This is Tuesday. By Friday afternoon, I plan to have gone through this stack of replies to the ad enough to have hired an assistant. If you want to work until then, I'd be happy to have you."

Holly felt like hugging Mrs. Clausen. Her face beamed as she thanked her. "I'll be here every day right after school," she promised, and happily left before she could say anything wrong that might make Mrs. Clausen change her mind.

Anxious to tell her mom and dad, she practically ran all the way home, but when she arrived, no one else was there. Darn, she thought to herself, tonight's Mom's meeting and Dad is still coaching. Bursting to tell someone, she called Lani, only to have Lani's mother say that they were eating and Lani would call her back when the meal was finished.

By the time Lani called back, Holly's mood had calmed down considerably. After all, she still didn't have a job, and since none of her friends liked to cook, none of them would understand what could possibly be neat about rushing out after school to work in a kitchen for no pay. Still, Lani was interested, and Holly found herself sheepishly explaining that she had good and bad news. After listening to the whole story, Lani said, "Well, at least she didn't just kick you out. Maybe in the week you're there you'll meet some cute guy, and while the rest of us put up with the immature seniors, you'll be dating a college guy!"

Holly sighed. "I don't know, Lani. I mean, everything in me says she's never going to give me the job permanently. But suppose she's thinking about it. If I so much as smile at one of the guys, she'll for sure decide that I'm just like that other idiotic girl and give the job to someone else. I probably won't get the job, and won't get to meet a single guy, and yet, you know, this is really dumb, but I'm still excited about going back."

"Well, I don't know," replied Lani. "I think she sounds awful. I wouldn't even want to work for her. But still, how can she not give you the job?" She laughed. "Of course, it might be worth it to be in the KOE house. Tell me again what it looked like on the inside. Did any of the guys talk to you?"

Holly again described the living room of the KOE house, thinking it was too bad that none of her friends really understood how thrilling it was to try a difficult recipe, modify it for a large group, and then have it turn out perfectly. It was such a triumph, and there was so much that she could learn from Mrs. Clausen. Still, there was no point to getting her hopes up; Mrs. Clausen had a whole file folder of replies to the ad; surely one of them would be just the right person and then Holly would be out of the picture.

F^{our}

The next three days were a roller coaster
ride for Holly as her hopes alternately rose
and fell about being able to stay on. On
Wednesday, she and Mrs. Clausen made
lasagna for fifty, and Holly thought Mrs.
Clausen's Italian sauce was the best that
she'd ever tasted. She carefully copied down
the recipe and, as they laid noodles in the
large pans, Holly assured Mrs. Clausen that
if she ever opened a restaurant that served
lasagna, it would be noted as a "Mrs. Clausen
specialty of the house."

The two of them worked together beautifully, and it was hard for Holly to remember
that she'd ever thought of Mrs. Clausen as
intimidating. They talked as they worked,
and Holly found out that at one time Mrs.
Clausen and her husband had been the chefs
for one of the finest hotels in New York, but
they'd needed a change and ended up in

Arizona and the KOE house. Mrs. Clausen chuckled. "We could've left for higher-paying jobs, but James and I decided we enjoyed all the boys. We never had kids of our own and this was like getting fifty all at one time."

Tales of her work at the New York hotel and the fancy cooking techniques she showed Holly were high points of the week's work, but unfortunately the week had its low points, too. Every day Mrs. Clausen would interrupt their time together with at least one or two interviews for the assistant cook's position. Holly would glare silently at the prospective job thief and mentally cross her fingers that the person would leave without finding employment. It had worked on Wednesday and most of Thursday, but late Thursday afternoon Mrs. Clausen talked to a woman on the phone for quite a while. Hanging up, she turned to Holly and said, "I do believe I've found my assistant cook. She's coming in for a final interview tomorrow."

If there had been any possibility of Holly's arguing for herself, her hopes were dashed when Greg pushed open the door to the kitchen and saw Holly there. "Well, well," he said with that same infuriating smirk he'd used the first day they'd met, "if it isn't Holly hard at work for dear old KOE, and here I didn't think you'd get the job." Holly tried not even to look at him, hoping against hope that somehow he would just disappear. But he loomed even larger than life as he continued, "Mrs. Clausen, what a choice you've made. Good thing we left it all up to you. The guys will definitely appreciate the visual interest you're adding to our meals." With that he took an apple from the fruit dish, winked, and sauntered back out the door.

Holly glared after him. "That Greg!" she exclaimed under her breath.

Mrs. Clausen was watching her carefully. "I thought you didn't really know any of the boys in the house."

Holly could feel her face redden. "I don't. He was at the front door the first time I came, and I was nervous about being here. I asked him where the kitchen was and he gave me a hard time." It was a simple enough explanation and it was the truth. If only her face wouldn't keep getting a darker and darker shade of red, maybe Mrs. Clausen might even believe her.

But Mrs. Clausen gave no indication of what she was really thinking. All she said was, "That Greg is something else. He certainly keeps things jumping around here. You never know quite what he's up to."

By Thursday night when she got home, Holly sank into a hot bath feeling as if she were going to collapse. She wasn't used to this hectic pace. Rushing out of school to work for four hours and then rushing home to dinner and still trying to get her homework done didn't give her any time for relaxing at all. Not that it much mattered; tomorrow was the last day she'd be at KOE anyway. Holly tried to tell herself that it was probably just as well, but deep down she knew it wasn't at all.

On Friday, when Holly arrived at the KOE kitchen, she was almost afraid to ask Mrs. Clausen if the woman she wanted to hire had arrived for the final interview yet. Maybe if I don't say anything, she thought to herself, somehow the woman won't show up. Mrs. Clausen was demonstrating how to make a special refrigerator cookie. Holly listened, so fascinated that she forgot about the time, and when she did finally look up at the clock it was almost five. The woman must not be coming, she joyously decided. Maybe she could convince Mrs. Clausen to keep her on another week.

Finally, Holly's curiosity overcame her better judgment and she had to ask. Trying to keep her voice indifferent, she said, "I thought you had some lady coming in for an interview today."

Mrs. Clausen sighed. "Oh, I did. She came at ten this morning, and I tell you, Holly, she'd be perfect. She's about my age, and she worked in a restaurant as a salad and side server. I offered her the job, but she said she had another interview at four, and she'd definitely let me know one way or the other late this afternoon."

Just then, almost as if it were cued in a movie script, the telephone rang. Mrs. Clausen answered, "KOE kitchen." There was a pause. "Oh, Mrs. Metzer, yes, yes." Holly felt as if she were dying. Without being able to hear both sides of the conversation, she couldn't begin to figure out what was going on. "Oh, I know what you mean." Mrs. Clausen's voice remained friendly. "No, it was a firm offer." It seemed to Holly that the conversation was dragging on forever, and forgetting all about the last batch of cookies that she was supposed to watch, she suddenly smelled burned pastry.

Holly ran to the oven to try to salvage some of the fancy dessert, and in doing so could no longer hear even Mrs. Clausen's part of the conversation. When Mrs. Clausen hung up the phone, she turned toward Holly and frowned. "I'm really so sorry, Mrs. Clausen; I'll stay late and make some more."

"Huh, what — Oh, the cookies. Don't worry about them, we've got enough without them." Mrs. Clausen sat down on the stool in the corner and wiped her hands on her white apron. Almost more to herself than to Holly she said, "I can't believe she didn't take the job. I just can't believe it."

Holly's heart lifted. She still had a chance. "Please, Mrs. Clausen. Let me try it. I know you don't want to hire me because I'm young, but I want to be a chef more than anything in the world. I love working here; just give me a chance and you'll see that it will work."

Mrs. Clausen sighed deeply. "Holly, I really like you. You're conscientious, polite, and talented, but you're also a cute girl in a boy-filled fraternity house. Believe me, girls are the most important topic in this house, and it would just be a matter of time until the boys were hanging around the kitchen or you were off madly in love or furiously angry with one of them. It's bound to happen. Any way you look at it, just as I start to really count on you, you'll disappear." Holly started to protest, but Mrs. Clausen held up her hand. "Holly, Greg hasn't been in this kitchen for an apple since school started. Why do you suppose he happened in today?"

Holly's face reddened. "I — I don't know. Maybe he just decided he wanted to start eating more nutritious food."

Mrs. Clausen folded her hands and refused to look at Holly. "Look, you've been a great help. I'll at least make sure that you get paid for this week."

The temper that had gotten Holly in trouble so many times before flared, and she blurted, "It's not fair. I don't care about the guys in this house. I care about becoming a great chef." The tears she was fighting added fury to her voice. "I care about going to the Cordon Bleu in France, but they only accept one out of every hundred applicants. Here I could get the kind of cooking knowledge I need to impress the board of directors; here I could start to earn the $2000 tuition that I'll have to pay if I ever do get accepted, only you're going to keep me from all that. Why? Have I shown up late? Have I been busy flirting? No, it's just that some day I might. Well, maybe the old person you hire will meet another old person on the way to work and never even show up." Holly tore off her apron and attempted to hang it on the hook. She was so angry that she missed twice.

Just then the smell of something burning again filled the air. Mrs. Clausen ran for the oven and Holly froze in horror. She'd done it again. "The garlic bread," she whispered as Mrs. Clausen pulled a charred loaf from the oven. "I put it in and then I got so upset. . . ." Her voice trailed off, but the statement didn't need finishing anyway. It was already obvious what had happened to the garlic bread.

That made two items she'd burned in less than an hour. A tall boy with freckles stuck his head in the door of the kitchen. "Everything okay? I was studying in the dining room, and I smelled. . . ." He stopped and sniffed. "Boy, it smells terrible in here! What happened, Mrs. C?"

Mrs. Clausen let him know that she had things firmly under control, and he left. Holly reached for her coat and her purse. No wonder Mrs. Clausen didn't want her around. She'd probably burn the house down. "Well," she said, trying to keep her lower lip from trembling, "thanks for letting me help these last few days; it was fun and I learned a lot." She started toward the kitchen door and then turned. "I'm sorry about the stuff I said. I hope you find a real good assistant. You deserve it."

"Holly," Mrs. Clausen said, her deep voice barking the name, "be here Monday at four. You work three hours every afternoon Monday through Friday and Saturday mornings from seven to eleven. The pay is four dollars an hour."

Usually not at a loss for words, Holly stood with her mouth open, unable to speak.

"Well, you want the job or not?"

"Want it? I'd love it," Holly said, still in a state of shock. "I'm never going to burn anything else the whole time I'm here. Oh, Mrs. Clausen, you won't be sorry; I promise you that you really won't. I'm going to work so hard, and don't you worry about my flirting or not being around when you need me. I don't care a thing about the boys of Kappa Omega Epsilon! The only thing I care about is this kitchen." Holly blissfully skipped out the door and headed for home, not having any idea how those words would come back to haunt her.

F*ive*

Friday night passed in a haze because Holly still couldn't believe that she'd gotten the job. Though her parents seemed delighted and proud, they didn't understand just how hard it had been to convince Mrs. Clausen. Even Holly couldn't figure out what had finally worked. After dinner, she'd retreated to her room to call Lani. Maybe when she told Lani the whole thing, she'd be able to see exactly what had finally changed Mrs. Clausen's mind. Holly dialed Lani's number, thinking she knew it better than her own phone number. The phone rang twice and then Lani answered. "Guess what," Holly exclaimed. "I've got great news!"

"You got the job permanently!" replied Lani.

Holly flopped on her bed. "How'd you know?"

"You just had to; I mean, you wanted it

so bad. I've been keeping my fingers crossed all day long that somehow that lady would change her mind and hire you." Holly beamed; no one could have a better friend than Lani.

"Listen, this thing could work out great for the whole crowd," Lani continued. "You can have your job, and the rest of us can get fixed up with college guys. How long do you think it will be before you know any of them well enough to set up blind dates?"

Holly sucked in her breath. This wasn't going to be easy, and she just hoped that somehow her friend would understand. "Lani, I can't fix you or anyone up with guys. I can't even have anything to do with the men of KOE. The whole reason Mrs. Clausen didn't want to give me the job was because she was sure I'd spend my time with the guys instead of in the kitchen working. I gave her my absolute promise that I didn't care anything about them. If I start trying to set up blind dates for you, and the guys start coming in the kitchen to ask about all of you, well, I'll lose the job I just killed myself to get."

There was a long pause on the other end of the phone. "You mean you're going to be around all those adorable guys every single day and none of us even gets to meet them? Oh, Holly."

For a minute Holly didn't know what to say. She could understand why Lani was disappointed. If the situation had been reversed, she'd have been upset herself, but that's the way it had to be. She just couldn't risk losing her job. "Listen, I'm probably not even going to get to know the guys. They really don't come in the kitchen much, and I'm certainly not going to go floating through the fraternity house."

"Well," replied Lani, "it's too bad." She giggled, and Holly knew that everything was going to be all right between them. "All I've got to say is that with all the creative cooking you like to do, I wish you could work on a recipe for romance."

Lani and Holly had been talking for almost an hour when Mrs. Hanson picked up an extension phone, saying she really needed to make a couple of calls. "Besides, you don't want that phone to permanently grow out of your ear."

Holly groaned at her mother's attempt at a joke, but agreed to hang up. Feeling contentedly tired, she decided to take a hot bath and go to bed, but as she was climbing into bed, her mom came in her room. "Dad and I have signed up for this ten mile bike-a-thon tomorrow. Why don't you come with us? It's going to be so much fun." Holly said that she was sure it was, but she'd pass. This was going to be her last Saturday of leisure, for after this weekend she'd be a working woman! The words whispered thrillingly in her mind as she fell asleep.

The next morning, Holly fuzzily awoke to

the insistent ringing of a bell. Rubbing the sleep from her eyes, she pounded on her alarm clock, wondering why she'd set it in the first place. But in spite of her pressing the off switch, the bell continued to sound. Holly shook her head, rubbed her eyes again, and stared at the clock. How could it possibly already be eleven? She never slept that late. The ringing bell sounded again, and suddenly awake, Holly realized that it wasn't her alarm at all. It was the doorbell, and since her parents were gone on their bike ride it was up to her to get it.

"I'm coming," she shouted, although there was no way that the person ringing the bell could hear her. She grabbed a robe and threw it on as she ran toward the door. Though her mother had warned her against it a hundred times, she flung open the door without even asking who it was, and then froze.

"Ah, I see we're dressed and ready to tackle the morning head on." With his familiar smirk, Greg was leaning up against the doorpost.

A jumble of thoughts filled Holly's mind, but she couldn't translate any of them into words. What was he doing here? What if Mrs. Clausen found out? How did he even know where she lived?

Greg waited for her to break the silence and when she didn't he said, "Well, this is a pretty interesting conversation. Care to join in? Actually, now that I think about it, it's fascinating to be standing on the doorstep of your house. Most people invite guests in, but this probably keeps the house cleaner."

Holly blushed. "Sorry, come on in," she said. "If you want to watch tv in the family room, I, uh, I'll be back in a few minutes." Greg walked into the family room and Holly beat a hasty retreat to her room to get dressed. She picked up a pair of old Levi's and then tossed them back in the bottom drawer, taking her new navy shorts instead.

"This can't be a good idea," she told herself, pulling on a cream-colored top. "He's arrogant, impossible, and I don't even like him. If Mrs. Clausen finds out he's here, I could lose my job before I ever start it. I don't know why I ever even let him in." Yet she continued to brush her hair, and apply a coat of the blue eye shadow she'd vowed to save for special occasions. "I'll just go right back out there and tell him that he has to leave."

She headed for the family room, but Greg didn't see her approach. He was deeply involved in a football game, and for the first time Holly had a chance to observe him without his blue eyes mockingly appraising her. In spite of herself, Holly was startled. He was without a doubt one of the cutest boys she'd ever seen. With his broad shoulders, sandy hair, and golden tan, he looked a lot like the guys the magazines used to advertise swim trunks, and as unbelievable as it seemed, he was sitting right here in her family room.

"Good game?" she said, entering the room and trying to keep her voice noncommittal.

"Hey, that's quite a transformation!" he exclaimed, looking up from the television. "When you first opened the door, I almost forgot why I came." Before Holly could say anything further, Greg shouted, "Oh no, a pass interception. Every time the Raiders really have a chance, they blow it!" He got up from his chair and snapped off the set. "I can't stand watching another stupid loss."

Greg turned around toward Holly and smiled. Her heart began doing flip flops, and she knew that kicking him out of her life wasn't going to be the easiest thing she'd ever done. There was an awkward silence, and then Greg recovered his wry grin. "Being the nice guy I am, I decided that since you're going to be waiting on me for the rest of the year, I'd get on your good side and take you to lunch first. That way I should be in line for extra helpings all year."

Holly blushed again and silently cursed the fair skin that showed her emotions so easily. "Greg, thanks, but I really can't."

"That's right." He snapped his fingers. "Of course not, I forgot. From the way you looked when you opened the door, you can't even have had breakfast yet. Okay, forget lunch. We'll try breakfast. Name the spot."

Holly looked at his sparkling blue eyes and rationalized that one breakfast couldn't hurt. After all, he had come all the way over to her house and he was really being quite nice.

She'd just go out to breakfast with him and explain that it was nothing personal but that she couldn't see him because she didn't want to lose her job. That was the adult way to handle the whole situation, and that was what she would do.

"How about Humpty Dumpty's right around the corner?" she asked, and then as soon as the words were out she wished she could take them back. Lots of her friends from school were there on Saturday mornings and she didn't need to run into them. Lani would never understand why after Holly's whole lecture about not being able to fix Lani up with a KOE that it was okay the very next morning for Holly to have breakfast with the cutest guy in the fraternity.

"Wait," Holly said, "let's go to Colony Kitchen instead."

"Ah, I like a decisive woman. We haven't even gotten to the car and she's already changed her mind." Fortunately, the top was down on the little MG to which he led her, and the whizzing wind and the roar of the motor prevented conversation and meant that she couldn't possibly stick her foot in her mouth anymore until breakfast. She didn't quite know why herself, but she had a growing suspicion that she should have told Greg he couldn't come in when she'd first seen him standing at the front door.

Well, I didn't, and we're here, she thought.

Besides, I can handle this, she bravely told herself.

Reaching the restaurant, Greg leaned across her to open her car door. She could smell the scent of his masculine after-shave lotion, and feel the warm pressure of his arm as it brushed her leg when he reached for the door handle. Oh Holly, she said silently, I think you're in trouble.

S^{ix}

There was no wait when they walked into Colony Kitchen. The college-aged hostess flashed a big smile at Greg, which he acknowledged as if it were his usual due from girls. She led the two of them to a table. "Your waitress will be right over, sir," she said, depositing two menus and giving another parting smile to Greg.

Holly took a menu and opened it quickly to cover her growing embarrassment. "Ah-ha," he said, eyes twinkling, "the poor girl is starving to death." Opening his own menu, he glanced for a minute and continued, "No wonder you like this place; it serves breakfast twenty-four hours a day."

"Greg, I don't usually get up this late. In fact, actually, I practically never — "

"Uh-huh, I know all about how you great-looking girls have to get your beauty sleep. You don't have to explain." He flashed that twenty-megawatt grin again, and Holly felt her stomach doing flip flops. Even if it was just a line, it was really quite wonderful that this gorgeous hunk of an older guy was sitting across from her telling her she was great-looking.

Realizing that the conversation had come to a halt, Holly began casting for something to get it going again. "How did you find out where I lived?"

In an exaggerated hush, Greg explained, "We spies have our ways of finding out important things, you know."

Holly laughed. "Aren't you ever serious about anything?"

"Sure," he replied, "I'm real serious about eating." Examining the menu again, he added, "I think I'll have a double burger, an order of fries, and a Coke float. What about you?"

"Oh, I'm not real hungry, I think I'll just get something to drink." Actually, Holly's stomach was feeling far too nervous to even consider the idea of receiving food.

Greg's blue eyes looked immediately troubled. "Hey, you know, I was just teasing you before. I don't care if you eat breakfast or lunch, or both if you want."

With that a gray-haired waitress appeared, ready to take their order. "I'll just have a Coke," Holly said.

Greg frowned and ordered his meal. "Will that be all?" asked the waitress.

"Well, I guess," he began, and then a smile

started across his face again. "No, actually, my friend would like the full pancake breakfast and a burger special."

The waitress stood staring for a minute as if she weren't sure whether she was being made fun of, but while Holly sat, too surprised to protest, Greg quickly reassured the waitress that he was quite serious about the order.

"I'm not sure that she'll really want both." The waitress had totally excluded Holly in the discussion. "There's quite a bit of food in each of those dishes. Either one is usually a full meal."

"I know," Greg said, shaking his head, "but she'll eat it all, I'll tell you; she eats every penny I make!"

Unable to quite believe what was going on, Holly watched the waitress turn on her heel and leave. "Greg!" Holly protested, finding her voice at last. "You can't be serious. We'd better call the waitress back right away. I can't even begin to eat all that food. Why on earth did you do that?"

"Well," he said, running a hand through his perfectly feathered golden hair, "I really love a good joke. Besides, I'd feel pretty stupid wolfing down lunch if you weren't even going to eat any breakfast. So what do you think?"

Holly's head was spinning. She'd never met anyone like this boy. He was handsome and exciting, but she continually felt as if she were on the edge of a precipice when he was around. She didn't mind not having the upper hand, but she'd at least like a shot at equal footing. "Well," she began, treading carefully, "I really don't think you should have ordered all that food, and I'll bet we can still call the waitress back and cancel some of it."

"Nah, it'll be worth it to see her put all that food in front of you and try to figure out how you eat like that and still keep that terrific figure you've got. But that wasn't what I was talking about. I mean, what do you think about us seeing each other, let's say, for example, my asking you out for a date on Friday night?"

"Me?"

Greg laughed, enjoying her shocked response. "Ah Holly, you're on to me. No, it really isn't you I want to ask out. You see, actually, I'm madly in love with our waitress and you're my way to get her insanely jealous."

Their waitress had to be at least fifty, and Holly blushed at Greg's teasing.

Before she could even respond, he continued, "So, should I take your lack of communication as a yes, pick-me-up-at-eight-o'clock, or a no, get-lost-creep-type answer?" He leaned across the table, and the smell of his after-shave didn't exactly make it easy to think. "Really, I'd recommend your saying yes."

Holly could tell that in spite of all his teasing, Greg was serious about asking her out.

She sighed deeply. For one moment she thought about forgetting Mrs. Clausen, forgetting her job, even forgetting the Cordon Bleu. Here she was sitting across from this incredible guy who'd just told her that she had a terrific figure and he wanted to take her out. "Greg," she replied slowly, "I'd really like that, but I just can't go out with you."

"Hmm, seeing another guy pretty regularly, huh?" Holly could detect a sudden change in Greg's confidence level and it made her like him even better.

"No, that's not it," she explained. "It's just that Mrs. Clausen wasn't too thrilled about hiring me in the first place, and to prove to her that I was serious about wanting to work, I promised her that I had absolutely no interest in any of the boys at KOE at all. So I just can't accept a date with you the very day after I made the promise. Do you understand?"

Before Greg could answer, the waitress arrived carrying a platter that was loaded with food. It looked as if she were getting ready to serve four instead of two. Placing Greg's burger and fries in front of him, she then cleared the condiments and napkin holder to his side of the table. First she put a plate of four gigantic pancakes in front of Holly. That was followed by a plate with four strips of bacon and a glass of orange juice. Next to that she squeezed in a bowl containing a tossed salad, a hamburger plate, an order of french fries, and a Coke. Still left on the waitress's tray were small containers of syrup and salad dressings. "I don't think these will fit on your table. Maybe you could just tell me which salad dressing and which syrup you want and I'll take the rest away."

"Oh, I think you can fit them in right here," said Greg, pulling his dishes closer to the edge of the tabletop. The waitress shook her head, plunked both items down, and marched away.

Greg and Holly looked at all the food on the table and simultaneously burst into laughter. Just as they'd regained some measure of composure, Greg noticed their waitress pointing them out to another waitress. "You know, I think you're going to be famous by the time we leave."

"Well, I'll have only you to thank," Holly laughed.

"Hey, I've got a great idea. Mrs. Clausen hates wasted food. I know because we guys get a lecture about the subject at least once a month. So why don't you just tell Mrs. Clausen you're going out with me until you use up the surplus of food I provided you."

Holly didn't say anything. "Okay," Greg continued, "bad idea, huh? Why does this job mean so much to you anyway?"

Holly stopped to think for a minute. After all, she barely knew this boy. Was she willing to share a dream? She began slowly, "Well, for one thing, I need the money, and for a second, I don't like to break promises once I make them, and for a third," Holly paused for a minute and then the words rushed out, "I want to be a chef one day, and this is good starting experience."

To her relief, Greg didn't even make one flip remark about her career choice. Instead, he seemed genuinely interested, and Holly found herself telling him all about why she wanted to be a chef and how hard it was for a woman to break into the ranks of the professionals. "The cooking school I want to go to is in Europe, and it only accepts one for every hundred who applies. I need whatever edge I can get, and I really think that I'll learn a lot from working for Mrs. Clausen." Holly continued her explanation. "If Mrs. Clausen knew me better, she'd know that I am not anything like that girl she hired as an assistant cook last year. She'd know that I could date a guy in the house and not have it affect my job, but she doesn't know that, and after last year, she's not exactly anxious to trust the word of a teenage girl."

The rest of breakfast seemed strangely subdued. Holly had a feeling that Greg didn't get turned down by very many girls for any reason, and it was easy to see why. She felt like pinching herself to make sure that this whole moment was real. In a way, she wished that a few of her friends could have at least seen her sitting here with Greg, but it was probably just as well that they didn't. It would only fuel their hopes that she could fix them up with Greg's friends.

Ignoring the fact that the table was still filled with food, the waitress returned to ask if they'd like some dessert. "No thanks," Holly replied quickly.

"Well, what do you have?" asked Greg.

"Oh, Greg, you're not . . ." Holly protested, and then they both started to laugh.

"I guess we'll pass, though I'm tempted to keep ordering," Greg told the waitress. "You see," he continued confidentially, "when you've got a first, last, and only breakfast with a girl, you have to make it a good one."

The waitress glanced at both of them as if they were nuts and said she'd return with the check. Greg looked at Holly appraisingly and, feeling his stare, she tried not to let it show that she was aware of his attention or that it was embarrassing her. "So," he began with that slow smile that made her heart pound, "does Cinderella have to get home immediately after the ball or would she like to go for a ride in her waiting carriage first?"

Holly knew she should probably just go home. With every additional minute they spent together, she was hating herself more and more for not being able to go out with Greg again. Part of her said that there was no point to continuing to torture herself. "But," said a small, nagging voice inside her, "you really want to be with Greg, and you won't get to after today. Besides, it isn't like you're accepting a whole other date with him, and it's such a pretty day for a ride in a convertible."

The next thing she knew, Holly was ensconced in Greg's car and they were practically flying down the freeway. The warmth of the sun filled the MG and Holly's heart as the miles passed quickly by. Because the wind and the sounds of the motor prevented Greg from making any more of the flip remarks that left Holly frantically searching for a clever retort, she was able to relax and enjoy the scenery around her. The desert had never looked more beautiful than it did today. Whether that was because of all the rain they'd had or because Greg was sitting in the seat next to her, Holly couldn't have said.

The two of them rode in silence for almost an hour, but it seemed to Holly that it had been no time at all before Greg was pulling the car back into her driveway. He switched off the motor, and suddenly it was very silent in the car.

Greg turned to look at her, and Holly tried to fight the lump that she felt was about to prevent her from speaking. "Thanks, Greg," she said, opening the car door, "I really had fun today, and I'm glad you came over." Her voice wavered in indecision for a minute, and then she continued, "And even though I'd really like to go out with you, I hope you understand why I just can't."

Holly knew how close she was to not understanding herself, and before she ended up risking the very job she'd practically killed herself to get, she called good-bye and hurried into her house. Shutting the door behind her, Holly flopped down on the living room sofa to review all that had happened that morning. The house was so quiet, she could hear the ticking of the hallway grandfather clock. Darn, she thought to herself, I didn't think anything in the world could lessen my excitement about getting this job! Part of her wished that Greg had never shown up to complicate things, but another, more knowing part of herself realized that she'd enjoyed this immensely and wouldn't have wanted to miss it for anything. "Well," she said aloud to the empty house, "it doesn't matter either way. Today was the beginning and the end of Greg, but someday, it will be worth it. I am going to be a famous chef, and nothing is going to stop me."

Just then the doorbell rang. Holly looked at the clock. Her parents. She certainly hoped they'd survived their grueling bike-a-thon. They usually only rode around the neighborhood, and she was sure they were going to be sore tomorrow, but at least they couldn't be in too bad a shape because they were getting back at a fairly respectable time. The doorbell rang again.

"Coming," she called, unlatching the door. "Did you guys survive?" she asked while flinging open the front door.

"Hi," said Greg as if he hadn't a care in the world. "I was just in the neighborhood; mind if I stop in?"

Seven

Oh, no, Holly said to herself, but aloud, she found herself inviting Greg in the house for the second time that day. As he comfortably settled himself in the family room, Holly could feel a sense of anger creeping into her infatuation. After all, hadn't she just explained that getting this job had meant the world to her and she'd risk losing it if she went out with him? Was he just ignoring everything she'd said because he was getting a kick out of manipulating some little high school kid? Her temper was just about to take over and tell him a thing or two when he beat it to the punch.

"Listen," he said, "I was thinking after I left you that I really do want to take you out. Of course, I understand how much your job means to you, and I certainly don't want you to lose it. So what if I pretended I didn't even know you around the frat house. Who'd have to know that I was seeing you?"

Holly's heart began to beat a little faster, but a part of her was compelled to say, "But that would be lying to Mrs. Clausen after I promised—"

Greg cut in. "Hey, I don't say you should go around lying. It's just that you explained it yourself. Mrs. Clausen isn't being fair. You know you're not like the girl last year. You're going to do a great job, and eventually, Mrs. Clausen will recognize that. Why should we get penalized from going out until she does?"

It sounded valid to Holly, and then Greg continued, "Of course, if all that was just some line because you don't want to go out with me, well, I guess my ego can stand the truth. Just tell me, and I'll get out of your life." He looked at her questioningly and in his look there was such a sense of vulnerability.

Holly found herself saying, "Oh, no, I'd really like to go out with you."

Greg grinned as if he'd known that was the answer she'd give. "Well, I'm glad that's settled. How about if we go to a movie this Friday night?"

After Holly agreed, Greg stayed around for another half hour talking and kidding. He was just getting ready to leave when the doorbell rang and her parents arrived. "Oh, lord," said Mr. Hanson, sinking into the easy chair in the family room. "I think I'm going to die."

Holly introduced Greg to her folks and explained that they'd just finished a bike-a-thon. "I think," said her mother, "that it might be more appropriate to say that the bike-a-thon finished us."

Greg laughed. "I sympathize. One time the guys in the fraternity pledged to swim laps for charity. I got all these sponsors, so everyone was egging me on to keep swimming so we'd get more money. By the time I finished, I was so tired that I thought I'd rather drown than have to get out of the pool. Of course, that was the bad news; the good news is that with a hot bath and some sleep, I felt much better the next day. What was your bike-a-thon for, anyway?"

Mrs. Hanson explained that they were teachers at Tempe High, and every year the faculty did a different project to raise scholarship money for outstanding senior students. "This project," said Mr. Hanson, "must have been thought up by a kid who wanted to kill his teachers."

The Hansons and Greg chatted for a few minutes longer, and unlike the high school boys that Holly knew, Greg didn't seem the least bit nervous or intimidated by being around parents. In fact, it looked as if everyone was really enjoying the conversation.

After he left, her father raised one quizzical eyebrow. "One of the side benefits of working at the KOE house?" he questioned.

"Well, sort of," she explained, telling her parents of her promise to Mrs. Clausen and the reason she'd had to make it. Holly never lied to her parents, and in turn, they believed that unless she was doing something dangerous to herself or others, she should make her own decisions and learn from her own mistakes. "I know I can do the job and still see Greg. It's just that until Mrs. Clausen knows that, too, I'm not going to let anyone in the fraternity find out that I'm dating Greg." Holly sighed. "Mrs. Clausen is a nice lady, and I really didn't get the job there to meet the guys, but it doesn't seem right that because I did meet one I liked, I can't be with him. I guess the worst part of this whole setup is that I can't tell my friends I'm going to go out with Greg."

"You know, Holly, you might remember that once you start a lie, it's sometimes pretty hard to keep up with it," warned her mother.

"I know, Mom, and I'll tell everyone the truth as soon as I can. Besides, it's probably no big deal." Half to her parents and half to herself, she continued, "He may not even want to take me out a second time."

Lani called a few minutes later and asked what was going on, and Holly felt a momentary pang when she said, "Oh, nothing much. How about you?"

"Well, I was leafing through a copy of one of my mom's magazines, and I saw an article that said you could make your budget stretch further if you made casseroles, so I thought I'd call you and tell you. Then you could tell Mrs. Clausen, and she'd be real impressed."

"Thanks, Lani, that's really sweet," Holly said, "but I've a feeling that Mrs. Clausen already knows about casseroles."

"Maybe so, but I'll keep trying. The sooner Mrs. Clausen quits being an absolute witch, the sooner we can all meet the KOE guys."

Hanging up the phone, Holly thought to herself that Lani just didn't understand. Mrs. Clausen wasn't a witch at all, unless you considered the magic she could create in a kitchen. She made everything look absolutely effortless, and Holly hoped that one day she could be as accomplished. Holly just knew that once Mrs. Clausen discovered how serious she was about becoming a chef, they'd be good friends.

The rest of the weekend passed uneventfully, but far too slowly for Holly's taste. By Sunday night, she was so excited that her stomach was turning somersaults. "This is dumb," she told herself. "It isn't going to be one bit different to walk into the KOE kitchen tomorrow than it was last week." But somehow, that wasn't true. Last week she'd been too busy fighting to get the job to let nervousness get in her way. But now that she actually had it, she didn't want to do anything to let Mrs. Clausen down.

Tossing and turning for what seemed like

forever, Holly worried that she might burn some food again, follow one of Mrs. Clausen's recipes incorrectly, or worst of all, have Greg show up in the kitchen again. Mrs. Clausen was a very perceptive person, and Holly was worried that Mrs. Clausen would see that Holly had lied to her if Greg happened to pop in the kitchen this week. But Holly couldn't very well call him in the middle of the night and tell him of her fears. Instead she crossed her fingers, hoped for the best, and eventually fell asleep.

At lunch the next day, Lani announced to the whole crowd that Holly had actually gotten the job at the KOE house. Marlene had been looking for a job for the past two months, Alicia had, too, and Becky was on a waiting list to do volunteer work, so everyone was pretty impressed with Holly's accomplishment. But Lani was taking no chances. She built the story up to her own exaggerated peak. "And there were at least twenty other people for the job. Holly was the youngest one, and the cook at the fraternity house is a mean old woman who would barely even speak to Holly. But one day she was so far behind that she let Holly help her. When she saw that Holly was ten times better than anyone else she could possibly hire, she had to give her the job!"

"Can't you just see it?" said Marlene. "After our ten-year high school reunion, Holly will invite us all to come visit her in

Europe where she'll probably be the Queen of England's personal chef."

"Ah, come on, you guys," said Holly modestly, but to herself she thought, Why not? After all, someone had to get the job. It might take more than ten years, but Holly just knew that one day she really was going to be a great chef. As conversation swirled around her, Holly imagined herself working at Buckingham Palace. The picture was a little fuzzy because she'd never even seen photographs of Buckingham Palace. Maybe I'll work in the White House, she thought, and the very idea sent chills up and down her spine.

There she'd be, called into the Oval Office waiting to have her menu accepted for an important state dinner. The President would be sitting at his desk explaining that he was entertaining a world leader, and she'd assure the President that the dinner would be flawless. He'd say, "I know it, Holly. That's why I asked you to be the White House chef."

"Holly, what do you think?"

"Huh?" said Holly.

"Do you agree with Alicia or not?"

"I uh. . . ." Holly stumbled realizing that she'd been totally oblivious to the conversation. "I'm not sure."

"You seem like you're a million miles away. What are you thinking about anyway?" asked Alicia.

Holly blushed. She couldn't very well say

that she'd been thinking about becoming the White House chef. It sounded absolutely ridiculous, so she changed the subject. "I was just wondering how hard Mrs. McIntee's English test is going to be. Has anybody heard?"

"How hard are Mrs. McIntee's tests, usually?" Alicia groaned.

"Don't you wonder," asked Lani, "if her face would crack if she ever really smiled?"

"Ugh, I can never remember the difference between a restrictive and a nonrestrictive clause. Anybody know?" asked Becky, and without waiting for an answer she added, "It doesn't matter. I don't have a prayer of a chance of passing this test. I never have understood punctuation very well."

Holly glanced through her book. Even though her parents were very proud of her getting the job at the fraternity house, they'd made it perfectly clear that she could only work if her grades didn't drop. There was absolutely no arguing with two school teachers that grades weren't important, and Holly had learned long ago that it was easier not even to try. Since there was no way she wanted to risk the job she'd just worked so hard to get, she began going over her notes again.

When the last bell of the day finally rang, Holly slammed her notebook shut, heading quickly for her locker. Jamming books in her backpack, she slung it over her shoulder, grimaced at the weight, and headed for the front door of Tempe High. It was going to be such a relief to get to concentrate on working instead of worrying about the people who were being interviewed to be her replacement. She wondered what Mrs. Clausen was going to be cooking for tonight's dinner. Did she have menus posted for the week or for a whole month? Did the boys get a say in what Mrs. Clausen made?

Her mind racing furiously with unanswered questions, Holly arrived in front of the KOE house. As she approached the front walk, she thought of the first day that she'd arrived here, and the way Greg had watched her standing at the front door. Quickly, she looked around, but there were no boys in sight. Even the fraternity living room was empty today. Good, she thought to herself. The less she saw of Greg at the fraternity house, the fewer people who were likely to guess that he was someone special to her.

Entering the kitchen, she called, "Hi, Mrs. Clausen. I'll just wash my hands, and then I'll be ready to start."

Mrs. Clausen looked at the clock in surprise. "You're a half an hour early!" she exclaimed.

Holly blushed, "Well, school was out, and I was anxious to get here. I mean, now that I'm a real employee and everything."

"All right." Mrs. Clausen chuckled. "The first thing a real employee does is quit cutting through the living room of the fraternity house. There's a back door over here," she said, showing it to Holly, "and from it you can come directly into the kitchen." Holly had wondered where that door led last week, but she hadn't felt that she had the right to ask.

"Now, today, I want you to start by peeling those potatoes." Holly's heart sank, but she tried not to let it show. Peeling potatoes wasn't like real cooking at all, and she crossed her fingers mentally, and hoped that Mrs. Clausen wasn't going to make her spend every day doing it. "Oh, and there's an extra apron over there. You're welcome to use it. It'll probably keep your clothes cleaner."

Holly went to the hook and pulled the starched white apron over her head, tying the string around her waist. Appraising herself, she decided that with a tall white hat, she might even look like a chef. Walking over to the big stainless steel sink, she began to scrub the potatoes. "So," she asked Mrs. Clausen, "what are these going to be used for?"

"What?" shouted Mrs. Clausen from across the kitchen.

"Oh, nothing," called Holly, feeling silly. It was impossible to make small talk with Mrs. Clausen way over on the other side of the kitchen. She wished that she could see what Mrs. Clausen was making at the pastry board, but even when she craned her neck, she couldn't see exactly what the cook was doing, and so Holly resigned herself to facing the pile of potatoes that lay in front of her.

She thought that if her friends could see her now, they might not think her job was so glamorous. There was no doubt that today's task was certainly a long, long way from becoming the White House chef, but, she told herself, putting down one potato and beginning fiercely to peel another, it was a beginning, and everyone had to start somewhere.

Eight

The potatoes Holly had finished peeling were put into a wonderful-smelling stew which was going to be served for dinner along with loaves of bread that Mrs. Clausen had made from scratch.

"Holly, check the sign-out sheet for dinner, please, and leave a count for the hashers as to how many table settings they'll need," Mrs. Clausen said.

Holly looked perplexed.

"Hashers," said Mrs. Clausen, "is the name the boys use for the food servers, and the sign-up sheet allows the boys to bring a guest for dinner. However, no boy can bring more than two guests a month."

Holly went into the dining room and checked the bulletin board. The guest slots on the sign-up sheet for that night were completely filled. No wonder! thought Holly, as her stomach growled, and the smell of the stew wafted through the air. Her cousin Marie would never believe that college food could taste like this. Last time she'd been home from her college in Maine, Marie had complained bitterly that eating the food on campus was like being force-fed garbage. Holly smiled to herself, wondering what Marie would say after seeing one of Mrs. Clausen's meals.

Dinner was just about ready, and Holly was dying for at least a little taste of the stew Mrs. Clausen had made, but she didn't yet begin to have enough confidence in herself or her job status to ask for it. Maybe, she thought, it was unprofessional for a cook's assistant to ask for tastes of the food. She hoped right up until the time she left that Mrs. Clausen would ask her if she'd like a little sample, but nothing was said, and Holly left the fraternity house starved. Ironic that after spending the afternoon immersed in food, she had eaten nothing. Her hungry stomach pushed her quickly toward home.

"So, how does it feel to have finished your first day of work as an official employee of the KOE house?" asked Holly's father over their dinner.

Holly grinned. "I love it, I really do, but I'm absolutely beat." The full extent of that exhaustion hit her as she flopped on her bed to begin her homework. Doing only that which absolutely had to be done, she went to sleep early. The next few days were almost as tiring. Her status among her friends, however, had immediately increased. At first, each lunch period, her friends demanded a full run-down of her previous day at work. However, they lost interest in her job rather quickly after she assured them that she hadn't even so much as been in the dining room when the guys were there eating and she didn't plan to be. "Listen," she told her friends, "I probably wouldn't even recognize a KOE on campus unless he was wearing a fraternity sweat shirt with the Greek letters clearly printed on the front."

"What about Jeff?" Lani asked.

"Well, yeah, Jeff's a KOE, but we all knew him from school last year."

"I thought you kinda liked him," Alicia said.

"I did," Holly replied. "But that was more than a year ago, and nothing ever came of it. Truthfully, I haven't even seen him at KOE except for the one day I ran into him when he told me about Mrs. Clausen. Actually, I probably should thank him for helping me get the job. If I see him, I will. Anyway, Alicia, I'm not at all interested in him now, which is probably just as well. After all, I'm sure he knows I got the job, and he hasn't even stopped in to congratulate me, so he certainly couldn't be very interested in me."

"Boy, Holly, how can you work in a whole house filled with cute college fraternity guys and have no romance in your life!" commented Becky.

Holly just smiled. Friday was approaching very rapidly, and with its arrival would come her date with Greg. In fact, that evening after work, he'd called to ask if she had anything special in mind. When she said it didn't matter, he laughed. "Good, prepare for a surprise!" he said. "I'll pick you up at seven-thirty."

Holly was left listening to a dial tone and wondering just what exactly she was getting herself into this time. She wished she could call Lani and tell her all about Greg, and then ask her what to wear tomorrow night, but of course that was out of the question.

Friday, Holly tried to hurry through her kitchen duties. Darn, she said to herself, I should have told Greg to pick me up at eight o'clock instead of seven-thirty, so I'd have enough time to get ready without rushing so fast.

"Holly, please soften that peanut butter a little," Mrs. Clausen called. "I'll put it out with bread for the boys for snacks tomorrow. On Saturdays some of the boys' sleep schedules don't correspond too well with mealtimes, and I always try to leave some food out that can keep all day."

Holly took a gigantic jar of peanut butter from the pantry shelf and carried it to the countertop. Even with the jar opener, she strained to get the lid off. Finally succeeding, she wondered exactly what she was supposed to do next. The peanut butter didn't exactly look creamy. In fact, it didn't look as if it was ever coming out of the jar. In the camp kitchen, she'd sometimes taken a knife, run it in hot water, and then swirled it through the peanut butter, but that wasn't going to be sufficient for this huge mess.

Mrs. Clausen must have seen her staring at the peanut butter looking perplexed, for the next thing she knew, Mrs. Clausen was at her side with a bottle of sesame oil. "Add this one drop at a time and then stir. Besides making it creamier, the peanut butter will taste nuttier."

Holly did as she was told and with amazement watched the peanut butter look as good as it had when it had been fresh. It was a tip she'd try to remember, although she really didn't think she'd be serving much peanut butter as a fancy chef. Still, Mrs. Clausen was always pulling food saving tips out of her head. She was amazing, seeming to have a solution to every problem. Starting a notebook of hints at the beginning of the week, Holly had already filled four pages in it. She'd probably have added even more, but since she didn't know Mrs. Clausen that well yet, she hadn't brought the notebook to work and had only added what she'd remembered after she'd gotten home each night.

At five o'clock Holly gave up all thoughts of getting out of the kitchen early that night. Mrs. Clausen seemed to have a hundred little things for her to do to help get ready for weekend meals. Trying not to let her impatience show, Holly mentally checked off the things she wouldn't have time to do when she got home from work. Scratch the leisurely bath, and trying on both of the outfits again that she was still trying to choose between.

"Holly?"

"Yes, Mrs. Clausen," Holly said, interrupting her mental check list and hoping that Mrs. Clausen was about to send her on her way.

"You seem rather jumpy today. Is everything okay? I mean, you don't have any regrets about taking this job, do you?"

Holly's eyes widened. Mrs. Clausen didn't miss a thing. "Oh no," she emphasized. "I love the job, and I'm really learning a whole lot. I really appreciate your hiring me."

Mrs. Clausen looked at Holly with a fixed eye and a half a smile. "Good. I guess maybe you're just tired from the week. You seem preoccupied, but I want you to know that you've done a good job this week, real good. Now, just don't go getting all flighty on me."

"Oh, I won't," promised Holly. Five minutes later, she was finally out the door of the fraternity house and on her way home, feeling a giggly sort of anticipation. It's a good thing Mrs. Clausen can't see me now! she thought.

Holly didn't think that her date was for dinner because Greg hadn't said anything about dinner. Of course, she thought, kicking a stone and watching it bounce along the street, he really hadn't said it wasn't for dinner, either.

Upon arriving home, she decided that she really didn't have time to eat either way. "I'm skipping dinner," she told her mom, and took an apple to her room to munch while she got ready. At least it would keep her stomach from growling if they didn't eat again, but leave her hungry enough in case they did.

Dressing carefully, she pulled on her navy slacks and her white button-down shirt, and finished the outfit with the plaid sweater vest she'd gotten the previous weekend. Putting a brush through her dark hair, she looked in the mirror and added a touch more lip gloss. The doorbell rang just as she was finishing dressing, and before going into the living room, she fixed her reflection with a look and warned it to quit letting Greg have the upper hand. She told herself that though her two brothers were grown and gone now, they'd given her plenty of training in how to take teasing and how to give it right back.

"Holly, are you coming?" called her mother.

Holly gave her reflection one last glance. "I hope you know what you're doing," she told it. "If Mrs. Clausen hears about this, you're dead."

Once they were seated in Greg's car, Holly asked Greg what he'd planned for the evening. "You don't give a girl much information that helps her know what to wear."

"You look great. Don't worry about a thing," he replied, putting his key in the ignition and starting the motor. But this time, Holly was not to be deterred by its roar, and she insisted on knowing what was up.

Reluctantly, Greg said, "Okay, okay, I give in. But you're spoiling a terrific surprise. We're going to a chocolate-tasting festival in Scottsdale. I figured you like to cook, you want to be a gourmet chef, so you might as well get right to the best part of the meal. It's supposed to be a big deal. Dessert people from all over the Valley could enter chocolate desserts, and they're giving prizes for the best ones."

On the one hand, Holly was really touched that he'd gone to so much trouble to tailor their date to something unusual that he thought she'd like. On the other hand, she was horrified, and that's what popped out of her mouth.

"Greg, we can't go there. We're bound to run into Mrs. Clausen. I mean, that sounds like her perfect idea of how to spend an evening."

"I agree," Greg said earnestly, while continuing to steer the car toward Scottsdale. "That's why I told her all about it. I even showed her an article in the paper about the chocolate festival."

"You did what?" Holly sputtered.

They'd pulled up to a light, and her words pierced the air as the car came to a stop. "I invited Mrs. Clausen to go to the chocolate festival, told her I was sure she'd love it there, but don't worry, we're covered." From under the seat, he pulled out two plastic noses attached to glasses and eyebrows. "Put one on; no one will ever recognize you."

Holly was a mixture of so furious and hurt that she couldn't speak at all. How dare he purposely try to get her fired? She'd kill him. She'd. . . .

Greg pulled into a parking place. "You know, I know it's a cliché, but you really are awfully cute when you get mad. I guess I forgot to tell you that Mrs. Clausen wasn't at all interested in attending this festival. Matter of fact, she pulled me into the kitchen to see some award she'd won in France for pastry-making, and said that there was no way she'd go watch some amateurs in some silly little contest in Arizona. So the coast is clear, but I still think the masks would be funny."

He slipped one on his face. "So what do you think? Is it an improvement?"

"Absolutely," she said, feeling her anger melting away. She smiled and fixed him with a look that she hoped was winsome and yet still indignant. "You know, there's an old Chinese proverb. He who teases, gets teased back, and you better watch out because I've had two older brothers for practice."

"Hmmm," he grinned, "that sounds like a direct challenge, and I never turn down a challenge." With that, Greg took her hand to help her out of the car and then kept it tucked in his own as they began to walk toward the festival grounds.

Nine

They entered a large building. Greg handed a lady wearing an apron that said I LOVE CHOCOLATE two tickets, and in return, she gave him plates, plastic knives, and forks. "Welcome. Are you familiar with the set-up?" Greg and Holly shook their heads no. "Cut yourselves pieces of whatever desserts you wish to try. You're also welcome to help yourselves to any of the recipes that are next to the desserts. At ten-thirty a panel of judges will announce this year's Chocolate Fantasy winners." The woman turned her attention to the next arriving group, and Holly and Greg walked into a huge room filled with tables covered with white cloths and laden with fantastic chocolate delights.

Chocolate-orange cheesecake, chocolate lace cookies, chocolate refrigerator cake, chocolate dipped strawberries, chocolate mousse cake. The list went on and on, and Holly and

Greg sampled until their eyes and their stomachs could absolutely hold no more. "So," said Greg, "it's almost ten-thirty. Which recipe does one of America's future great chefs think will win?"

"The mousse cake. No, the chocolate almond bark. No — oh, I don't know. What do you think?"

Greg shook his head, and his sapphire-blue eyes twinkled. "Hey, you're supposed to be the expert. Guess the chef-in-training still has some learning to do." He looked at the recipes clutched in Holly's hand, "Hmmm, I knew it would work. I bring you here on a date, you collect lots of great recipes, then we start having chocolate feasts at the frat house, right?"

Holly laughed, but secretly, a little part of her wondered if that was indeed why he'd taken her to the chocolate festival. The magical glow of the evening faded as she tried to ignore a nagging sort of doubt about his motives. All the way home, she rode in silence, brooding inwardly. So what if he doesn't ask me out again? It would probably be for the best anyway, she tried to convince herself, unconvincingly.

The top was down on the car, and the sky was filled with stars. Reaching her house, Greg made no rush to open Holly's door. "Well," he said, his rugged profile reflected in the moonlight, "you never answered me. Do I get more of these great chocolate desserts or not?"

"Gee, I'm sure if you asked Mrs. Clausen, she'd be happy to help you make some of them," Holly said with a sweet sense of sarcasm.

"Cute, real cute." Greg cocked his head and grinned. His long arms seemed to stretch casually out in a yawn, and then Holly felt them slip around her shoulders. His face was only inches away from hers as he softly said, "Holly, maybe it's not really the chocolate I'm interested in."

Holly felt her breath suck in. But before she could say or do anything, Greg released her, jumped out of his side of the car, and came around to open her door. Just before she walked in the front door, he added, "On the other hand, I really do love good desserts."

Since she couldn't tell any of her friends about Greg, and her parents weren't particularly pleased with her deceit in the matter, there was no one she could talk to about him and no one she could ask about how to tell when he was kidding and when he was being serious. She tried to put him out of her mind while she plodded through geometry homework, but there in the middle of a difficult proof, she could still see his smiling face. I wish I could put some sort of realometer on him, she thought. Then maybe I could know when he's telling the truth and when he's not.

Sunday faded its way into Monday morning, which slowly made its way to lunchtime. The girls at Holly's table were full of discussion of their weekend plans, but Holly was strangely silent. "You okay?" Lani asked.

"Yeah, I'm fine. I guess I'm just a little tired." And she thought to herself that if Greg continued to ask her out, she was going to have to come up with something better than always being too tired to be with her friends.

When the final bell rang, Holly was more than ready for it to happen. Stopping for a snack, she made her way to the fraternity house, and Mrs. Clausen's kitchen. However, much to her surprise, Mrs. Clausen had company when Holly walked in the door.

"Holly, this is Jeff Leonard."

"Hi," Holly stammered awkwardly, wondering what on earth Jeff was doing in the kitchen and whether she should pretend that she didn't know him.

Jeff took the decision out of her hands. "Oh yeah," he said, barely glancing up, "we've met. She used to be in some class of mine in high school." With that he turned his full attention back to Mrs. Clausen, and the two of them huddled over some papers, making notations as they went.

Holly stood helplessly waiting for some instructions from Mrs. Clausen and wishing that she could at least look efficient while Jeff was in the kitchen. Finally, Mrs. Clausen looked up and said, "Oh, you want to peel those potatoes over there? We're having french fries tonight."

Holly trudged to the sink and began to peel. At this rate, she'd be more ready for KP duty in the army than training for a world class chef. As she peeled, she stared at Jeff and Mrs. Clausen, wondering what on earth they might be discussing. Holly decided that the KOE boys certainly didn't possess any one look. Jeff and Greg couldn't have been more dissimilar. Greg's sandy blond hair and twinkling blue eyes were quite a contrast to Jeff's curly dark locks and big brown eyes. There was something rather kind and decent-looking about Jeff, while Greg spelled danger with every glance. Her heart began racing a little at just the thought of him.

The back door to the kitchen banged open and the housewares man strolled in. "Ah," he said, looking at Holly, "so you're still around. Well, good for you. Helen, I've got those knives you ordered."

Mrs. Clausen excused herself from Jeff and went to see the houseware man's wares. Jeff winked at Holly. "Congratulations," he whispered softly. Holly glanced to see if Mrs. Clausen was watching them, and Jeff caught her look. "Don't worry," he continued, "I won't do a thing to spoil your chances for continued employment. Mrs. Clausen will never even know that we're friends."

"Thanks," Holly whispered back.

After Jeff left, Holly was dying to ask Mrs. Clausen what Jeff had been doing in the kitchen, but she said nothing.

"So," inquired Mrs. Clausen, wiping her hands on her large white apron and fixing Holly with a no-nonsense look. "How was your weekend?"

Taken aback at Mrs. Clausen's interest, and wondering if this was her way of saying that she knew Holly had broken her promise and gone out with a KOE boy, Holly nervously gulped, "I uh, I went to a chocolate festival."

"Really?" Mrs. Clausen said questioningly. "It certainly couldn't have been very good. Most of the people who cook with chocolate don't know what they're doing!" She sighed. "You should have seen the wonderful creations that James, my husband, made in New York." She sighed again, and the faraway look in her eyes told Holly that Mrs. Clausen was lost in memories. Realizing that Holly was watching, Mrs. Clausen looked embarrassed, and said, "That reminds me, I planned to make a big chocolate sheet cake for tonight. I do it once a month for all the boys who have birthdays during the month. Would you go flour the pan?"

Holly took out the large sheet cake pan, and got out the margarine and white flour. Having greased the pan, she began to flour it. "What are you doing?" called Mrs. Clausen.

Holly stopped, confused. "Didn't you ask me to flour the pan?"

Mrs. Clausen walked over to her. "Ah, yes, but definitely not with this." As she talked she took the pan from Holly's hands and dumped out the white flour. "Always use cocoa to flour your pan," she said, handing it to her. "Chocolate cakes taste ever so much better that way."

"Right," said Holly, making a mental note of the information. There was so much she wanted to ask Mrs. Clausen, and patience was certainly not one of Holly's long suits, but something told her that she'd better not push the cook.

That night as she trudged home, questions not only of food filled her mind. She thought again about Jeff and wondered what on earth he'd been doing in the kitchen and why he and Mrs. Clausen had looked so busy. At least Mrs. Clausen didn't suspect that she and Jeff even really knew each other. It was sweet of him to congratulate her and let her know that he was pleased she'd gotten the job.

Now, if Greg had been in the kitchen, she told herself, he'd have teased me by making me think he was going to slip and say something that would get me in trouble. I'd have been dying inside, sure that Mrs. Clausen would figure everything out, and he'd be enjoying my embarrassment. She sighed. It didn't really matter, because she'd not heard a word from Greg since their date. Maybe he had only taken her out to make sure she'd have lots of good dessert recipes for the fraternity. After all, he had said that he'd asked Mrs. Clausen if she was interested in going to the festival. Maybe he'd only asked Holly as a last resort.

By the time she reached the house, Holly had a splitting headache. Knowing that she still had a geometry test to study for definitely did not lessen the pain she was feeling.

When Holly saw the geometry test the next day, she wondered why she'd tried to wade through studying at all. The test was absolutely impossible. At one point she erased so hard that she actually tore her paper.

Hmm, she thought, finally giving up and turning in her paper, if I own a restaurant and my geometry teacher comes in to eat, I'm going to tell him that I can't possibly take his reservation for dinner. Holly was really getting into her daydream. She could just see Mr. Hall, dressed in his same rumpled suit, looking defeated and sad as he watched all the people inside Holly's restaurant having a wonderful time. Good, she thought, it would serve him exactly right. Defeated and sad is just the way he leaves all his students feeling!

Somehow, visualizing Mr. Hall in front of her restaurant helped the day go faster. When school ended, Holly rushed toward the KOE house, not even stopping for her customary ice cream cone on the way. She told herself that it was just because she wasn't hungry, but she knew the possibility of running into Greg had something to do with it. Today was Thursday already, and she hadn't heard a word from him.

In spite of her earlier arrival, Holly did not run into anyone at all except, of course, Mrs. Clausen who was looking rather hot and bedraggled. "I've been baking bread all day today," said Mrs. Clausen, "and I'm beat! I guess I'm just not as young as I used to be. How would you feel if I sat in this chair and supervised, and you made the meal tonight?"

"Really?" exclaimed Holly. "You mean it?"

Mrs. Clausen laughed. "Yes, I mean it, but you better pay careful attention to what I say. My boys aren't used to having their dinners destroyed."

At first Holly was so nervous that she was sure she would make a terrible mistake, but Mrs. Clausen's instructions were clear and to the point, and her explanations and tips were fascinating. She made it seem so easy to juggle the preparation of three or four things at one time. The two hours simply flew by as Holly worked. She felt as if she should be paying Mrs. Clausen instead of the other way around.

"Well, I guess that's about everything," said Mrs. Clausen. "The hashers should be coming in soon, and you've got the food all ready to serve."

Holly looked around in amazement. Everything really was finished. Maybe it wasn't the most complex meal in the world, but Holly had managed to time finishing two vegetables, salad, and meat loaf so that all would be done perfectly when served. She'd even managed to create a dessert to be served after dinner.

One of the two hashers who had been hired to be waiters for the fraternity dinners walked in the kitchen door. As far as Holly could tell, neither of them had any personality at all. Even Mrs. Clausen seemed to sense that they definitely were no threat to distracting her assistant cook from the duties at hand.

Holly gathered her things reluctantly. She hated to leave this place with its oversized pots and pans, and wonderful aromas. "Maybe," said Mrs. Clausen, "you should stay around until dinner starts. If you want, once the boys are seated, I'll introduce you as the cook of this meal."

Holly's eyes widened. Her first thought was that it would be a perfect opportunity to see Greg and to remind him that she was still around. Her next thought was that she looked a mess. Glancing in the stainless steel refrigerator door, she saw a somewhat distorted reflection, but it was good enough to convince her that her hair had frizzed from the heat of the cooking, and her outfit was smudged where food had spattered and missed the apron she was wearing. But her final thought clinched her decision. What if Mrs. Clausen is testing me? What if she wants to see if I really am interested in meeting the boys instead of in cooking?

In the space of an instant, Holly smiled at Mrs. Clausen and said casually, "Thanks, but I think I'll be going home. It was sure fun to get to make everything, but I don't care about getting credit for it from a bunch of boys I don't even know."

Holly could see Mrs. Clausen fighting a smile. Score one for me, Holly thought. That's what Mrs. Clausen wanted to hear.

All the way home, Holly thought of the steps in preparing the meal. She'd helped the cook with parts of a meal at camp, and she'd peeled a ton of potatoes for Mrs. Clausen at the KOE house, but this was the first time she'd really had a chance to make a whole meal for fifty people. More than ever, Holly was sure that she wanted to be a chef. To create delectable food that people enjoyed eating would be a tremendous thrill.

"Mom," she called, excitedly swinging open the front door of her house. "Guess what I got to do today?" All through dinner her parents heard the step-by-step recreation of the KOE meal, and after dinner as she helped her mother with the dishes, Holly was still bubbling over her accomplishments. "You know, one good thing about being an important chef is that I'll just get to make the food and I won't ever have to clean up dirty dishes."

Mrs. Hanson laughed. "Well, until then, I appreciate your help in the kitchen. And when we're through here, you'd better go finish your homework. You know our deal. If your grades drop, your job ends."

Holly frowned, laid down the terry cloth

dish towel she'd been using to dry dishes with, and grabbed her backpack, which she'd dropped just inside the front door. Turquoise blue in color, it was always easy to spot, especially among the lavender and pink backpacks that all the other girls at school had. At the beginning of the year, everyone was calling everyone else to decide on what colors would be in, and as soon as they'd all decided, Holly had deliberately chosen something different. It was her way of saying she didn't want to be just like everyone else. Heaving the backpack over her shoulder, Holly stifled a yawn, and headed toward her room. The sudden exhaustion that engulfed her would have to wait. She couldn't risk losing this incredible job to bad grades in school.

Dropping everything on her bed, she kicked off her loafers and sat cross-legged on her bed. Unzipping her backpack, she pulled out her geometry book, and gasped. I don't believe it, she thought. How could this possibly be?

Ten

Holly picked up the piece of notebook paper that was lying on top of her geometry book and read the scribbled pencil words again. "Are we on for this Friday night?" she read aloud. There was no signature, but Holly knew exactly from whom the note had come.

How had Greg gotten this in her backpack without her knowledge? Before she could figure out an answer to that question, her mind jumped ahead. He had actually asked her out again. He must have had a good time last Friday! She squeezed her hands together in anticipation of going out with Greg again, but then a puzzled look crossed her face.

How would he even know if she could go out or not? What kind of a way was this to ask someone out? Indignantly, she thought, It's Thursday night. How dare he just assume that I'm around whenever he shows up in my life! Does he just plan to show up here tomorow night? she wondered angrily. How am I supposed to react? Maybe he'll still call tonight . . . but should I tell him I already have plans since it's so late?

A terrified look crossed her face as she wondered what on earth she'd do if he wandered into the kitchen of the KOE house tomorrow afternoon to finalize plans. He wouldn't do that! she tried to comfort herself, but then she had to admit that with Greg there was no telling what he'd do.

Holly crossed her room and stared at the mirror on her dresser. She wished she could discuss the whole situation with Lani. Goodness knows it would help her sort her own thoughts out. Holly frowned at her reflection, and it frowned right back at her. Okay, she said aloud to it, how am I supposed to handle this whole thing? The reflection stared back blankly in response.

Holly flopped on her bed, put her head in her hands, and thought, but nothing brilliant or even close to it popped in her mind. Her eye caught her geometry book, and she sighed. Dealing with Greg was even more frustrating than trying to figure out geometry, but she had to get through geometry, and she didn't have to deal with Greg. He wasn't worth the problems he caused, and that's what she'd tell him the next time she talked to him.

Holly glanced at the telephone that was

sitting on her nightstand, hoping but not really expecting that it would ring. She stared back at her geometry book. She hadn't yet worked a single problem. She sighed and dug in, resolutely decided that this dumb class would not keep her from her goal of good grades. She wanted every advantage in getting a scholarship to the Cordon Bleu, and along with recommendations and cooking experience, good grades were probably bound to help. Deep in concentration, she didn't even realize that the phone had begun ringing, until her father called, "Holly, it's for you."

It had to be Lani. Holly decided that she'd only talk for a minute, and then call Lani back after she'd finished her geometry.

"Hello," Holly said.

"Hi! Were you surprised to get my note?"

Holly took a deep breath. So Greg had called. "Oh, I was surprised all right," Holly stalled.

"Well, what's the answer?"

In spite of her earlier resolution to put Greg firmly out of her life, Holly suddenly knew that a part of her very much wanted to say yes to tomorrow night's proposed date. Maybe, she rationalized to herself, I could just let him suffer a little and then still say yes.

Holly began, "Gosh, Greg, I've got some tentative plans with someone else. I'm really sorry, but you know it is Thursday night."

Greg sounded really contrite. "You know," he said, "it serves me right. I wanted to come up with some really great way to ask you out again, but it just took me too long, I guess. Tell me, were you at least surprised?"

Holly could feel her anger melting, and she started to try to figure out how to tell Greg her tentative plans had fallen through so that she could be with him. "Hey, you still there?" he asked. "Are you mad?"

Jarred from her thoughts, Holly laughed. "No, I'm not mad. I was sure shocked, though, to open my backpack and find your note. Just how did you manage that?"

"Ah, I told you, we spies have our ways."

"Seriously. . . ."

"I'm always serious. Can't you tell?"

The bantering went on back and forth, and Holly found herself thoroughly enjoying the conversation. She had to be on her toes every minute to keep up with Greg's quick sense of humor, but it was a fun challenge.

Suddenly, Holly could hear a voice in the background, and Greg's tone changed. "Listen," he said, "my roommate is desperate to use the phone. I'm sorry about this Friday. How would you like to go out next Friday instead?"

"That would be great," Holly said, feeling both a sense of elation at having won a point and a feeling of great disappointment that she wouldn't be able to see Greg this Friday night, too.

Holly was trying to decide if she should tell Greg to call her tomorrow afternoon to see if her plans had fallen through when he said, "Gotta go. See you next Friday, and Holly, don't have too good a time this weekend."

The line went dead, and Holly replaced the receiver. Carefully, she went over the conversation in her mind. She still didn't know how he'd managed to get the note in her backpack. That backpack had been in the kitchen, and she and Mrs. Clausen had been in the kitchen. Surely, if anyone had come in, unzipped her backpack, stuck a piece of paper in it, and then zipped it again, she'd have noticed. So how did the note get there?

Holly shook her head and smiled, understanding that if Greg sensed it was bugging her and that she really wanted to know, he'd never tell her. She'd only get the answer if he figured she didn't really care.

She looked back at her geometry book. Okay, she admitted to herself, even though Greg and geometry both add grief to my life, there are a lot of differences. For one thing, the mere thought of geometry does not make my heart beat faster every time I think about it!

Finally finishing her homework, Holly pulled out the current issue of *Gourmet* magazine and began leafing through it. The subscription had been a birthday present from Lani. Lani had laughed when Holly thanked her for the gift, saying that Holly was probably the only teenager in the country who'd rather read *Gourmet* than *Seventeen*.

Feeling guilty about her deception, Holly picked up the phone and dialed Lani's number. "Want to go to a movie tomorrow night?" she asked.

"Sure," Lani replied. "Marlene and Alicia mentioned something about doing something tomorrow, too. Maybe we could all go. You've been so busy with work, nobody's gotten a chance to see much of you."

School on Friday passed uneventfully, and Holly rushed to the KOE house. Yesterday, she'd shown Mrs. Clausen that she could follow directions to complete a full meal, which had to mean that Mrs. Clausen was going to start giving her more responsibility around the kitchen! It was exciting just to think of what they might create today. There was so much to learn!

"I'm here!" she called to Mrs. Clausen, slamming the outside door to the kitchen behind her, and throwing her backpack in the corner.

"So I see!" observed Mrs. Clausen. "You look happy. Did you have a good day at school?"

Holly blushed. She was too embarrassed to tell Mrs. Clausen that the reason for her happiness was anticipation of a productive afternoon in the kitchen. "You look as if you're feeling better yourself today," said Holly, changing the subject.

"I do feel much better. I don't know what came over me yesterday, but I'm real proud of the way you got everything organized."

Holly could feel herself standing up a little straighter in Mrs. Clausen's praise. "So what do we have up for today?" she asked.

Mrs. Clausen shook her head. "Look in the sink, and you'll see." Holly walked over to the deep stainless steel sinks, and peeked in.

"Oh no," she gulped, looking at the sink full of scorched and blackened pots. "What happened?"

"That's exactly what I called Jeff Leonard in here to ask this morning!"

"Did he make this awful mess?" gasped Holly. It was on the tip of her tongue to say that Jeff just wasn't the type of person to do something like this, but she caught herself in time.

"No, no," Mrs. Clausen explained. "Jeff wouldn't do something like this, but as house steward, he's the one who's responsible for finding out. I'm afraid he caught quite an earful this morning. I was really angry. At any rate, I think the pots can still be salvaged with some good scrubbing. Here's some special steel wool, and a pair of rubber gloves to protect your hands."

Holly's eyes widened. "You, uh, want me to try to clean all of these?" She mentally crossed her fingers and hoped that somehow she had misunderstood Mrs. Clausen.

"I'm afraid so," Mrs. Clausen said. "I ought to wait until Jeff finds out who made the mess and have the guilty party clean it up, but I need those pots. I can't wait for him to play detective."

"Okay," said Holly, pulling on one of the long yellow rubber gloves, and trying not to let the tears she felt climb to the surface of her eyes. It was just that she'd had such high hopes after yesterday, and now instead of creating she had been relegated to cleaning ruined pans. She was so discouraged that she didn't even try to watch what Mrs. Clausen was making over on her pastry board.

The time ticked slowly away. Holly's arms and back hurt from scrubbing. Her legs were tired of standing, and her hands were sweating inside the impossible gloves she was wearing. For the first time since she'd walked through the door of the KOE house, she was almost sorry she'd worked so hard to get this job.

It seemed to Holly that there was an overwhelming silence in the kitchen broken only by the scrubbing sounds of her steel wool. Was it this quiet every day? Had she never noticed before because she'd been so intent on what Mrs. Clausen was doing? Holly sighed, put the pot she was working on back in the sink, and stretched for a moment. Picking up the pot again, she inwardly groaned. It still looked black on the bottom. What on earth had someone done to get it this way? Wishing it were time to go, she glanced at the back door, and in that instant, she saw what she otherwise would certainly have missed. Pretending not to stare at the back door, Holly suppressed a giggle and watched carefully.

E*leven*

Several minutes passed in which Holly continued to look and yet not appear as if she was looking at the kitchen door to the outside. Then ever so quietly the door opened, and the same hand that had reached in to get her backpack replaced it on the floor. So that's how he did it! Holly thought to herself. She hadn't stopped to think how close to the back door she tossed her backpack every day. Part of Holly was dying to see what on earth Greg had put in her backpack now, but after thinking about it for a minute, she decided to wait until she was off work and could savor the contents without being watched by Mrs. Clausen. Holly smiled to herself. For once she had the upper hand. Greg would be expecting her to keep questioning him about his mysterious feat, but she wouldn't say a word. Matter of fact, if she moved her backpack just a foot to the left, he wouldn't be able to reach it unless he walked all the way in the kitchen. With that gleeful thought, she attacked the pot she was cleaning with renewed vigor. "I think I've finally got this one. It looks as good as new," she called to Mrs. Clausen happily.

Mrs. Clausen wiped her floured hands on her apron and walked over to Holly. "So it does," she said, observing the pot. "Most of the rest of them look pretty good, too. Only one more and you'll be done. What do you suppose those boys got into last night?"

"Gosh, I don't know," Holly said, "but I guess Jeff will find out." And curiosity overcoming her she added, "Just what is a fraternity steward anyway?"

Mrs. Clausen laughed. "Well, I'd say that depends on whom you ask for a definition. Officially, it's the boy selected by the fraternity to be the coordinator between the boys and the cook. He relays their requests and complaints, and goes over proposed menus with me. The position was set up as a way for the boys to have some input into what they got to eat, and for the cook to have one boy to remind the others of the kitchen rules. Of course, that's just the official definition. I've heard rumors around here that it's the toughest office in the entire fraternity, because dealing with the 'kitchen witch' is an intimidating experience."

"Oh, I'm sure no one thinks you're a witch," Holly protested. "The KOE house is known for having the best food on campus."

Mrs. Clausen picked up a sponge and began to wipe off the counter. Holly had noticed that the cook was rarely still. Even when chatting, her hands deftly moved to complete something that had to be done in the kitchen. "Holly, I wouldn't blame them for thinking I'm a witch. I give the boys excellence, and I expect it in return. I can make the life of a steward absolutely miserable if he doesn't complete his duties. We'll see how Jeff handles the responsibility. Frankly, it's pretty unusual for a freshman to take the job. It's easier for the house steward to stand up to the boys if he's a senior." It was almost as if she'd forgotten Holly. "Well, we'll see," she said to herself.

Holly continued scrubbing the pots, but as she scrubbed, she wondered. Why had Jeff taken on this office? He didn't seem interested in anything having to do with cooking, and he certainly didn't seem the type to enjoy self-punishment. Holly tried to remember more about him from the past year's Spanish class. He'd seemed really nice and more mature than most of the guys in the class, which may have been part of the reason she'd liked him. Finally, she concluded that she just really didn't know him well enough to have any reasonable understanding of why he'd chosen to get himself elected house steward. Perhaps he was just really dedicated to the fraternity and wanted to help out any way he could.

Deep in thought, Holly looked up and realized that Mrs. Clausen was standing next to her. "You've worked hard today," she said, and looking over all the pots critically, she added, "Why don't you go ahead and leave a few minutes early."

"That's okay," replied Holly, wondering if this was another of Mrs. Clausen's tests. No wonder the boys were intimidated by her. There was something about her no nonsense attitude and her steely blue eyes that pierced right through a person. Most people probably wanted to stay on Mrs. Clausen's good side.

Right now those eyes were assessing Holly carefully. "Did you enjoy today?" Mrs. Clausen asked.

Holly wasn't quite sure what to say, not wanting Mrs. Clausen to think she'd hired a complainer, but on the other hand, who could enjoy scrubbing burned pots? Mrs. Clausen's eyes continued to stare at Holly until she uncomfortably said, "I didn't mind."

"That's not what I asked you. Let's be honest with each other. Did you enjoy yourself today?"

"No." Holly's reply came out in a half-whisper.

"Good," said Mrs. Clausen, as Holly wondered if she really had gone to work for a witch. Then Mrs. Clausen cleared her throat. "A person who just wants to put in hours and get paid doesn't particularly care if the time is spent washing dishes, setting tables, or cooking. But a person who really wants to be a chef, well that person just aches to get to the food and create."

"That's right!" Holly said, surprised to hear her own voice. "I loved yesterday. I never wanted it to end. I was learning so much, and when I finished the whole meal, I was so proud of myself. I almost felt that I should pay you for yesterday. I could hardly wait to get here today, and then when I did and I saw that all I was going to do was clean pots all day, well I almost felt like quitting." Holly's hand flew to cover her mouth. "I mean, I didn't really want to quit. I want to keep working here. I'm really glad you gave me the job, and I really am learning a whole lot. I — "

Mrs. Clausen held up her hand. "Enough, already. I understand." She turned to take a pot of vegetables from the burner, and then, looking back at Holly, she appeared to be weighing something in her mind.

"Holly, this is a tough business to be in, and it's even tougher for a woman than a man. The standards for excellence are high and the kitchen politics not always fair. You still think it's something you want?"

Holly nodded her head yes, and then in emphasis, she added, "I know I want it more than anything in the world."

"Now tell me," Mrs. Clausen said, her blue eyes twinkling. "Those pots had to be cleaned today. We did not know which boys burned them, so we couldn't have the culprit remedy his deed. Ah, then who should have cleaned them? Perhaps you thought it should be I, the master chef, so that my novice assistant could play at cooking when she arrived?"

Before Holly could answer, Mrs. Clausen waved her on. "Be off for today. It's already past time for you to have left."

Holly took her backpack and headed out the door with Mrs. Clausen's words still ringing in her mind. One thing was for sure. Holly considered that her life had always been quite orderly, but everything was certainly in a constant state of turmoil now. Between Mrs. Clausen and Greg, Holly never knew quite what to expect next.

Greg, she thought suddenly, and quickly took her backpack from her shoulders. The note — how could she have forgotten! What was Greg's message?

Grabbing her geometry book, she scanned the cover, but there was obviously no note attached. He must have used a different book this time, she decided, and quickly pulled the other books from her backpack, but there was nothing on her English or her French books. I wasn't dreaming, she told herself. I did see him take my backpack and put it back. Why would he do that if he didn't intend to leave a note?

Holly took her books one at a time and rifled through the pages to see if the note had been put inside, but there was nothing in any of the books. Stuffing them back into her backpack, she looked around sheepishly, hoping that no one had seen her actions over the past few minutes. If so, the person would surely think she'd lost her mind. For a minute, she almost expected Greg to pop out from one of the bushes, laughing that he'd fooled her again, but sheepishly, she realized that was absurd. Greg was probably halfway through dinner at the fraternity house right now. She couldn't help but wonder what he was going to do with the rest of the evening. Would he have found another date, and for that matter, why hadn't he asked her out for Saturday instead of waiting for next Friday? She pondered those questions all the way home, and it wasn't until she was almost at her front door that she decided maybe he had thought it was too late to ask for this Saturday after she'd made such a big deal about the lateness of his Friday request. Darn me, she decided, I've got to stop being so stupidly unbending about things. What difference did it make if he asked me at the last minute? I really want to be with him!

As Holly walked in the front door, her parents were just on their way out of it. Mr. Hanson had a football game to coach, and her mother was going to watch. Holly felt a little guilty. When she'd been younger, she'd never missed one of her father's high school football games, but this season she hadn't yet been to one. "Want to come with us?" her dad asked. "You'll have to hurry, but we can wait a few minutes for you to get ready."

"Sorry, Dad, I've got other plans with the girls tonight."

"Oh, of course, you're probably going to your own game. Tell me, when we play your high school, are you going to root for your school team or your old dad?"

Holly laughed. "Dad, I'm always rooting for you. Actually, we girls are going to see a movie tonight." It seemed to her that her dad looked slightly displeased, and she was pretty sure it was because he felt that Holly should be out there supporting some football team, but if so he gave no indication, saying only, "Don't be too late tonight." As she went upstairs to dress, she thought about the many years that her family had spent at Friday night football games. Her father had been head coach at Mesa High ever since she could remember. Maybe that's why she didn't find her own high school football games so exciting. Of course, on the other hand, none of her friends seemed to care much about them, either, so maybe it was just that Tempe High had such a bad team this year.

Holly rushed to get ready, grabbing a piece of cold chicken to eat as she dressed. She'd barely finished changing into a pair of jeans and a sweater, and running a brush through her hair when she heard Lani honking in front of the house. Holly ran out to the car and climbed in the backseat. Since the four of them had already agreed during lunch which movie they'd see that night, they headed directly for the theater.

After the film ended, they decided to cancel their perpetual diets and head for Pizza Etc. Conversation wound its way from food in general to the movie they'd just seen to the place most of their talks usually ended — boys.

"Are you going to Judy's party tomorrow night?" Alicia asked.

"I guess," said Marlene. "Do you know which boys she's invited?"

"I think it was just a kind of general invitation to whoever wants to come," said Lani.

"It doesn't really matter. All the guys at Tempe High are such jerks. They're so immature. Holly, don't you think that cook is ever going to let up enough so that we can meet the guys at the KOE house? Who'd ever believe that our best friend spends every day with the finest guys at ASU, and she doesn't even know who any of them are!" moaned Marlene.

Holly thought of Greg and winced inwardly. If they ever found out about him, she could forget having any friends left at all. She started to try to figure out how to explain the situation with Greg to them when the waitress put down the piping hot pizza in front of them. The conversation immediately ceased as everyone dug in, and Holly, deciding that perhaps the timing was some kind of an omen, kept her comments about Greg to herself.

By Sunday night at eight, she could no

longer rationalize why she should do her homework later, and so Holly retrieved the backpack that she'd thrown on the floor of her closet Friday afternoon. Might as well get the worst over first, she thought, and opened her geometry book to try to complete the assignment. There were five proofs to work, and she took a pencil and opened her spiral notebook to get paper. Oh no, she whispered, her mouth dropping open. There, inside the notebook on the first blank piece of paper was scribbled, "Did you miss me this weekend?"

Holly could feel the rush of blood at her temples. Greg was unbelievable. Even when she thought she had everything figured out, he still surprised her. "Yes, Greg," she said out loud to no one, "I really did miss you, and next weekend is going to be great!"

Twelve

Walking into the KOE kitchen on Monday afternoon, Holly put her backpack just a foot further away from the door than usual. Smiling to herself, she thought that it would be really funny to see Greg's hand groping for the backpack he couldn't quite reach. She looked around the kitchen but she didn't see Mrs. Clausen. She must be talking to the housemother, thought Holly, and then, surveying the empty kitchen, she walked quickly to the large stainless steel sink. Thank goodness — no scalded pans and no potatoes were waiting. It was going to be a good afternoon, Holly could just feel it! The kitchen seemed unnaturally quiet without Mrs. Clausen's presence, and Holly looked around, wondering whether Mrs. Clausen was expecting her to be doing something, but there appeared to be nothing waiting. Holly glanced again at her backpack by the back door. Had she put it just enough out of Greg's reach so he could barely touch it, or was it too far away all together? She glanced around the kitchen again, and figuring that there was no one in sight, she walked out the back door to the kitchen and reached her hand in as if to try to grasp her backpack. Too far away, she thought. It's only going to bug Greg if he can almost pull it out but not quite.

Holly walked back in the kitchen and placed her backpack a little closer to the back door, then returned outside to test if the placement had been right. Shaking her head at herself, she knew that she was being ridiculous. This is like first grade, she told herself, and besides, he probably won't even try to take my backpack today.

True, said another part of herself, but what if he does? For once he'll be the one retreating in embarrassment. With that gleeful thought in mind, she reached her arm through the door, and groped for her backpack. She felt the nylon mesh, but only with her finger tips; the spot was perfect. She began to withdraw her hand when someone grabbed it and wouldn't let go.

Embarrassment flooded her face, and if she could have gotten her hand away, Holly was more than ready to disappear totally rather than try to explain why she'd been outside groping through a crack in a door for her own backpack. It was only seconds, but it seemed like hours while Holly still crouched outside, tried to figure out what to do, and the person inside still held tightly to her hand. Then the back door opened slowly, and Holly found herself looking at the face of the person grasping her hand.

"Jeff." She smiled weakly, looking at the surprise in his eyes, and trying to stand up gracefully as if it were no big deal to have been groping around for a backpack.

"What on earth. . . ." He still held her hand as if he couldn't quite believe the whole thing, and her hand were positive reassurance that he hadn't been imagining it.

"Oh, well, uh, you probably want to know what I was doing out there, right? . . . Well, I was, uh, well, actually, I was just. . . ." At that moment swinging doors from the dining room opened, and Mrs. Clausen marched in.

"What," she said, softly but furiously, "is going on in my kitchen?" Jeff dropped Holly's hand like a hot potato. "It's not what you think," Holly stuttered. How ironic it would be if she'd gone to such lengths so that Mrs. Clausen wouldn't know she was dating Greg, and then got fired because Mrs. Clausen thought she was interested in Jeff.

Mrs. Clausen said nothing. She simply stared at the two of them. "Actually, Holly managed to get her backpack caught in the door, and as she tried to extricate it, the door slammed on her hand. Why don't you take a look at it?" Jeff said casually. "I only came in to tell you that I know who damaged the pots, and why, and to tell you how the house council is handling it."

"Oh?" said Mrs. Clausen questioningly, and Holly could tell that the cook was interested. For that matter so was Holly. Mrs. Clausen looked at her. "Go call the produce man and ask him where my hundred ears of corn are. Tell him I don't need them after the meal is served, and remind him that we already agreed on the price."

Holly left to do as she was told, wondering if Mrs. Clausen believed Jeff. She felt both grateful to him for saving her job, and very curious about what had happened to the pots and pans. Holly dialed the number. "Best Produce, hold on, will ya?" Holly was left dangling on hold for so long that she was sure the produce man had forgotten all about her. Finally, he returned to the phone. "All right. You got your corn. But your boss is breaking me. Tell her a man needs to earn a living. There has to be a little profit." He continued, but Holly only half-listened. This appeared to be some sort of almost daily ongoing game between Mrs. Clausen and the produce man. He complained that Mrs. Clausen was unreasonable, and she threatened to go elsewhere, but one day Mrs. Clausen had mentioned to Holly that she'd been using the same produce man ever since she'd arrived at the KOE house, so Holly guessed the two of them must enjoy the bickering.

By the time Holly heard the end of the litany of complaints from the produce man, Jeff had left the kitchen. Too bad; now she would probably never know who had spoiled the pots or what was being done about it.

"So, Holly, tonight's spaghetti sauce is already simmering. It's too early to start the pasta. Why don't you knead that bread dough I started?"

Holly looked at the huge mass of dough, uncertain exactly what Mrs. Clausen wanted. She considered winging it, and then decided that she'd better not take a chance on ruining the dough.

Actually, Mrs. Clausen didn't mind the question. She walked over to the bread board. "Kneading serves two purposes. It helps mix the ingredients more thoroughly and makes it sticky. We begin by flouring the board lightly." She motioned to Holly, who spread flour on the board. "Too much," Mrs. Clausen said, brushing some off. "Only use enough flour to keep the dough from sticking to the board. If you used as much as you had there, the bread would be tough and dry."

Following Mrs. Clausen's instructions, Holly did what the cook proclaimed to be a perfectly satisfactory job. "Next time you'll know just how to do it right," said Mrs. Clausen when they were finished. "One more thing. Until you really know what you're doing, follow directions carefully. Knead the dough for exactly the amount of time the recipe specifies. Some doughs require only seconds; some require eight to ten minutes." Mrs. Clausen shook her head. "I can't tell you how much good food gets wasted because amateurs don't read directions carefully."

As Holly hung up her apron and prepared to leave, she thought about how much fun the afternoon's instruction in breadmaking had been. If only geometry could be this interesting, she wouldn't even mind doing the homework for it.

Remembering her earlier episode with it, Holly picked up her backpack, sheepishly called "Bye" to Mrs. Clausen, and headed out the back door.

Walking quickly toward home, Holly mentally reviewed what she'd learned about kneading dough that day. At camp, Chef Strand had always bought commercially prepared breads and rolls. Maybe, this summer, she'd bake bread for everyone. She daydreamed about the comments the kids would make when they walked into the kitchen and smelled it fresh from the ovens. Why, she'd be the most loved person in the whole camp.

"Hey, Holly, wait up," came a masculine voice, breaking into her daydream, and she turned, expecting to see Greg's twinkling blue eyes. But to her surprise, it was Jeff who was coming toward her. "Say," he began, "I'm really sorry about this afternoon. I know how much this job means to you, and I wouldn't blow it for you for the world. Did Mrs. Clausen get mad at you?"

"Actually, you must have defused the situation fine because she never said another word. Listen, I really do appreciate it. If it hadn't been for you, I'd have probably never even gotten the job in the first place, and if you hadn't calmed Mrs. Clausen down today, I'd have probably lost it."

"Glad to help," Jeff said, falling in stride with her. "So tell me," he said, "how do you feel about becoming a chef after a week of working at the KOE house?" Holly answered briefly, but Jeff asked lots of questions and seemed genuinely interested in knowing the answers. Holly began explaining everything about the past week. Before she realized it, they were in front of her house. Holly blushed. "Sorry, I guess I sort of talked your ear off."

Jeff laughed, a nice, warm kind of laughter. "Not at all, it was pretty interesting. See ya."

After he left, Holly realized that she'd gotten so involved in talking about herself that she'd missed the perfect opportunity to find out who ruined the pots, what was going to happen to them, or for that matter, even why Jeff had decided to become the house steward.

Darn! she thought to herself. That's probably a lost chance I'll never get again. She peeked out the window and saw that Jeff had continued down Lawrence Street. He must live somewhere around here, she deduced, but she couldn't remember ever having run into him in the neighborhood.

After she had finished dinner, and helped her mother with the dishes, Holly went to her room to add her newfound knowledge about kneading dough to her hints and tips book. Good thing she'd bought a big loose-leaf notebook. That way she could continuously add material. Holly had put dividers in for each letter of the alphabet, and briefly she wondered whether she should put the things she'd learned on kneading under B for bread, D for dough, or K for kneading. Finally, she compromised. She'd enter it under D and cross-reference a note under B and K. That finished, she looked at the red notebook with pride. Not only was it neat and well-organized, but it already contained a great deal that she'd learned about cooking.

She stared at it for a few minutes and then carefully put the notebook in her backpack, thinking that it couldn't hurt to have it with her while she was at work. If Mrs. Clausen seemed in a good mood, Holly could pull the notebook out and ask permission to write down tips as soon as she learned them.

Actually, as it turned out, she didn't have to ask Mrs. Clausen at all. The next day, after she'd inquired for the third time about a procedure for making fried chicken batter, Mrs. Clausen suggested that she get a little notebook in which to keep track of the things she was learning. Holly reddened, and then pulled the loose-leaf from her backpack. "Uh, I've been kind of doing that on my own at home, but sometimes, I can't remember everything you've said by then."

Mrs. Clausen took the notebook from Holly's hands and scrutinized it carefully. Her penetrating blue eyes showed no emotion as she read many of Holly's entries. "It's not a bad beginning," she allowed, handing the book back to Holly. "I'll try to make certain that you get something valuable to add to it each day, that is if you don't burn out after a few weeks."

"Thanks, Mrs. Clausen. I'd really appreciate it, and I won't ever want to quit getting new tips." Holly sighed to herself and wondered what it was going to take to make Mrs. Clausen truly believe that she was serious about this whole thing.

The week passed unbelievably quickly, and Holly's book of hints became fatter each day. If cookies were doughy, they were either not baked long enough or the oven temperature was too low. If muffins had a dry, crumbly texture, they had too much flour. If bread was uneven in color, the liquid ingredients hadn't been mixed well enough. Holly glanced through her book in amazement. Mrs. Clausen was absolutely a walking encyclopedia when it came to anything about cooking.

After waiting and wondering all week about what her date with Greg would be like, it turned out to be quite nice. He even suggested that they go to a movie theater in Phoenix, a ten-mile drive from Tempe, so that they definitely wouldn't run into Mrs. Clausen.

Greg's personality was as teasing and taunting as ever, but tonight, Holly felt more able to handle the challenge and meet him on even ground. A couple of times she even felt as though she'd gotten the better of him. It seemed to her that the night had ended much too soon when they pulled up in front of her house. How could she already have spent five hours with Greg?

He walked her to the door, and his broad-shouldered frame towered over her. Bending, he kissed her gently, and then pulled her close once again and kissed her more passionately. Holly felt as if the world were exploding inside her. Releasing her, he took her hand and said, "I think maybe we should make this a weekly activity."

Trying to get control of her own emotions, Holly joked, "The kiss or the date?"

Greg's eyes penetrated right through her. "Both."

"Okay," said Holly breathlessly. Greg smiled, and then he was gone. Holly sat on her bed in her room trying to believe this whole thing was for real. No girl could possibly be this lucky, to have both the perfect job and the most exciting boy in the world, like her. She fell asleep with a grin on her face.

The next day Holly woke up to come to terms with the only unpleasant side of this whole thing. It was one thing not to mention Greg to her friends if she was only going to see him once or twice, but it was quite another to keep lying if he was going to be a very important part of her life. She really hadn't liked lying in the first place, and, somehow hoping that they'd understand, she called Lani and then Marlene, Alicia, and Becky and asked them to meet her at Mulligan's at two o'clock.

When she arrived, she saw them sitting in a back booth. "Hi, everyone. Sorry I'm late," she apologized. "Cokes are on me today."

Lani was looking at her carefully. "Okay, Holly, we're dying to know. What's this all about?"

"Well," began Holly, and suddenly she wished she were back at home, or that she'd rehearsed this whole thing before she'd said it. "I met this guy. . . ." It sounded trite and unsophisticated to her ears even as she said it, and besides, Greg was definitely not just this guy. She took a deep breath and started again. Finally she got the whole story out, from the time that she'd first met Greg through his parting words Friday night.

Becky, who was the romantic among them, said that she had goosebumps at just the thought of the whole thing, and when did they get to see this gorgeous hunk? But Alicia, who was always more cynical, looked at Holly skeptically. "Is what I'm hearing right? You're going to be seeing a handsome, wonderful KOE guy every single weekend, and that's okay, but you still can't introduce any of your friends to any of his other KOE friends."

Her tone put Holly immediately on the defensive. "It's not like it sounds at all. I didn't expect to meet him. I really didn't even try to meet him. Even though we don't do things around campus, I'm still taking a tremendous chance of losing my job just by seeing him at all. The more people who get involved, the more likely Mrs. Clausen will find out. Look," Holly pleaded, "just give me another month or so. Maybe then Mrs. Clausen will give in a little about things. As soon as she does, I promise, I'll find a way to introduce you to all the guys in the house."

"Meanwhile," said Marlene, "you'll just continue to go out with Greg and have a great time with a KOE guy yourself." Lani didn't say anything at all, but she looked confused. There was a strained silence about the table instead of the normal laughter and chatter. Well, so be it, Holly thought resolutely to herself on her way home. I haven't done anything wrong. They'll realize that in a few days. I know they will. But in spite of her brave words, she wasn't so sure.

Thirteen

The girls virtually ignored her on Monday during lunch, and Mrs. Clausen had a migraine headache when Holly arrived after school and barely spoke to her during work. She began walking home, feeling lonely and disgruntled. "Hi," said a friendly voice popping up by her side.

"Jeff," Holly said in surprise. "What are you doing here?"

"Heading home," he replied. "Mind if I walk with you?"

"I'd love it," she said, grateful for friendly companionship. As it had been the previous week, again, it was so easy to talk to Jeff. "You know, last week, I about talked your ear off, and after you left, I kicked myself for not finding out how you got to be house steward, what it means, and if you like it."

Jeff laughed. "Well, I wish I had some great story to tell you, but I really don't. In

122

an insane moment, I actually volunteered for the job, and that's about all there is to how I got it. I didn't exactly have to battle any of the other guys for the opportunity. Actually, it really isn't so bad. In spite of her gruff exterior, Mrs. Clausen is a pretty good person except, of course, when she's furious at three dumb sophomore guys who decide to try to make popcorn balls on a bet, and ruin her pots."

"Ah, so that's what happened!" exclaimed Holly. "I hope Mrs. Clausen killed them. My arms and fingers ached for three days after trying to return those pots to usability."

Conversation continued effortlessly until they reached Holly's house. They stood outside her front door and talked for another twenty minutes. Finally, Jeff said that he should get going. "My mom's waiting for me for dinner."

"Oh, is it a special occasion at your house?"

Jeff's face reddened, and his voice got a little scratchy. "My dad died a couple of months before I started college. My mom was pretty broken up. I offered to live at home for another year or so, but she insisted I should go ahead with all the plans I'd made, so I try to go home at least on Monday nights for dinner. Sometimes she cooks, and sometimes I take her out. It works out pretty well, and maybe it makes it a little easier for her to get through the week."

Holly watched Jeff leave, thinking what a nice person he was. Some girl was going to be really lucky to get him for a boyfriend. Maybe she could eventually fix Jeff up with one of her friends, that is, if she still had any friends by then.

After a few days, a pattern clearly emerged. Her friends weren't going to desert her totally, but on the other hand, they weren't going to completely let her forget that they were hurt and angry. For the time being there wasn't much she could do about that.

Life began at last to settle into a predictable routine. School during the day, work at the KOE house in the afternoons, and Friday nights with Greg. Each date with him, however, was still a challenging ride on a rollercoaster. She watched her every word, prepared at any second to try to counter his sarcasm or humor with an equally clever remark of her own. Every time she thought she had him figured out, he fooled her again. Dating him was hard work, but definitely worth the effort.

In a very different way Jeff, too, had become a part of Holly's life. Every Monday night, he walked home with her, always careful to meet her a block away from the KOE house so that Mrs. Clausen wouldn't see. Never had she been able to talk to any boy as easily and comfortably as she spoke with Jeff. In many ways, he seemed to understand her better than she had ever understood herself. From time to time, she wondered what would have happened if they'd ever started dating when he was still at Tempe High and she'd had such a crush on him.

Holly sighed, wishing that Jeff were the one she needed to discuss a problem with rather than Greg. She had spent almost a month trying to figure out just the right way to cleverly present her idea to Greg. She wanted to go out with him on Saturdays instead of Fridays. Holly was really exhausted on Friday nights, after a full week of school and work. Besides, she was left with so little time to get ready for their dates that she had to rush. Everything would be so much easier on Saturday when she only worked in the morning.

Holly didn't want to admit even to herself that maybe, just maybe, she had another underlying reason for wanting to change the day of her and Greg's date. Its name was jealousy.

Holly knew from being around the house helping Mrs. Clausen prepare refreshments that the guys had parties almost every Saturday night. She'd never asked Greg anything about them, but she figured if he wasn't with her, he was probably at the parties. And, if he was at the parties, he certainly couldn't be dancing by himself. She'd tried asking Jeff about the parties in a discreet way, but all he'd said was that the parties were one of the main reasons a guy joined a fraternity. Dating could get quite expensive and parties gave guys a place to take girls without spending a fortune. Jeff said that most of the guys showed up to make sure the parties had some excitement, and they got pretty wild sometimes.

He didn't really seem to want to talk about the party scene at the KOE house any further, and Holly had decided that Jeff was going to be no help in this matter. She was going to have to bring the idea of Saturday dates up to Greg without some clever plan.

Ironically, her opportunity came on their very next date. It was right after Greg had finished kissing her good-night.

"I could do that every night," he proclaimed.

Holly saw her opportunity. "Good, why don't we add Saturdays?" she bantered.

Greg still smiled, but Holly thought she detected a wariness in his eyes. "What do you mean?"

Holly felt herself wanting to retreat. She didn't want him to think she was monopolizing all of his time, and she hurried to clarify herself. "I mean instead of Friday nights, we could go out on Saturdays. It's just that everything seems so rushed on Fridays. I thought it might be easier on Saturdays."

"Holly, that'd be great," Greg said, but it seemed to Holly that his face didn't look as if he meant it. He said, "It's just that there are fraternity parties most Saturday nights, and Mrs. Clausen would surely find out we're dating if we showed up at a fraternity party."

Holly couldn't make herself look up at Greg, but the stubborn streak in her couldn't let go yet. Very quietly, she said, "We wouldn't have to go to the fraternity parties."

Greg looked shocked. "Holly, I'm a KOE. I've got to support the house functions. The guys are expected to be at those parties."

Holly sighed. Part of her felt like crying and wistfully, she said, "Maybe I've been there long enough now that Mrs. Clausen believes how serious I am about being a chef and won't care if you and I are going out."

Greg took a deep breath. "Holly, there's, uh, there's another little problem I haven't told you about. You remember when you told me about the assistant cook from last year, and how the situation with her kept Mrs. Clausen from hiring you? Well, she caused quite a few problems and not just for Mrs. Clausen. Because of her, the guys decided at that point that no KOE could ever again date an employee of the house while she was still an employee."

"But that's not fair," Holly protested.

"Listen," said Greg with an increasing sense of urgency in his voice, "it may not be fair, but I could get booted right out of the house if anyone found out I was dating you. So I'd better keep showing up at those parties on Saturday night, even though I'd rather be with you." He kissed her again, and Holly floated into the house. In spite of his constant teasing, underneath he was quite a wonderful person because Holly knew how much he loved being a KOE, and he was risking it all for her. She wished she could find that assistant cook from last year and wring her neck.

It was hard to believe that she'd been working at the KOE house almost two full months. Her red notebook was crammed with information. She leafed through it. "Acidic food slows down the softening of fiber, so it takes longer to cook," she had written. In parentheses, to make certain she'd understand, she had continued, "If you're making a stew with a tomato and want to add sliced carrots and potatoes, add the carrots first. The tomato has acid and means the high fiber carrots will take longer to cook than the potatoes." Sometimes Holly wondered if she'd even need to go to the Cordon Bleu by the time she could meet Mrs. Clausen's exacting standards and absorb her wealth of information.

One day Holly walked jauntily in to the KOE house and was shocked to find Mrs. Clausen sobbing with her head buried in her hands. She felt tremendous fear and sadness for the older woman she had come to like and respect so much.

It was the first time Holly had ever seen Mrs. Clausen exhibit extreme emotion about anything. She wanted to do something to help, but she didn't want to embarrass her employer or invade her right to privacy. Had Mrs. Clausen heard her come in? Holly stood for a moment uncertainly, and then natural instinct took over. Without even realizing what she was doing, Holly walked over to Mrs. Clausen and put her arms around her. For a few minutes neither of them spoke, and feeling the older woman's pain, Holly's own eyes brimmed with tears.

Finally Mrs. Clausen's sobs abated, and Holly stood back. Mrs. Clausen dried her tears with her apron and looked at Holly. Her voice breaking she said simply, "My sister is dead. There is no one left in my family now, and I must go back to New York to bury her."

A chill ran down Holly's spine, and not knowing exactly what the right thing to say was, she offered only, "I'm so sorry."

Mrs. Clausen continued mechanically. "I've put dinner up for tonight. It will be all ready for them. I called the college temporary service, but the two spare cooks are already filling in. I must go."

At that moment Jeff walked through the swinging doors from the dining room, and Holly looked gratefully at him. "One of the guys caught me right after class and told me. I hurried back. Don't worry, Mrs. Clausen, you just leave."

She nodded her head and continued mechanically as if the only way she could speak was to remove herself completely from her emotions. "The boys can have cereal or toast for breakfast. I've sliced lots of cold cuts that should hold them for lunch, but dinners. . . ." She shrugged helplessly and repeated, "The temporary cooks are already filling in elsewhere."

"It's okay, Mrs. Clausen," Jeff said authoritatively. "I'll come in and help out in the afternoons and Holly here will be in charge, won't you, Holly?"

"Sure," she said, her own voice not at all too steady. "Don't worry, Mrs. Clausen, I've got my whole book full of your hints."

Mrs. Clausen seemed as if her mind were already in New York. "Thank you both," she whispered. "I must go pack." Her eyes again filled with tears, and she moved almost by rote out the back door. For a few minutes, Jeff and Holly stood looking at the door almost as if it would be disrespectful to say anything at all.

Then Jeff walked over to her and put his hand on Holly's shoulder. "Do we need to do something to keep anything from burning? I mean I'll do whatever you say, but you'll have to be in charge. I don't know anything about running this kitchen."

Holly turned toward the myriad pots and pans simmering on the stove and gulped as the realization hit her that for the next few days she was supposed to produce nightly dinners for fifty people. With a sinking feeling, she was almost positive that she didn't yet have the knowledge to pull it off.

"Jeff," she said, a note of panic creeping into her voice, "I really don't think I can do this until Mrs. Clausen gets back."

His big brown eyes looked supportive and

compassionate. "Let's not even worry about 'until Mrs. Clausen gets back.' Let's just worry about dinner tonight. Do you know what Mrs. Clausen had planned?"

Holly walked over to the menu sheet on the wall. "Roast, baked potatoes, jello, and brownies," she read. Looking at Jeff, she smiled weakly. "At least this isn't one of Mrs. Clausen's exotic dinners." Checking the oven, she found that the roasts were already cooking, and she knew she'd helped make jello molds yesterday.

"Okay," she said, half to herself and half to Jeff. "All we have to do is scrub the potatoes and put them in to bake and make some brownies for dessert."

"That doesn't sound bad at all," Jeff said encouragingly.

"Actually, I think our hardest part of dinner tonight is going to be carving the roasts. I've never carved meat in my life."

"Me, either," said Jeff, "but if it's any help, I was always pretty handy with a knife. You should have seen the things I whittled at camp as a kid."

In spite of herself, Holly laughed. "Somehow, I don't think the guys would appreciate having whittled roast. Have you ever made brownies before?"

"No, but I'm great at eating them," Jeff offered.

"Some assistant cook I've got!" Holly groaned in mock horror.

"Now you know what Mrs. Clausen probably felt like when you started," Jeff started to joke, but the mention of Mrs. Clausen sobered the two of them and made them think once again of the cook's sad situation.

The brownies got made, and even the one jello mold that always stuck came right out this time. The potatoes were almost finished baking, and the kitchen aromas wafted invitingly toward the dining room. A buzzer pierced the air. "What's that?" Jeff jumped.

"Mrs. Clausen must have set it. The roasts are through."

"Uh-oh, that means they've got to be carved, huh?"

"Well, we've still got a few minutes. Mrs. Clausen says that you're supposed to let meat stand for a bit after you cook it. That way it retains the juices better when you cut it." Holly walked to the big pantry closet and took out a cookbook.

"What are you doing?" asked Jeff.

"Trying to get us some help in carving these things. I'll read, you cut." Holly handed him a big knife.

"Yikes," he said. "Is there a first-aid book in there, too?"

The pieces were definitely not cut as evenly and perfectly as they would have been if Mrs. Clausen had carved the roast, but at least it was sliced, and Jeff hadn't even cut his finger. He looked around the kitchen, and seeing everything finished, he proudly stated, "We did it. We turned out a terrific meal."

Holly felt pretty pleased about their accomplishment herself, but on the way home, she reminded herself that tonight was the easy meal. Mrs. Clausen had already done a lot of it. Suddenly, she realized that she'd been so busy worrying about tonight's dinner, that she hadn't even checked the menu to see what was scheduled for tomorrow.

When she arrived home, she told her folks all about what had happened. "I feel so bad for Mrs. Clausen," she said. "I wish there was something I could do."

"I think you're already doing it. From what you've said, the KOE kitchen is Mrs. Clausen's life, and you're keeping it running smoothly while she's gone."

"Well, I'm trying, although I'm still not sure that I'm going to be able to do it," Holly said, and to her surprise, she found herself adding, "But it sure makes it easier to know that Jeff will be there pitching in to help."

Fourteen

Because of the strain that the KOE house had put on Holly's friendship with the girls at school, she rarely mentioned anything about work, but today, at lunch, when Marlene said that she looked preoccupied, Holly told the group about Mrs. Clausen. "You mean you've got to cook for fifty all by yourself? I'd be scared to death!" Alicia said.

"I am," Holly admitted. "I mean last night, Mrs. Clausen had everything pretty well started, but tonight I'm on my own."

"We'd come help," Becky offered, "if you'd let us near your precious KOE guys."

"It would be fun," Lani admitted. "Too bad Holly's the only one who knows anything about cooking. I knew there was a reason I should have paid attention in home ec. What are you supposed to be making tonight, anyway?"

Holly blushed. "I don't actually know. I

got so involved with getting through last night's meal that I forgot to even look at the menu for tonight. Not too smart, huh?"

The bell rang, ending further conversation, and Holly went to her afternoon classes, but her mind wasn't on her teachers' lectures at all. Instead, she tried to figure out what Mrs. Clausen might have left for dinner tonight. I only hope she hasn't planned one of her around-the-world gourmet evenings for one night this week, Holly thought to herself.

Figuring that there would probably be a lot to do in the kitchen, Holly rushed to the KOE house as soon as school was out. The lights and the radio were turned off in the kitchen, and Holly felt a tremendous sense of loneliness upon entering. On the counters were remnants of the lunches and breakfasts the boys had put together for themselves. It seemed so strange to see the stove devoid of any pots and pans, and to not smell the aromas of something good cooking. Holly stood near the back door holding her backpack as if she were frozen to the spot. She almost felt like hanging a DO NOT DISTURB sign on the kitchen and disappearing until Mrs. Clausen got back.

Holly Hanson! she admonished herself. Get a hold of yourself! What's the matter with you? You say you're going to be a great chef, but you're scared to even make a meal for fifty people. What kind of chef will you ever make? Pep talk over, Holly put her backpack down, and went to the menu board to see what Mrs. Clausen had planned for this week's food. Tonight was supposed to be spaghetti. I can handle that, Holly told herself reassuringly. Tomorrow was baked chicken. Today, she'd have to call the meat market and make sure Mrs. Clausen had ordered the chicken. Holly's eyes fell on Thursday night's menu. Oh, no, she breathed. There's just no way I can ever attempt that. Of all the weeks for Mrs. Clausen to plan an Oriental dinner.

Trying to decide how to handle everything, Holly walked to the counter and began putting away the things the guys had left out from breakfast and lunch. The doors from the dining room swung open, and Jeff strode in. "Hi, boss," he called. "Am I late or were you early? I hope this doesn't mean I'll get fired."

Holly laughed. "You're right on time, and I'm sure glad you're here."

Jeff picked up a knife and fork and with a phony French accent, he said, "Ah, Madamoiselle, zis is what all ze great chefs tell me." Dropping the accent, he continued, "How are we set for today?"

"Well, Mrs. Clausen has spaghetti planned, and her recipe for sauce should have been started — " Holly looked at the clock " — about two hours and twenty-five minutes ago."

"Uh-oh, so what now?"

"So, we improvise. We just won't be able

to start from scratch." Holly was surprised to hear the confidence in her voice.

"Great, let's get started."

The afternoon passed quickly. Jeff was funny, and genuinely helpful. Holly realized that in spite of her earlier feelings about not even wanting to come in the kitchen, she was actually having fun.

As they were finishing the meal, Jeff exclaimed, "Pretty good. It looks to me as if we're two for two. Why don't you stay and eat some of your creation tonight?"

"Oh, I don't really think so. . . ."

"Ah-hah, I knew it. You're afraid you've poisoned everyone, and you don't want to die."

"No, really, it's going to be good."

"Then you stay and eat it, too."

Thus, Holly found herself staying for dinner. At first, Jeff tried to convince her that she should just join everyone in the dining room, but Holly was adamant about not doing that. "The chef doesn't belong there," she told Jeff, and besides, she thought to herself, I don't want to have to sit near Greg and pretend that I don't even know him.

Finally, seeing that she was absolutely not going to eat in the dining room, Jeff insisted that he, too, would eat in the kitchen. "But you belong out there with the guys," Holly protested.

"No way; tonight I'm the assistant chef, and I belong right wherever the chef is," Jeff assured her. Holly didn't argue any more. In fact, as she walked home, she reflected that she was glad she'd stayed for dinner and that it had really been fun to talk to Jeff as they'd eaten. He was turning out to be quite a terrific friend.

The next day she could hardly wait to get back to KOE's kitchen. This evening's dinner was going to be a cinch, and she knew that she and Jeff would have fun making it. Tomorrow night's dinner might be a different story. She'd told Jeff that there was no way they were going to attempt Mrs. Clausen's wok cooking, but she wasn't sure what they were going to do. She glanced at the clock. Jeff had been here by this time yesterday and the day before. Maybe he'd decided she'd be okay now, and he wasn't coming. After all, it really wasn't the steward's job. It doesn't matter, Holly told herself. I can do it by myself. But there was no doubt from her exuberant cry of "Jeff!" when he walked in the kitchen that she was really glad he'd come.

"Well, I've got my part of the Chinese dinner for tomorrow night," he said confidently.

"You do?"

"Yep!" He laughed and held up two pairs of chop sticks. "Whatever you decide to make tomorrow is fine, but we're using these in honor of Mrs. Clausen's missed Oriental dinner."

"That's a deal," smiled Holly, "but before we worry about tomorrow night's dinner,

138

we'd better get ready for tonight's." The two worked in tandem, and as she had predicted, the meal's preparation went extremely smoothly. As she took the golden brown chicken from the oven and arranged it on serving platters, Holly felt a sense of pride. It looked good, and it smelled wonderful.

"This tastes super," said Jeff, as the two of them sat on stools pulled up to the counter in the kitchen. They talked and joked throughout dinner, and afterwards Jeff offered to walk Holly home.

"Oh, you don't have to do that," Holly protested. "I'll be fine." But she was glad when Jeff said it would be no problem.

The walk home was pleasant and comfortable, and deep in conversation, Holly and Jeff stood outside her house for almost an hour before he left.

The next day Holly walked into the KOE kitchen and got to work. It seemed hard to believe that she'd been so intimidated by the whole thing just a few days ago. Still aware of her limitations, she canceled what she could of the Chinese food, and froze whatever was left. They were going to have meat loaf, mashed potatoes, peas and carrots, tossed salad, and sundaes for dessert. Checking her ingredient list again, Holly proudly decided that she was serving a well-balanced meal that most of the guys would eat, even if it wasn't quite what Mrs. Clausen had had in mind for this evening.

True to his word, Jeff produced the chopsticks, and while everyone else calmly ate in the dining room, Jeff and Holly tried hysterically to cut and eat meat loaf with their chopsticks. At the meal's conclusion, Jeff grabbed Holly's hand and pulled her out into the main dining room.

Whistling to get the group's attention, he called, "As you know, Mrs. Clausen had to leave town for her sister's funeral, and she'll be back tomorrow night. None of us starved while she was gone, and that's thanks to Holly Hanson. I think we owe her a rousing KOE cheer."

Blushing and wishing she were back in the kitchen, Holly couldn't stop herself from searching out Greg. He was sitting in the back of the room, a smirk on his face. He was wearing a blue KOE T-shirt that made his eyes even bluer, and when he saw that she was looking at him, he winked, which made Holly blush even more furiously.

Cheer over, Holly thanked everyone and retreated quickly to the safety of the kitchen. "You shouldn't have done that!" she scolded Jeff, but he just laughed and said she deserved the recognition.

"Besides, it was about time that you met the men of KOE," Jeff asserted.

Holly had been on the verge of answering that she already knew one of the men of KOE quite well, but she bit her tongue. It seemed strange to have to suddenly watch her words around Jeff. Over the past few days, they'd talked about everything. He'd told her how he'd felt after his father died, and she'd shared things with him that she'd never even told to Marlene or Lani. She was sure she could trust him to tell him about Greg, too, but still, if anything went wrong, and it meant Greg got kicked out of the fraternity. . . . She stopped herself mid-thought. It was too awful to think about.

Instead, she changed the subject. "You know, I'm glad that Mrs. Clausen is coming back tomorrow. This week showed me that I can do it. I can be in charge of getting a meal out for lots of people, and get everything done and served at the same time, but it also showed me how much I still have to learn. If I'd been left in charge for very many more days, I'd have run out of things I knew how to do. Your being here has really been great. It took what would have been a very scary experience and made it into a lot of fun."

Jeff started to wave her compliment off, but Holly continued, "Listen, I know you did a lot more than you had to do as the house steward. You've been super, and I really want to thank you."

Jeff leaned over and gave Holly a hug. "My mother would never believe I was saying this about working in a kitchen, but I had a lot of fun, too, I really did, so there's no need for thanks."

Holly thought about the conversation on the way home. She hadn't been embarrassed or tongue-tied to tell Jeff just how she'd felt about his help. What if she'd had to thank Greg? She rolled her eyes just thinking about it. They'd have joked that he was lucky she'd let him in the kitchen.

Well, there was no need to worry about that. Greg hadn't set foot in the kitchen the whole week. Holly frowned thinking about that. But it was just as well, she rationalized. It would only have made the guys in the house suspicious that there was something between him and Holly. After all, she reasoned, it was logical for Jeff to be there as the house steward. It was not logical for Greg to have any reason to be in the KOE kitchen.

Just the thought of Greg made her pick up her pace and walk home faster. He was supposed to call her tonight to let her know what they were doing tomorrow night, and Holly definitely didn't want to miss his call.

She'd only been home about five minutes when the phone rang. "Is this the princess of the pots?" laughed Greg.

"Careful," she bantered back, "it's the only princess you'll probably ever know." Then, in spite of everything she'd told herself on the way home, she added, "I thought you might stop in this week, with Mrs. Clausen gone and all."

Greg countered, "Ah, I thought about it, but I hated to watch you work, and I certainly didn't want to stop the progress of dinner."

"You could have helped," Holly offered.

"Me, help in the kitchen?" Greg laughed. "Believe me, you wouldn't have wanted my help. Besides, looks to me like you already got enough help from our house steward. Was he putting the moves on you or what?"

Holly was amazed. "Jeff?" she said, in a puzzled voice.

Before she could decide what else to say about the subject, Greg dropped it completely. They debated about what to do on their date for the next half hour before finally deciding just to go to a movie.

"Well, good-bye, my princess of the pots," Greg said.

Hanging up the phone, Holly felt the same rush of excitement that she'd felt ever since the first day she met him. She was half tempted to greet him tomorrow wearing a big pot as a crown and holding a dish scrubber as a scepter. He'd probably get a big kick out of that, but she wasn't sure if it would mess up her hair and make them late for the movie while she tried to fix it.

Actually, the movie they'd chosen to see didn't sound too great. It was just that they were running out of things to do. It was pretty hard to stay away from his friends, stay away from her friends, and still go places and do things.

Holly could hardly wait to have Greg meet all her friends, and to be able to fix some of them up with other KOE boys. Then they'd have lots of things to do. For a few minutes, she allowed herself to daydream. They were all at a big KOE party together. Lani, Marlene, Becky, Alicia, and Holly. Everyone was dancing and having a wonderful time. All the girls agreed that though their dates were nice, none were as cute as Greg. Holly smiled at the daydream, and then flopped on her bed, propping up her elbows and putting her chin in her hands. Too bad it was only a daydream, and at least for now, she couldn't see any way to turn it into reality.

F*ifteen*

All through school the next day, Holly worried about seeing Mrs. Clausen, wondering what the right thing to say and do was. When she'd asked her mother over breakfast that morning, Mrs. Hanson said that all Holly could do was let Mrs. Clausen know that she was sorry about her sister and make her feel appreciated to be back. It sounded easy but Holly was still nervous. What if she hadn't kept the kitchen the way Mrs. Clausen wanted it? What if Mrs. Clausen was angry about Holly's not having served the Chinese dinner that had been planned? What if she was just different now?

As she walked to the KOE house, her stomach nervously bounced up to her throat. Getting to the back door, Holly stood stalling for a minute and then, taking a deep breath, she pulled on the metal handle, and the door opened. I've got to be cheery, Holly warned herself, pasting on a smile and walking into the kitchen. Even if Mrs. Clausen is depressed, I've got to try to act like everything is okay. But the smile turned absolutely genuine as Holly saw Mrs. Clausen in her white apron bent over the pastry board, humming to herself in front of a gigantic mound of chocolate chip cookie dough.

"Holly!" Mrs. Clausen exclaimed, "what a job you did here! If I'd been gone much longer, they might have written me and told me not to come back, that they'd hired you permanently."

"Not really," replied Holly, basking in the compliment. "They missed you unbelievably, and we're all really glad you're back."

Mrs. Clausen smiled broadly and her eyes rested on a bouquet of flowers and a big welcome home sign on the silverware counter. Holly was glad that the guys appreciated Mrs. Clausen. What a neat thing it was for them to have gotten her the flowers, she thought. The KOE house was a pretty special place.

Almost as if she'd read Holly's thought, Mrs. Clausen acknowledged, "It's good to be home; it was good to be missed. I'm baking a bunch of the boys' favorite cookies. Don't just stand there watching. Put your apron on, come help, and tell me all about what it was like to run the kitchen alone."

For the next hour, the two of them made cookies and talked. Holly explained every detail of what had gone on. "I started by posting a list of every single thing I had to do each day, and you were right about its working. If I hadn't done that, I'd have forgotten all about making the sauce for the vegetables until it was too late." Mrs. Clausen chuckled when Holly told her that she'd gotten the produce man to give her the green beans for less than he'd originally quoted.

"So, after all this do you still want to be a chef?" Mrs. Clausen inquired, and her no-nonsense blue eyes demanded an honest answer.

"I sure do!" Holly replied. "More than ever, but I've still got so much to learn. I got so scared right after you left, that if it hadn't been for Jeff Leonard, I'd have probably fallen apart the first day."

Mrs. Clausen stuck another batch of cookies in the oven. There must have been almost two hundred of them already piled high on plates, and the kitchen smelled heavenly. She wiped her hands and fixed Holly with a look. "Well, get out your notebook. Tonight, I'm going to give you a lesson on Swedish meatballs."

Holly went to get her notebook out of her backpack, and as she bent over to retrieve it, Mrs. Clausen said, "Holly, you know that Jeff is a pretty nice boy. You don't only have to see him in this kitchen, you know."

Holly stood up very slowly. Had Mrs. Clausen meant what Holly thought she'd meant? The answer was very important and it had nothing at all to do with Jeff. Careful, thought Holly in warning to herself, but she had to proceed. She had to know. "Remember when you hired me?"

"I certainly do," said Mrs. Clausen, suppressing a smile. "You didn't give me any choice."

"Well, you said that you didn't want some flighty girl who was only interested in the boys here. I promised you that I wouldn't care about any of the guys in the KOE house."

"Yes . . . and now. . . ." Mrs. Clausen certainly wasn't going to make this easy.

"Well, and now, you're telling me that you think I should see Jeff."

Mrs. Clausen began adding ingredients to the ground meat she'd taken from the refrigerator. "Holly, I really do believe that there is absolutely nothing that is going to stop you from becoming a chef, but you've got to have a little fun along the way. Now, are you going to bring that notebook over here in time to learn something or not?"

Holly took careful notes, and helped shape the meatballs just as she was told so they'd stay fluffy during cooking. As they finished, Mrs. Clausen said, "Next week, you can get ready to really take notes. We're going to start baking for the KOE Winter Formal, and we'll turn out the most perfect French pastries you've ever seen."

"What's the Winter Formal?"

"Ah, you should see my boys. They get all dressed up, and so do their dates. They have

148

a beautiful dinner dance at the best hotel in town, and every year I make all the French pastries for their dessert."

"That's wonderful," Holly said. However, she had to admit that it wasn't just learning to make French pastries that was so exciting. Before leaving for the weekend, Holly walked over and threw her arms around Mrs. Clausen's ample shoulders. "I'm so glad you're back, and I love working here."

All the way home, she thought how perfect life was. Mrs. Clausen had said she, Holly Hanson, was going to make a good chef. Mrs. Clausen had also said that Holly could be with a KOE without fear of getting fired. That meant that she could introduce her friends to some of the guys and her friends would no longer be mad at her, which would be nothing short of great.

Her friends could go to KOE parties together, and everyone could finally meet Greg and see how handsome he was. Wait until he found out that they could go to the KOE Winter Formal together.

But there was just one more little problem that had to be solved first. Something had to be done about that dumb KOE rule that was preventing her and Greg from being together around the fraternity house. Certainly, if Mrs. Clausen could see that there was no problem with it, the guys in the house could, too. Holly began to grin. She wouldn't even say a word to Greg about Mrs. Clausen. She'd tell him all at once, after she'd seen about getting the KOE rule changed. Boy, would he be surprised. For once, she'd finally get to leave him looking flabbergasted, just the way he'd so often left her. She laughed aloud at the mere thought.

Hurrying in the front door of her house, Holly rushed in the dining room to tell her parents that everything was okay with Mrs. Clausen. "She wasn't even mad that I didn't make the Chinese dinner, and she said that she really believes I will be a chef one day. I still feel so bad about her sister, but I'm so glad she's back. I love working there." The words tumbled out in rapid succession. "I've gotta run. Greg's picking me up in twenty minutes, and I haven't even taken a shower yet."

Mr. and Mrs. Hanson looked at each other, and Holly saw the look. "And don't worry about my going out with Greg. I don't like deceiving anyone, either, and I'm about to get it all worked out. I'll be able to introduce him to my friends, and he'll introduce me to his. I promise."

Greg picked her up right on time, and as Holly walked into the entryway to greet him, she was again struck by his rugged good looks. Sometimes, she almost felt like pinching herself to convince herself that a boy this cute actually cared about her.

Walking out the door, he took her hand and began examining it. "What are you doing?" Holly asked.

"Just checking."

"Just checking what?"

Greg's blue eyes were twinkling. "Jeff's been telling everybody how you just worked your fingers to the bone saving us all from starvation while Mrs. Clausen was gone, so I thought I'd check it out for myself. Actually, your fingers still look very nice to me. As a matter of fact," he said, his eyes appraising Holly and taking in the new Esprit outfit she was wearing, "the rest of you looks very nice, too."

"I'm so glad it all meets with your approval," Holly joked, but inside she was very pleased by his compliment.

While they were waiting in line for the movie, Holly said, "Tell me about the plans for the Winter Formal."

Greg looked uncomfortable. "Ah, Holly, let's not even talk about that."

"But it's the biggest event of the whole fraternity. Mrs. Clausen and I are going to start baking French pastries for your dessert next week, and I'd like to know about the rest of it."

"Holly, you know we can't go together, so why make ourselves miserable talking about it?"

Holly bit her lip to keep from blurting out everything. There was just one thing she had to make sure of before she continued with her plan. Looking up into his eyes, she asked, "But if we could go, would you want to take me?"

Greg put his arm around Holly and pulled

her close. "Is my Holly fishing for compliments or what here? Isn't it enough that I practically risk my KOE membership every time I take you out, and I'm still taking you out?"

The movie they saw was awful, but it didn't matter; the evening was wonderful. As Greg walked her to the door, he said, "What do you suppose is making Holly grin like a Cheshire cat tonight?"

"I read that men think mysterious women are sexy. What do you think?" she teased.

Leaning over, he wrapped his arms around her and kissed her tenderly. "What do you think I think?" he echoed, and he leaned toward her to kiss her again.

By the time Holly got to her room, she was certain that she had floated instead of walked there. Too keyed up to sleep, she sat on her bed and thought about what her formal might look like. She'd try to find something blue, since Greg had once told her it was his favorite color, and maybe something with some rhinestones on it to add a little flash. She pictured herself dancing with Greg, her head resting on his shoulder, and it was a picture she thought she could hold in her mind forever. There was just one little problem — she hadn't gotten the KOE rule changed yet. Better get first things done first, Holly, she warned herself.

Just how was she going to get that darn rule changed anyway? For the next hour, she sat deep in thought. In spite of the fact that she'd now been working in the house for several months, she really didn't know very many of the boys. She certainly couldn't march into a fraternity meeting, and she didn't know the president well enough to ask to see him. Obviously, Mrs. Clausen didn't even know about the KOE rule, so she certainly couldn't help.

Holly drummed her fingers on her nightstand and continued to think. "Jeff," she said aloud. "How stupid of me not to think of Jeff in the first place. On Monday, when he walks me to my house, I'll explain the whole thing to him, and he'll be able to tell me just whom I should talk to. Maybe he could even set up a meeting for me." That resolved, Holly climbed into bed, and quickly fell asleep, a smile still playing on her lips.

S*ixteen*

Thank goodness Monday afternoon's lesson on making cream puff shells was fascinating, or Holly would never have been able to survive the day. Now that she'd decided to talk to Jeff, she could hardly wait to do it and get things resolved once and for all. At last dinner was ready, and calling good-bye, Holly quickly left the KOE house kitchen and began looking for Jeff. He didn't seem to be anywhere around, and with a sinking feeling Holly hoped that he was going to his mom's tonight. She hadn't really confirmed anything with him; it was just a given on Monday nights. She stood indecisively for a few minutes, and finally she decided that she might as well start walking home. She'd covered less than half a block when she heard, "Hey, wait up."

Turning, she waved to Jeff and waited for him to catch up to her. As he got closer, she said, "I waited for a while, but when you didn't come, I decided that maybe you got tied up tonight."

"Sorry," he replied. "I was studying for a biochemistry test tomorrow, and I didn't realize what time it was. Well, how were things in the KOE kitchen today?"

"I missed my second assistant chef, but it was good to have Mrs. Clausen in charge again. I told her what a big help you were last week." Holly felt she should wait before just plunging in to tell Jeff her problem, but she was too excited. "And, Jeff, I need your help on something else."

"Sure, what is it?"

"Well, first of all, you're sworn to secrecy, promise?"

Jeff looked a little perplexed, but he said that if it was that important he wouldn't say anything to anyone. Holly took a deep breath. "Okay," she began. "I'll try to make a long story short. I've been seeing Greg Lane every Friday night for the last few months, and well, we really like each other a lot. We'd see each other more, but there've been two problems. One, I was afraid Mrs. Clausen would fire me if she found out, and two, you guys have that dumb fraternity rule about not dating employees."

"What's any of this got to do with me?" Jeff said.

Ignoring the tone of annoyance in his question, Holly continued, "I'm getting to that. Today, Mrs. Clausen said that she didn't care if I dated KOE guys." Holly blushed a little, thinking that Mrs. Clausen had specified which KOE it should be, but Holly left out that part.

"So," she continued, "I don't have to worry about that." The next words tumbled out in a rush. "I want to surprise Greg. I want to get that KOE rule against dating employees changed. It's a dumb rule. It's not even fair. The maids are all old, the gardener is a man, and so are the hashers. Mrs. Clausen and the housemother could be everyone's grandmothers, so the only employee anyone even could date is me, and I've proven that I can do my job and that I'm not some airhead."

Finally, Holly had to stop to take a breath. "Jeff, I want you to tell me whom I can talk to or what I should do to get that rule changed. If anyone could ever help me, it would be you."

"I'll check into it," Jeff said, but there was no enthusiasm in his voice.

"Thanks, Jeff, I knew you'd help." Holly stepped up on her tip toes and kissed Jeff lightly on the cheek.

"Would you not do that, please," he said in response.

Holly was shocked. "I'm sorry. I . . . didn't mean anything by it."

They walked together in silence, Holly so wrapped up in thoughts of Greg that she barely noticed. "Here's my phone number," she said, tearing out a small piece of pink paper and handing it to Jeff. "As soon as you know anything, will you give me a call?"

On Tuesday, Mrs. Clausen taught Holly how to make eclair shells, and on Wednesday, she covered napoleons, admonishing Holly never to use tap water. "It must be ice water, if you want the pastry to turn out correctly." Holly listened, but her heart wasn't in it. She had neither heard from nor seen Jeff, and she was beginning to be very disappointed in him. He knew how important it was to her to get this rule changed, especially with the Winter Formal coming up. After all, she hadn't asked him to try to get it changed, just to find out whom she should talk to about it.

As Holly left the fraternity house on Wednesday, instead of heading out the back door, she even walked boldly through the living room in hopes that she'd see Jeff, but the living room was empty. She brooded all the way home, and finally, she decided that if she hadn't heard anything from Jeff by the week's end, she'd have to forget the surprise angle, and tell Greg so that he could get the rule changed in time for the formal. It might be better that way anyway.

When Holly got home, she found a note on the refrigerator from her parents saying they were both at a school board meeting, and to help herself to leftovers for dinner. She flipped on the tv, to cover the silence of the house, and when the doorbell first rang, she almost thought that it was part of the television program. Then she realized that it was her doorbell.

Rushing to the front door, she called, "I'm coming," and peeking out the peep hole, she saw it was Jeff. All at once, she felt a rush of guilt for doubting him, and opening the door wide, she said enthusiastically, "Come on in. Am I ever glad to see you."

Jeff ignored her invitation to come inside. "I just wanted to let you know that there is no KOE rule against an employee dating a guy in the house."

"Oh, Jeff," Holly breathed in gratefulness, "you're the most incredible friend. How'd you ever get it dropped so fast?"

Jeff's face remained absolutely impassive, but there was a hardness in his eyes as he said, "You don't understand. I didn't get anything changed. There never was any such rule."

Holly's mind was spinning. None of this made any sense. "Maybe, because you're just a freshman, you didn't know about it," Holly offered. "I mean there must be a ton of rules, and you can't know them all right off the bat."

"Holly." Jeff's voice was flat and cold. "You asked me to check. I checked. There is no rule preventing employees from dating the guys in the house." He started to leave.

"Wait!" Holly called. "Wait a minute. If there wasn't any rule, why would Greg say there was?"

"Why don't you ask your boyfriend that

question?" Jeff called over his shoulder as he continued down the front walkway.

Suddenly, nothing made any sense at all. Holly felt as if something was terribly wrong and somehow it was Jeff's fault.

She walked back into the house and slammed the front door. Tears were streaming down her face, and she thought to herself that she didn't care if she never saw Jeff Leonard again.

Why she was so angry at him, she wasn't sure. Maybe because he'd been the one to burst her perfect world. Somehow there had to be a logical answer to all of this, and Friday night, when she and Greg went out, Holly resolved to find out exactly what that answer was.

The next day, Mrs. Clausen sent Holly on an emergency run to get a jar of thyme. "I should take my own good advice, and always make a list before I start, no?" she said to Holly.

"It's the first time since I've been here that you've ever forgotten anything," said Holly loyally. "It'll only take me a few minutes to run to the grocery across from campus and get a jar." She hurried quickly out the door, and headed for the grocery.

Walking through the door to the small store, she saw Jeff. I'll ignore him, was her first thought, but looking up and seeing his right eye black and blue, and practically swollen shut, she was so shocked, the words just popped out of her mouth. "Oh, Jeff, your eye. What happened? Does it hurt?"

"Yes," he said coldly, "as a matter of fact it does. Now if you'll just get out of the doorway, I can get through."

"What's the matter with you?" Holly stood her ground. "Why are you so mad at me?"

"Why don't you grow up?" Jeff said.

"Oh, and I suppose you're the perfect example of that." Holly could feel her voice rising in anger.

There was a controlled fury in Jeff's voice as he said, "Well, at least I wouldn't let someone string me along with some dumb lie about a nonexistent rule." He gave her a cold look. "But I am dumb enough to get into a fight with Greg because he told you that lie. So I guess we're even."

"Greg wouldn't do that," Holly defended.

"Oh, yeah. How can you be so blind? The truth is your Greg has been dating two girls, you on Friday nights and the other girl only on Saturday nights. He managed to convince the other girl he worked on Friday nights. But he couldn't invite both girls to the Winter Formal, and some of his friends bet Greg that he couldn't keep both girls strung along if he excluded one of them from the formal."

"Oh, no," Holly breathed, "I don't believe it."

Jeff ignored her and continued, "But Greg just laughed, and he bet his friends ten bucks that it would be no problem to keep dating both girls even after the formal was over."

The two of them stood in the entryway of the grocery, and in the eyes of each was a mixture of pain, anger, and disbelief. Then Jeff shoved past Holly, and walked quickly away.

Heading into the grocery in a daze, Holly told herself that this whole thing couldn't be true. She picked up the small jar of thyme, and it felt as if it weighed a million tons. Jumbled thoughts filled her head, and the way back to the KOE house was blurred by her tears.

Holly didn't see Jeff again on Thursday or Friday, and she was glad. Friday night, she dressed especially carefully for her date with Greg. She wasn't quite sure why, but she knew it was important to look as perfect as she could.

When Greg called to confirm the time he'd be picking her up, she decided he sounded perfectly normal. He said that he was looking forward to a great evening. Thinking of his words and the way he'd sounded, Holly was tempted to try to forget about everything Jeff had said. Why risk spoiling anything between you and Greg? a part of her said. Yes, said another part of her, but don't you want to know the truth?

The two parts of her subconscious were still waging battle when Greg rang the doorbell. Holly had decided to wear a pair of designer jeans and a stylish shirt, and had managed to mousse her hair into a more sophisticated style. She looked in the mirror and added a touch of blue eye shadow to make her eyes an even deeper shade of blue. She knew she looked great, but that didn't change how she felt. She wished that she never had to walk out to see Greg. It was too scary to think that everything could soon be spoiled.

"Hi," she said, walking out in the entryway, and feeling more nervous than she had since their first date.

"Hi." A slow grin spread across his face. They said good-bye to her folks, and headed out the front door.

"Hey," he said, slipping his arm around her, "you look pretty terrific tonight." The sparkle in his eyes told her that his words weren't just a line. He opened the door to his red sports car. "Your chariot awaits. I hope you're ready for the unusual, because I have a most unusual evening planned for us."

She and Greg had fun; he made her laugh all night as usual. Every time Holly thought about bringing up the subject of the Winter Formal, the words stuck in her throat. In a way, she wished Mrs. Clausen had never given her permission to date a KOE. If she had to find out that Greg was stringing her along, she didn't know what she'd do.

It was four hours later, and they were back at Holly's house about to say goodnight, when she knew that she had to say something. The top was down on Greg's car, the wind was blowing softly, and the sky was gleaming with stars. This night is too perfect to have anything go wrong. If I ask Greg right now, everything's bound to work out. Besides, I'll be miserable again all week if I don't, she told herself. I've got to make some sense of all this.

Greg leaned over. "You seem a thousand miles away. What are you thinking about?"

"That I'd like to go to the Winter Formal with you." Holly looked into his deep blue eyes.

He grinned and shrugged. "And I'd like to go with you, but you know how things are."

"You know," she said, hating the part of herself that was pushing her on, "Mrs. Clausen doesn't care anymore if I date a KOE."

"She doesn't?" Greg looked genuinely shocked. "Well, uh, then it's really too bad about the KOE rule."

"It's too bad about Jeff's eye, too," Holly said, although why those words had popped into her mouth at that point, she couldn't have said.

Greg took a deep breath, and half to himself, he said, "So Jeff just couldn't wait to fill you in. Some frat brother." Then, turning to look at Holly, he said, "Well, you might as well know the whole story. I'm not quite the jerk he'd have you think I am.

"Holly, I don't even know how to start. Actually, all this would never have happened if you hadn't been so terrific. When I first saw you, I thought you were cute, but I was kind of dating a girl at school. I stopped by your house that first time on the spur of the moment, and I asked you out to breakfast just as spontaneously. I thought I'd take you out once or twice, and that would be that. How could I have known we'd have so much fun together? Just as I decided I'd better say something to this other girl, you said you couldn't date me around the house because you'd lose your job." He grinned that slow, smooth grin that Holly had been hooked on from the first day she'd met him. "I really was supposed to be at the fraternity parties, and so the simplest solution seemed to be to keep seeing both of you. Hey, I really am sorry about the formal. It was easy to decide to ask this other girl, because neither you nor I thought that you could go."

"And Jeff's black eye? . . ." Holly didn't know why that had suddenly become so important to her, but she had to know.

Greg laughed. "Weird. It's like the guy's out of another era. Can you believe he tried to start a fist fight? He was all hot under the collar because you didn't know about the other girl I was dating. Anyway, it was none of his business in the first place. And a guy doesn't rat on a fraternity brother in the second place. You know all about everything now. Besides, you'd have hated the formal. It's stuffy."

Greg jumped out of the car without opening his door, and in a flash he was at Holly's side, opening her door. "Think they should use a sword or a rope or a guillotine?" he asked.

"For what?"

"Why, to behead me for my dastardly deed. It'll happen at sun up. They'll ask if I have any last words, and I'll say that I just want to say good-bye to the fair maiden Holly Hanson." He leaned so close to her that his aftershave filled the air, and his eyes looked beseechingly into hers. "Say something," he begged.

"I don't think they use guillotines anymore."

Greg laughed. "That's my girl." He took her hand and pulled Holly from the car. Tilting her head up, he bent and kissed her tenderly. "I'd sure hate to miss out on that."

Walking her to the door, Greg kept his arm tightly around her shoulder. "So everything's still okay between us, right?"

Holly couldn't make herself speak at all. She allowed herself one long look into Greg's perfect blue eyes and then she shook her head no. "Good-night, Greg," she said, opening the door and shutting it behind her. Then her tears fell freely. "And good-bye," she whispered softly to herself.

Seventeen

"And so I'm going to have to quit," Holly told her mother and father over Saturday morning breakfast. "I just can't work there with all the guys knowing what a fool I was after Greg bet them ten dollars that I'd still go out with him after the Winter Formal. And I can't face Greg again knowing that he just conveniently made up a rule to suit his dating pleasure. I feel so gullible."

"Well," said Mr. Hanson, buttering a piece of toast, "you might want to think that one out a little more. For one thing, you love the job. For another, you'll end up disappointing Mrs. Clausen and proving to her that young girls can't be hired to work for her because they get too hung up on boy problems."

Holly pushed some hair out of her eyes. "All right. Then I'll stay there and work, but I'll . . . I ought to put poison in their fancy French pastries. They could have their dinner dance, and for dessert they could all drop dead!"

Holly's mother laughed. "I think you've been watching too many soap operas," she said, and then she looked sympathetically at Holly. "But I don't blame you a bit for being hurt and angry."

"Frankly," said her father, "I feel sorry for Jeff Leonard. All he did was try to be helpful, and all he got for it was a black eye."

Holly sighed. "I guess I owe him an apology, but I just can't do it yet. Everything hurts too much." Holly left the table grateful that her parents had not given her a lecture about how deception only leads to more deception. They hadn't liked her lying and sneaking to date Greg in the first place, and it would have been very easy for them to say I told you so.

The weekend passed slowly, and the next week even more so. On Monday afternoon, although she'd waited a few minutes, she had a hunch that Jeff wouldn't be walking home with her, and her feeling was correct. The route seemed longer than usual and the solitary walk very lonely.

Around the fraternity house there was more and more talk about the Winter Formal, and every time Holly caught a whisper of it, she felt depressed all over again. She'd been so immersed in her own thoughts on Thursday that she'd put too many eggs in the cake batter she was making and had to start over again.

On Thursday night, Greg called as if nothing at all had gone wrong between them. "Let's try Big Surf tomorrow night," he'd suggested.

"I don't think so," Holly replied, thinking of the anguish he'd put her through.

"Okay, I'm flexible. Where do you want to go?"

"Greg," Holly said, measuring each word, "I am not going out with you tomorrow night."

"Tell you what," he replied, seemingly unfazed. "If you're ticked off about Friday nights, we'll skip this one, and right after Winter Formal, we'll go out on a Saturday night. If you want, we'll even go to a house party."

"I don't think so," Holly said.

"Why not?" Greg said, sounding puzzled. "I thought you wanted to go to parties at the house."

"I did, Greg, but that was before I knew you were lying to me the whole while we were going out," she said angrily.

"Oh, come on, Holly. I was just having a little fun. It's not such a big deal."

"It is a big deal to me," Holly said, more sad than angry now. "And if you really understood or cared about me, the way I thought you did, then you'd know why," she continued. "I thought you were my boyfriend. How do you think I felt when I found out I'd been sharing you with another girl?"

"Well, like I always say, what you don't know can't hurt you," Greg said lightly.

"You did hurt me, Greg," Holly said slowly. "And I don't want to see you anymore."

"Well, have it your way," Greg concluded. "But you'll change your mind. We have too much fun together, and you know it. When you're through being mad, give me a call."

The line went dead. Holly was so angry that she threw on a windbreaker and called to her parents that she was going for a walk. She walked briskly and it helped to let the anger out. Having no destination in mind, she paid little attention to where her feet were taking her. She'd crossed several streets before she looked up at a street sign and noticed that she was on Lawrence Street. Jeff lived on Lawrence, she remembered.

Curiosity about what his house looked like sent her down his street. She didn't exactly remember the address, but that was okay. She wasn't really planning to visit or anything. In fact, it was rather a fun game to stare at each house and wonder if it looked like a "Jeff Leonard-type house."

The third house from the corner on the south side of the street looked like it could be his. Holly could almost imagine him walking out the heavy oak front door, but she figured her imagination was working overtime when she heard what she was sure was Jeff's voice saying, "What on earth are you doing here?"

Holly jumped. The voice had come not from the house in front of her, but from behind her. She whirled around to see Jeff across the street. He came toward her. "What are you doing here?" he asked again.

"I uh. . . ." There was no way she was going to say that she'd been wondering which was his house. "I was just taking a walk."

Holly looked at his face. She was glad to see that the black and blue area around his eye was pretty well faded.

"Look, as long as I ran into you," she said, "I'd just like to tell you that I'm sorry. I should never have gotten you involved in this whole thing and I hope we can still be friends."

Jeff had been rather wary at first, but soon the two of them were immersed in conversation. Finally, Jeff said, "You could come in. We really don't have to stand out in the street."

"I probably should get going," Holly said. "I just told my folks I was going for a short walk, and I don't want them to worry."

"Well, hop in my car and I'll give you a ride."

Holly took him up on the offer, and as they rode home she wondered why he'd never driven home on Monday nights. "Is this new?" she asked.

"Nah, I've had it since school started, but sometimes I just like to walk."

They pulled up in front of Holly's house.

"Holly, I'm glad we're still going to be friends," he said. "I've missed you." He leaned over, opened her door to let her out, and then shut the car door.

Just before he gunned the motor to leave, he added, "And I guess we might as well be honest with each other. I left my car at school on Monday nights because I wanted to walk with you."

Holly stood watching the gray Camaro disappear from view and letting Jeff's words sink into her mind. Everything about the last few months suddenly seemed so topsy turvy. How could she have seen nothing the way it actually was? Holly walked into the house slowly, trying to make all the pieces fit together.

Her mom greeted her in the living room. "Are you okay? Dad and I were getting worried."

"I think I'm fine," Holly said, "but I've got a lot of things to sort out."

For the rest of the weekend, Holly replayed the events of the last few months. Brushing her hair on Sunday night, she looked in the mirror and told her reflection, I'll bet Jeff doesn't even like to cook, but he was there because he knew I needed support. She couldn't help but compare him to Greg. Where had Greg been while she'd been frightened and needed support? Holly's blue eyes stared back penetratingly from the mirror as if to answer. Greg never gave my problems a thought because from the beginning the only one he was concerned about was himself and his own good times.

Sinking back down on the bed she shook her head, and for a few minutes she let her mind wander, imagining what it would have been like to have had Jeff as a boyfriend the last few months instead of Greg. It might not have been as dramatically exciting, but she had the feeling that it would have been more worthwhile. Well, she told herself, it's too late for that now. At least Jeff and I will still be friends.

The thought made her feel guilty about all her school friends. She'd distanced herself from everyone, just expecting them to understand because of her mysterious boyfriend. Monday, she'd ask Jeff if any of the guys in the house needed a blind date for the Winter Formal. How ironic, she told herself, that some of my friends will probably get to go to the KOE formal while I sit home.

When Holly got to work on Monday afternoon, Mrs. Clausen was busy making more French pastry shells. She greeted Holly's arrival by bemoaning the fact that in her days as a fine chef, she'd never frozen any kind of pastry. But, since the kitchen here was so small, it was the only way she could make enough for the Winter Formal.

"Ah, but it hurts me to put these in the freezer!" she lamented. "When you are at the dance, please taste one of each kind and then report if they are okay."

"I'm not going to the dance," Holly said, trying not to show her sense of regret.

"Why not?" Mrs. Clausen demanded.

Holly felt herself redden. "Well, because no one asked me."

"Too bad." Mrs. Clausen shook her head. "It's such a fairy tale evening." She appraised Holly carefully. "Which of my boys did you want to go with?"

Holly suppressed a smile, imagining Mrs. Clausen ordering one of the boys into the kitchen and demanding that he take her assistant cook to the Winter Formal. "Oh, I don't know," she hedged. "I don't even know most of the boys."

Mrs. Clausen dropped the subject and told Holly to start boiling noodles for lasagna. She worked on the Italian meal the rest of the afternoon and wondered whether Jeff would still walk home with her on Mondays or whether he'd just drive now.

As she was leaving, Jeff stopped her outside the kitchen to say that he was in the middle of studying for biochem and he was going home later.

That night as Holly slept, Mrs. Clausen's question reappeared in a dream. Holly was rushing around to finish dressing. "Hurry," called her dad, "I've got the camera all loaded and I want to take some pictures before you leave." She walked in the living room wearing a blue dress with rhinestones. Her father just finished shooting a roll of film when the doorbell rang, and her dad and mom went to answer it. She could hear them making small talk with a boy. He was wearing a tuxedo, and he looked very handsome, but Holly couldn't see his face. Anticipation and excitement filled her mind. Then he turned directly toward Holly, and his face was visible. It was Greg. "Oh, no," she said, "I didn't want to go with you. I thought you were going to be Jeff."

Holly awakened with a start, sat up in bed, and looked around her room realizing that in spite of how real it had all seemed, it was just a dream. But now, feeling wide awake, she decided to see if she could make some sense of her dream.

Lani had said that dreams were really subconscious thoughts, and Holly wondered if that's what this dream had been. I really did want to go to the Winter Formal with Greg, she reasoned, but maybe that's because I didn't really know him. She thought of the long talks she and Jeff had shared, eating meat loaf with chopsticks together, and his appearance whenever her life needed straightening out. Holly Hanson, she told herself, you're a prize jerk.

She shook her head sadly. The formal was less than two weeks away. No doubt Jeff had a date, and even if he didn't, after the way she'd botched things up, she wasn't going to be his choice. She'd ruined everything by not being perceptive enough to know what was really important.

Holly stared at the nightlight gleaming

against her wall. "I'm just unlucky, I guess," she said aloud to no one.

She could almost hear the firm voice of her father reply that such a comment was nonsense. How many times had he said that you make your own luck in life, and that if you want something, you've got to go after it.

That's been drummed into my head since I was a little girl, Holly thought, and it's true. I wouldn't have had this job at all if I hadn't gone after it. Her dad had always told her to think like a winner or she'd never be one.

She slept little the rest of the night, knowing both that she was going to put a plan in action and that she was terrified to do so. If only I didn't have to wait clear until next Monday before I'll see Jeff again, she thought. However, to her surprise, Jeff came bounding in the kitchen the very next afternoon.

"You wanted me?" he asked Mrs. Clausen.

"Ah, yes, Jeff," she said. "About this meal for tomorrow. I can't get good green beans. What do you say we substitute squash?"

"Ah, Mrs. C, you know the guys hate squash. If we have to have a vegetable, at least make it peas."

Holly saw Jeff start to walk out of the kitchen, and digging her nails into her palms to give herself courage, she said, "Uh, Jeff, could you stop down when I get done tonight? I wanted to talk to you."

Jeff looked a little puzzled, but agreed, and then left. Holly was so busy watching him go that she almost missed the smile playing about Mrs. Clausen's lips.

Holly was all thumbs for the rest of the afternoon, and both she and Mrs. Clausen were relieved when it was time for her to go. Holly hung up her apron and walked out the back door, feeling much like a reluctant soldier sent to do battle. Jeff was sitting on the back steps, and stood up as she came out. "What's up?" he asked.

The easy camaradarie that had existed between them had been replaced by a nervous awkwardness on both their parts. "Uh, are you walking to your house today?" Holly asked, hoping that it would be easier to walk and talk.

"No," Jeff replied, "I went to see my mom last night after I finished studying, and I probably won't get back for a few days." He offered no further comment.

Suddenly, Holly wondered if he'd really been working on a biochem lab or if he'd just wanted to avoid walking with her. Stop it, she told herself, or you'll lose your nerve altogether.

Drawing on what some called her stubborn forcefulness, she took a deep breath. "Look, I won't keep you because dinner at the KOE house is good tonight. I have it on good advice that the lasagna is excellent," she joked.

She began again. "I, uh, I just wanted to say thank you for everything you've done for me, and I wondered if you'd let me treat you to dinner one night soon to show my appreciation." The words sounded stiff even as she said them.

Jeff looked very wary. "No thanks. I don't need you to try to repay me. Whatever I did, I did because I wanted to."

Holly looked into Jeff's soft brown eyes, and saw how guarded they were. "What if I said that I'd just like to be with you," she said. She felt a little awkward at being so forward, but it seemed the only possible way to salvage the situation.

"Why?"

Holly looked at him, and smiled. "Why not?"

Jeff shook his head, and half muttered to himself, "I'm probably going to be sorry." Then he returned Holly's smile. "Come on. Let's go."

"Where are we going?" Holly asked.

"How quickly she forgets. Didn't you offer to treat me to dinner?"

Sitting at a hamburger place right off campus called the Chuckbox, the two found that ease of conversation had returned, to the point that Holly looked at her watch and gasped. "I don't believe what time it is. I've got to get home before my folks think I've disappeared altogether."

They walked back to the fraternity house, and Jeff drove her home. Sitting outside her house, Holly thought how much she hated for the evening to end. Maybe some day, she and Jeff were going to be more than just friends, but it wasn't going to happen before the

Winter Formal, and she really hated to even bring the subject up.

Still, she'd been selfish long enough, and she owed her friends the chance to get to go. "Listen," she said, taking a deep breath, "I promised some of my good friends that I'd check and see if any of the KOE guys needed dates for the formal. If they do, will you let me know, and maybe we could play dating bureau."

"I'll check around," Jeff replied noncommittally. He appeared to be deep in thought, and then he said, "In fact, I might even know of one guy right now, but he's pretty particular."

Holly was all business. "Great," she said, thinking how to make a good match. "Why don't you describe him to me, and tell me what kind of girl you think he'd like, and then I'll tell you which of my friends would be best."

"Okay." Jeff stopped to think. "But why don't I just describe the kind of girl he'd probably like. I'd say she'd have to be about five feet tall with wavy dark hair and blue eyes. Personality — smart, but pretty stubborn. Hobbies — well, he likes to eat, so she should like to cook."

Holly began to blush. "But that sounds like me."

Jeff appeared to think that over and then said, "No, it couldn't be you. This guy is only interested in a girl who's unattached, and you're involved with Greg."

"Oh, no, I'm not!" Holly said indignantly. "That is definitely over!"

Jeff grinned. "Really — well, then, the guy I have in mind sounds a lot like me. Do you think that couple would work out or not?"

Holly felt herself blush an even deeper shade of red, but she looked straight into Jeff's eyes. "Yes, I really do."

They were both silent for a moment. Then Jeff leaned toward Holly and kissed her gently. They gazed into each other's eyes for a long moment. Then Jeff turned back to the steering wheel.

"Good, then it's all set," was all he said.

Jeff's kiss was still lingering sweetly in her memory after he'd left. She walked slowly into the house in awe at the way things had turned out. Just when she'd been sure her chance at love was over, life was providing a very exciting new beginning. She just knew that she and Jeff were going to have a wonderful time at the Winter Formal.

Holly thought that it was a good thing Mrs. Clausen had happened to need Jeff in the kitchen today, or she'd have never ended up talking to him in time for the Winter Formal.

"Holly, is that you? We're in the family room," called her mother. Holly walked in to join her parents, unable to erase the silly grin that kept appearing on her face.

"Gee, honey, you're really late tonight," Mrs. Hanson said. "Was Mrs. Clausen demonstrating some very exciting recipe?"

At the mention of the cook's name, Holly's mind flashed back to Mrs. Clausen's calling Jeff in the kitchen today to inform him that she'd have to substitute another vegetable for green beans. Suddenly, Holly remembered glancing at the menu board when she'd first arrived. Green beans had never even been scheduled for an evening meal. The smile on Holly's face broadened.

"Actually, Mom, I think Mrs. Clausen was trying to help me finally figure out the right recipe for romance." Holly's eyes twinkled. "And you know what? I think she succeeded."